OLD PALS ACT
a novel

C.J.BROADBENT

&
AMPERSAND

Copyright © C.J.Broadbent 2000

First published in Great Britain in 2000 by
Ampersand
Finboro, Helmshore Road,
Helmshore,
Rossendale,
Lancashire BB4 4AE.

Printed by
Dalton & Co. (Printers) Ltd.,
Oxford Street, Accrington, Lancashire.

ISBN 0 9533690 1 3

A catalogue number for this book is available
from the British Library

The right of C.J.Broadbent to be identified as the author of
this work has been asserted by him in accordance with
the Copyright, Designs and Patents Act 1988.
This book is sold subject to the condition that it shall not,
by way of trade or otherwise, be lent, re-sold, hired out or otherwise
circulated without the publisher's prior consent in any form
of binding or cover other than that in which it is published
and without a similar condition including this condition being
imposed on the subsequent purchaser.
No part of this publication may be reproduced or transmitted in any form
or by any means, electronic or mechanical, including photocopying,
recording or any information storage or retrieval system, without either
the prior permission in writing from the publisher or a licence,
permitting restricted copying. In the UK, such licences are issued by the
Copyright Licensing Agency.

Dedicated to the memory of
the 11th (Service) Battalion (Accrington)
of the East Lancashire Regiment:
the Accrington Pals.

ACKNOWLEDGEMENTS

To Angela, Keith and Richard, who first took me to
the battlefields of the Somme.

To Suzanne Alderson for the cover design.

To William Turner, for supplying me with much of the
factual information in his books "The Accrington Pals"
and "Accrington Pals Trail" (Pen and Sword Books)

To Stephanie Speight, for information about life at
Charlotte Mason College in the 1960s.

To everyone who has offered ideas and information,
without which this book could not have been written.

This is a work of fiction.
All the characters in it are imaginary,
with the exception of John Harwood,
Lieutenant-Colonel A.W.Rickman
and Sergeant James Rigby.

OLD PALS ACT

Contents

Prologue..Page 1
Chapter 1: East Anglia: Gone.............................Page 19
Chapter 2: East Anglia: Gone Forever.....................Page 41
Chapter 3: East Anglia: Puzzles..........................Page 62
Chapter 4: Oxford: Shocks................................Page 82
Chapter 5: Oxford: Shame.................................Page 107
Chapter 6: East Anglia: Bill.............................Page 125
Chapter 7: The Good Book ....Page 146
Chapter 8: A Northern Pilgrimage.........................Page 160
Chapter 9: Phil's Story..................................Page 184
Chapter 10: Accrington ....Page 205
Chapter 11: Albert Lord's Story: Meetings....... ....Page 218
Chapter 12: Albert Lord's Story: Bonding.................Page 236
Chapter 13: Albert Lord's Story: Ever Nearer.........Page 252
Chapter 14: Albert Lord's Story: Abroad...............Page 274
Chapter 15: Albert Lord's Story: Betrayal.............Page 293
Chapter 16: East Anglia: Realisation.....................Page 319
Chapter 17: For Anne: Early Days.........................Page 328
Chapter 18: For Anne: Discoveries........................Page 346
Chapter 19: For Anne: Fruition...........................Page 365
Chapter 20: Visits: The Shadow Lifts.....................Page 383

Old Pals Act

Prologue

1916

The soldier joined the line of men getting off the train at the dockside station, blending in with the endless column of stretchers, crutches and bandages. Everywhere there were men in pain, wounded and maimed for the rest of their lives. Who could tell he hadn't been with them all the time? Who would care ? What was one more amongst all these?

There was only a cursory glance at the papers he offered, as he hobbled up the gangplank of the ship, carrying his kit bag over his shoulder. There were far too many fellow travellers for a strict check. Anyway he was sure they were in order, everyone had said so before he left.

He leant out over the rail of the ship. This was just too easy, he thought to himself, yet deep down inside there remained a horrible feeling that something might still go wrong. As he turned and limped to the uncomfortable wooden seats, he scanned the crowd of fellow soldiers to see if he recognised anyone, at the same time carefully keeping his face tucked down well behind the turned up collar of his tunic. There was no one he knew, there never was. The men he had fought with were probably all dead by now or still back there, suffering and waiting for the merciful release that death brings. A pang of guilt pricked his brain, but only momentarily. He soon shut it out of his mind.

Congratulating himself on his success, he settled down for the voyage. He thought back to the last three months. He had been happy, mixing with like-minded individuals, who made no demands on his time or emotions. He had enjoyed their company, but knew he had to return to England. His comrades accepted this and indeed helped him on his way by covering, watching and guiding. They were good friends. He lit a cigarette, a habit he had only acquired recently, and inhaled deeply, tucking his hands inside his tunic for protection against the cold November wind blowing off the sea.

Sleep was out of the question, but he meant to rest as much as possible. He didn't know how long he would be on the move or indeed what conditions he would have to face before reaching his destination. There would be nobody to help him when he landed on the other side. Still, he had always shunned assistance in the past, except of course from his new-found friends and one other person, and he was no doubt long dead by now. He didn't mind being alone, having always preferred his own company. He comforted himself with that thought.

There was a slight moving sensation as the ship slid gracefully out of the harbour and headed into the rougher waters of the English Channel. Three, maybe four hours and I should be back on dry land again, he thought, thank God for that. He was not a natural sailor and there was always the chance of the ship being torpedoed, but he put that thought out of his mind. Somehow he knew a watery grave was not his destiny, though he still anticipated he would die violently at some stage in his life. He had suffered that premonition for over two years and it was still as strong as ever.

In the distance he could hear someone playing a mouth organ. How he hated that sound, it reminded him of the past, something he was keen to forget. Luckily the swell became worse as they approached mid-channel and the playing died down as no doubt the perpetrator had decided it was safer to have both his hands free as the ship rolled drunkenly from side to side.

His hand strayed to his inside pocket; the papers and money were still there, they must not be lost, they were his ticket out of this horror, forever. He cursed the day he had ever got involved, swept along by the tide of youthful enthusiasm and an overwhelming desire to do his duty. That was a laugh. What he had seen and done could never be classed as duty. A grim smile creased his face, but there was no humour in it. Still, he had found a way out and hopefully would soon see his loved one again.

"Got a light mate ?" asked someone sitting close beside him, waking him from his thoughts. He smiled and handed across a matchbox, but then realised that he would have to light the cigarette for him, as the man's right hand was heavily bandaged. Cupping the flame he lit the cigarette and passed it across.

" Blown off at Beaumont Hamel," continued his companion waving his bandaged stump in the air. "Lucky really, could have been my bloody head."

He laughed and coughed at the same time making a horrible rasping noise in his chest.

"What about you ?"

This was exactly what he didn't want, but he could hardly ignore the man.

"Shot in the leg at Serre." He patted the injured leg gently. " Going back to convalesce, might be forever, who knows."

It would be forever, he knew that, but he kept it deliberately vague. His travelling companion nodded, but didn't ask more. The soldier was glad of that; his story might not stand up to too many questions. To avoid any more talk he feigned sleep. He needn't have bothered; his travelling companion somehow did drift off into that blissful state, the cigarette, now out, still dangling from his mouth.

Alone with his thoughts again, the soldier contemplated his next move. He had no real need, it had all been worked out beforehand, everyone had contributed ideas, until finally a plan had been drawn up. Once he was away, then he would have to think out the next step more carefully. He hoped his luck would hold.

After what seemed an eternity, there was a general excitement amongst the men sitting near him. Land had been sighted; they were nearly there, on friendly soil once again. He smiled to himself, checking his papers once more, and waited for the ship to dock. Ropes were thrown down onto the quayside and finally the ship was made secure against the harbour wall. Those men who could move began to make their way to the nearest gangplank, hastily made fast by the ship's crew. The soldier shuffled his way behind a line of men onto dry land once more. When the way was clear, a team of medical orderlies made the reverse journey to collect the men unable to walk for themselves.

He blended easily into the confusion and followed a line heading towards a train, hissing and snorting as it waited in the station. Without pushing or drawing attention to himself, he boarded the train and positioned himself near the door. He had no idea where the train was heading. He didn't much care at the moment. All he knew was that it was taking him away from the coast.

As the train slowly filled up he sank lower beneath his tunic collar once more, but he needn't have worried, as the other occupants of the compartment were all unknown to him. They showed no interest in him at all, indeed nobody spoke. He gazed out of the window and waited for the departure. There was no heat in the train, but crushed in, as they all were, he didn't feel the cold. That would come later. The train moved slowly out of the station and he relaxed even more. Nobody had requested to see his papers, or even asked his name or company. This was easy.

As they rumbled slowly on their journey, his fellow travellers all drifted into sleep, the lullaby of the wheels soothing them away from the nightmare of reality into the dream of unconsciousness. Not he, his mind had to be kept alert if the plan were to work. The moment had to be right. The train continued its laborious journey, never seeming to vary in speed. The first hour ticked by and he was starting to feel anxious. Surely it must stop soon. It did. He felt the lurching sensation of it slowing down and he heard the grinding of the brakes. Gradually the train slowed down to a halt. He glanced out of the window. They were not in a station, and he could just make out a hedge and fields in the gloom. Glancing round the compartment one final time, he flung open the door and tumbled out. As he slid down the embankment he could just make out the cursing and swearing of soldiers woken from sleep by an icy blast of air. He heard the carriage door being pulled shut. He neither knew nor cared if anyone reported the incident when the train arrived at its destination. It would be too late to do anything about it by then. Keeping low, the soldier disappeared into the Kent countryside.

* * * * * * * * * * * * * * * * * *

1958

It was her first funeral. She was, after all, only just 16. As she sat in church, next to her parents, she recalled that awful moment about a week ago, when her father had gently broken the news to her that her grandfather had died. He had lovingly cradled her in his arms, rocking her slowly backwards and forwards, in an effort to soften the blow. It was not unexpected; she knew that, but it was a shock nevertheless. She somehow thought he would recover, her granddad who was so tough, tough enough to come through that terrible war.

She remembered the times when she had toddled along next to her grandfather, her special pal, as he liked to be called, clinging tightly to his hand as he took her to the park near the house. It was such a steep slope up to the monument, for a small child, her little legs taking a dozen steps to his one. He used to sit for what seemed like hours staring at the list of names carved on the stone plaques. She had tried to count them all once, but there were too many.

As she got older, he told her what the names were all about. She asked him where his name was, but all he had said, with a tear in his eye, was,

Old Pals Act

"I didn't die."

She had implored him to tell her all about the war. What had he done? Had he killed anyone? Had he been wounded? As usual he had given in, as most people did when she pestered them. He told her of some of the horrors of the trenches. She had shuddered when he mentioned the rats. He told her how he had been wounded, twice in fact. He told her how he had won a medal. She in turn had told everyone at school about her grandfather's medal for bravery. She had taken it round every child in the class, swelling with pride. Her teacher had told all of them about the Accrington Pals. She felt slightly jealous when she found out that many of her friend's grandfathers had been Pals as well.

" Yes, but mine lived," she would say, feeling she had got one up on most of them.

There was one story he had always refused to tell her. She had met her match, and recognised that he could dig his heels in deeper than she could. Her father had known it, she was sure of that, but he just said,

" When you are old enough."

She had not pursued it, nor had she speculated what it might be, and over the years it had disappeared readily from her mind, which filled with the preoccupations of her early teens.

It was an awful day when she got home from school to be met by her mother saying her granddad was in hospital. She could tell from the tone of her voice that it was serious. She had insisted that she visited him every night. She had watched the frail old man fading away in front of her eyes. She used to hold his hand for the entire duration of the visit. On her last visit he had given her a letter, saying

"Read it when I've gone."

They were the last words he ever uttered to her. He passed away the next day.

The funeral party left the church and headed for the cemetery, the coffin easily carried by four black coated men, who lowered it into the ground with dignity.

"Goodbye old Pal," she said aloud as she clung tightly to her parent's hands.

Her first funeral was over. She carefully opened the envelope when she got back home. It was a letter written in her grandfather's beautiful writing, but she didn't understand it. What on earth could he mean? Six biblical references were printed on another sheet of paper; she looked them up and jotted them down on the back of the paper. They, like the letter, made no sense. Shrugging her shoulders she replaced them in the envelope and tucked it safely between the pages of her bible. Her father would decide to tell her when he thought the time was right, her grandfather's letter said so.

She trusted her Pal.

* * * * * * * * * * * * * * * * * *

Old Pals Act

1971

The sophisticated young lady, dressed in a smart black suit, a stylish, wide brimmed hat perched on top of shoulder length auburn hair, stared at the open grave as her mother's coffin was lowered down. A tear trickled its way down her cheek. She had not really said goodbye when she had stormed out six years ago. Her intelligent eyes scanned the mourners, people she was only vaguely familiar with, except one of course. Her gaze locked on the figure of her father, as well dressed and athletic looking as ever, head bowed, hands clasped together in front of him. Without thinking she took a handful of soil out of the small box offered to her and sprinkled it over the coffin, the dirt making a rattling sound as it landed.

She looked across at her father once more, his head now lifted and staring straight back at her. Their eyes met across the open grave. It was not cold, yet a chill ran down her spine. The party walked slowly away from the grave and to the waiting car. As they picked their way through the town towards the house, she closed her eyes and wondered what her father would have to say to her when they were alone once more.

She had arrived two days ago, their first meeting for six years. The greeting had been frosty, to say the least. Yet they had been brought together once more, bonded by common grief. He had not spoken as he opened the door to the weary, travel-stained young lady; he had merely stepped to one side to allow her entry. There had been no smiles of welcome, no embraces, nothing. She felt sad that he had not held her in his arms, as he always did when she was a child. He indicated that she should have her old room, which she had left for the final time six years ago. She felt a jolt of happy memories as she entered and noted that nothing had been touched. Her posters were still on the wall; her books were just as she had left them, falling over on the shelf as ever. The clothes she hadn't been able to carry with her when she left were still in the wardrobe, dated now. She doubted that anyone had entered the room apart to give it a token dusting from time to time. Tears welled up as she sat on her bed. She wondered why had it ever happened. She had asked this question of herself many times over the years since she had left, but she had never come up with an answer.

She took her washing bag out of her suitcase and made her way to the toilet. There were still signs of her mother, half-used bottles of perfume, talcum powder and, saddest of all, a toothbrush, with the white deposit of toothpaste drying on the handle. Her face was still red and blotchy as she returned to the bedroom and slowly unpacked, carefully taking out her black suit and placing it on an empty hanger in the wardrobe. Sitting down on the bed once more she began to think of the events of the previous day.

She had wept when she got the telephone call from her father, surprised that he knew her number. She could not think how he had got hold of it. She had always loved her parents, her father more than her mother, but in spite of this, the sense of loss was great, though she had really lost both of them six years ago when she had made her decision. She had set off that morning, leaving her husband and young son behind, an overwhelming sense of foreboding heightening as she headed north.

So now the funeral was over, the small gathering in a local hotel had finished, and father and daughter had returned to the empty house. They sat down in the expensively furnished lounge, looked at each other and she said,

" Well, now are you going to tell me? I think it's time don't you?"

Without saying a word, her father stood up and left the room. He returned minutes later with a large brown envelope, which he handed to her.

"Read, read it all and then you will understand."

She carefully opened the envelope with the letter opener lying on the small pine coffee table, and took out the document. She recognised the handwriting straight away, though it was not as neat as it usually was. Three photographs also tumbled out. She smiled as she recognised one of the faces looking at her, and then she began to read.

It was early evening when she put down the document, tears freely rolling down her cheeks. She stood up and embraced her father, who was also crying openly.

" You should have told me, things would have been so different," she sobbed, salty tears trickling into her mouth as she spoke.

" I realise that now." he replied, " But you were off before I got the chance. After that, well, you know how our family never likes to give in. I suppose it was a sort of matter of pride, like. I never thought you would go through with it, leaving and all."

His words came out in a disjointed fashion, not like the articulate man she had once known. She could feel her temper rising up inside her, and in a sudden moment of fury, she ripped one of the photographs in two and threw the offending half into the litter bin. The other half she carefully put in her handbag. She glanced across at her father with a questioning look on her face.

" So what do I do?"

He joined her on the settee and quietly told her there were two things he required of her. She stood up when he had finished folding her arms across her chest.

"Impossible!" she cried out, "I could never do that! The first, maybe, but the second, never!"

He shrugged his shoulders, realising perhaps that she would never agree to his terms.

"Then there can be no way back. We will not talk again."

He stood up and left the room. The following day she returned home, knowing she would never again speak to her father. Both of them were stubborn, neither of them would ever give in, it simply was not in either of their natures.

When she arrived back home her first job was to pull out her bible and retrieve the envelope carefully placed there when she was a teenager. Now she understood, understood it all. She knew what course of action to take.

* * * * * * * * * * * * * * * *

1997

She was making the same journey, for the same reason. Another funeral, this time her father. She was now in her fifties, but she had retained her style and poise. As she drove north she reflected on her life.

Her stubbornness had so often dictated the outcome of events, yet she would not change anything if she could have her life all over again. Well, perhaps one thing, but then again, no. She thought of her son. He would be confused by her sudden and mysterious disappearance, and she knew she would have to explain everything to him when she got back. She didn't really want him to find out, but deep down inside she knew she would have to tell him one day. He was the one person who was most affected by events, and if he knew, then he could decide. Decide what, though? What could he do? It was a problem, a burden she had carried for nearly thirty years.

She pulled off the motorway and found the hotel where she had booked a room that morning when she had found out. That had been a rush, but she had sorted everything out with her usual efficiency. There was no real need to leave so suddenly, as the funeral was not until Thursday, but she felt she wanted to get away before she had to explain her actions to her son. He was always likely to lose that temper of his, so it would be better to wait until it was all over. She checked into her room, unpacked and headed off to see Robinson, the solicitor who had written to her.

Everything had been sorted out, the funeral arrangements, the clearing of the house and its sale, once she had removed any personal things. This had been well planned, she thought; her father must have known in advance. If only he had told her instead of keeping it bottled up. *Typical of our family*, she thought. There again, she was just as bad.

Once he was satisfied she was who she said she was, Mr. Robinson shook her warmly by the hand, indicating a chair, and, as she made herself comfortable, he explained in a deep, formal voice all the details. The funeral had been organised by himself personally, following the specific instructions of her late father.

"To the letter, I might add, even down to the hymns in church and the get together afterwards."

There was almost pride in his voice as he spoke.

"Perhaps you could sort out whatever you wanted to keep as soon as possible," he added, "so that the house can be cleared quickly."

He handed her an envelope with her name on, which he had been instructed by his late client to give her only after his death. He also gave her a set of keys to the house. She thanked him and left, saying she would be in touch.

She drove to the house and let herself in. Nothing had changed. Every room was just as she remembered, except hers. That had been stripped clean, everything had gone, all traces of her had been removed. It was as if she had never existed. This upset her more than her father's death. She gazed around her for a long while before she finally left.

Locking the house up once more, she drove back to her hotel. Leaving the envelope unopened she lay on her bed and slept. It was early evening when she woke, coughing. She took a minute or two to remember where she was. It all came flooding back. She took her final antibiotic and rang her son; he would be going frantic with worry. She tried to be as cheery as possible on the phone, to put his mind at rest. She put the phone down, hoping he was reassured that she was all right. She couldn't explain over the phone, it was too complicated. He would understand, though, and he would draw everything out of her. He was like that.

The following day, she returned to the house and began to sort out things she wanted to keep. There was precious little - various certificates, a few ornaments, rings and odd bits of jewellery, father's pocket watch, but that seemed to be it. These she put in a cardboard box. *I'll wrap them properly in newspaper at the hotel*, she thought. It took her quite a while to find what she wanted most of all, her grandfather's war medals. They eventually turned up in a small box, right at the bottom of the wardrobe. She took them out and kissed each one lovingly. She smiled to herself as she thought of her beloved grandfather. The document she had read over twenty years ago was lying flat on the top of the wardrobe. She gave a little shudder as she put it in the box along with the other items. She had no desire to read it ever again.

As she loaded the box into the car she took one last look at the house. There had been happy memories here, but sadly many years ago. She pulled carefully onto the busy main road and headed for the offices of Mr. Robinson to return the house key. He wasn't there, so she left a message with his secretary, saying there was nothing else she wanted in the house and he could arrange for the disposal of all the contents. She made her way back to her hotel, carried the box up into her room, and cried her eyes out. Another call to her son cheered her up. It was good to hear his voice again, though the signs were there he was very confused, and, predictably, his temper was almost at boiling point.

She woke bright and early the next day, feeling much better. The funeral was at 11.30, so she had plenty of time. After breakfast she returned to her room and put on her beautifully tailored black suit and drove slowly to the church. As always she was early, so she spent a while in silent prayer before the funeral began. The church filled up steadily. Her father had been a well thought of member of the community and many people had come to pay their last respects. There was, of course, no other family present, she being an only child, so she felt rather like a stranger in the crowd. Several people nodded to her, but nobody spoke. After all, it was well over twenty years since she'd last been in Accrington.

The printed Order of Service card she placed carefully in her bag - no expense spared, she thought - before leaving the church heading to the graveyard where her father's body was laid to rest next to her mother's. She took one final, lingering look at the scene before setting off back to the hotel. It didn't seem appropriate somehow to go to the gathering afterwards. She wondered if her father would have been pleased to see her at his funeral. She had crossed him, and that was something he was not used to.

She rang her son later that same evening, saying she would be home the following day. That was when the problems would arise. After her evening meal she returned to her room and wrapped the ornaments carefully in newspaper provided by the hotel. That done, she caught sight of the unopened envelope on the table by the bed. Taking her nail file out of her handbag she carefully opened it up and took out the typewritten document and began to read. It was a letter from her father. Perhaps letter was rather an understatement, tome would have been better. Her eyes widened as she read more and more.

She finally finished reading the letter, scarcely able to believe its contents. Shaking her head she returned it to the envelope, which she placed in the box, and stared into space. Shock waves vibrated through her body. In an effort to erase everything she had just read from her memory, she placed the box in the wardrobe. Out of sight, out of mind. She could hardly believe the story as it unfolded in front of her. There was no way it could be true, yet it must be, otherwise, why write it at all? Feeling numb, she lay on the bed, dreading even more the meeting with her son the next day. Now there was even more to tell him.

Unsteadily, she got to her feet, undressed and took a welcoming shower. She settled back into the room and opened the wardrobe once more and looked at the box. Giving an involuntary shudder, she closed the door again, uncertain of how to proceed. She slipped out of her dressing gown and got into bed.

She hardly slept that night, unable to put the latest revelations out of her mind. As she lay awake she decided what to do. The answer was not totally satisfactory, but it would at least delay the inevitable. The box would remain in the wardrobe and she would pretend to have forgotten it. One of Robinson's minions would pick it up, to be stored until she could arrange for its collection. It was a purely symbolic act, but if the box were not in her possession, then it was as if it and the contents did not exist. She need not tell her son about what it contained, at least not straight away, that had always been her way. In her tired and confused state of mind this seemed like a good plan.

By the time daylight filtered through the window, she felt only slightly better. Her night-dress and bedclothes were soaked in sweat; her hair hung in strands down her face. She stripped and had a long refreshing shower, which made her feel more human. She carefully packed her clothes, folding every item neatly as she always did, with the exception of the soaking night-dress, which she placed in a plastic bag and deposited in the litter bin. She closed the wardrobe door, taking one last look at the box as she did so. Buying time perhaps, putting off the inevitable certainly, but she had made her mind up and she was not one for changing. She had a light breakfast, paid her bill and left, carefully dropping down the slip road onto the motorway taking her towards home. As she got to the A1 she pulled in at a cafe and made a phone call to Mr. Robinson, explaining she had left the box in the hotel and please could he send someone to collect it and store it for her until she could arrange to have it sent on. He was only too pleased to help and promised to organise it straight away. Lies come easily when you have been telling them for so long.

She continued her journey south until she was forced to stop again for a break. She ordered a cup of black coffee. Her head was still splitting, as she went into the toilets and splashed her face with cold water until she felt better. Returning to the car, she carried on driving, until weariness and confusion overcame her. The car left the road, slamming into a tree. The pain lasted only a split second until she knew no more. She would never feel pain again, ever.

Chapter 1

EAST ANGLIA: GONE

There comes a time in most people's lives when events of the past finally catch up with them. Some are less dramatic than others, but are inescapable none the less. Mine started to catch up with me earlier this year when that little ticking time bomb finally went off. Why it happens at a certain time, no one can say. There could be umpteen little triggers just waiting round the corner for someone to set them in motion. I suppose the events I am about to unfold to you all started with a broken boot lace, or could it be a letter arriving at my mother's house, or even a chance meeting in a dance hall. Perhaps it was even a dose of antibiotics. Who knows ? You read on and draw your own conclusions.

My name is Peter Jackson. I am 30 years old, above average height, but you might say I was a little portly round the waist, due to my liking of the local beer. I could be classed as an artist - successful, even - my specialities being buildings and landscapes. I live in the town of Stradbroke in Suffolk. It is a pleasant place, boasting a 14th century church, several pubs, a small primary school, a larger high school and a statue of Bishop Grosseteste the 13th century Bishop of Lincoln, who was born here. All in all a picturesque little town, but one of contrasts. Parts of it are typically Suffolk, like the older cottages with their steeply pitched, thatched roofs, like mine, whilst there is also a more modern brick built council estate. The older buildings tend to have their plastered walls painted in delicate pastel colours of pink, green or pale yellow, a sight that pleases my artist's eye.

I have always lived here in Stradbroke, initially with my parents, though my father walked out on us when I was just four years old, and latterly on my own. My wife walked out on me after five years of marriage in 1995, due in no little part to my dramatic mood swings and volatile temper. Since then I have worked hard building up quite a reputation as an artist, owning my own shop in Diss, about 10 miles from Stradbroke.

My mother lives about a ten-minute walk away in an old brick built row of cottages, the house she moved into with my father, just before I was born. So we are close, but we can still lead our own lives. She is in her fifties, very attractive, with beautiful auburn hair. She is a great worker for the church, organising fund raising events. She also bakes simply delicious scones, which are the highlight of any church garden party. She gets heavily involved with the summer playgroup for the local children and is a well-respected member of the community. I, on the other hand, am not quite as gregarious, preferring to spend my time in my converted studio, painting away to my heart's content. Most of the people in the town refer to me as Anne Jackson's son, "you know, the artist bloke." That is if they refer to me at all.

I owe a lot to my mother. She brought me up single handed, eking out her schoolteacher's salary to feed and clothe me. She supported me through school, where I was always known affectionately as "Carrots " due to my shock of bright red hair. It used to bother me at first until my mother pointed out that Winston Churchill, one of the greatest Prime Ministers of England, also had red hair. My mother always knew how to make things all right again.

She guided me through university, keeping me motivated to continue my studies, when I was quite prepared to let them slip and drop out. In fact she gave me the biggest telling off of my life when I came home at the end of term and announced I was giving up my course. I had never seen her lose her temper before. I suppose it was her comment about me reverting to family type and walking away when the going got tough that hurt me most. It was obviously a reference to my father. I didn't like being compared to the man who had walked out and left us on our own. There was no talk of me quitting university again. I graduated with a degree in business studies, which has proved to be of little use. All I ever wanted to do was paint.

She helped me a great deal to open up my own art shop, due in no little part to her foresight of her taking out an insurance policy when I was born, maturing when I was 21. She never speaks of my father, or indeed of any of her family. All I know about her past is that she is a northern lass, from Accrington actually, who went to teacher training college in Ambleside in 1961. She met my father whilst she was at college.

When she finished her course in 1964 she returned to Accrington and, much to the disapproval of her parents, married my father in 1965 after they had moved down to work in Ipswich. My mother was a school teacher and my father, as far as I could gather, was a motor mechanic. I was born in 1967, shortly after they moved from

Ipswich to live in Stradbroke. To the best of my knowledge she has not communicated with her parents since the day she left. I can only assume they are both dead as she never makes reference to them. I asked about her family once, several years ago and all she would say was she preferred not to talk about them.

"Let's just leave things in the past where they belong. Perhaps I will tell you one day," was all she would say.

I didn't pursue the matter, but I could never understand why she had to be so secretive about things. After all I was her son and I suppose I had a right to know.

She took early retirement from her teaching job in Ipswich last September, not sorry to leave behind the rigours of the National Curriculum, OFSTED inspections, whatever they were, and the like. Deep down, however, I knew she still missed her little charges and often visited them when she was in the area, clutching packets of sweets for every child in school.

So, since the traumas of my divorce, my life has been very much on an even keel for two years. I have now got a good life here in East Anglia. I'm seeing a very pleasant young lady and, who knows, we may even marry one day. Sara has her own house in Hoxne, which is very close to Stradbroke, so we don't exactly cohabit, but we see a lot of each other. However, the most well regulated lives can be thrown into disarray very quickly, as happened in February of this year.

Mother had been ill for the last month and a half, suffering from a bout of pneumonia, and was just about recovering, I was quite worried about her and I found myself being more protective than usual. I had always regarded myself as the man of the house since father left and I tended to be somewhat over fussy at times. So you can imagine how I felt one bitterly cold Tuesday morning, about 8 o' clock, with a typical East Anglian frost lying thick on the ground, half way through my breakfast of toast and Earl Grey tea, when the phone rang. It was my mother, normally a very calm person, but on this occasion I could tell she was agitated.

"Listen Pete," she said, " I've got to go away for a few days. Will you look after Tiger ? You know where everything is, don't you ?"
" Of course," I replied, " but what's the matter? What's going on? Where are you going?"
" Sorry, no time to explain, something important has come up," she replied evasively. " I'll ring you tonight. Bye."

With that, the phone was hurriedly put down. I was left staring at the handset. I rang back immediately, but all I got was the answer phone. There you are again: her secretive gene kicks in. It was almost as if she didn't trust something ..... or me. Or was I being paranoid?

Anyway, as I said before, we lived close to each other, so I quickly got dressed and walked round to her house. It couldn't have been more than twenty minutes since her call, but her car was gone, and the house was locked up. Like good organised people we've always had keys to each other's houses, so I let myself in. As I entered the kitchen there were all the signs of a hurried departure. Her tea cup and breakfast plate had been left to drain by the sink, something mother never did; she always dried up and put the crockery back in its rightful place in the cupboard. On the table was an empty envelope, meticulously opened as always with the silver paper knife, which was still lying on the table. Of the contents there was no sign. I tried to make out the postmark, but it was badly smudged. I glanced around the room to see if there were any other clues indicating the reason for my mother's hasty departure. There were none. It was almost as if she knew I would go round to her house and she wanted to be away to wherever before I arrived. I am paranoid!

I suddenly became aware of a rubbing sensation around my ankle. I looked down and there was Tiger, my mother's ginger cat, obviously wanting feeding, a duty I duly performed, after which the cat's interest in me disappeared. Over the years mother had always had a cat around the house. Each one had been cosseted and totally spoilt. She used to sit with the things on her knee, tickling them under the chin, always saying the same thing:

"No one will ever hurt you."

Leaving Tiger to its own devices, I made my way upstairs to my mother's bedroom. Here again were signs of a quick exit. She had removed some clothes from the wardrobe, but not closed the door properly. Again, mother would never do this. She always insisted on a place for everything and everything in its place, I suppose it was the teacher in her. She must have been in a real hurry. Her small suitcase was missing, and when I checked the bathroom so was her toothpaste, toothbrush and other sundry items she always took with her on trips away. I closed the door of the wardrobe and returned downstairs. Tiger had finished breakfast and was settling down to a hard day's sleeping on the windowsill. Unable to work out the reason for her departure, I carefully locked up and returned home.

I am the kind of person who, when presented with a mystery, likes to solve it. And this, to me, was a mystery. My mother was not given to impulsive actions, unless there was a real good reason, so I figured it must have been something important to have called her away so suddenly. Normally I would not have been so worried - puzzled, yes, but after all she was not fully over pneumonia and the doctor had advised her not to be out in the cold for too long, and she was still taking antibiotics, which made her rather light-headed at times. I needed to talk to someone. The obvious choice was Sara.

One of the big advantages of being your own boss is that you can come and go as you please. So I rang through to the shop and informed Elaine, my trusty assistant, that I would not be in that day. I blessed my foresight in having given Elaine a set of shop keys. Then I made another call, this time to Sara to see if she was going to be around during the day. Sara is a mobile hairdresser and worked unusual hours, trying to fit around her customers. I was lucky, and I heard her familiar voice at the other end of the phone.

"Hello darling, " she said, "Not at work today?"
"Can I come round ?" I asked. "Mother has upped and gone somewhere in a hurried fashion, packed a suitcase and gone."
"Gone ? Gone where?"

Her voice sounded genuinely puzzled. She knew my mother's habits, and that she was not one for hasty decisions.

"That's just it, I don't know."

I hoped my voice didn't sound too abrupt as I replied

"OK, but I've got an appointment in Harleston at 11.30, so don't be long."

I blew a kiss down the phone and hung up.

I set off straight away, pulling the BMW out of the drive. As I drove to Hoxne I began to think about Sara and how much I loved her. It was nearly 18 months since we met. I had gone round to see mother about something and there she was, expertly restoring mother's greying hair back to its original shade of auburn, though according to mother she was just "adding extra highlights".

The first things that struck me about Sara were her eyes. They were a beautiful shade of green, and gave the impression of being permanently happy. Her hair was short and blonde, neatly cut and styled back over the ears. She smiled across at me and wrinkled her slightly upturned nose, a habit she still does to this day. Mother introduced us and I settled down to wait for her to finish. Unconsciously I found myself glancing across at Sara, hastily averting my eyes if she looked back at me. I pretended to read the newspaper, shaking my head at times to give the charade authenticity. When she had finished, mother made us a cup of tea and we fell to chatting. Sara, like me, was divorced, the difference being she was the one who walked out after a stormy relationship with a doctor in Norwich. She moved to Hoxne about a year ago and set up her own business. She met my mother after being recommended to her by one of the church-going group mother was friendly with. I found her a very easy person to talk to and enjoyed her company.

I escorted her to the door and, much to my surprise, asked to see her again. What was even more surprising was the fact that she agreed. I arranged to pick her up the following Friday to take her out for a meal. I returned indoors, only to see mother grinning from ear to ear. It was if she knew what had passed between us on the drive. Mothers are like that sometimes!

Our relationship went from strength to strength over the next few weeks and we were constant companions. Given our unsuccessful attempts at marriage in the past, we had no desire to rush things, but without doubt, the magic spark was there. It was with these thoughts in mind I pulled up outside her little, pink painted cottage in Hoxne.

Sara greeted me at the door with her usual smile, followed by a welcoming kiss. I followed her inside where I found to my pleasure that a cup of coffee was already waiting for me. She turned off the CD player as I slipped out of my fleece jacket. She was wearing blue jeans and a magenta overall with "Sara" carefully embroidered across the top. Even after so long, I still found it difficult to take my eyes off her.

"Well, tell me all," she said, sounding for the entire world like a schoolteacher demanding some explanation from a naughty child.

As I sipped my coffee, I did my best to explain the events of the morning. Actually, as I related them to her, I started to think that I had over reacted, a tendency of mine, and that there was nothing amiss at all. I said as much to Sara. To my dismay, she agreed with me.

"I'm sure there is some reasonable explanation, " she said. " Your mother is a rational person."
"Exactly, " I replied. "Exactly. So why would she rush off so quickly ?"

I suppose I felt slightly hurt that mother had not seen fit to inform me of her plans.

After mulling things over for a while, neither of us could come up with any feasible explanation for mother's flight, to who knows where, so we both decided that there was nothing we could do except wait and see what she had to say when she rang that night. Sara promised to come round after she had finished work. With that I left, feeling a little better. I just wanted to talk to someone. I began to realise how much I relied upon Sara and how much I missed her when we were apart.

I arrived back home, and on entering the living room I saw the red light was flashing on the answer phone. I hurriedly pressed the button, thinking it might be a message from mother. It wasn't. It was from Elaine, saying she had sold my latest painting of Stradbroke Church for £350 (yes, my pictures do fetch that sort of price). Normally I would have been delighted, but on this occasion it hardly registered.

At a loss for what to do for the rest of the afternoon, I retired to my studio and tried to work on my latest painting, a local scene. As I worked, I started to think about mother. Her actions of that morning were totally out of character. Mother, as far as I knew, had never made a hasty decision in her life and she would always tell me about any trip she was planning. Something had happened, but what?

I went downstairs, poured myself a whisky and lit a cigarette. I glanced at the clock and was surprised to see the time, 5 o' clock. I refused to have any means of telling the time in the studio on the grounds that being a compulsive clock-watcher inhibited my creative flow.

Sara, bless her, arrived at about 5.30, (see what I mean) full of the joys of one who has finished work for the day and was about to spend the evening with one she loves. To my delight she had called at home and brought a change of clothes with her. That meant she would spend the night with me. She threw off her coat and planted a passionate kiss on my receptive lips. The closeness of her body meant I could clearly smell the traces of hair spray she used on her customers. On some days the smell of sulphur indicated she had been giving some person a perm. Call me strange if you like, but it was a smell I found incredibly erotic. Her green eyes sparkled in my direction.

"Any news, sweetheart?"
"Not a word," I replied.

She must have detected a note of disappointment in my voice, because she proceeded to kiss me once again, this time with an air of " don't worry, babe, I'm here." We went upstairs and made love with gentle passion. We then lay exhausted on the bed, looking lovingly into each other's eyes. In true unromantic fashion, I lit a cigarette and inhaled deeply. I resisted the temptation to ask "how was it for you?" on the grounds that I might receive a kick between the legs.

We both shot up in bed as the strident rings of the telephone broke the silence. I grasped the phone and almost shouted

"Hello"

There, on the other end of the phone and much to my relief, was the familiar voice of my mother.

"Hi Pete, how are you?"
"Mother is that you?" I mindlessly asked, knowing full well who it was.

"Who else did you expect? " she asked, " Anyway, she's probably there already"
"Hi Anne," Sara called out, " you've whipped your son into quite a frenzy today!"
"I thought I might have, but things happened so suddenly there was no time to explain"
"What happened so bloody suddenly?" I shouted down the phone, more out of relief than anything else.

"It's too complicated to explain over the phone, just trust me. I'm OK, I'll tell you everything when I get back. Let me speak to Sara will you ?"

She emphasised the word "everything" in her schoolteacher voice. I handed the handset rather grudgingly over to Sara.

"Try to persuade him not to worry about me. I'm fine, honest, it's something I had to do."

I just about made out what she was saying.

"Put him back on will you?"

Sara handed the phone back to me.

"Look, Pete, I'm perfectly OK, there's nothing to worry about. I realise I've a lot of explaining to do when I get back, but just try to be patient. Ring you tomorrow. Bye."

With that she put the phone down. Mother could be very infuriating at times! I pressed the green button, terminating the call. The look of relief mingled with hurt must have been evident on my face; Sara kissed me full on the lips, saying,

"Don't worry, things are OK."

"What was it she had to do?" I puzzled out loud.
"You heard what she said. She'll explain everything when she gets back. So don't worry."

We made love again, and then lay in bed for about an hour intertwined in each other's arms.

It is an unexplained phenomenon that making love gives one an appetite. Or at least it is with me! It is also an unexplained phenomenon that the last thing you want to do is prepare any food. The same thought passed between us, yes we should go out for something to eat. The symbiotic nature of our relationship was growing stronger.

We showered, dressed and strolled hand in hand the 100 yards up the road to the Queen's Head. This was a pub we both enjoyed visiting. The beer was good, the food was excellent and the company was first class if you wanted it. Not that I ever did, especially if Sara was with me. We found a table in the restaurant and sat down. As always, I forgot to duck my head and received a hearty blow on my forehead from the typically low Suffolk beam, an act that always brought a smile from Sara's imp-like face followed by a wrinkling of her nose. Sara ordered a lasagne whilst I had my favourite steak and ale pie. We both had tiramisu for our second course. After the meal we went to sit in the main bar area at a little table halfway between the poolroom and what could, I suppose, be called the snug. I went to the bar and ordered a pint of Adnam's bitter and a gin and tonic, with ice but no lemon.

The pub had filled up by now, and all around were the faces of people I knew by sight. The people on the next table were enthusiastically discussing the next production by the Stradbroke Players. A crowd of intellectual people opposite were engrossed in the Times crossword, whilst a clutch of Stradbroke youth were playing pool. Sara and I were content to smile at each other, happy in the silence that true love brings. As usual I ended up staring into her eyes, wishing I could recreate them on canvas, something I had never been able to manage. We decided to have another drink before leaving. I was feeling relaxed for the first time that day and was determined to make the most of it. I made my way to the bar and ordered the same again. Landlords are good at remembering your last round, and the same drinks duly were placed in front of me.

Just as I was picking up the glasses, I felt a tap on the shoulder. I spun round, taking great care not to spill the drinks. There confronting me was a semi-familiar face. It was a man I had seen around the village a few times, a man who for some reason always took time to pass the time of day with me, despite the fact I wasn't sure of his name. He was wearing a green jumper and some tatty blue jeans. His face was unshaven and his hair, looking as though it hadn't been washed since the late seventies, flopped wildly around his head. He was clutching a half-finished pint of beer in his hand, which he waved menacingly about.

"Hello there old boy," said the face, breathing alcoholic fumes all over me, "How are you?"

"Fine," I replied, "Couldn't be better."

With that I made to sit down, but his burly frame blocked my way.

"Now that mother of yours, how's she?"
"Fine," I replied once again. "Matter of fact she's away at the moment."

I realised I couldn't add any more, because I didn't know any more, so I made a noncommittal grunt, a habit of mine which always drives Sara to distraction.

"Away is she?" the man continued. "I expect she's visiting that father of hers ? Well, when you see her, tell her Bill Garnett was asking after her."

I returned to our table with the phrase "that father of hers" bouncing around my head. Mother had never mentioned a father to me, but a relative stranger apparently knew of his existence. For the second time that day I began to look on my mother in a different light. She was now a mother with secrets; a mother with things she had seen fit to hide from me. I had grown up thinking I had no family, and now to my surprise it seems I had a grandfather, and goodness knows what else.

Sara could see something had upset me as I sat down. I told her what Garnett had said. I expected her to be as surprised as me, but she sat in silence, staring down into her glass. Then it dawned on me. Sara knew about my grandfather! I confronted her with this. She didn't deny it, and her silence confirmed it.

"She let it slip by accident, months ago, when I was doing her hair. We were talking about families. She asked me not to mention it to you, I don't know why. "

Her words spilled out, and tears welled up as she saw the hurt look on my face.

"I'm sorry, Pete, I really am, it's just...."
"Just what?" I snapped.

I must have raised my voice as the Stradbroke players at the next table turned and looked in our direction. I glowered back at them and they resumed their conversations.

" Drink up and let's go," I said, draining my glass rather too quickly and banging it hard on the table, shattering it in the process and cutting my hand into the bargain.

Silence roared across the pub. Sara put her unfinished drink down in embarrassment and we both got up to leave. As we opened the door, there was an ironic "goodnight" from the landlord. Sara smiled at him. I just walked out.

"You and your temper." was all she said.

It was snowing gently as we walked back home, and there was a slight covering on the road. We walked in silence. Sara knew I was upset by the events of the evening and that I felt betrayed by the two people I held most dear in my life. I cursed the bond that forms between women, excluding everyone of the male sex. Now you might think that I was making a fuss about this, but consider my feelings. It was obvious that I had jumped to the wrong conclusion about her family being dead, but why had mother never enlightened me? I could understand her never mentioning my father, after his walk out, but why not my grandfather ? There might even be a whole family somewhere I knew nothing about. She must have had her reasons, but I could not for the life of me think what they might be.

As we reached home, Sara took her car keys out of her bag and made for her car. Plans of staying the night seemed to have evaporated; still she hesitated before turning the key in the lock as though she expected me to try to persuade her to stay. I didn't.

"Well goodnight then," she said, still not getting into the car. " I'll see you tomorrow ?"

"Goodnight, drive carefully."

With that I gave her a kiss on the cheek and turned towards my front door, unlocked it and went inside without saying another word. Her car started up and she disappeared into the night. That was probably the most childish thing I had ever done. Talk about sulking. Sara rang after about 10 minutes to say she was home safely, a little tradition of ours, originally initiated by my mother. I made a clumsy attempt to apologise, but I suspect I failed miserably. We rang off with the promise of further contact the next day. I consumed another large whisky before retiring to bed.

I woke early the next morning with a raging hangover and an overwhelming feeling of guilt and remorse. Had I really treated my beloved Sara so badly last night? I knew the answer and immediately reached for the phone by the bed. I dialled Sara's number and before the end of the first ring the phone was answered.

"Hello," Sara's clear voice answered.
"Hi, it's me." I said almost apologetically down the phone.

Her reply was polite if rather frosty.

"Look, Pete, I'm going away to stay with Kate for a few days. I'll ring when I get back. I need time to think."
"About last night," I began, but Sara cut me short.

" forgotten," she said, an unconvincing tone in her voice. "I'll be back early next week. I'll ring you then. Bye."

With that the phone went dead. I was left staring blankly at the handset. The most important person in my life had just walked out of it. I rang straight back, but she had switched on the answer phone and even if she was there she had obviously no intention of answering it. I've been here before, I thought.

I got out of bed, showered, dressed and went downstairs. There were two letters on the mat, both junk mail from companies virtually begging me to take out a loan with them. I threw them in the bin straight away and settled to make breakfast. A cup of Earl Grey and a bowl of muesli later, I was feeling a bit more human. An overwhelming sense of injustice engulfed me, replacing the earlier feeling of guilt. After all, I said to myself, I was the one who had been kept in the dark. I was the one who had been treated badly by the two women I thought I could trust. Or was I, as usual, over-reacting? Probably. My fatal character flaw was showing itself once again.

Deciding there was no more I could do at the present, I set off to work. The weather was still cold and the roads were rather icy. I drove slowly, negotiating the numerous bends between Stradbroke and Diss with great care. As I passed the top of the road leading to Hoxne, I was tempted to turn down it, to see if Sara was still there. I resisted and carried straight on. I arrived in the thriving market town of Diss, parked up and strolled past the Mere, a charming little lake situated near the centre of the town, on the way to my shop.

As I walked through the door I could see Elaine, hard at work, talking to a potential customer. Elaine is one of those faithful people, an Earth Mother, quite happy with her job and with no intention of doing anything else. She has long black hair almost down to her waist. I suppose you might call her attractive, but she never went out of her way to make the best of her features. She looked at me over the top of her wire-rimmed glasses as I walked towards my office. In my fantasies I have always wanted to paint her in the nude, but I could just imagine the reaction if I ever broached the subject ! Still you can always dream. The shop itself, cleverly called "CHIAROSCURO", caters for all budding artists, selling paper, paints and brushes. It also provides a perfect outlet for the sale of my own watercolours. A lucrative little trade, now I was becoming quite well known. It certainly kept me in the manner I was getting used to.

Elaine finished serving the customer and looked questioningly at me, as if wanting some explanation for my absence yesterday. I offered none. Sod it, I'm the boss, I thought and went into the office to check the mail. As I sat there I realised I had done it again, and now it was Elaine who had received the Jackson cold shoulder. I went back into the shop and apologised, saying there had been some problem with mother.

"Not ill again, I hope?" asked Elaine.
"No, no," I replied. "She's just had to go away for a few days."

I pre-empted Elaine's next question by simply saying "up North", an assumption I had made after what Bill Garnett had said the previous evening.

For a horrible moment I thought Elaine was going to say, "to see her father ?" but she didn't. She simply said "Oh ?".

Elaine is not one of nature's curious people.

The day went quite quickly after that, and quite successfully. Mr. Jones of Southwold called in to ask if I would undertake the commission of doing a painting of his house. I said I would call the next day to have a look. I like doing commissions as they pay well, and this particular one meant a pleasant day out on the coast. I left for home shortly after five, and this time I did a detour through Hoxne village to see if there was any sign of Sara. The house was in darkness and the car was not parked outside. I drove back home and waited for mother to ring.

I had just poured myself a whisky - this is becoming a habit, I thought - when I had an awful thought. Tiger ! That damned cat ! I had to feed the blessed animal. Grabbing my coat I rushed around to mother's house and let myself in. The hungry looking animal gave me a look of disdain and positioned itself next to its now empty feeding bowl. I don't think the animal had ever liked me, a feeling heartily reciprocated, I might add, but now that dislike would probably have turned to positive hate. I scraped out its food into the bowl, filled up its water, changed the kitty litter and retired to the lounge. I noticed with interest that the light was flashing on the answer phone. Out of sheer curiosity I pressed the message button. It was a woman's voice, one that I vaguely recognised.

"Anne ? Sorry you're not in at the moment, but I just had to tell you the latest news. I met Phil the other day. He was down in Oxford on business, so he gave me a call. He asked after you, and of course Pete. Will try again later. Bye."

The city of Oxford was the clue. Mother's closest friend at college, Sue Greenwood, lived in the city of dreaming spires, so I presumed it must have been her making the call. However, the surprise was the name Phil. That was my father's name. The man who left when I was four. The man of whom I had no recollection. He asked after both of us. A rather strange action from someone who had made no contact with his son for so long. I walked round the house, checking that everything was as it should be. I even remembered to water mother's collection of plants. Just as I was leaving the phone rang. I managed to answer it before the machine took over.

"Hello, " I said.
"Oh, hello."

The voice on the other end of the phone sounded surprised, expecting to hear my mother's voice.

"Is that Sue, Sue Greenwood?" I enquired, knowing full well that it was, as I recognised the voice from the answer phone message.

"Why yes, how did you know? That's Pete isn't it? How are you?"

I resisted the temptation to ask if I could answer the questions in any order. I'd upset enough people lately, without adding another to my list. I explained that mother was away for a few days and I was at present house, plant and cat sitting. The phone went quiet at the other end. Another silence, I thought. This was becoming boring.

"Up North."

For the second time that day I pre-empted the question.

"Gone to visit friends has she?" Sue asked rather guardedly.
"I expect so, she didn't say," I replied equally guardedly.
"Well, tell her I rang, just for a chat, she gets back will you?"

I suppose she thought she had better indulge in some pleasantries before she rang off, so she continued.

"And how are you? And the business?"
"Fine on both counts, and yourself?"
"Pretty much as usual," replied Sue.

I had only met the woman about half a dozen times, the last time being at my wedding, so I was unsure what "usual" was, but I said I was pleased to hear it. With that we said our goodbyes and hung up.

I walked slowly back to my house, deep in thought. I settled back into my favourite armchair and continued with my whisky. Mother rang up later in the evening. She was, as usual, not very forthcoming. However, she did assure me that all was well and that she was staying in a lovely hotel called Sykeside House in Haslingden. I put the phone down and went to get the road atlas out of the car. I looked it up. Sure enough, Haslingden was about five miles from Accrington, my mother's birthplace. This seemed to confirm the theory that she was visiting relatives, probably my grandfather. Sara did not ring that evening. I went to bed feeling tired and depressed.

Chapter 2

EAST ANGLIA: GONE FOREVER

I couldn't sleep that night. My troubled mind took me on a journey from Stradbroke, to Accrington, Oxford and back to Stradbroke again. I suppose I must have slept, but I was unsure of exactly when. I was constantly churning over in my mind just what had happened to my world in the last twenty-four hours. I had lost my mother, on a temporary basis. I had lost my lover, hopefully on a temporary basis. On the other side of the coin I had gained a grandfather, and a father who apparently still asked about my welfare twenty six years after turning his back on me. Is it any wonder that I was confused ?

When morning did eventually arrive I was still tired and in need of sleep. It was cold and I did not want to get up one little bit. However, I forced myself to make a move. I had my ritual shower, Earl Grey and muesli. I now felt able to face the world once again, though a glance in the mirror suggested otherwise. I looked like death. At least the run out to the coast to meet Mr. Jones might wake me up a bit, especially if I drove with the windows open.

I set off towards Southwold; my appointment was not until 12 o'clock so there was plenty of time. The weather was much better that day; the frosts had disappeared, which made driving easier. I got there in good time, arriving in Southwold at about 11 o'clock. I tend to arrive everywhere early, rather than run the risk of being late. Having an hour to kill I thought I would take a stroll along the promenade, something I remember doing as a child. The wind blowing off the North Sea was certainly bracing and served to clear my head. I sat for a while, skimming pebbles, of which there was an abundance, into the sea, but try as I might I could not break the four bounce barrier. I have always enjoyed the pleasure of my own company. I suppose that was the artist in me surfacing. I thought mainly of Sara. I was already starting to miss her. She was perhaps the one person I would rather be with, than in my own splendid solitude. I made a conscious decision to ring her when I got home and to try to persuade her to come back. I was sure I had Kate's number somewhere.

My appointment with Mr. Jones went well. I was commissioned to paint his house, which in all fairness was a rather beautiful place, standing as it did near the shoreline. Painted at the right angle, I could incorporate the sea in the background, blending with the sky. I got a mental picture of the end product. I could really do justice to it, I was sure. As we sat down in his lounge for a cup of tea, I put forward my idea to Mr. Jones, and he seemed impressed. We arranged for me to come back in the spring to make preliminary sketches.

By the time I had got back to Stradbroke, I was feeling, for me, quite cheerful. I pulled into the drive and let myself in. I saw with slight amusement the yellow, sticky label that said TIGER!!! on the whisky bottle. I would be bound to notice that at some point in the not too distant future. So before I settled myself, I walked round to mother's house to feed the beast. There was no mail, nor were there any messages on the answer phone, much to my relief. So I did my duty towards Tiger, for which I received a begrudging miaow, and left.

I put a call through to Elaine at the shop to see if anything urgent had cropped up in my absence, but she assured me that there was nothing she couldn't take care of and that there was no point in me driving over that afternoon. I thanked my "little jewel" and rang off.

I looked across at the whisky bottle again. Should I ? No, it was too early in the day, so I contented myself with a cup of coffee and contemplated Sara. I knew I was going to call her, but I was afraid of the answer I might receive. I cursed my childish behaviour the other night, promising myself I would not act like that again.

I eventually found Kate's number. Kate was Sara's sister, who lived in Birmingham, Bartley Green to be precise, with her husband and two small children. I had met her several times and she shared Sara's good humour, blonde hair and green eyes. I keyed in the number on the pad, stopping before I pressed the final digit, my courage failing me at the last moment. I sat and stared at the phone. No doubt Sara and Kate had discussed matters, probably over a few glasses of red wine, and I was to be told where I got off. My confidence was at rock bottom. Nobody likes to be rejected, as I was convinced I was about to be. I tried again, not even getting to the last digit this time. I stood up and walked out into the garden to get some fresh air, disgusted with myself. It was on the third attempt that I finally dialled Kate's number. The phone rang about half a dozen times before Geoff, Kate's husband, finally answered it. I announced who I was and asked if I could speak to Sara. There was a silence until finally I heard Sara's voice.

" Well?"

The question was fired down the phone like a bullet; things did not sound too good, I feared the worst and my stomach began to churn. I had mentally prepared what I was going to say: how much I regretted snapping at her, how much I loved her, how it was all my fault, but it came out all wrong.

" Please come back, I'm sorry," was all I managed to blurt down the phone.
" OK. I've missed you, love you, I'll be back tomorrow."

The phone went dead. My heart gave a leap. I wanted to turn several cartwheels, but I thought better of it and poured myself a welcome glass of whisky! With a broad grin permanently etched on my face, I made myself a meal of egg and chips, since it was all that was left in the house. I promised myself I would make a celebratory dinner tomorrow when Sara had returned. I felt happy again. I didn't know it at the time, but that happiness would shortly be blown up in my face.

I decided that I would ask Sara to marry me as soon as she got back. Yes, I know we had both decided not to rush into things after our respective divorces, but the thought of losing her was a prospect too unpleasant to contemplate, and besides we had known each other for eighteen months. I was confident she would accept. I began to make plans for the wedding. It would of course have to be at the registry office as we were both divorced, but the reception would be a splendid affair, with no expense spared. I shook my head clear of these thoughts - careful, Pete, this is not like you at all. One thing at a time. I sat and stared at nothing in particular and thought of Sara. My reverie was broken by the telephone. Before I answered it I couldn't help thinking how big a part the telephone had played in my life over the last thirty-six hours. It was mother.

She sounded a little flat, but she wouldn't say why. I silently cursed the way she insisted on playing things close to her chest. The good news was she would be returning tomorrow, probably late afternoon, and would I make sure the central heating was switched back on. How typical of mother to think of such matters. I didn't have the heart to tell her that the central heating had not been turned off!

As I put the phone down I didn't realise that would be the last time I would speak to my beloved mother.

Not wanting to stay in the house on my own, I decided I would go to the Queen's Head and apologise to mine host for my rudeness the other night, to offer to pay for the glass and also to see if Bill Garnett was prepared to tell me more about my mother and her father. I washed up and set off to the pub. The place was deserted as I opened the door, which made me feel slightly better about the task in hand. I ferreted out the landlord and apologised for my rudeness. He gave me a noncommittal smile, said to forget about the glass and pulled my pint. I retired to the table Sara and I sat at two nights ago. I checked the highly polished surface by rubbing my hand over it, to see if my broken glass had done any damage. Thankfully, all seemed OK. I smiled inwardly to myself. I was feeling better; tomorrow would see the return of Sara and, of course, mother.

I began to plan my course of action. How would I play it with mother ? Should I greet her with all guns blazing, demanding an explanation, or should I let her tell me in her own good time? Knowing my mother, I decided on the latter, aware that she would not be forced into doing anything she did not want. All I did know is that I would get to the bottom of this once and for all. I could be stubborn as well. I forced another pint of Adnams down me. I think a combination of the whisky and beer was starting to take effect, so

I decided the best course of action would be home and bed. Just as I was leaving, who should appear but Bill Garnett. I nodded to him. I didn't feel sober enough to ask him about my mother. He nodded back and asked if she had returned yet.

"Tomorrow " I replied.
"Perhaps I'll pop round and see how the little old boy is getting on," said Garnett in his deep Suffolk drawl, but before I could reply he had moved over to the bar and was ordering a drink.

I half made to follow him, but decided against it. As I walked home I was pondering his last remark. I presumed that by the "little old boy", he meant my grandfather. This was going to take some getting used to. My family was going to extend beyond Mother and myself. Another thought crossed my mind: just how did Bill Garnett know so much, and what relationship did he have with my mother? Surely not a physical one ? But after all mother would only have been around twenty-eight when my father left, and very attractive. I shut my eyes. Bill Garnett would probably be about the same age as my mother. Oh God, things were getting complicated ! I needed to talk to her, and how.

My head was really starting to spin as I unlocked the front door and went inside. I decided, surprisingly, given my habits of the last few days, against having another whisky. Instead I made myself a strong cup of coffee. I smiled to myself - perhaps I should start calling it a "brew" to please my grandfather! A friend at university came from the north and always referred to his coffee as that. I retired to bed and slept soundly until the alarm went off next morning.

I followed my usual morning ritual, shower, breakfast, then a quick stroll to mother's to feed that damned cat. I actually whistled as I walked along, feeling happy that Sara and Mother would both return to my life later that day. All tasks being accomplished, I drove to work. Elaine was already there busying herself with tidying the shelves, although to me they already looked perfectly presentable. I gave her a peck on the cheek, something that I never did. It took the poor woman quite by surprise and she became quite flustered. Seeing the effect I'd had on her I apologised,

"I'm sorry, it's just that I'm in quite a good mood this morning. Look, why don't you take the day off ? I'll look after things here." Elaine did not take second bidding.
"If you're sure," she paused, " there are some things I have to do."

With that she got her coat and was off. I could not for the life in me think what Elaine would have to do, she was far too organised not to have allotted time to do them already. However, off she went.

The day turned out to be pretty run of the mill. I made the odd sale of artist's paper, the occasional print, but nothing out of the ordinary. I closed up at 5 o'clock and drove steadily home. I called at mother's just to see if she had arrived back yet. There was no car in the drive. I glanced at the dashboard clock, which glowed 5.30. Must have been held up, I thought. I turned the car round and drove home.

"Sod it ! " I exclaimed, realising I hadn't got any food in for Sara's return. Oh well, we would go out to eat, and hang the expense. I had a quick shower and rang mother's house to see if she was back yet, but there was no reply. At about 6.30 I heard the sound of a car on the drive. Sara, I thought to myself, and rushed to the door, which I flung open anticipating a passionate welcome. It was perhaps as well that I didn't embrace the party standing on the doorstep. For there were two police officers standing there, one of whom I recognised as being the local constable, P.C. Rothwell, also an inhabitant of Stradbroke. My first thought was of the shop.

Someone had broken in, stolen some pictures and trashed the place. However, a glance at their faces indicated something more serious.

"Mr. Jackson ?" asked P.C. Rothwell.
"You know damned well I am," I snapped back.
"May we come in ?" asked the second one, whom I did not recognise.

Without speaking, I stood to one side and let them pass. I directed them into the living room and indicated for them to sit down. Preferring to stand, the two police officers looked at each other rather awkwardly as if they didn't know where to begin.

"I'm afraid we've got some bad news for you. There's been a crash."
"And ?" I almost shouted, though I knew deep down inside what was coming next.
"I'm afraid she's been killed, the driver of the car that is."

P.C. Rothwell quoted the number and make of my mother's car, currently being kept at her address, pointing out that being local to the village he knew that I was the obvious person to contact, once the confirmatory telex had been received at the police station in Ipswich. Apparently a phone call is not enough, due to the possibility of hoax calls! Obviously without formal identification he could not say for definite that it was mother. However, he did say after consulting his notebook that the deceased was female, aged probably mid-fifties and wearing jeans and a yellow sweatshirt bearing the Lacoste logo. I knew mother possessed such a top. P.C. Rothwell then stated that I should prepare myself that the deceased might be my mother.

It was unlikely that they had made a mistake. I stood up and walked to the window. I breathed deeply, turned and sat down. I stared at one policeman and then the other. To this day I don't know why I said it but I did.

"But what about the cat ?"

In a state of shock I broke down and wept. I suppose that the police are used to situations like this, so neither of them spoke for several minutes. When they did, it was words of condolence. At that moment another car pulled into the drive. I heard footsteps running on the gravel. It was Sara. She had seen the police car parked outside and come rushing in.

"What's happened ?" she cried out. " What's going on?"

She took one look at my face and I swear she knew. She rushed over to my side and put her small, cold hand in mine.

"It's Anne isn't it?"

I nodded, tears welling up. I stifled a sob.

"She's been killed in a car crash."

She hugged me and I felt the warmth of her body against mine. I noticed that she too was crying openly. A sorry pair we must have made for the two officers, who, with all credit to them, said not a word.

I regained my composure first.

"So what happens now?" I asked, surprised at the steadiness of my voice.

P.C. Rothwell explained that the body would have to be formally identified.

"So where is the, the..... body ?" I asked. It took me a long time to say that last word.
"At the hospital in Peterborough, " responded P.C. Rothwell.
"When do I.....?" I could feel myself going again.
"Tomorrow, if possible," replied the officer, knowing what my question was going to be.
"Report to the police station in Peterborough first and ask for the family liaison officer. They will be expecting you." He gave me the address.
"I'll drive you there," Sara offered, a gesture for which I was grateful.

P.C. Rothwell and his colleague stood up to leave and I followed them to the door. I almost said "thank you", but I realised just in time how ridiculous such a statement that would be under the circumstances.

"Well, goodbye sir, " they both said as they climbed back into their car. I remained outside, staring at the drive for several minutes before going back inside.

Sara and I held each other for a long time, comforted by each other's grief. We didn't speak for at least half an hour, though it may have been longer, or it may only have been for a few minutes, I couldn't tell. At last Sara broke the silence.

"I'll make a drink," she said in a flat voice, and disappeared into the kitchen. I sat down on the settee, staring into space, uncertain of what to do or say. Sara reappeared after a while, carrying two cups of coffee which, I noticed, had been liberally laced with whisky.

Illogically I thought that whisky bottle must be nearly empty by now.

We drank in silence, content to be alone with our thoughts. I had lost a mother, Sara had lost a friend and, I suspect, a confidant. My mother was gone. I must confess I didn't know what to do next. Sara did not go home that night, instead we went to bed and cried each other to sleep.

I woke early next morning, thinking perhaps it had all been a dream, which I suppose is the natural reaction under the circumstances. I knew deep down inside, of course, that it hadn't. Sara came downstairs and we had a silent breakfast before setting off on the journey to Peterborough. We called at Sara's house, so she could get changed. I rang Elaine from Sara's, informing her of the sad events of the previous day. Efficient as ever, she told me not to worry about anything at that end, she would take care of everything. Somehow I just knew she would. Elaine, bless her, seemed to thrive on a crisis.

I remember very little about the journey to Peterborough. Sara drove slowly, in a subconscious attempt to delay the inevitable. I sat staring out of the rapidly steaming up window of the car. Even the dark threatening clouds seemed to reflect my sombre mood. Illogically, I wanted to paint them to capture my melancholy for all time. I said nothing of these thoughts to Sara, who said not a word as she negotiated the traffic heading towards the A1.

Being Saturday, the town centre traffic was heavy and slow moving as people searched for a car parking space. After getting lost once, we finally arrived at the police station in the town. We presented ourselves at the desk and were directed to an interview room, where Sergeant Wilson, who was the family liaison officer for the case, met us. He informed us that the crash had taken place yesterday afternoon at about 2 o'clock. It appeared that the car had left the road and had smashed into a tree. Death, he added, almost as a consolation, would have been instantaneous. He explained that I would have to formally identify the body before the coroner would release it from the hospital morgue.

Sergeant Wilson and a colleague drove us to Peterborough District Hospital; not a word was spoken as we picked our way through the traffic. The hospital was a large tower block. We entered reception from where we were directed to the mortuary. It was in the form of a small chapel of rest, with a crucifix positioned at one end and flowers arranged around the side in small alcoves. The body lay on a trolley, underneath a white sheet, which was respectfully raised by the attendant. Mother's lifeless face stared back at me. There could be no mistake. It was definitely her. Strands of her beautiful auburn hair, carefully combed and arranged, just as mother would have liked it, framed her bruised face. She looked strangely peaceful as she lay there. I closed my eyes and thought about my mother. How she had struggled to bring me up on her own. How she had put my interests first in everything. How she had been there for me when I divorced Linda. There would be no more phone calls telling me what she had done that day, or asking how my day had gone. No more secret huddles and giggles with Sara when I went out of the room. No more celebrations when she won £10 on the lottery. No more silly little gifts for me when she returned from shopping trips. The sense of loss overwhelmed me, as I stood there not moving for several minutes. The faint rumble of trains coming from nearby Peterborough station brought me out of my trance. It would take a long time before I would be able to hear railway noises again without shuddering. I nodded and the sheet was lowered again. Tears in my eyes, I walked slowly out of the room and held Sara in my arms.

We returned to the police station where we were given a cup of hot sweet tea. I signed a form filled in by Sergeant Wilson, with my assistance. Mother's full name, her address, date of birth, maiden name, occupation were all details that had to be recorded. Sergeant Wilson explained there would have to be an inquest, but he was sure a verdict of accidental death would be returned. He did ask if mother had been upset about anything, as the car appeared to have left the road for no reason. I explained that mother had not been well recently and she had been up to the North of England to see relatives. As far as I knew she had not been worried about anything. The coroner would release the body on the following Monday. I would have to make arrangements with an undertaker to take it back home. He then gave me mother's belongings found in the car, her suitcase, some tapes and of course the money and jewellery found on the body. I signed for this, not really taking much notice of what was going on.

The next few days went by in a blur. Undertakers were contacted and all arrangements were made. Death certificates were made out and sent off to the relevant parties, insurance companies, and mother's solicitor. I do not wish to dwell too much on the details, but suffice it to say the funeral was arranged for the following Friday at 11.30. The service was to take place at Stradbroke Parish church, followed by an interment at the cemetery down the road. My mother did not believe in cremation. Everyone says that the most difficult part of the death of a loved one is the waiting for the funeral. I have to agree with them. I suppose it's not knowing how you will react that makes things difficult. I pride myself on always being in control, unless my temper gets the better of me, but I had no idea how I would take things on Friday.

There was an endless stream of callers to the house as soon as word got round the village. Every postal delivery brought piles of sympathy cards, filling every available shelf, nook and cranny. I did not realise how many people my mother knew in and around the Stradbroke area. Bill Garnett came to the house, tears in his eyes, and he showed more emotion than one would expect from someone who merely lived in the same village. I was in no mood to ask him any questions about his relationship with my mother, but even in my upset state, I made a note to talk to him about the matter after the funeral.

Sue Greenwood, mother's best friend, arrived from Oxford and took up residence on the Thursday night. She was a small, rather intense woman with long grey hair gathered together in a ponytail. Not what you would call traditionally beautiful, but I was sure she would have been attractive when she was younger. Considering she was the same age as my mother, she looked a lot older, due in no little part to the fact that her clothes were rather dated, to say the least. Perhaps I was being hard, comparing her with mother, who even in her fifties always dressed in the height of fashion. She prided herself on still being able to make men's heads turn when she entered a room.

Sue was obviously very upset, and talked non-stop about mother, without really saying anything. She seemed most distressed by the fact that she never got to say goodbye. Natural sentiments, but I hadn't the heart to tell her that nobody really got to say goodbye. Sudden death is like that. Again I decided I had to talk to her at a later date, to find out more about mother. I wondered about my father, and whether he should be informed. Sue would probably know how to contact him.

I was just about to ask her this, but she saved me the trouble by telling me that she had phoned him and relayed the sad news. I sat there stunned, when she said that he would try to attend the funeral. I wasn't sure if I wanted that, but what could I do ? I was not up to arguing the point, but the prospect of seeing my father again filled me with a feeling of foreboding, tinged with curiosity.

Sara appeared later that evening and Sue tactfully retired to her room. I can honestly say that without Sara I don't think I would have managed. She was a real tower of strength. She accompanied me every day, making the visits to registrars, undertakers and church. My proposal of marriage had been put on hold, but now I was even more determined to ask her. We sat down on the settee and held each other closely. Sara glanced over into the corner of the room. There was mother's suitcase given to me in Peterborough. I followed her gaze and shook my head.

"I haven't had the heart to open it yet, I just can't bring myself to even think about it," I explained.
"Quite understandable," she replied, giving me a quick kiss on the top of my head, which was now cradled in her arms, "I'll sort it out for you after tomorrow."

Sara realised that it would probably be too painful a process for me. She was right. However, the real anguish would come when mother's house had to be cleared and eventually put on the market. I went sick at the prospect. Sara must have read my mind.

"Don't think about that just yet," she whispered, and squeezed my hand in that familiar reassuring fashion. We kissed and sat in silence, each wanting to be alone with our thoughts. After about an hour of this spectacular silence, Sara got up to go. I really wanted her to stay the night, but it didn't seem appropriate somehow.

"See you tomorrow," she said. "I'll be with you."

I took great comfort from that last remark. Without Sara I would have felt very alone. Whilst I was waiting for her traditional "home safe" call I wondered if I could have done more about trying to contact my grandfather in Accrington. I knew he was called Lord, because that was my mother's maiden name, but I had no address or even an initial to go on. I could have asked Sue if she knew any details, but I thought better of it. After all, I wasn't even supposed to know of his existence. He had shown no interest in me for thirty years, so I felt no loyalty towards him. Hard sentiments, but understandable, I justified to myself. Sara rang after about fifteen minutes; she was back at home. The call was even more important to me now after mother's death.

The next day duly arrived, the cold wintry sun shining brightly, which mother would have liked. She was always fond of this time of year.

"Spring is just around the corner," she would say.

The church was packed for the service. Not one of the little wooden pews were empty, indeed some people were actually standing at the back. So many wanted to pay their last respects. There were people I had never seen before: colleagues from work, old pupils and of course the majority of the village. Little tears of pride pricked the back of my eyes as I gazed around me. Sara, Sue and I, the chief mourners, followed the coffin down the aisle to the accompaniment of Mendelssohn's Funeral March. The single wreath of lilies rested peacefully on top of the coffin. We took up our seats in the pew at the front.

"I am the resurrection and the life: he that believeth in me, though he were dead, yet shall he live," began the vicar, commanding the attention of the assembled gathering.

The service was .... I don't suppose lovely is the appropriate word, but it was not as unpleasant as I had presupposed. The vicar gave an overview of mother's life, extolling her virtues and her service to the community. All the time he was talking I stared at the red, black and white tiles making a tessellating pattern on the floor. Sara sat next to me and held my hand throughout the service. I nearly broke down as we sang the 23rd Psalm to the tune of Crimond, a particular favourite of mother's. She once told me it was one of the first tunes she learned to play on the piano.

Sue had asked to say a few words, so she walked slowly to the front of the church and told of the fun she had had with my mother over the years. She ended up with a few words from a poem written by mother when she was at college, apparently dedicated to her friendship with Sue. Tears rolled down my cheeks as I heard Sue's clear voice ring out through the church, turning towards the coffin as she spoke.

"Seasons go, years go, but friends go on for always - you will always be my pal, even after death...."

After the service, the coffin was carefully carried back out of the Church to the graveyard, where, after the final committal, mother's body was finally laid to rest.

I noticed as we were leaving that Sue was walking with a man. That, I thought to myself, must be my father. He was about as tall as me, but lacking the red hair. I knew I had to talk to him at some point during the afternoon, a prospect that did not exactly make me feel any better. We arrived back at my house, the three of us by car, whilst the rest of the mourners walked, since it was no distance.

Outside caterers, organised of course by Sara, had made the traditional funeral breakfast. I didn't feel like eating. I much preferred the odd glass of whisky to keep me going.

Throughout the afternoon people kept coming up to me offering their condolences. People I hardly knew would shake me by the hand, give me a kiss on the cheek, or hug me. I found it all overwhelming. Then came the moment I had been dreading. Sue was walking towards me with the man who must be my father. He was wearing an expensive-looking suit, beautifully tailored, showing all the signs of affluence. I could see myself in him as he walked across the room. In fact, take twenty-five or so years off him and give him ginger hair, and it could have been me. He avoided eye contact until Sue introduced us.

"Pete," she began, "Pete, this is your father."

He offered his hand, and to my surprise I took it. It was a rough hand, the hand of one used to hard manual work. He looked as nervous as I felt.

"Hello son," he said, and smiled at me.

Try as I might, I could not bring myself to say "hello dad." After all, I had not seen him for over twenty years, and during that time he had made no effort to see me or even send me a birthday card. I couldn't help thinking what a cold-hearted man he must be, and that my mother was well rid of him all those years ago. However, like it or not, he was my natural father, so I felt obliged to speak to him.

"Hello," I mumbled back. " Good of you to come." I couldn't hide the touch of irony in my voice. Whether he detected it or not, I did not know or really care.
"Listen son, we need to talk. There's a lot to catch up on."
"There needn't have been if you'd stayed around." I replied. " You were the one who went away, remember".

I began to turn away, indicating that as far as I was concerned the conversation was over. I really felt as if I couldn't bring myself to be civil to this man if we continued talking any longer. My eyes searched the room for Sara. When I located her she was in conversation with Elaine. I started to walk towards them, but to my surprise, my father moved in front of me and blocked my path.

"Look," he said, " I know how it must seem, but it's not like that at all. I didn't walk out and leave you. Anne made my life so miserable I had to go."

I could feel my temper rising and it took a real conscious effort to stop myself from hitting him.

"Perhaps this is not the best day to speak ill of the dead," I replied in a rather acidic tone, the irony in my voice replaced now with disgust. He seemed to shrink visibly before my eyes, realising the wisdom of my remark and the unpleasantness of his.

"I'm sorry," he mumbled, "but could we have a talk sometime?"

I couldn't help detecting a note of pleading in his voice, though the words sounded genuine enough. I agreed coolly, asking him to leave me his number so that I could ring him. I glanced at the business card he handed me. Jackson's Garage, it said, and 01422 preceded the number. I looked enquiringly at him.

"I have my own garage, in Halifax." he said. "I'm doing quite well. I'd love for you to come and see it."

There was a note of pride in his voice, which was not lost on me. He was trying to hold out an olive branch, to restore contact, to have his son back. I shuddered at the thought. He would have to do some pretty impressive talking to make me change the way I thought about him. I made my excuses and moved away.

People were starting to leave by now and I felt it my duty to bid them farewell. I positioned myself near the door, wishing Sara would come and join me, not just for moral support, but because I wanted to hold her hand. Bill Garnett was heading, rather unsteadily, towards me. He was wearing an ill-fitting dark blue suit and a badly stained black tie. Sausage roll crumbs had gathered in the creases of his shirt. He looked a mess. Here was another man who was involved in my mother's past, to what degree I wasn't certain, but I was determined to find out. He shook my hand as he was leaving. I flinched as he breathed alcohol fumes in my face.

"Goodbye," he said. "A pity he had to come." He nodded towards my father, who was talking to Sue, and nearly fell over in the process. I didn't comment, but just thanked him for coming and suggested we had a chat about mother in the future. He seemed to think that might be a good idea.

"I'm in the pub most nights."

That I could well believe. Putting my hand in my pocket, I surreptitiously wiped it with a handkerchief in an effort to rid my self of the greasy deposit Garnett had left there.

My father was next to go. He smiled at me as he approached; did I detect some paternal affection and pride? Surely not after all these years ? We parted, again, but this time I did promise to get in touch with him when things had been sorted out and my life had returned to normal. He said he understood perfectly and would await my call. I must admit I was intrigued by his earlier comments and wanted to know more. Again the feeling of not really knowing my mother was driven into my mind.

Eventually everyone had left. The three of us sat down with relieved expressions on all our faces. Sara went into the kitchen to make coffee, whilst Sue remained in the lounge with me. I looked across at her and she smiled. I couldn't help but think there was something behind that smile.

"Well, just what do you know about mother's past ?" I enquired.
"More than can be told now," she replied. "Much more."
"We need to meet up, and then you can enlighten me," I responded.

She looked me straight in the face and agreed. I wrote down her number on the back of the business card my father had given me. Sara came back at that point, and no more was said about the matter. We began to clear up, chatting about the events of the day. Sara and Sue seemed to have become quite friendly, but Sara was like that, she got on with most people.

I had an overwhelming sense of relief that the funeral was over and perhaps, just perhaps, I could start unravelling the parts of my life mother had seen fit not to tell me about, not the least of which was the prospect of having a grandfather somewhere in the north of England. Why, oh why had his existence been kept from me? More to the point, why had he not kept in touch with his daughter and grandson ? Oh mother, I thought, there is so much you should have told me. Still, I was determined to find out, somehow. Sara stayed that night. We needed each other. After making love, I lay awake for a long time, wondering what was going to happen next.

Chapter 3

EAST ANGLIA: PUZZLES

Sue left for Oxford the following day. It was an emotional farewell; I had grown to like her over the last couple of days. I wished we could have met under more pleasant circumstances. Sara liked her as well, which was good enough for me. As she manoeuvred her Citroen 2CV out of the drive she paused, and I made her promise to ring as soon as she got back home, thus encompassing her in the Jackson "travelled home safely" umbrella. She of course said she would.

"How like your mother you are, to insist upon such things." she said.

Tears began to appear in her eyes as she waved a final farewell out of the car window. She and mother must have been close, as close as sisters in their earlier lives. I knew I must visit Sue and find more about their life together at teacher training college. Perhaps she could tell me more about the mother I thought I knew so well. Sara and I went back into the house. Alone at last, we collapsed on the settee and embraced each other. We had promised ourselves a completely relaxing Saturday and Sunday before we started the daunting task of sorting out mother's home, a job I was not looking forward to in the least. Being our own bosses, it was easy for us to take the following week off to try to get things moving. I had promoted Elaine to manageress for the duration, whilst Sara had passed all her appointments for the following week onto a colleague, who gladly accommodated them.

I wanted to get away from Stradbroke for at least one day, so I suggested a trip to Ipswich to do some shopping. We both realised that this was pure escapism, but Sara, true to her sex, readily agreed. The day was largely uneventful. I bought a new pair of jeans and a sweatshirt, whilst Sara indulged herself in a new skirt and top and sundry other items that she insisted were needed to supplement her wardrobe. She wrinkled her nose in pleasure as I bought her a silver bracelet to say thank you for all her help over the last week. It was just nice to be together in a different environment. I have always liked Ipswich, ever since mother used to take me there as a small boy. She once pointed out where she lived before I was born, but I have never been able to find it since. As we strolled round the town mother's death inevitably kept creeping back into my thoughts. I don't wish to sound heartless, I loved my mother very much, but we all have our own ways of dealing with grief. You never really know how until it happens to you. In my case, now that the funeral was over I wanted to find out more, much more, about mother's family and the reasons for her secretive behaviour. That would be my mourning, my comfort, my shoulder to cry on. Easier said than done, I suppose, but I was determined to try. No doubt my resolve would waver a little as we started to clear her personal effects.

We called in at the town of Framlingham on the way back for a meal. We had put out of our minds the upsets of the last few days and enjoyed ourselves to the full. I was driving, so could only drink orange juice, but I'm sure my liver appreciated the rest. We even respectfully said "hello" to the statue of the bishop, driving past it as we arrived back in Stradbroke. As we turned down the main street, a man was lurching around in the middle of the road. I saw him just in time. I slammed my brakes on and swerved to the side, missing him by only a few feet. I jumped out of the car to find a very drunk and wild-eyed Bill Garnett lying on the pavement outside the post office. He was wearing the same suit he wore at the funeral, so crumpled that I doubted he had taken it off since yesterday. As I approached him I could see he was actually crying, trying to get up and failing miserably.

"I loved her, I really loved her," he was saying over and over again, "oh I know she used me, but I didn't mind. That bastard, glad he went !"

He looked up, and seeing who I was, began to crawl away, nervously glancing over his shoulder as he went.

"Bill ..... Bill !" I called after him. "Are you all right?"

He didn't so much answer, as vomit in the gutter, then managed to pick himself up and proceeded rather unsteadily on his way.

His words echoed in my head. I tried to dismiss them as the ramblings of a drunken man, but for some reason, I couldn't help thinking they had something to do with mother. I got back in the car and we continued our journey home. I told Sara what Garnett had said, but since she didn't know my thoughts about his relationship with mother, she simply thought that he was talking about a woman in one of the neighbouring villages, with whom, she had heard, he was having an affair. Hairdressers do, after all, pick up a lot of gossip. I wasn't convinced, but made no further comment.

A hungry looking Tiger, who incidentally was in full time residence with me now, rubbed himself around our legs in greeting. Sara actually liked the creature, and the feeling was reciprocated. I decided that this must be a flaw in her character, but Tiger went up a few rating points with me. I dropped several hints about Sara taking him back to her house, but I don't think she liked him that much. I noticed out of the corner of my eye that the answer phone light was flashing. I pressed the button and there was Sue's voice announcing her safe return home. We looked at each other in a guilty fashion. We had both forgotten she was going to ring. It was too late to call back that night, but I would contact her the next day to apologise.

Sara was up first next morning. I could hear her busying herself in the kitchen. She entered the bedroom wearing one of my shirts, which barely covered her modesty, and carrying a cup of tea and a slice of toast.

"Here you are, lazy bones, but don't ever think this will become a normal procedure in the future."

With that she walked out of the room and downstairs. I must train her to fetch a paper, I thought, but I would never be brave enough to speak it out loud. However, I liked the remark about in the future. I drank my tea - not Earl Grey, she would have to be told about my early morning foibles, but only when hell freezes over - and ate my toast. I had just finished when I heard her coming up the stairs again. Thoughts of bacon and egg were quickly dispelled as I saw her visibly shaken, pale face coming through the door. In her hand she was carrying what looked for all the world like a wedding invitation card. She silently handed it over. I opened it up and read the words inside:

ORDER OF SERVICE
FOR THE FUNERAL OF
MR. F.J.LORD

6th February 1997

"Where did you find this ?" I asked in a puzzled voice.
"I started to look through Anne's suitcase, and there it was on the top," she replied, hardly able to keep the sadness out of her voice.

I had no need to read any further. Here in front of me was the reason for mother's trip north. Her father had died and she had gone to his funeral. I looked at the date; it was exactly a week and a day before her own, the day before she had herself died. I was speechless. Sara held me close to her, equally stunned. I had gained a grandfather and lost him again in a matter of days. I read the black-edged card again. The words stayed the same. The service had taken place at the parish church in Accrington. I decided there and then that a trip to the North of England was essential for me, if only to find out more about the circumstances of this latest death. Though where I would go and whom I would contact was still a puzzle.

I got out of bed, showered and dressed. I made my way downstairs to find Sara sitting on the settee reading what appeared to be an official letter. She passed it over to me.

"Here's part of the mystery solved, " was her only comment.

I took the letter and began to read. It was from Messrs. Robinson and Robinson, a firm of solicitors in Accrington, Lancashire. The gist of the letter was that a Mr. F.J.Lord had passed away on the 30th of January in Queens Park Hospital, Blackburn. He had left instructions that a Mrs. Anne Jackson should be informed, but only after his death. Here the letter gave mother's address. She was to be his sole beneficiary. Could she present herself to the office with proof of identification as soon as possible, in order for the details of the estate to be worked out quickly ? The letter added, almost as an afterthought, that the funeral would be held on the 6th of February, at Accrington Parish Church. This would, of course, account for mother's rapid departure on that Tuesday morning. I noted the letter was dated the 31st of January. I could only assume that the intervening weekend had slowed down the delivery.

I was beginning to feel rather sickened. What sort of rift had occurred between my mother and her father to have caused such a cold-hearted attitude on his part? I could not imagine any circumstances which would drive a family apart to such an extent. Grandfather had left his estate to mother, so he had tried so bring about some reconciliation, but only after his death. I was starting to wonder just what sort of family I belonged to.

I immediately dialled the number of the solicitors, forgetting that even solicitors don't work on a Sunday. I simply got a recorded message saying the office would be open again on Monday. I glanced over at Sara, who was holding mother's passport, which she had just taken out of the suitcase.

"Proof of identification," she mused.

There was nothing further we could do that day so we went for a walk into the village. The snow was starting to fall again as we returned about an hour later. We were both feeling much healthier after the walk, and we spent the rest of the afternoon and evening curled up in front of the fire. Not much was said, as we were both feeling rather shell shocked after the latest revelation. I commented at one point to Sara that I didn't think I could take many more surprises. I would have to before I had finished.

Sara went home that night at about 9.30, claiming a lack of clean clothes. As she drove away she said she would be round the next day to make a start on mother's house.

"Not too early, " I smiled, not because I didn't want to see Sara but because I wanted to put off going round to mother's for as long as possible. Who knew what we would unearth when we started to search ?

I poured myself a whisky - I felt like I deserved it - and sat down and read again the letter from the solicitors. I still could make no sense of the whole affair. No doubt Messrs. Robinson and Robinson would be able to shed some light on matters in the morning. I had consumed half of the drink, when Sara rang to announce her safe return.

"Goodnight sweetheart," were her closing words to me. I wished she were still here. I then began to realise just how tired I was feeling, so I drained the rest of the whisky, patted Tiger and set off for bed. I was just going upstairs when the phone began to ring. Should I let it ring and let the answer phone take over, or should I answer it? I decided it might be Sara, so I picked it up. It wasn't Sara, It was Sue Greenwood. Damn ! I still hadn't contacted her.

"So I've caught you at last," were Sue's opening comments.
"Not quite in the act," I laughingly replied, surprised at my humorous retort. I was pleased to hear Sue's voice again; she was a link to mother, and one which I was keen to hang on to.

"Well, better luck next time," she replied, entering into the spirit of things. "Look, Peter, we really must meet up again to talk about your mother. I'm sure there are a lot of questions you would like to ask. Perhaps, just perhaps, I may be able to answer them."
"Why didn't she tell me about her father still being alive?" I dived straight in. There was silence at the other end of the phone. I didn't prompt, I just waited. Sue realised this and answered.
"How did you find out? I thought I was the only other person to know about him."
"Think again, Sue." I related the meeting with Bill Garnett in the pub.
"Bill Garnett, of course, he *would* know. " She emphasised the word.

I was slightly shaken when Sue confessed to knowing about the very existence of Bill Garnett, and said as much.

"We really need to talk, but I don't think the phone is the best place to do it," she replied. "Can you come over to Oxford sometime and I can tell you things face to face ?"
"Of course I can, but there is something you should know first."

I related the account of my grandfather's death. Again there was a stunned silence.
"So the old sod has died, has he ?" Sue asked rhetorically. "This doesn't really change things. I ought to see you. How about this Wednesday ?"
"Fine by me," I replied. "Better give me instructions on how to find your place. Let me get a pen."

I balanced the phone between my shoulder and ear, jotting down the instructions as she spoke. I arranged to arrive at about 11 o'clock. I put the phone down, all thoughts of sleep now gone; I poured myself another whisky and lit a cigarette. I inhaled deeply and blew smoke into the room. So Sue thinks my grandfather was an "old sod", I mused. I must confess I agreed with her if the contents of the solicitor's letter were to be believed. I finished the whisky and cigarette and went to bed.

Sleep came quickly that night and I slept soundly until about 8 the next morning, when I was awakened by the postman pushing letters through the letter box. Slipping on my dressing gown I went downstairs to inspect the mail. There was the usual clutch of junk mail, but one letter in particular caught my eye. It was an official-looking letter, neatly typed, with a local postmark. Like most people I began to guess who it might be from, rather than actually opening it straight away. I couldn't guess, so I opened it. It was from mother's solicitors in Diss. I read it through, and the upshot was that they were in possession of mother's will and would I go to their office at a date and time convenient to me and ask for a Mr. Taylor, who was dealing with the matter. Never before did I realise the number of formalities you had to go through when there had been a death in the family, but there again, why should I? Death had never touched me this closely before.

Sara arrived shortly after breakfast, carrying two suitcases and dressed in an old pair of jeans and a baggy T-shirt, with "Hairdressers do it with style" written across it. I looked enquiringly at the suitcases.

"I've decided to economise on petrol, seeing I'm losing all my business this week, so I'm moving in. " She gave me a sly grin, her eyes looking down at the floor in mock coyness. "That's if you don't object."
"Rather presumptuous of you, young lady," I remarked, pretending to weigh up all the options in my mind. "Oh, go on then." We held each other tightly for several minutes. A delicious soapy smell entered my nostrils.

"I'll make up the spare room," I said, a comment which was rewarded with a playful clip round the ear. I told Sara about Sue's call the night before and my proposed visit to Oxford on Wednesday. Sara thought it best if I went on my own.

"Besides," she said, "it'll give me a chance to take your mother's clothes to the charity shop in Ipswich."

I felt a little disappointed that Sara would not be joining me, though I could see the wisdom of her remarks.

I had two phone calls to make before we could start on mother's house, ironically both to solicitors and both about wills. I rang through to mother's solicitors in Diss first, gave my name and asked to speak to Mr. Taylor. I did not have to wait long before a well-educated voice was speaking to me on the other end of the phone.

"Ah, Mr. Jackson, good of you to get in touch so quickly. I was deeply sorry to hear about your mother's untimely death. Please do accept the company's condolences."

I thanked him for his kind remarks, but got straight down to business.

"You said something about making an appointment concerning mother's will."
"Quite," Mr Taylor responded. "When would be convenient ?"
"How about tomorrow ?" I asked, aware as soon as I spoke of what seemed like indecent haste. "Or is that too soon ?" I continued, trying to sound less eager.
"No, tomorrow will be fine," Mr. Taylor answered. "Now let me see, around 10, will that suit ?"
I replied in the affirmative, said goodbye and rang off.

"Well that's phase one completed, " I shouted to Sara, who was busy unpacking upstairs. "Now for phase two."

I dialled the number of Robinson and Robinson in Accrington, wondering if this call would be as easy as the first. The phone was engaged the first time I tried. I managed to get through at the second attempt.

"Robinson and Robinson, Gill speaking, how can I help you?"

The voice had an unmistakable northern lilt. I waited for a few seconds to see if she would add, "chuck" onto the end. She didn't, so I replied,
"My name is Peter Jackson. Could I speak to someone who has been dealing with the business of the late Mr.F.J.Lord ?"

Gill replied that she would see what she could do, and would I please hold ? A crackling version of Rossini's Thieving Magpie came over the phone. Within a couple of minutes, the hold music stopped.

"Hello Mr. Jackson, " It was Gill again. "I'm connecting you to Mr. Robinson now."

I wonder if that's Mr. Robinson senior or junior, I mused to myself.

"Hello Mr. Jackson." But for the northern accent I might have been speaking to Mr. Taylor again. "How can I help you ?"

I explained who I was, but before I could continue Mr. Robinson interrupted,

"I'm sorry to have to stop you there, but our dealings are with your mother, and I'm not prepared to discuss the business with you, at the express request of the late Mr. Lord."

"What ? He actually said not to talk to me ?" I was flabbergasted.

"Yes, I'm afraid so," replied Mr. Robinson, "so you see my hands are tied. Any communication regarding the will must be with your mother."

"You might have a problem there," I replied. "You see.... you see, she's dead."

I almost choked on the last word. I think it was the first time I had actually used the word "dead" with reference to mother. There was silence at the other end of the phone. I was getting good at stopping people in their tracks of late.

"Well, of course, that puts things in a different light," came the response from Mr. Robinson. "A very different light. I fear things could get rather complicated from now on."

He didn't know the half of it. I explained that mother had left a will naming me as sole beneficiary, so that meant, in my layman's eyes, that the contents of grandfather's estate should now become contents of mother's estate, which would now become mine, warts and all, by the sound of it.

"So it would seem," agreed Mr. Robinson, sounding rather crestfallen. "So it would seem."

There was a pause, then he continued. "You had better give me the name of your mother's solicitors so that we can contact them, in an effort to sort things out."

This I duly did, adding my own address and phone number. Mr. Robinson promised he would get back to me as soon as possible.

I put the phone down and grimaced. Why had grandfather said I was not to be communicated with ? What the hell could I have done to upset a man I had never even seen, a man of whose very existence I was ignorant until a few days ago? The puzzle was getting deeper. Feeling very depressed, I went upstairs to seek solace in Sara. I saw to my horror as I walked in the bedroom that a teddy bear had taken up residence on the bed. Sara noticed my look of shock.

"Meet B4," she said.
"No, don't tell me," I grinned, " B4 bear." She threw her arms round me and pulled me down onto the bed.
"I love you," she whispered.
"Snap," I responded.

We made love there and then.

We showered, got dressed and went downstairs again. I phoned Mr. Taylor once more, but he wasn't in, so I left a message with his secretary telling him to expect a Mr. Robinson to ring him about mother's will. I felt happy knowing that they would have to earn their fees sorting this one out.

Then came the moment I was dreading. Mother's house. We drove down there in Sara's car and let ourselves in. We had decided to drive because we knew there would be things to pack into her boot for the journey to the charity shop in Ipswich. When I entered the living room I half expected to hear mother's voice offering to put the kettle on. It didn't happen. I checked the post. There was nothing urgent to attend to, as any communication from the bank, building society or insurance company would have been forwarded to her executors, in the form of Mr. Taylor.

Old Pals Act

Sara, as organised as ever, had brought a pile of black bin liners to put mother's clothes in, a job which I could not bring myself to do. Instead I looked through her "special drawer", a place I was forbidden to look in when I was a child and a place I had shown no interest in as an adult, until today. Feeling like a thief I opened the drawer and tipped out the contents onto the bed. There were two scrapbooks, a pile of letters tied together in a bundle, and a jewellery case. It was the scrapbooks I was most interested in. I sat on the bed and opened up the first one.

Inside was a collection of photographs, all neatly pasted in and carefully labelled. My mother was always well organised, an occupational hazard. The first picture was that of a soldier, obviously with his arm around another person, but for some reason that half had been torn off. "Granddad Lord 1915" said the label. The next picture was labelled "Granddad Lord and I, aged 2 months. Accrington, January 1943." It showed a man gingerly holding a child, which was probably one of the first pictures taken of my mother. A lump came to my throat. Fifty-five was no age to die. There followed sundry pictures of my mother as a child. Learning to walk, on holiday, the usual family snapshots to be found in thousands of albums world-wide. The interesting things were the photographs containing her parents. "Dad and I in Blackpool, Summer 1951" or "Mum and I in Oak Hill Park, Spring 1953". There was obviously a time when the Lords were a happy family; that was apparent from the joy shouting at you from the photographs. How times must have changed. There followed many pictures following mother's schooldays, from a toothless 5 year old to a rather attractive young lady in the sixth form.

The next section was obviously taken when Mother was at college in Ambleside. The picture that leapt off the page was a picture of mother sitting on a stone wall in front of a curious little house, with her arm round a man, my father. "Phil and I C.M.C. 1962" was written neatly underneath. It took me a while to work out what C.M.C. was until I remembered that the name of the place Mother had trained was Charlotte Mason College. There was also a picture of mother and Sue proudly standing on top of a hill, looking for all the world like Hilary and Tensing at the top of Everest. "Sue and I on top of Wansfell, 1963" was written neatly underneath. There were many pictures taken in the Lake District, mostly of Mother, Sue and Phil. There was a group photograph, presumably of mother's year at college. I felt immense pride as mother's beautiful face leapt out at me, putting the others in the shade, or was I being a slightly biased son ?

I skipped on further until I found the wedding photographs. Mother and Phil cutting the cake, mother and Sue, her bridesmaid, outside church, father and his best man, my parents standing next to a quaint old lady. "Granny Jackson", mother had written neatly underneath. The wedding group photograph caught my eye. A couple I presumed to be my father's parents were standing next to mother, but curiously, her mother and father were missing. I knew they disapproved of the marriage, but surely they would have gone to their only child's wedding ? Obviously not !

I made my first appearance, well almost, on the next page. It was a picture of mother, heavily pregnant. "Great Yarmouth April 1967." Very close, I thought, I was born in May. I dominated the next pages. As with mother there were early steps, first teeth and the like. I had my own copies of these so I took little or no notice of them.

It was the next picture that made me sit up with a jolt. There, jumping out of the page at me, was a picture of a young Bill Garnett holding my hand walking down a beach ! "Bill and Peter, Southwold, June 1971" was written neatly underneath. In a curious twist of fate, I could just about make out Mr. Jones' house in the background. I racked my brains trying to remember when father left. I knew it was 1971, but when exactly, I did not know. Perhaps Sue would be able to tell me. I prayed to God he left before June. I searched the scrapbook for any more pictures of Bill Garnett, but I found none. The last set of pictures were of my wedding in 1990 to Linda. I felt no emotions at all when I looked through them again. Linda and I were never really compatible. We simply fell in lust, but when that wore off there was nothing. She walked out on me after a blazing row, probably my fault, as my temper was even worse then. Sara has mellowed me a great deal. I have never set eyes on Linda since.

Right at the back of the book was a beautiful pencil drawing of some ruined church, the shadows creating a wonderful effect. I couldn't make out the title at the bottom, but it was signed, A.L. I presumed it was a picture drawn by mother in her younger days. I found it odd she had never thought fit to mention it to her artist son. Still, mother was apparently riddled with secrets; another one did not surprise me. I replaced the picture once more in the book and thought no more about it.

I could hear Sara calling from the next room. She was asking what we were going to do for lunch as she was getting hungry. I glanced at my watch, it was 1.30. I had been looking at the photographs for nearly two hours. I walked into where Sara was filling sacks with mother's clothes.

"Well, here's one load for the charity shop. They'll have a field day when they see these. Your mother certainly dressed with style," she said. I showed her the picture of Bill Garnett and pointed out the date.
"So what does it prove?" she asked. "I really think you're becoming obsessed with that man."

Perhaps I was, but I was determined to find out more. I was becoming more and more intrigued about the whole situation. Just what the hell had gone on ? We walked to the fish and chip shop in Stradbroke, only to find that they had finished serving and there was nothing left. We went to the baker's shop in the same street, where the best they could offer was a steak and kidney pie and a cheese and onion pasty, so we hungrily took that option. Lunch was eaten on the wing as we walked back to mother's house. I was keen to look at the second scrapbook whilst Sara was intent on bagging up the rest of the clothes.

We settled to our tasks with enthusiasm. Or at least I did. Sara was less than happy about mother's gargantuan collection of shoes. I settled back into the spare room and opened the second scrapbook. Unlike the first, there were no photographs to be seen. This seemed to house a collection of assorted newspaper cuttings. Again mother had carefully organised them into chronological order.

The first cutting was from the Accrington Observer and Times, dated June 17th 1940. It announced the marriage of Frank James Lord and Emily Davies at Accrington Parish church the previous Saturday. I glanced back at the photographs to refresh my memory of what my grandparents looked like. The next event chronicled was the birth of my mother, on November the 11th 1942. To Frank and Emily the blessed gift of a daughter, Anne.

The next cutting, dated December the 12th 1958, was an announcement of a death, my great grandfather or so I presumed.

Death of a Pal
The death was announced today of a former Accrington Pal,
Mr. Albert Lord, of Blackburn Road, Accrington.
Mr. Lord was one of the original Pals, enlisting in 1914.
He saw service in Egypt and France before being

> *wounded in battle. He was awarded the Military Medal*
> *in 1917.*
> *He was a local amateur artist, and some of his work*
> *can be seen hanging in local art galleries.*
> *The funeral will take place on Thursday next at*
> *Accrington Parish Church at 3.30 p.m.*
> *Will friends please accept this as the only intimation.*

I had no idea of what a Pal was, but my limited knowledge and the dates mentioned indicated to me it must be something to do with World War One. This apparently was my great-grandfather, on the face of it a bit of a war hero. He was also an artist, obviously where I got my talents from.

There seemed to be a bit of a gap before the next cutting, which announced the marriage of Phil and Anne, my mother and father. This, I noticed, was from the East Anglian Gazette, dated April 24th 1965. There was a newspaper photograph alongside the announcement. Mother and Phil smiled back at me from the scrapbook. I couldn't help but notice the strong similarity between Phil and myself at a similar age, confirming my thoughts on the subject at the funeral. Perhaps he had a temper, which led to the downfall of the marriage between the two of them. Perhaps he was a womaniser, a drunkard ? I wanted the reason for the break-up to be placed firmly at his door, making my mother the innocent party.
There then followed a series of cuttings relating to events at mother's school, concerts, school fayres, fund raising activities and the like. Mother was always very proud of her school and what it stood for in the community.

"For the children's sake," she used to quote her old college motto at me, as I was dragged along to Saturday morning netball matches, or evening concerts, as a small boy. She never missed any school event. Unfortunately, neither did I !

The next cutting shocked me to the core. It was from the Oxford Times, dated May 3rd 1965. It was a story about a window cleaner seeing the unconscious body of a woman lying on the floor of her flat. His prompt action of calling the ambulance had saved her life. Miss Sue Greenwood had apparently tried to commit suicide by taking an overdose of aspirins. I looked at the date of the cutting again; it was only 8 days after my parents' wedding. Surely that must have been a coincidence. I returned to the wedding photographs in the first scrap book, and looked carefully at the picture of Sue. She appeared to be happy and smiling, showing no indication of what she would try to do a week later. More to the point, where the hell had mother got this cutting from ?

I was tempted to rush into the next room and show Sara the cutting, but my eye was attracted to the next cutting. It was yet another announcement of a death. This time it was dated 30th of April 1971. It was a Mrs. Emily Lord, wife of Frank and mother of Anne. After a long illness, patiently borne, said the Accrington Times. I would have been about four, but why did I never meet her ?

There were only two more entries in the scrapbook. First was the marriage of Peter Jackson and Linda Dawson in 1990, and secondly the opening of my shop in 1991. The latter was highlighted in yellow pen with obvious pride. I closed the book and went in search of Sara. She had just filled the last bag and was lugging it towards the door, ready for its journey to Ipswich. I showed her the cutting about Sue and she looked shocked. Sara was one who tried to explain things rationally; she failed on this occasion. I now had another question to put to Sue when we met on Wednesday, but how the hell was I to broach it ?

We loaded the bags of mother's clothes into Sara's car and drove back to my house. By now it was about 4 o'clock and we were ready for a good shower and a change of clothes, Sara more so than I, as she had done most of the work. We showered together, enjoying the sensation of soapy bodies in close proximity.

Lunch had not been very substantial, so Sara made an enormous spaghetti bolognaise, whilst I walked to the off license for a bottle of Frascati, our favourite wine of the moment. We ate in virtual silence. I wanted to think about the new shocks I had received that day. Sara, sensing this, made no effort to make conversation. Try as I might, I could make no sense of the situation. We decided on an early night, retiring about 10.30. I wondered what the next day would bring.

Chapter 4

OXFORD: SHOCKS

Tuesday dawned with a grey, leaden sky, full of snow. By the time we had finished breakfast the world outside had turned white. I did not really fancy travelling to Diss to see Mr.Taylor if the conditions continued to worsen. I am not famous for my ability to drive in snow and ice. Luckily, just as we had finished breakfast, there was a call from the aforementioned Mr. Taylor.

"Mr. Jackson ?"
"Speaking," I replied.
"I had a call from a Mr. Robinson, your late mother's solicitors in Accrington, yesterday," he continued. "In the light of the developments, I think it would be best if we postponed your visit until we can sort out the new complications. We should be clear by next week. Could you contact me then in order to proceed ?"
I said I would, and asked if there were any problems.
"Not really," replied Mr. Taylor, "it's just that I need to see a copy of your late grandfather's will to add his estate to your mother's.

Mr. Robinson is going to fax it to me but these things take time. I'm sure you will appreciate that."
The last comment was more of a command than a question.
"OK then, I'll ring you next Monday."
"That will be fine," said Mr. Taylor and rang off.
I stared vacantly at the handset before returning it to the cradle.

It felt very strange for someone to refer to this mystery man in the North of England as my grandfather. I had only ever had my mother as family before, my father didn't really count. Having a day off, as it were, Sara and I continued sorting out things at mother's house. There were no more little skeletons crawling out of mother's cupboards, wardrobes or drawers. Just lots of memories - ornaments brought back from holidays, some of my old annuals and toys, which mother kept for the day when I had children, items of jewellery, each one bringing back some little memory of my mother. I was thoroughly miserable by the end of the day. Still, it was a job which had to be done, and we were gradually getting there. Again I wondered how I would have managed without Sara. I'm sure I would have given up long since without her driving me on. Mother always said she was good for me. If only she could have lived to see how accurate her prediction was. We sorted everything out into three piles, a keeping pile, a throwing away pile and a give away pile. I was tempted to keep everything, but, as Sara pointed out, a lot of the items were of no value to me, and things like mugs and cutlery would be of more value given away to people who might make some use of them. I could not argue with this kind of common sense. Given different circumstances I would probably have said the same, but disposing of a loved one's possessions is like pressing the delete key on their life.

The snow had stopped as we made our way back to my house and the roads were clear again. The weather forecast was much better for the next day and my trip to Oxford to see Sue.

I proposed to Sara that evening, and she accepted. It was a sort of "if you could see your way clear....." affair rather than a down on one knee job. Throughout my life I have never been what you could call a true romantic. We decided to get married as soon as possible after all the legal formalities regarding mother's death had been sorted out and I had found out a bit more about my family.

It was with a feeling of elation, then, that I set off at about 7.30 the next morning, kissing Sara goodbye and pointing my car towards Cambridge and the M11, and from there onto the M25 which would take me eventually to the M40 heading towards Oxford. I worked out the trip would take about three hours. I was not one for breaking up a journey once I got going. Luckily I didn't encounter any hold ups, so it was around 10.30 as I approached the Headington roundabout just outside the City of Oxford. Not being used to the technique required at a busy roundabout - go, no matter how much traffic is coming - I waited until the road was totally clear before I pulled out into the traffic. This did not please the driver of the car behind me who blew his horn violently in an effort to make me move. I simply made a rude sign at him through the mirror.

I drove through the busy suburb of Headington, surprised to see a shark sticking out of a roof at one point as I crawled along. I thought to myself, this is the city, and they do things differently here. I negotiated the traffic lights and dropped down Headington Hill, where I started to run up against the real Oxford traffic. Living in Suffolk, I was not used to traffic jams. Three cars in a row constituted heavy traffic in Stradbroke, but here was different. Progress was very slow, but eventually I arrived at the roundabout at St. Clements. I followed the sign for city centre and drove carefully over Magdalen Bridge past Magdalen College on my right, just as Sue said I would. The thing that struck me very forcibly was the number of buses. I was in a queue of four before I turned right at the traffic lights onto Longwall Street. Luckily the buses all went straight on towards the city centre.

According to Sue's directions, I should drive along here until I came to the University Parks, follow the road round to the left, before turning right onto Parks Road. Norham Gardens, the location of her flat, was at the end. Here, said Sue, I should make an attempt to park and walk. After several tours round the block I eventually found a place to stop and endeavoured to find Sue's flat.

As soon as I got out of the car I was struck by the overwhelming feeling of academia. It positively shouted at you. Everywhere I looked there seemed to be students, or possibly tutors, carrying folders and files, no doubt containing lecture notes, dissertations or perhaps even research papers. Everyone seemed to be in a hurry. I was not used to this and felt fairly vulnerable. Country boys, especially ones who paint for a living, have this tendency! I located Sue's flat and rang the bell. I looked at the window and wondered if this was the one through which the window cleaner saw Sue's prostrate body. Perhaps I was being a trifle morbid. Sue's cheery face appeared at the door, and she stood to one side and beckoned me in. Once inside she planted a big kiss on my cheek.

"Good to see you again, Pete," she beamed at me.

As we entered her living room I was amazed at the number of books, which seemed to be everywhere. There was a floor to ceiling bookcase, completely full, there were books on the floor, on the coffee table and on the windowsill. Sue, I knew, had taken early retirement from teaching, like mother, and now wrote children's stories, more as a hobby than a living. She could see I was staring at the books.

"Everyone does that the first time they enter this room," she smiled.

"I'm sorry, " I responded, "it's just that I've ....."
"Never seen so many books in your life ?" she said, finishing my sentence for me.
"Well, yes." I smiled at her.
"Oxford is a place where it's almost compulsory to buy books," she replied. "I've lived here all my life, so it's only natural I should have a lot of books. Now, how about coffee ?"

I accepted readily. She went out into the kitchen whilst I sat down, still fascinated by the tremendous amount of reading material. I wondered if Sue had actually waded through them all. Probably, I decided. One section of the big bookcase caught my eye. There were at least six books all written by Sue herself. I pulled one off the shelf and began looking at it. It was obviously a children's book, as it was called "Little Betty Beetle Buys a Brush." I flicked open the first page and read the contents.

"Little Betty Beetle saw her house was dusty".

Hardly a Booker prize candidate, but I'm sure young children would enjoy it. Especially the cartoon of the aforementioned Betty Beetle wearing a pink skirt and examining a dusty bookshelf. Sue came back into the room, carrying a tray on which were two mugs and a plate of chocolate biscuits.

"Ah, I see you've found my contribution to the literature of this country," she said, laughing. "It's all good stuff, you know"

I returned the book to the shelf and made a grunt of agreement.

"How like your father you are," she said, "except the hair, of course, that is definitely from your mother."

Old Pals Act

I got a mental picture of mother's hair, that beautiful auburn colour, not quite as ginger as mine. It felt very strange to be told that I was like my father, a man I had been taught to put out of my mind ever since I could think.

"It's that smile and, of course, the noncommittal grunt that seals it," she continued, " and the way you sit with your feet wrapped around each other."

I glanced down. She was right. I did always sit in the manner she described, especially when I was unsure of myself, as I was at present. I decided to dive straight in.

"How well did you know my father ?" I asked.
"And that direct, no frills approach," she continued. I noticed she was staring blankly out of the window as she said this. As if awakening from a dream, she shook her head and looked me full in the face.
"Perhaps we'd better start at the very beginning," she said, sipping her coffee.
"A very good place to start," I sang tunelessly, cursing my flippancy as soon as I said it. Sue made no comment. I settled down comfortably and prepared to listen to Sue's story. Perhaps at last, a piece of the jigsaw might be put in place.

Sue started to talk. Her voice was that of a schoolteacher, slow, clear and very precise. I got a picture of her telling a story to a class of young children and holding them spellbound. Perhaps I should sit cross-legged and suck my thumb.

> *I first met your mother in September 1961, when we both started at Charlotte Mason college, together. Lottie's, as it was affectionately known, was a predominantly girl's college tucked away in Ambleside in the Lake District.*

I arrived from Oxford early one Sunday afternoon. I travelled alone on the train to Windermere and finally by bus to Ambleside. My parents didn't have a car at the time but if they did I doubt they would have undertaken such a journey. I was very nervous as I walked up the steep drive to Scale How, a large, white painted building, surrounded by beautiful trees and greenery. This was the administrative part of the college and the place, according to my acceptance letter, where I had to report on my arrival. I entered through a big black door and made my way inside. I was met by an intense looking girl, smelling strongly of carbolic soap. It's funny what you remember. Anyway, she directed me down a corridor into a huge room full of equally nervous and lost looking young ladies like myself. I gave my name at the desk. A man with serious horn-rimmed glasses checked down a list of names in front of him.....

At this point Sue paused and looked at me.
"Have you ever visited the Lakes ?" she asked.
I replied in the negative. She looked on me with a sense of pity.
"You really must get up there one day, its well worth the trip."
I smiled and said I would try.
"Sara would love it, you know," Sue continued. "Perhaps your honeymoon ?"
She had a wry smile on her face, just like my mother used to have. I was amazed at the intuitiveness of women.
"How did you know ?"
I was puzzled. After all, I had only known about it myself for about 12 hours !
"Just watching the two of you together, that was a real give away, and of course your mother told me months ago."
"Have you ever married ? " I asked, trying to divert attention from my own transparencies.

"Nearly, very nearly, but that was a long time ago."
The tone of voice suggested that she was not going to enlighten me any further. Instead she continued her story.

> *The man eventually found my name on the list.*
> *"Ah, here we are, Miss Greenwood."*
> *We were never referred to by our Christian names by members of staff.*
> *He informed me that I had been allocated a double room in Scale How, which, as well as being the administrative centre, also housed students' rooms. He handed me a key to the room and signalled to another girl who was standing nearby and instructed her to show me where room 7 was.*
> *I nervously picked up my two suitcases and followed the girl upstairs through a maze of corridors until we arrived at the room, my home for the foreseeable future. The door was not locked, so we went straight in. My roommate had apparently not arrived, as there was no evidence of any other suitcases or clothes. My guide, who was called Mary, wished me good luck and departed. I gazed round the room. It had a double wardrobe, two rather uncomfortable looking single beds, and two tables and chairs. I threw my suitcases on one of the beds and sat down and cried my eyes out. I don't know if it was weariness after the long journey, or the overwhelming feeling of being alone, but I had never felt so miserable in all my life.*
> *Once I had pulled myself together, I unpacked and put my clothes away. Sensibly, I only used half of the wardrobe, knowing that there would be another occupant at some point. There was a knock on the door. I opened it and there stood a girl probably just a little older than me. I remember her very clearly. She was wearing a grey skirt*

and a white blouse. She had long blonde hair tied up in a ponytail. Her teeth stuck out like a rabbit's. I wanted to twitch my nose, but didn't. She stared at me intently through a ridiculously thick pair of spectacles. She introduced herself as Elizabeth White, Liz to her friends.
"Pleased to meet you, I'm Sue."
Liz, it turned out, was the senior student living in the hostel. I was to go to her if I had any problems or wanted to know anything. I said I would, and after giving me a toothy smile, she left. There were lots of things I wanted to ask at that point, but somehow I could not bring any to mind.
When I had finished unpacking, I locked the door of my room and ventured downstairs. An uninspiring tea of salad was being served. Perhaps Liz decided the menu, I thought cruelly. I nervously made my way into the dining area and presented myself at the serving hatch. I was handed a plate of cheese salad and a bowl of peaches. I manoeuvred my way to an empty seat and sat down to eat my first meal at college. As I gazed around there seemed to be a lot of other girls looking equally lonely, but none of us seemed to have the confidence to introduce ourselves. I finished my meal and walked out of the dining room.
Not being able to face the lonely room, and it being a pleasant, sunny, autumnal afternoon, I decided to go for a stroll into the village. I made my way down the steep drive and out onto the main road. I headed towards the village, stopping to admire the famous bridge house on my right.

"I've seen a picture of it in one of mother's scrap books," I interrupted.

"More than likely," Sue replied. "It's probably the most photographed sight in the Lakes. Though your mother used to joke that people took more photographs of her !"
I could well imagine mother uttering such a statement.

> *I continued walking until I reached a right-angled bend in the road, by a pub called The Salutation Hotel. I crossed the road and looked in the shop windows on the other side. As I did so, a smart-looking car stopped beside me. The window was wound down and a very prim and proper lady sitting in the passenger seat asked me where the college was. Feeling almost like a local, I told them to follow the road round and to turn right after about a hundred yards. The lady smiled and thanked me. As the car pulled away I caught a glimpse of someone sitting in the back seat, someone with beautiful auburn hair.*

"Mother ?" I asked.
"Correct," replied Sue. "That was my first sight of Anne Lord, and of course her parents."
Sue glanced across at me at this point and sighed.
"We haven't got very far, but that seems like a good place to stop. How about some lunch ?"
With the exception of two chocolate biscuits with my coffee, I hadn't eaten since breakfast, so I readily agreed.
"Let's go for a pub lunch. My treat," I added. "Where would you suggest ?"
"We could walk into the city," said Sue. "I know a place."

We set off and ambled slowly into the centre of Oxford. Sue was the perfect guide as we walked, pointing out all the places of interest as we passed. We walked up Parks Road, turned left onto Holywell Street and then through an intricate series of passages down Bath Place, until we got to a place called the Turf Tavern. It was a charming place, a little courtyard of calm situated in the middle of Oxford. In the summer one could sit outside in an intimate beer garden. Being only February, we went inside and ordered a baked potato with cheese each and sat and ate. I treated myself to a pint of bitter, whilst Sue had an orange juice. During the meal Sue turned questioner, asking me about Sara and our plans for the future. I wasn't sure I liked her expert probing, but I answered her questions as best I could. Another pint of beer later, we set off walking again. We continued up the passages onto New College Lane, under the Bridge of Sighs and back towards Sue's flat. As we passed Keble College gates, Sue glanced at her watch.

"It's still open. Lets go inside," she said. "You're an artist, you'll appreciate this."

We walked through the traditional Oxford college archway and we arrived in a quadrangle. The lawn, sunken and immaculately manicured, formed a beautiful centrepiece. We walked round the outside of the grass until we reached a small doorway. We made our way inside and found ourselves in Keble College Chapel. As we went into the chapel, Sue directed me through a door on the right.

"Feast your eyes on this, and weep." she said.

We walked into a small side chapel. Sue pressed a red button and the most beautiful picture I had ever seen was illuminated. It was "The Light of the World" by Holman Hunt, a picture I of course had heard of, but never seen. As an artist I could appreciate the magnificence of the picture, but my words cannot describe its brilliance. It was a picture of Christ holding a lantern knocking at a door, and yet not gaining admittance. The fact that the picture was under glass gave it a wonderful three-dimensional effect, which seemed to jump out at the viewer. My breath was literally taken away.

"Well ?" asked Sue. "What about that ?"

I was speechless, totally overcome by its beauty. We stood for a while, gazing at the technical perfection of the picture. Neither of us spoke. After a few minutes the light went out and a feeling of anti-climax came over me.

"I thought you might like that," said a self satisfied Sue. "Seen enough ?"

I couldn't resist pressing the button again, and stared in awe at the picture once more. Happy that I had absorbed all I could of the beauty of the picture, I made a move towards the door. We walked out of the chapel and back towards the porter's lodge where I bought a postcard of the picture. I was determined to put my copying skills to good use and see if I could use some of the techniques in the picture. We made our way back to the flat and settled ourselves down once more. Sue continued with her story.

> *I decided I would go back to my room, if I could ever find it again, and start to write a letter home. This was my first time away from Oxford and home. Already I was missing my parents and little brother. I'd waved them off tearfully earlier in the day at Oxford railway station before my long journey north....*

"Before you ask," Sue said, "they're both dead. Charles, my brother, now lives in Australia with his wife and three children. I haven't seen him for years."
I nodded and continued listening.

> *I made my way back through the village, marvelling at the magnificent hills on both sides of me. I had no idea of their names at that point. I promised myself I would walk*

to the top of those before I left Ambleside. After getting lost in the labyrinth that was Scale How, I eventually located my room again.

As I entered, I immediately saw there was another suitcase and a trunk on the floor, as yet unpacked. This was obviously the property of my roommate. What was she called ? What would she be like ? Would we get on ? All these questions whizzed through my mind. I sat down at one of the desks and started my letter home. Funnily enough this simple act made me feel slightly better and I began to cheer up.

Before long, I heard the door being opened. I glanced across and in walked your mother, complete with tear stained eyes. She was wearing a flowery dress and a yellow cardigan, draped over her shoulders, quite the fashion at the time. We introduced ourselves. That was to be the start of a friendship that would last for over thirty years, until her death nearly two weeks ago, in fact.

The first thing that struck me about Anne was her beautiful hair. It was an autumn shade of auburn, worn down to her shoulders at the side, but fastened back from her forehead with hair clips. Her eyes were deep blue and sparkled with happiness. Her face was oval and her mouth turned up slightly at the corners, giving the illusion of always smiling. I felt quite plain by comparison.

As with most students going to college for the first time, we compared our backgrounds. Anne told me she came from Accrington, and was the only child of Frank and Emily Lord. I got the impression that she was very close to her parents....

"So what happened ?" I interrupted again, receiving a withering stare from Sue.

"All in good time," she answered. "Your mother could be impatient too."
Feeling suitably chastised I fell silent and listened as Sue continued.

> Anne told me she had had a meal with her parents on the journey to college, whilst I told her the delights of the college tea. She screwed up her nose; she didn't look very impressed. We sat and chatted for a while as she unpacked her clothes. I observed every garment as it was taken out of her case and trunk. She was quite a follower of fashion, your mother. There were colourful skirts, blouses, lacy tops, and at least eight pairs of shoes, all reflecting the current fashions. I thought of my own array of clothes and began to feel drab as well as plain. Seeing my envious gaze, she told me that her father owned a dress shop in Accrington. That, if anything, made me feel worse. She had obviously noticed my limited supply of clothes. I pointed out that I had a trunk following on, containing more clothes. I failed to add, however, that they were no more fashionable than the ones I had already installed. I felt better over the subsequent months as I observed that very few of the girls at college could compete with your mother in the fashion stakes.
> Anne, always the one with initiative, suggested we explore the village to see if we could find a nice pub and have a drink. I, always the cautious one, pointed out the 10 o'clock curfew mentioned in the rules we had all been sent. Your mother didn't seem too concerned about this, muttering something about rules being there to be broken. So we set off once more down Scale How drive.
> With all the homing instinct of a pigeon, Anne located a pub within yards of the college gates. It was up a fairly steep hill, called Smithy Brow.

"Understand, Pete, that in The Lake District you are either going up a hill or coming down one," Sue said laughingly.
I waved a cigarette in the air, asking if it was all right if I smoked. Sue nodded and went to fetch me an ashtray, placing it on the coffee table in front of me.
"Bet your mother doesn't, er... didn't approve," she added.
"Correct," I responded, drawing deeply on the cigarette. "A nasty little habit I picked up at university."

So in we went. The pub was called The Golden Rule. We would spend a lot of time in that pub, and many others, before we finally left Ambleside three years later! As we walked through the door an eerie silence descended on the place as everyone turned round to look at us. I was all for going straight out again, but Anne was not thrown by it at all, and she made her way confidently to the bar and ordered a lemonade for me and a gin and orange for herself. The landlord didn't blink an eye and went to get the drinks. I heard one of the men at the bar mumble something about "Charlotte's Harlots" being back. I felt myself blushing. We took the drinks and sat down at an empty table where I confessed to Anne that I had never been in a pub without my parents before. She raised her eyebrows in disbelief. As we chatted I gained in confidence, laughing at her sly remarks about the locals standing round the bar.
We finished our drinks. Anne was keen for another one, but I pointed out it was nearly 10 o'clock and we had better go back to our room. She wavered, but after weighing it up carefully, she agreed. Even your mother didn't want to make a bad impression on her first night. We made our way back into Scale How, entering the door just as Liz was about to lock it. We looked at each other and breathed a sigh of relief. Giggling, we made our way

back to our room. I'm sure we must have woken up the inhabitants of the rooms along our corridor as we went on our merry way. Feeling tired, we undressed and went straight to bed.

"I like you, lots," your mother said as she turned out the light. I felt quite flattered, but I didn't commit myself as quickly as she did.

I hardly slept that night. Not being used to sharing a bedroom with anyone, I was always aware of the slightest movement Anne made. She, however, seemed to be having no problems sleeping, judging by the little snuffly snores coming from her side of the room.

The next morning saw us up bright and early ready for our first full day at college. The September sun streamed through the window, and all seemed well with the world that we were about to enter. Both of us dressed quickly. I put on my prettiest dress of pale yellow with a huge floral pattern, whilst Anne sported black ski-pants, a white blouse, and a bright red scarf tied round her neck. We headed downstairs for breakfast. As we entered the dining room we were both struck by the noise of female voices talking excitedly. We both elected to have cornflakes and tea; neither of us really fancied a cooked breakfast. One table was reasonably empty, so we headed for that one. We were soon joined by four other students, who smiled nervously at us. It transpired that they too were first years and, like us, were rather unsure of what to do.

I consulted my timetable for the first week. 9.00 a.m. Monday morning, a talk by the principal in the Barn. It sounded a rather strange location for a serious talk, but on asking Liz, whom we spotted at the other end of the dining room, we were informed it was actually a hall, also the venue for the once a month dances.

We all trooped up there and sat down facing the stage at one end. The principal entered the room and welcomed us all to Charlotte Mason College, and proceeded to outline what would be expected of us over the duration of our three-year stay. It all sounded rather exciting, but at the same time, for me at least, rather formidable.
However, we soon fell into the routine of college life and things became less strange for your mother and me. We worked hard, your mother especially. It became apparent that she was a very intelligent girl, with her mind set on a teaching career. Though she not only worked hard, she played hard too. She dragged me along in her wake, and because of her I began to grow in confidence. We went to the college dances. I had done ballroom dancing as a teenager, so I cut quite a dash on the dance floor. I actually outshone your mother at times. I don't think she ever forgave me that.
There were boys, too. Ambleside was the haunt of weekend climbers, who congregated in a pub in the village called The Royal Oak. They then used to make their way up to the dance. Being an all girl college, their attendance provided light relief. Anne's looks and extrovert personality had them flocking round her. She had only to wink her eye or flick her hair and they came running. I benefited too, of course, but it was Anne who attracted them. Nothing serious, just good fun.
We used to go to the pictures. 1/6d, it cost, about 8p to you, Peter. I remember going to see "Breakfast at Tiffany's". We walked back through the streets, arm in arm, singing "Moon River", until we were stopped by the local policeman. College life was fun, and Anne made it even more so....

There was silence for a few minutes. I glanced across at Sue and saw a distant look on her face as if she were in a trance. I too sat silently, reluctant to interrupt her thoughts and remembrances. This must have been difficult for Sue, but it made me realise, once again, just how close they must have been all those years ago. I stubbed out my cigarette, aimlessly making patterns in the ash as I waited.

> *She was a funny mix, your mother. The college vamp one minute, the little angel the next. I remember how she went to church every Sunday without fail, in fact she occasionally sang in the church choir. She was very musical, you know, a brilliant pianist. Her church-going was because of her grandfather she once told me. He had been a soldier in the First World War, an Accrington Pal or something. Apparently he was a devout Christian, and the horrors of the war had made him even more so. Anne adored him. She used to call him her own special pal. He was dead when Anne came to college, but she talked of him often. His death had hit her hard. I could never imagine being that close to my grandfather, who was a crusty old man, totally lacking a sense of humour. Despite being a gregarious character, your mother enjoyed her own company. She used to go off on her own and wander round the churchyard. Once when she was doing this she found Charlotte Mason's grave, and every month after that, without fail, she placed a bunch of flowers on it. Yet she was quite a rebel as well....*

Finding it hard to believe, I looked enquiringly across at Sue, who smiled back at me.
"Oh yes, quite a rebel. I suppose it must be difficult for a son to imagine his mother was a bit of a tearaway in her youth, but she was."

> *We were not allowed to put posters or pictures up in our room, in case it damaged the walls. Remember it was the days before Blu-Tac. Anne did not let this rule put her off. In no time at all, she had sellotaped pictures of Cliff Richard and Elvis Presley all over the walls. She got a good telling-off by the cleaners for that. She didn't care, nor did she take them off as requested. There were other instances too. The evening meal was a formal affair, attended by members of staff. Grace was said and polite conversation was expected. No girl was allowed to turn up in trousers, oh no, it was dresses only. But not our Anne. She made a point, at least once a week, of turning up in her ski-pants. The principal was angry with her many times, but Anne still did it....*

"Why ?" I asked.
"I suppose she was making a statement. Sorry to say this Pete, but her parents over-indulged her, and consequently she thought she could get away with anything and she usually did !"

I shook my head, amazed at how little you could know a person despite having lived with them virtually all your life. Mother had kept a lot hidden from me. I wished she had seen fit to share some of her past, but of course it was too late now.

"So you see, Pete, we were blissfully happy at college. But soon I was, for a time anyway, going to be made even more happy."

> *It was the end of the Spring term. By now we had become inseparable friends. Anne suggested I went to stay with her family in Accrington. I had grown in confidence over the last six or seven months and readily agreed. Once upon a time I would never have dreamt of going to stay with strangers. Anne's father picked us up on the last day*

of term, and we made the long journey to Accrington. There was no M6 in 1962. We arrived mid-afternoon at the Lord residence. Their house was pretty impressive, a Victorian semi on Manchester Road leading out of Accrington.

Emily, your grandmother, was waiting by the window for us as we arrived. She made me feel very welcome, and I was treated to typical northern hospitality. Once you have been accepted as a friend by a northerner you are in for life. The house was beautiful. I knew that Anne's parents were well off, because Anne never had a grant, she was paid for by her father. My grant, by the way, was about £32 a term. But seeing the house made me realise just how wealthy they must be. Apparently, Frank had started out buying and selling clothes from a stall on Accrington market. However, it was not until Emily's father gave them a considerable sum of money that he got rid of the stall and opened the shop. He never looked back, and was now a wealthy man. "Not bad," he used to say, "for a market lad." He was very proud of what he had achieved, and rightly so, though Anne once told me he had been a bit of a rogue after the war, trading on the black market and the like.

I stayed with them for a week, and it was one of the happiest times of my life. I was charmed by the little town of Accrington, its rows of houses, the friendly people and its gentle pace of life, so different from the hurly-burly of Oxford, which even then was a busy, bustling city. I met many of your mother's friends. She was very popular. I was also introduced to her former boyfriend, Jim, who was one of the nicest lads you could wish to meet, full of fun, and handsome as well. Anne, being Anne, had finished with him just before she went to college. "You can't keep up a relationship up with anyone who lives eighty miles away," was the reason she gave.

It was the Friday night. I was due to go home to Oxford on Sunday. Anne's parents took us out for a meal to a big hotel nearby, the name escapes me, but it was very lavish. Never before had I set foot in such a place. Frank and Emily treated me like another daughter. I was truly happy. They were such nice people, or so I thought at the time.

*It was the next night when things started to happen. Anne had decided - note, **Anne** decided, that seeing it was my last night in the north we should go to the dance hall in Burnley. I thought it was a splendid idea, but felt a little apprehensive. On the Saturday afternoon we decided to go for a stroll together, before getting ready for the dance. We walked arm in arm to see the War Memorial in Oak Hill Park, which was no distance from the house. We made our way into the park and climbed steadily towards an impressive stone obelisk at the very top. Carved in stone at the base of the monument was a plaque honouring the men of Accrington who gave their lives in the Great War. We climbed the steps at the side of the monument and gazed up at it. The list of names seemed endless. Understand, Pete, I had no real concept of the Great War, but your mother, of course, was much more knowledgeable on the subject, her grandfather being a soldier. Anne told me as we made our way down again that her "pal", as she always called her grandfather, had died in 1958, not killed in action like the men listed on the monument.*

"He and I spent a lot of time up there," she said, *flicking her head back towards the monument. "He used to tell me stories of when he was in the trenches. Some of them were quite horrific. There was one story, though, that he always*

refused to tell me. "When you're older," he always used to say. He never got to tell me."
By this time we were back at the house. Emily had made us a cup of tea and put out a plate of sandwiches. We ate hungrily, what with the fresh air and all that. We laughed and joked with Emily all afternoon. I felt truly happy, and sorry to be leaving the following day.
It was soon time to get ready for the dance. I went upstairs and put on my prettiest skirt and white blouse. After a few minutes Anne burst into the room, took one look at me and rushed out again. She re-appeared in no time at all carrying a new skirt, bright red, covered in white polka dots. Over her other arm was a starched petticoat to make the dress stand out wide.
"Try these on," she ordered, thrusting the clothes towards me. At first I refused, but Anne insisted. I had never worn anything like this before, so I felt rather self-conscious as I did my fashion parade for Anne and Emily. They both agreed that it was just me, so I wore it to the ball, as it were.
Frank ran us into Burnley, several miles away. He stopped the car outside a place called Burnley Mecca. "I'll pick you up at 11," he called out of the window as he drove away. Anne was really amazing, the way she got him running round after her. There was no way my father would have done that. He, of course, did not have Anne as his daughter !
We paid the entrance fee and went inside a huge dance hall, much bigger than our little "barn" at college. Your mother was in her element, as we walked across the floor. We met some of her old school friends inside and began to dance round the pile of handbags placed on the floor, all of us hoping to be asked to dance by the boys who were clustered around the edge. Anne, as usual, was asked

first. He was a callow youth, with terrible acne. Anne, being Anne, didn't refuse, and disappeared onto the dance floor to do the twist, the rage dance at the time.
It was whilst I was waiting at the side that I saw him. He just had to be the most handsome boy I had ever set eyes on. He had jet-black hair, carefully combed and greased back. He was wearing a dark blue, pretend mohair suit, narrow cut. His tie was horizontal stripes of blue and white. On his feet were a pair of winklepicker shoes. He was with his mates, the whole gang of which were obviously out for a good Saturday night. I had very little experience of boys at the time, despite my two terms at college, so I didn't know what to do to attract his attention. Anne would have had no trouble, that I was sure of.
I pointed him out to Anne, who, in her usual fashion, said she would get him and one of his friends to come over for a dance. She was as good as her word, and very shortly my dream boy, accompanied by a friend, appeared and we began to dance. My usual confidence on a dance floor took over, and I must admit we did make a handsome couple as we jived away to the band. Anne seemed to be getting on well with her beau, but then again, she always did.
The four of us made our way to some empty seats and collapsed onto them. The boys went to get us some drinks. Anne and I disappeared to the toilet as soon as they returned, for a secret conference. Anne didn't really want to stay with her boy, but she promised she would lure him away so I could remain alone with mine. She was very good at this sort of thing, your mother. I nervously agreed and we sat back down. We sipped our drinks and talked about nothing much, it was too loud to have any real

> *conversations. Then, as if by magic, Anne and her boy disappeared onto the dance floor.*
> *We were left alone. He looked around to see where his mate had gone, but the room was so crowded he couldn't see them. Well-done, Anne, I thought. There being no alternative, he turned round to talk to me, or perhaps it should be shout to me.*
> *"Hello," he said, "I'm Phil...."*

Sue looked across the room at me when she said the name. Its significance was not lost on me.

"Phil," I said slowly. "My father."
"One Philip Jackson, bachelor of the Parish of Oswaldtwistle, son of Jackson the butcher, apprentice motor mechanic, the same," she sighed.
I glanced at my watch. It was nearly 6 o'clock, and I had a feeling the story was nowhere near finished.
"Why don't you ring Sara and tell her you'll be home tomorrow ?" Sue suggested. Being keen to hear the end of the story, I readily agreed.

"Hi, sweetheart," I said as soon as she answered the phone.
"I know, I know - you've decided to stay the night and journey back tomorrow. Am I right, or am I right ?"
"I don't know how you knew it, but yes, you're right."
"No problem," she said, but whispered cheekily under her breath, "don't end up in bed with her, will you ?"
"No I won't. Look, I'll see you tomorrow. Bye love."
I put the phone down feeling rather flustered.
"Won't what ?" queried Sue.
"Er, won't stop up talking all night."
A classic example of thinking on one's feet.

Sue made the bed up in the spare room and then I helped her prepare a meal. She was obviously enjoying herself, as she started singing.

"It's nice to have visitors," she said. "The last person I had for a meal in this flat was your mother, about two years ago."

I wanted to know more, but Sue was obviously not going to tell me any more that night. She poured out two large brandies and both of us became rather drunk. I found myself as the storyteller now: explaining the break up of my marriage and how I knew it would be different with Sara. All the time I was talking, Sue was listening intently and staring at me, no doubt comparing me with my mother, and probably my father. It felt very odd. The evening passed off pleasantly enough, but I could feel myself getting weary and I begged leave to go to bed. Sue showed me where the spare room was and I retired. Like the living room, this too was full of books. Tired as I was, I couldn't help thinking of some of the things Sue had told me about my mother, and, of course, that last revelation about her and my father. How had my mother and father ended up together, when it was Sue who made the first move towards him ? So what had happened ? None of it made any sense. I lay on my back and stared at the ceiling, not certain what to make of the latest revelations. I was seeing a side of mother I had never even thought existed. I eventually dropped off to sleep, dreaming of Christ carrying a lantern knocking on the door of the bridge house, which was finally opened by a life sized rabbit, wearing a polka dot dress.

Chapter 5

OXFORD: SHAME

The smell of bacon and eggs and the distant voice of someone singing "Moon River" awakened me the next morning. Where the hell was I ? For several seconds my mind would not function. Then it all came flooding back to me, Sue, mother, college, everything. Sue had thoughtfully left a spare towel and a brand new toothbrush on the dressing table. I dressed quickly and made my way to the bathroom, where I had a good wash, but unfortunately not a shave. I hated the prickly sensation an unshaven face gave me. Even Sue could not conjure up a razor. I walked into the kitchen where an appetising breakfast was being laid on the table.

"Sleep well ?" she enquired.
"Like the proverbial log," I replied. "That smells good."

I sat down and began to eat. I don't usually have a cooked breakfast, but I must admit I enjoyed this one. I washed up as Sue made a second cup of tea. We took the drinks into the lounge and sat down. My eyes strayed once more to the vast collection of books. Sue smiled across at me.

"I thought it might be a good idea if we continued the story as we walked today," she said. "Oxford has some rather splendid walks, you know."

I glanced out of the lounge window; a pale winter's sun was filtering through the clouds. The idea sounded appealing.

We set off at about ten o'clock. Sue wrapped a green, yellow and brown scarf round her neck.
"My old college scarf," she smiled at me. "I thought it was appropriate to wear it today. Your mother refused to buy one, you know. She said the colour scheme was awful !"

We walked back into the city, this time down Broad Street, Cornmarket Street and down St. Aldates towards a place Sue called Folly Bridge. Buses were everywhere. The green and white open-topped "Guide Friday" double deckers seemed to appear around every corner with the guide telling the eager tourists all about this lovely city. Even this early in the year the place was packed with hordes of tourists and students. As we walked, Sue continued her story, her clear narration pulling me in once more.

> *Phil and I spent the rest of the evening together, dancing and talking about ourselves. He was interested to learn I came from Oxford, a place he had never visited, but would like to one day. To see where they make the Morris Oxford, he joked. We exchanged addresses; I gave him both my Oxford address and my Ambleside one. We both promised to write. He offered to walk me home, but I declined, saying I was staying at Anne's house in Accrington and her father was going to pick us up. He*

grunted, saying he understood. Phil always understood, though I do believe he would have walked me home if I had asked, even the seven or so miles to Accrington. Or was that just wishful thinking? We found your mother at the end of the dance. Phil's mate was ancient history as far as Anne was concerned. She told Phil that she had last seen him over in the general direction of the toilets. Phil went in search of his friend, giving me a farewell kiss on the cheek. I beamed with joy, glancing over at Anne as if seeking her approval and - possibly - her envy.

We walked out of the dance hall together and made our way to the place where we were to be picked up. True to his word, Frank was there waiting for us. We climbed in the car and were driven back to Accrington. Frank went straight to bed when we arrived at the house, but Anne and I stayed up talking about the evening. Unusually, I did most of the chattering. I was keen to tell Anne about my new friend, Phil. Your mother, bless her, listened patiently. She seemed pleased that I had hit it off with someone, though I did notice a hint of jealousy in one or two of her replies. I thought nothing of it at the time. Perhaps I should have done, in retrospect.

I caught the bus to Preston the next morning, and then the train to Oxford. All through the journey I was thinking about Phil. Then, with a typical fatalistic sigh, I resigned myself to the possibility that I might never see him again. All our lives would have been simpler if I hadn't.

After the fun I had with Anne in Accrington, life in Oxford seemed quite dull. However, I had some college work to do so I kept myself busy, writing essays and the like. Then on the Friday, it arrived. There on the mat was a letter addressed to me. At first, seeing the Lancashire postmark, I thought it was from Anne, but it wasn't her writing. I tore it open, and to my delight it was from Phil. Just a

> *brief note, saying how much he had enjoyed meeting me and how he would like to see me again, hopefully very soon. It was signed Phil at the bottom, with a kiss. I still have the letter somewhere....*

Sue went quiet for a while and we just walked. We eventually arrived at a place she informed me was called Christchurch Meadow, a large expanse of grassland as the name suggests. We followed a rough gravel path towards the river. Considering the time of year, it was a pleasant morning, and I enjoyed staring at the boats moored along the banks. Occasionally a rowing boat would shoot past with the cox urgently shouting orders. Could this be the Oxford boat race crew in training? They were certainly moving at what seemed a fair old speed. After a while we sat down on a convenient bench and stared across the river. I could just make out a cricket pitch on the other side. Sue looked across at me and smiled.

"During the summer this place is full of punts. I used to love coming along here with Doug and watching them. It's amazing the lack of co-ordination some people have when you give them a punting pole."
"Who's Doug ?" I enquired.
"Oh, just someone, a long time ago."

She was starting to be as secretive as mother. Charlotte Mason training, I thought to myself. As we resumed walking, Sue carried on with her story.

> *I wrote back straight away, saying how nice it was to meet such a charming young man, and how the dance had been such fun, and I too was looking forward to meeting him again. I told him I would be back at college in a week, and would he write to me there. I signed Sue at the bottom,*

and added a kiss. You must realise, Peter, that in the early 1960s, relationships were not the same as they are today. I had never really had a proper boyfriend, but that state of affairs might be about to change. Anne's words came back to me about long distance relationships. What did she know?

The holidays soon came to an end, and I made my lonely journey north. I was glad to be back at college seeing all my friends again, but especially Anne. We were just like sisters, and we shared all our secrets. She seemed thrilled that Phil had written, and examined the letter closely. We giggled, and she gave me a big hug as if to say "well done". I watched the post every day but there was no letter from Phil. I had just about given up when there it was, on the next Monday morning. There was that familiar handwriting, again, on an envelope addressed to me. Remember, Pete, I had read and re-read his letter at least a hundred times, so I could tell it a mile off. I rushed into breakfast with a broad grin on my face, and sat down next to Anne. She knew straight away that I had received a letter, and shared my excitement.

I ripped the envelope open - Anne tutted, she was always so careful when she opened her mail - and pulled out the letter. My eyes grew wide with joy as I read the contents. Phil, remember, was a motor mechanic, and he had managed to borrow a car from the garage and was coming up to Ambleside the following Saturday and where could he meet me and would I ring him to let him know if this was convenient? He was also bringing up a mate for my friend Anne. I passed on this news to Anne and she looked delighted. She was genuinely happy for me. She seemed indifferent about her "blind date", Anne liked to choose her own men friends.

After lectures that day, I rushed to the public phone box in the centre of Ambleside, not wishing to use the one in Scale How, since it was just a little too public to make a personal call such as this. With trembling fingers I dialled the number Phil had given me in the letter. The phone started to ring at the other end. To my relief, it was Phil who answered. He sounded pleased to hear from me so soon, ecstatic in fact. He said he and Ian, his friend, would try to arrive in Ambleside mid-morning. I suggested he should drive through the centre of Ambleside and look out for the Bridge House, and I would be waiting close by. I also said I would sort out accommodation for the two of them for Saturday night....

Sue looked at me and smiled.
"There was no way boys could stay in the hostels, so I arranged for them to stay in a local B&B."
I smiled back at her; it was if she were trying to keep an air of respectability about the whole weekend. I thought of my own days at university, where no visitors ever stayed anywhere but in resident students' rooms. How times change.

The rest of the week dragged. I thought Saturday would never come, but of course it did. Your mother showed less enthusiasm for the visit than I did, but I suppose that was understandable. After all it was Phil coming to see me and not her, and she would end up with an unknown quantity, brought just to make up numbers. Anne was not used to situations like this.
We positioned ourselves next to the Bridge House, sitting on the low wall and looking at Stock Ghyll, the name of the river flowing beneath us as it wound its way through Ambleside, eventually joining Windermere at Waterhead about a mile down the road. I kept glancing nervously

down the road to see if I could see any sign of Phil's car. Not that I knew what it looked like, of course. Eventually my long wait was over. A small blue and white car, I think it was an old Ford Anglia, pulled up next to the kerb. Phil jumped out and flung his arms round me. This action took me by surprise, especially when he kissed me and held both my hands. His friend got out of the passenger side and Phil introduced him to us both as Ian. We all clambered back in the car and I directed Phil to the car park near Scale How.

I was keen to show Phil the college, so we strolled around the grounds. Phil and I walked hand in hand, whilst Anne and Ian walked behind us a distance apart. I could tell that Anne was not interested in Ian, but was going through the motions for my sake. After lunch we went to the guest house on Compston Road and the lads settled in. It was going to cost them the princely sum of 15 shillings per night; about 75p nowadays. We then went for a car ride to Rydal, parked the car and walked up the track to the caves. As we sat staring down on Rydal Water below, I could feel myself falling in love with Phil. He was so considerate and he listened to everything I had to say about the area and the beautiful sights to be seen, making intelligent comments and asking questions. Ian and Anne, I noticed, were not talking, they were just sitting staring across the valley. I started to feel sorry for my best friend. I would not inflict this on her again. Phil would have to come to see me on his own in future.

We went out for a drink later that evening, almost inevitably to the Golden Rule. We made our way to the back room and managed to sit together at a small circular table. I noticed that Anne was now virtually ignoring Ian and joining in the conversations Phil and I were having. Eventually Phil and Anne started to dominate the proceedings, talking about the places around Accrington and Oswaldtwistle. After all they were both natives of the area and had common experiences.

There was a sick feeling deep down inside my stomach. I could not hope to compete with Anne if it came to a straight contest for a boyfriend. I hoped, no, I prayed, she was not making a play for Phil. I confronted Anne with this as we made our traditional trip to the toilets together. Much to my relief, Anne assured me that this was not the case and we returned to the table. I was feeling much happier. That night Phil walked me back to Scale How and kissed me passionately on the doorstep. Anne had gone up to the room by this time and Ian was walking back to the guest house. Phil, who always wore his heart on his sleeve, declared his love for me. I told him I loved him too. Thinking this gave him carte blanche, he tried to put his hand on my breast. I recoiled and pushed him away. I was not ready for that just yet, and I said as much. Some boys would have lost interest straight away, but not Phil. He grunted an apology and said he understood. We arranged to meet in the morning, and said goodnight. I climbed the stairs to our room. I suppose I felt flattered, but also a little disappointed in myself for pushing him away so readily.

Anne was sitting up in bed when I entered the room. I could see she was not happy. I apologised for the evening and for landing her with Ian, who was not exactly the most desirable or interesting boy to spend the day with. Apparently his main topic of conversation was the workings of the internal combustion engine ! She said not to worry about it, but perhaps Phil could come up on his own next time. I gave Anne a sideways glance and said I would mention it to him.

"So do you think mother fancied Phil at that point ?" I asked Sue.
"Not straight away," she replied. "I'm sorry to say this about my friend and your mother, Pete, but she didn't like anyone to have something she hadn't got."
"So when did she start making a play for him ?" I asked, rather tactlessly.

Sue just sighed, and we continued our walk down a twisty path running next to the river until we arrived at the Botanic Gardens. We went through a gate and eventually found ourselves back in the High Street, more or less opposite Longwall Street where I had turned the day before. On our left as we walked down, Sue pointed out where William Morris had opened his first garage, heralding the arrival of Morris cars.

"Phil always wanted to visit me and see this, but he never did." she said, her voice tinged with sadness.
We slowly continued our walk back towards her flat, Sue talking as we went.

> *Your mother and I were on teaching practice for the next few weeks, so Phil didn't come up again. After that it was the summer vacation and I went back to Oxford. Phil and I wrote frequently all that summer. I even went out with him when I came to stay with your mother for a few days. We went out as a threesome once or twice, something which I found unusual, as Anne was never one to be without male company. Anyway I thought nothing of it. Anne promised me as I left for Oxford after the visit that she would keep an eye on him and stop him from meeting any other girls. That should have cheered me up, but for some reason it didn't....*

"Can you guess the rest, Pete, or shall I spell it out for you ?"

Sue's eyes were filling up with tears as she looked up at me and I felt an overwhelming sympathy for her.

"No, I think I know what happened. As soon as you returned to Oxford, mother started seeing Phil. Is that how it happened ?"
"Not quite that quickly," she replied.

By this time we had arrived back at her flat. It was about two in the afternoon. We went inside and Sue made a cup of coffee and brought out some nibbles to eat. We sat and ate and drank the coffee. I could tell she was keen to bring the story to an end.

> *I returned to college in September 1962 for my second year of study. Anne and I managed to get our old room back, and our friendship continued. Phil visited me several times over the year, on his own, I might add, but we always went out with Anne whenever he came....*

Here Sue dug out some old photographs of the three of them, very similar to the pictures I had seen in mother's scrapbook.

> *The writing was on the wall by the start of our third and final year at Charlotte Mason. Phil hardly ever wrote to me, but Anne made sure she got to the pigeonholes, where our mail was deposited, before I did every morning. I found out later that he wrote to her on a regular basis. I just couldn't compete. She had the looks, the poise, the style and elegance. She could have had any boy she wanted, but she chose mine. The only boy I ever wanted....*

Here Sue broke down and sobbed. I was overcome with guilt, albeit by proxy. After all, they were both my parents. I felt ashamed. I apologised. Sue smiled at me and wiped her eyes.

"Now why on earth should you apologise ? You weren't even born."

I reached across and held her hand. Sue squeezed mine tightly. We sat holding hands in silence for several minutes. I looked across into Sue's face. It was the face of a woman who had been wronged and never quite got over it, even after over thirty years. I let go of her hand. Sue had recovered her composure.

"I'm just a silly old fool," she said.
"No you're not," I replied. "You were hurt by two people who you thought you could trust. My parents," I added ironically. "But why East Anglia ? Why the split with her parents ? Why did Phil leave ? Is it too painful to finish the story ? Stop if you want to."
Sue assured me she could continue.

> *We finished our teaching course in June 1964, and we both were then qualified teachers. I think I had forgiven Anne by then, and our friendship was, if not quite as strong as before, still there. I returned to Oxford and managed to get a job at a primary school in Cowley. Anne was not so lucky, and for some reason found it difficult getting a job in Accrington. We kept in touch, of course; indeed Anne came to visit me in Oxford just after Christmas 1964. It was then that she told me that Phil had asked her to marry him. She was completely besotted by him at that point, and had accepted. I asked what Frank and Emily had said. She had not told them yet. Strangely out of character, for your mother. In fact she was going to introduce Phil to them both the following weekend, when she returned from Oxford. She wanted me to be the first to know, under the circumstances....*

"Was she being sensitive ? You know, wanting to tell you personally ?" I asked, looking Sue straight in the face. I was starting to feel rather ashamed of my mother.

"In her own way, I suppose she was, and indeed I was pleased I heard it from her own mouth, rather than getting a wedding invitation through the post. In fact she even asked me to be her bridesmaid."

"That was rather hard faced of her wasn't it ?" I asked.

"Not really. She was just being Anne. As far as she was concerned the race had been run and she had won, as always, and now everything was OK again."

I sat in stunned silence; this was a side of mother I had never seen before. She had always been so unselfish as far as I was concerned, always putting me first in everything. I didn't like this recently discovered character trait one little bit. Sue, on the other hand, appeared completely selfless.

> *So Anne left Oxford back in January 1965, with the sole intention of telling her parents that she was going to marry Phil. I used the word "telling" advisedly. Anne was not one for asking. If she wanted something she got it. I heard nothing from her until early April, and then it was a letter. I had received lots of letters from Anne in the past, but never one like this....*

Sue walked over to the cupboard and pulled out an envelope, carelessly torn open, and passed it to me. I unfolded the delicate pink sheets, instantly recognising mother's handwriting.

"You read it," said Sue. "I'll give my voice a rest."

I took the letter from Sue and began to read it to myself. I knew Sue could probably recite it by heart.

Old Pals Act

Dear Sue,

So how are you? Well, I hope. It seems such a long time since we saw each other in January, so I thought I'd bring you up to date on the marriage plans. Remember I told you I was going to take Phil home to meet mum and dad? Well I did. What an awful experience that turned out to be. At first everything went well. Mum and dad really took to Phil and were delighted that we were going to marry, after all he was a local lad with good prospects. He passed his exams, by the way, and now is a fully qualified mechanic, whatever that means. Well, mum and I went to make coffee whilst we left dad and Phil in the lounge. When we went back in dad was bright red in the face and was holding Phil by the throat in an attempt to strangle him. Mum screamed at dad to let him go, which thankfully he did. Phil backed towards the door, clutching his throat. I had never seen dad lose his temper like that before, he was proper blazing. He told Phil to leave straight away and never to come to his house again. He could also forget about marrying me as he would never let a daughter of his marry one of his kind. I rushed after Phil, who by this time had gone out into the street, to ask what was the matter. Phil said he didn't know and walked away. I went back into the house and confronted my father. He refused to tell me. Mum was trying to calm him down, and get some sense out of him, but he insisted that the marriage was off. I rushed upstairs to my room in tears. Mum came up in a few minutes. Dad had obviously told her the reason for his actions and she now agreed with him, just as she always did. The wedding was off. Not negotiable.

Dad followed her upstairs and apologised to me, but he was adamant he would not allow me to marry Phil under any circumstances, but he would not tell me why. Well, you know me, Sue. I dug my heels in and demanded an explanation, but neither of them would tell me. They simply asked me to trust them, saying he was not the boy for me. I then said something I will probably regret for the rest of my life. Either you give me an explanation or I walk out of this house and never come back. They called my bluff. I walked out and have never been back. I am now living with Phil and his parents in Oswaldtwistle.

However, best chum, it's not all doom and gloom. I've got a teaching job, in Ipswich of all places. I start after Easter.

But now - wait for it - Phil and I are to be married, in Ipswich on the 24th April. Please, please will you come and be my bridesmaid ? You will be my only friend there, apart from Ian, remember him ? Phil has asked him to be best man. Write soon and let me know. Please write to the address on the letter and not home. Love you lots.
Anne
XXX

I put the letter down on the coffee table and looked at Sue. She smiled back at me.
"So now you know." she said, carefully folding the letter and putting it back in the envelope.
"Do you know what happened ?" I asked, unable to keep the bewilderment out of my voice.
"No idea, not to this very day," she replied.
"So what about the wedding ?"
"You must have seen the photographs. Everything went off smoothly."
I could feel myself about to mention Sue's attempted suicide; she spared me the trouble.
"That was the first time I had seen Phil for almost a year. I thought I was over him, but I wasn't. I was happy for Anne, of course, but I

still wanted Phil. I knew I couldn't have him. It was all too much to bear."

Tears were starting to appear in Sue's eyes, tears of shame I suspect.

"I ..... I tried to kill myself, when I got back from the wedding," she blurted out, "I was so depressed and hurt and alone, I couldn't stand it."
I decided to feign ignorance, "So what happened ?"
"I took an overdose, passed out on the floor, but the bloody window cleaner saw me lying there and called an ambulance. A stomach pump later I was almost back to normal. It even made the papers. Can you believe it ? We do strange things at times. I actually sent a cutting to your mother. I suppose I was subconsciously trying to make her feel guilty."

I remained silent. It certainly explained how mother got hold of the cutting I had seen in her scrapbook.

"It's an ill wind, though," she went on. "I fell in love with the ambulance driver, Doug. He called on me a few days later to see how I was. I think he must have fancied me, lying there all pathetic and helpless."
"And ?" I asked, feeling for all the world like a chat show host drawing personal details out of a guest.
"We had a passionate love affair, for three years. We were very much in love. We nearly married."
"And ..... ?" I repeated.
"He died. Cancer." She looked at me as she said this, "I couldn't love again, there's too much pain."

I looked at the floor, then at Sue. I crossed the room and threw my arms round her. We stayed like that for several minutes.

"At least it got me over Phil," she said. " Well, almost. I still love him, you know."

Sue still hadn't finished. She stood up and positioned herself by the window. In the natural light, what there was left of it, I couldn't help thinking what an attractive woman she could be. She might still make someone a good wife.

> *We kept in touch over the next few years. You were born two years after the wedding; here - this is a photograph of you, cradled in your mother's arms. I came over to visit the three of you in 1969, just after you moved up to Stradbroke. I always liked that house, you know. Perhaps I should sell this place and buy it !*
> *Anyway, in 1971, Emily died. Anne went to the funeral, leaving you with Phil. I don't think he would have been very welcome in Accrington. She must have tried to make up with her father at the funeral; after all it was six years since she walked out. I don't know what exactly happened, but she rang me when she got back and dropped a bombshell. Frank had mellowed, and had told Anne the reason for his reaction when he tried to throttle Phil all those years ago. And as a result Anne was now was totally against her husband. She had real hate in her voice. She made it clear that he was never going to be part of her life again, and the sooner he went, the better....*

"Did she tell you why ?" I asked.
Sue shook her head.
"No. All she would say was that he had to go, her love for him was now gone and that she could hardly bring herself to look at him. I couldn't imagine what had turned love into hate so quickly and so irrevocably. Her father wanted Anne to let you go to live with him,

so that both of you would be out of her life. Your mother refused to leave you. So your grandfather cut all links with Anne once more."

I shook my head in disbelief. What could have happened to make Phil be hated so much, and what is more, why was I also a hate figure in my grandfather's eyes ? I could make no sense of it.

"Shortly after that," continued Sue, " your mother turned on the charm and had an affair with Bill Garnett, secretly at first, but then more openly. Your father walked out in November 1971."

I was stunned by this last revelation. I had my suspicions of course, but to have them confirmed was a body blow. The whole sad episode made no sense. I needed to speak to my father, to find out his side of the story.

"So mother never even hinted why she had the change in her feelings towards my father ?"
"No, never, though I did ask her once. All she would say was she preferred not to talk about it, to anyone. Sorry Pete, I can't help you on that score."

I glanced at my watch; it was nearly 4 o'clock, and dark outside. I hugged Sue again and got ready to leave. I had genuinely enjoyed listening to her. She had given me a clearer picture of my mother. Not all of it was pleasant, but she had not really solved anything. I was even more convinced now that the answer would be found in Accrington. Unfortunately, the people who could have told me anything were all now dead. My only hope was my father. Perhaps he could fill in some of the gaps.

I left the flat and returned to my car. It took me a long time to get back to Stradbroke that evening. The traffic leaving Oxford was slow moving and there had been a crash on the M25. I was almost sick as I drove slowly past the wrecked car. So it was nearly 8.30 when I pulled into my drive, where I was met by my beloved Sara. It was good to see her again. I felt that I needed her more than ever now. Ignoring the cold, we hugged each other on the doorstep for several minutes, Sara grimacing at the sight and feel of my stubbly chin.

My first job when I got inside was to ring Sue and tell of my safe return. She had seen on the news about the crash on the motorway and was starting to worry. I felt like I had gained another mother. After all, but for an accident of fate - or was it mother's intervention - I might have been her son.

Sara and I talked until the early hours about Sue's revelations, but we could not really make any sense of the whole affair, though she was shocked to hear about the way Anne had calmly taken Phil away from Sue.

"I would never have thought her capable of such a thing. She was always so selfless," Sara remarked, her comment echoing my earlier thoughts.

How wrong can you be?

As for the reaction of my grandfather towards my father, she could not even hazard a guess. We went lovingly to bed, older but no wiser.

Chapter 6

EAST ANGLIA: BILL

We slept in late the next morning, neither of us wanting to leave our blissfully warm bed, where we lay curled up together. I was the one who made the first move, putting on my dressing gown and going downstairs to make a cup of tea. There was no post, so I went back to bed and we drank the refreshing drink, but it was another hour before we both decided that we were achieving nothing luxuriating here in bed. We had what you could call brunch before setting off to mother's house again. Sara, in my absence, had completely stocked up with food, enough to withstand a siege, she laughingly pointed out. I was beginning to like having a "wife" again.

Mother's house was virtually clear now, except for the furniture. I congratulated Sara on her solitary endeavours. The pile of personal things was now rationalised into several large cardboard boxes ready to be taken to my house, where they would no doubt be placed in the loft. Things like washing machine, fridge, television and video we were going to advertise in the local paper, since neither of us had any real need for them. The furniture was going to a second-hand dealer in Diss, where it would be sold on for a commission.

I still felt very depressed about the whole concept of breaking up mother's home, but, as Sara pointed out, what else could we do ? I wondered if there was anything Sue would like as a memento of mother, and decided to ring her to see. Sara had also contacted the local estate agent to put the house on the market, a job I had not even thought of doing. Sara was wonderful. Where would I have been without her ?

It was just as we were leaving, probably around 5.30, when we encountered Bill Garnett. He was walking down the road in the general direction of the village, but in all probability he was going to the Queen's Head. I made a move to speak with him, in spite of Sara's restraining hand on my arm.

"Hello Bill," I said. " Sobered up, have we ?" He looked across at me and nodded in the affirmative.
"Just going down for a top-up though," he laughed.
"Mind if I join you ?" I asked before Sara could stop me. "Perhaps you could tell me a bit about my mother in the old days ?"
"Sure, always glad of a little company." He grinned at Sara, " ...and the little woman too?"
"No thanks, I've got one or two things to do," Sara responded, giving me a dirty look.
"I'll be down around eight," I said, giving Sara an enquiring glance as if to ask "is that OK ?". She nodded, but she didn't look too happy about the whole proceedings. I just hoped that Bill would stay sober enough so that I could get a proper tale out of him.

When we got back inside my house, Sara treated me to the burning martyr routine. Something about going away to Oxford for two days and leaving her. I apologised, but pointed out that I really would like to speak to Bill about mother as soon as possible. She agreed that would be a good idea, if only to get it out of my system. I think she was getting rather fed up of me trying to discover my past, when she wanted to plan our future. All in good time, I thought, all in good time. We had a light evening meal of baked potato with grated cheese filling, plus a bottle of wine which Sara made appear from the fridge as if by magic. I must admit to having the lion's share. I rapidly got showered and changed after washing up and made my way to the pub. Would he be able to put in place another piece of the jigsaw ?

Being a Friday night, the pub was quite busy already, full of the youth of Stradbroke, celebrating the weekend. It took me several minutes to locate Bill. I eventually spotted him sitting on a stool at the bar, talking to a group of people who were clustered round him. I waved across, making the traditional gesture asking him if he wanted a drink. He mouthed back at me a pint of Adnams. There was hope, if he had not been drinking spirits all night, that he might still be relatively sober. I ordered the drinks and went to stand next to him. Luckily, a table became free. I think they often did when Bill Garnett headed towards them ! We went to sit down. I offered him a cigarette, which he took gratefully. We sat looking at each other for a few minutes; neither of us was prepared to speak first. I studied him carefully. He was someone who looked to have aged beyond his years. His face was wrinkled, especially round the eyes. He had a huge red nose, due to excessive drinking I surmised. Surely my mother could not have been interested in him, not even twenty-plus years ago. Somehow I just couldn't see them together, or was it that I didn't want to accept it ? Yet how could I discount Sue's comment about mother having an affair with him ?

He seemed to be studying me with the same intensity, no doubt thinking of the period all those years ago when he was friendly with my mother.

"You're just like him, you know, except for the hair of course," he began.
"Tell me all you can remember about mother and father. It's important to me," I almost pleaded, ignoring the remark about my appearance. Besides, I was getting used to people saying that, and it no longer had any impact.

He stared at his glass for a long time and then he began to tell his story.

> *It was in 1967, or was it 1968 ? I can't really remember, it don't matter too much though, when your mother and father bought the house in the village. I remember it had been on the market for a long time, nobody seemed too interested in it for some reason. I was working as a farm hand at the time. I had lots of mates, we had good times, drunk most nights....*

I couldn't help comparing the way Sue told her story with the disjointed efforts of Bill Garnett. I hoped he was going to get his facts right and not go wandering off at a tangent. I needn't have worried: he soon got into the swing of things.

> *Well, your mum and dad moved in. All the men of the village fancied your mum. She was a real stunner, you know. Unfortunately for the rest of us, she only had eyes for your father. Of course, she would talk to us lads in the pub and the like, but she would never let us get close. So we all became just good friends. Your father was a decent old boy, talked all northern he did, had his own garage*

> business in Diss. Did quite well. He would fix our cars
> and tractors and stuff at weekends, good lad.
> "Lets have a look at it," he would say....

Here Bill pronounced the word "look" as you would the boy's name Luke. He laughed,
"We always took the piss out of him when he said that."
His laughter turned into a fit of coughing followed by a loud belch. Amazingly, even more space appeared around us at the same time.

> *Your mum, she was teaching in Ipswich. Travelled every day, quite a trip, but she was tough you know. Had to set off really early in the morning, got back late. Worked hard she did, they both did. They were popular in the village.*
> *Then you were born, in...... whenever. Not long after they moved here and then they were a proper little family. Everyone used to look at you in your pram and comment on your hair. Your mum gave up teaching for a while whilst you were growing....*

Bill was ready for another drink. I wasn't sure if he could cope with another pint and continue telling the story. Nevertheless, I got him another one, and a half for me. I knew I couldn't take everything in if I had much more to drink, and I cursed my greed with the wine earlier on.
"So Bill, why did father walk out on us ?" I asked.

> *You'd be about four or so - never was too good on ages - when I saw your mum in the village, all crying like. Turns out her mum had died. Didn't know your mum had any family till then....*

"Join the club," I whispered in a barely audible voice.

> *Your mum said she was going to the funeral, up north. I said that me and Lizzie would look after you for a day or two whilst your mum and dad were away. Lizzie, she was my girl at the time. Your mum thanked me kindly, always polite your mum, but said Phil would not be going, as he wasn't exactly popular with her dad. I must admit I was a bit surprised like, couldn't imagine anyone not liking him, but I said nothing. So she set off and left your dad and you to fend for yourself. I remember he took time off work to look after you. He was like that, your dad. I remember he brought you round to the farm one afternoon to have a look round, like, and you walked hand in hand as he showed you the machines and what they did....*

I felt a pang of love towards my father, but I still wanted to know what had happened. Why had he upped and left, what had gone wrong ? Bill Garnett looked across at me and smiled, well it was more of a grimace, and said.
"Look, boy, I'm getting rather pissed, perhaps we'd better continue this some other time."

I gathered from this that the conversation was at an end and I would glean no more information from him that night. I glanced at my watch. It was 9.30 or thereabouts. Perhaps it would be prudent to return home and see Sara, who no doubt would be still up, or I hoped she would.

I took my leave of Bill and asked when we could continue the conversation. He was rather noncommittal, but said he would be about the next day. I walked a little unsteadily towards the door and left. The blast of fresh air hit me as soon as I walked down the street. I was a little worse for wear and walked, as if on castors, down the road towards home, the short walk seeming much longer somehow.

Sara greeted me at the door. She seemed surprised that I had arrived back before closing time. I explained that Bill was getting rather "refreshed" and couldn't continue.

"Living in a glass house on that one," she remarked as I sat unsteadily down on the settee. I smiled and pulled her down and kissed her, and she responded readily. As we held each other I related Bill Garnett's story, probably, but only just, more coherently than he did.

"Look, forget about bloody Bill Garnett, will you, and forget about the past. It's all over now. Let it lie."

I was surprised at Sara's attitude towards the whole affair. After all, it was my past that I was trying to discover. Should I exclude her from it ? I didn't think so, unless, of course she wanted to be excluded. I pleaded with Sara to be patient with me; I think she agreed but I wasn't sure. All I know is that we went to bed and made love with a passion that surprised us both.

Once again we slept in the next morning, and it was nearly ten o'clock before either of us stirred. When we did it was as a result of the phone ringing. I reached across and answered it. There on the other end was Elaine.

"Hello, Mr. Jackson," came the voice. Elaine was always very formal when speaking to me.
"Good morning Elaine," I answered. " What can I do for you ?"
"Well," she replied, "it is Saturday and I wondered if I could take the day off ? I've worked all week without a break. I just thought

that if you were going to come in today, I could perhaps have some time to myself ?"

I cursed silently to myself. Poor Elaine ! She had done a full week on her own in the shop, and it was only fair I should return and give her some time away from work.

"Sorry, Elaine, a thousand times sorry. Look, give me an hour and I'll be over there and relieve you, is that OK ?"
"That's fine. Look, I'm sorry to have to ring you like this, but, well I'm sure you understand."
"Of course I do. See you in about an hour."

I hung up the phone and cursed aloud, rather unreasonably in retrospect. I explained the situation to Sara, and got up, showered and dressed. I gulped down a frugal breakfast and left, calling out to Sara that I would see her later. As I pulled out of the drive, I noticed the fuel gauge on the car was showing red so I had to call at the garage in the village for some petrol. Old Jack, who of course commiserated with me about my mother, served me.

"A fine woman," he said. "Full of life, and always got a kind word to say for everyone. Nice to see your dad in church. What a pity things turned out the way they did. I always liked him, you know. Don't know why he did what he did, a mystery to all of us. Such a loving couple, nice to see them together it was."

I handed over my credit card without saying a word. I was again confronted by the paradox of my father's actions. Why did he walk out ? What the hell had happened to make him take such a step ? Everyone who knew them seemed to think they were a perfect couple. It seemed every person I spoke to made the puzzle deepen, and yet at the same time revealed a little bit more about my parents.

I drove to Diss, alone with my thoughts. I could make no sense of the whole affair. Why had such a perfect couple, or at least on the face of it, blown themselves apart so quickly ? I could not fathom it. Thinking deeply, my mind was distracted from the road and I very nearly killed myself as I rounded a bend just outside Diss on the wrong side of the road, narrowly missing a large wagon going in the other direction. I must try to put these things out of my mind, at least until I was in the possession of a few more facts.

As I walked through the door of the shop Elaine, who was ready to leave, greeted me. I apologised most profusely and she bade me farewell. I settled down to what I thought would be a hard day's work in the shop. It was not the case, though. If anything, business was very slow, in fact non-existent. As I sat looking at some of my pictures, I was reminded about my great-grandfather. What was it the notice in the paper had said ? Something about his pictures being on display in local galleries. I wondered what style of pictures he had painted. Well, only one way to find out. I dialled directory enquiries and asked for tourist information in Accrington.

"Hello, tourist information, Lesley speaking, how may I help you ?" answered the cheerful voice at the other end.

I explained the situation, giving my name and reason for interest to the lady, quoting my great-grandfather's name and his age and date of death. She begged me to be patient whilst she consulted someone else in the office. After quite a while she came back with a sort of answer.
"My colleague seems to think that, given his age, he was most likely one of the "Accrington Pals", a regiment of World War One volunteers. One of the lucky ones who survived."
"Death of a Pal," I said down the phone.
"I beg your pardon ?" came the puzzled retort from the other end of the phone.

"Oh nothing," I replied.
"As for his paintings," Lesley continued, " it's possible that they may still be in the local art gallery, but the chances are they may have been removed, we honestly don't know."

I thanked her for her assistance and hung up. Was I any the wiser ? Perhaps, but if I was, I wasn't sure where all this was leading me. Professionally I would have liked to see the pictures, but that would mean a trip to Accrington to search for them myself, something I would probably do at some point. The rest of the day passed off without too much excitement, so at closing time, I locked up the shop and made my way home.

Sara, who had heard the car draw up, greeted me at the door. She rushed over to me and threw her arms around me.

"Bill Garnett called round this afternoon," she whispered in my ear. "He's a spooky man ! He kept asking for you, and even when I told him you were out he still asked to see you. I think he was rather drunk."
"More than likely," I replied. " Did he say he would call back ?"
"No, he just said he would be in the pub tonight, if you wanted to continue your little chat. Don't go Pete," she implored. " Don't leave me again."

I knew I shouldn't, but I knew I would. We walked into the living room. Sara, deep down inside, probably knew it too. She disappeared into the kitchen and made us both a drink.

"You do realise that I need to see him again," I began, after she returned with two cups of coffee.
"Yes, of course, but you are becoming totally obsessed with the whole thing. Why not leave it all in the past where it belongs ? Let's get on with our lives."

"Let me just listen to the end of the story, then perhaps I can forget the past, for good ..... please ?"
I gave Sara a pathetic, puppy dog look. She started to soften.
"You promise, once you have heard the end of his story, you will leave it be ?"
"Once I get to the bottom of it, I promise," I answered, congratulating myself on the evasive nature of my reply and grunting, just for good measure.
"That's not what I asked, now is it ?"
Sara was equal to my noncommittal answer.
"Not quite," I conceded. "But let's see where it takes us, eh ?"

Sara could see there was no use in continuing with the argument. The Jackson stubbornness had kicked in. Though I did feel that eventually it would meet its match with Sara. I looked across at her impish face as she sipped her coffee, staring back at me over the rim of the mug. I would never do anything to hurt her, she meant too much to me. I knew I could be putting our relationship at risk pursuing my mystery, yet I could not give up until I had discovered as much as I could.

After the evening meal I went upstairs to have a shower in readiness for my second meeting with Bill Garnett. I needn't have bothered. Just as I was drying myself there was a terrific hammering on the door. I stopped drying myself, made my way to the top of the stairs and cocked my head to one side to see if I could determine who it was. I heard Sara answer the door.

"Oh, its you. You'd better come in. He's in the shower."

I didn't hear a reply of any sort, just the door closing. I dressed as quickly as I could and made my way downstairs. There, sitting in the armchair, was Bill Garnett. Sara was on the settee, keeping as far away from him as possible. A look of relief spread across her face as I entered the room and joined her on the settee.

"Thought it might be easier if I came round here," Garnett said, slurring his words and belching.

I could see that Sara did not share his thoughts, but said nothing, just shuddered.
"Well, er... yes... you've saved me a trek down to the pub. Would you like a drink ?"
"Coffee or tea ?"
Sara was like lightning with her question.
He looked slightly taken aback with the speed of Sara's response, and said he would like a coffee.
"And for you, Pete ?"
"Coffee, that's fine." I smiled across at her.

She left the room to make the drinks. Bill looked rather disappointed and wore an "I wish I'd stayed in the pub until he arrived" look on his face. He glanced slyly at his watch and I could have sworn I heard his brain say, "Two hours to closing time. Might just be able to squeeze a couple in if I'm quick." Perhaps I misjudged the chap, but I think not.

"Maybe we should continue," I said hastily.
"You're right," came the reply. " Now where did I finish the tale last night ?"
"My mother had gone north for the funeral and dad was looking after me."
"Oh yes, I remember."
Pulling himself to the front of the chair and stroking his chin, he continued with his recollections.

Away a few days she was. I think I saw her again about a week later, in the shop with you she was. I asked her if everything had gone OK and she replied as well as could be expected under the circumstances. She said she was having a bit of a get-together at the house next Saturday night, to cheer her up, like, what with her mother dying and all. Would I like to come? Bring Lizzie, of course. I said I would ask her, but I thought it would be all right. I promised to let her know sometime either the following day or the one after that. She smiled that dazzling smile at me and said she would really like me to come if possible. She turned away and her hair - she had it long in those days - whirled out behind her. She took your hand and walked out of the shop. Lizzie said she was keen to go, so it was all arranged.

The following Saturday came and we arrived at her house. There were a lot of people there; your parents had plenty of friends. As we went in the house, your mother rushed up to us and kissed us both. Now that was unusual for her. Phil came up to us saying he was glad we could make it, but he contented himself with shaking our hands. The party was in full swing; people were chatting and generally making polite conversation. Lizzie had seen some friends and had gone over to talk to them. I was left on my own. I was never a real party lover, so I just stood by the stereo, studying the collection of records.

Suddenly there was a terrific clatter and everyone turned towards the kitchen door to see what had happened. Your mother had been carrying a plate of sandwiches out of the kitchen and had dropped the lot. Your father rushed across to help pick them up. Quick as a flash your mother pushed him away, quite hard, and said she could manage, and not to be so bloody fussy. It was said very loudly and everyone heard. I felt a little surprised. I had never heard

> *your mother snap at your father before, it seemed most unlike her. She started to clean up the mess whilst Phil walked away looking rather upset. Everyone continued as if nothing had happened, but no doubt feeling slightly embarrassed.*
> *After she had thrown the sandwiches away she walked over to where I was standing. She apologised for her outburst. She should have perhaps apologised to Phil, and not me. I grinned at her and made some comment about accidents happening. She looked me full in the face and asked me if we could talk, somewhere private, like....*

At that moment Sara came back into the room carrying our cups of coffee. Please God, don't let her drop them, I prayed to myself. She didn't, depositing them safely down in front of us. Bill's eyes lit up to find she had put a drop, or more than a drop, of whisky into the cups. She grinned across at us both and simply said,
"Just to keep out the chill of a cold night," and sat down next to me on the settee.
"Thank you very much, missy," said Bill. I nodded my thanks and kissed her lightly on the cheek.
"So where was I when all this was going on ? Surely not upstairs in bed ?" I asked, offering him a cigarette.
"Oh no," he replied, " you were sleeping down the road with some neighbours, friendly with their son. Moved away now, they have."
"So what did mother want to talk about ?"

> *We walked out of the kitchen door and into the back garden. It was very warm and stuffy in the house, so it was nice to be out in the fresh air. Your mother then opened her heart to me. How she was fed up with your father, how he wasn't the man she married. How he had slapped her the day she arrived back from the funeral. She also*

thought he had hit you whilst she had been away. "The bastard!", I thought....

"Sorry, miss," Bill apologised to Sara for using bad language, looking all embarrassed.

I found it hard to believe, but here she was telling me these things, and I was in no position to argue, now was I? As we walked around the garden she slipped her hand in mine and squeezed it gently. We walked back towards the door, and she let go of my hand, but only after she was sure the action had been seen by a couple of the guests. I didn't know what to make of that little show of affection. I put it down to her being drunk and still being slightly shocked after the death of her mother. I rejoined Lizzie when I got back inside, and explained I had been outside for some fresh air. She seemed quite happy chatting to people, so I poured myself another drink and thought about your mother's actions. I came to the conclusion there was nothing in it, but at the same time I felt rather flattered.
Things went from bad to worse with your mother and father after that. Somehow, whenever they were seen together they always seemed to be rowing and arguing. I remember they had a blazing row in the pub one night, all over your father not getting any ice in your mother's drink. She went wild, calling him inconsiderate and thoughtless, caring only for himself, bloody typical of his lot. Just like at the party. It was really embarrassing. So your father spent more time out drinking with his mates. He confided in me one night that he didn't know what had happened between the two of them. I didn't say a word. About three weeks after the party, your mother came round to see me one night, almost in tears. Phil had

> *slapped her quite hard across the face. Sure enough, her left cheek was red and starting to swell. She had just walked out of the house and come straight round to see me. She threw herself into my arms and sobbed. I comforted her as best I could, and eventually she calmed down. That was the start of my involvement. I'm not saying I caused them to split up, but I .... I might have had something to do with it....*

Bill Garnett looked across at me and apologised.
"It's not like you think," he said.
"And just what do I think ?" I snapped back at him.
I could feel my temper starting to boil and I made a move to stand up and confront him. Sara, spotting the danger signs, pulled my arm.
"Come on, Pete, let him finish."
I reluctantly relaxed back onto the settee.

> *Your mother made all the running. She would ring me at every opportunity, inviting me round to do simple little jobs in the house. Usually when your father was just coming home from work. Your mother had given up working to bring you up, remember. Phil would come in and barely speak to either of us. This happened far too often for my liking. Word got back to Lizzie, goodness knows how, and she finished with me. I felt very much like the pig in the middle....*

"Excuse me for a moment, would you Bill ?" I interrupted. "I want to show you something."
I stood up and went upstairs to fetch the photograph of us both on the beach at Southwold.
"About this time, was it ?"

I indicated the date. Bill took the picture and studied it, and his face broke into a slight smile.
"Yes, it would be. I'd forgotten all about that picture, but not the day itself."
I looked across at him with a puzzled look on my face, inviting him to elaborate.

> *I remember your mother rang me up early one morning, suggesting we set off for the day. As you know, I fancied your mother and didn't take second bidding. I drove round to the house. Thankfully your father had set off for work, so I didn't meet him. We piled you and everything we needed for a picnic into her car, and set off for Southwold. We had a lovely day, paddling on the beach, eating ice creams, a true family day out. Something I've never had, not having children of my own, like. I remember buying you a fishing net and taking you on the beach to see if we could catch anything. We didn't, but it was fun. It was nice to see your mother smiling again after the miserable time she had been having of late. I remember we sang songs all the way back, and you joined in 'til you fell asleep in the back seat. One of the nicest days of my life, it was....*

It felt very odd to hear Bill talk like this. I had no recollection of the day out, but he obviously had enjoyed the trip to be able to remember it so clearly. The more I listened to Bill's story, the less I liked of the situation which was arising. My father had apparently beaten my mother and me, though I cannot remember any such incident. My mother had started up a relationship with Bill, despising my father overnight, or so it seemed. As with Sue's story, everything seemed to revolve around the trip north to her mother's funeral. What the hell could have happened ? I recalled the telephone call my mother had made to Sue after the funeral, something about Phil never being part of her life again. Mother was true to her word, he was being phased out, and very skilfully, it seemed. My thoughts were brought to an end as Bill continued.

> *After that we became very much an item, as they say nowadays, and I spent lots of time with your mother. Goodness knows how it must have confused you. Phil was to be seen at your house less and less, until he could stand it no more, and he walked out in the November of that year. I was pleased to see him go. From what Anne had said he was a thoroughly bad lot, drunk most nights, violent and abusive. That was why she turned to me. I was such a steady chap, or so she said. I began looking forward to a Christmas spent with you and your mother. I think I had fallen in love with her. We spent hours talking about everything you could think of. She told me about her father in the north. I would have liked to meet him, he sounded quite a character. I was told about her friendship with that Sue woman, from college days, everything. However, not once did I sleep with her. Oh, I tried lots of times, but she always refused, saying it was too soon after her husband had gone....*

"You do realise he's dead ? " I interrupted.
"Who ?" he asked.
"Her father. That was why she went north the other week, to his funeral."
Bill obviously was ignorant of this fact, and his face dropped.
"You mean... ?"
"Yes, she was killed whilst returning from Accrington."
He went quiet for a second or two and shook his head.
"No, no I didn't know. That's badness, that is."

Old Pals Act

I indicated to Bill to continue his story, but he was obviously quite shaken by the news. His voice trembled slightly as he spoke.

> *It was early December when she dropped the bombshell. She didn't want to see me again ! You know how single minded your mother could be. Believe me, boy, this was not open to argument. She meant what she said. As quickly as I entered her life, I was kicked out. To this day I think she used me as a lever to get rid of your dad. If that was the case, it bloody well worked. I don't think I ever spoke to her again, except to pass the time of day, certainly not like before, sharing secrets and all. I still loved her. I think I still do, at least her memory....*

I looked across at the rapidly sobering Bill. There were tears in his eyes. I really think he did love my mother, even though he was under no illusions about her manipulations. Mother was very good at using her beauty to achieve her goals. However, the puzzle still remained. Why had she done this, and what had my father done to bring about such a situation ? Bill Garnett had not really provided an answer. He had, if anything, made the puzzle deeper. He had obviously no idea why mother had reacted the way she did. Judging from his comments at mother's funeral, he still believed my father's behaviour to be the reason. Yet I believed - no, knew - it went much deeper than that.

Bill got up to leave. I couldn't help feeling a little sorry for him. He had lost a lot through his involvement with my mother. Not the least of which was his girl Lizzie, who most likely would have made Bill happy. I really believed he was the victim of circumstances, an innocent rider on a manipulated roller-coaster, and one which was driven by an expert, my mother.

"Well, good night, then," he shook my hand and smiled at Sara.

"Thanks for your kindness. No doubt I'll see you both around the town or in the pub."

As he walked towards the door, I could have sworn he had visibly shrunk, his shoulders slightly hunched. He had the air of a man who had bared his soul. He turned on the doorstep and said good night to me:
"He caused it, you know, not your mother. She was a good sort. Don't think bad of her. I don't."

Even now he was not prepared to let mother take any of the blame. He must have truly loved her, but mother did have that effect on people. Neither Bill nor Sue had uttered one bad word against her, though heaven knows they both had good reason.

I locked the door behind him and turned to Sara, who was still sitting on the settee, looking very pensive.
"So what did you make of that ?" I asked.
"Sounds like poor old Bill was sucked into the whole situation by your mother. I'm sorry to sound disloyal to her memory, Pete."
"I tend to agree with you. She certainly seemed to have him under her spell."
"Do you think your father beat Anne and you, like she told Bill ?"

I thought for a moment. It was all so long ago. I certainly couldn't recall my father striking me, but I was only three or four at the time.
"I don't honestly remember anything like that happening, but I suppose it's possible."
"So, it was something your grandfather told your mother back in 1971 that changed your mother's opinion of Phil ? It must have been something bad to cause that sort of reaction," Sara continued. "He should have told her before she got married, instead of refusing, and all this trouble might have been averted."

"On the other side of the coin, mother should have never walked out without trying to find out the reason first," I retorted. "They were certainly alike, mother and her father - stubborn as mules."
Sara smiled across at me.
"It's continued into the next generation. I just know you will never rest until you get to the bottom of it."

I knew deep inside me that she was right.

Chapter 7

THE GOOD BOOK

Following the night with Bill Garnett, things settled down, and I made no further progress. I won't pretend I felt satisfied with this state of affairs, but what could I do ? I knew at some point I would have to communicate with my father, as he might be able to shed further light on the situation, but I was busy at work and I didn't have much time at my disposal. I wanted to extend the shop, incorporating a studio on the premises. Besides which, Sara was putting pressure on me to let the whole thing drop, which I probably would have done but for yet another twist of fate, which came initially through the unlikely medium of Elaine.

It was now the end of March and I had arrived at the shop quite late, due to an appointment with mother's solicitor. He had gone to great lengths to tell me that the whole double-will business was nearly settled and I should expect to inherit in about another month or so. Apparently, I would soon be the proud owner of my unseen grandfather's house in Accrington, which was on the market, as well as my mother's. Several people had viewed her terraced cottage in Stradbroke and a firm offer had been put in, pending all legal formalities being sorted out. I felt quite encouraged by this. I had no idea what was happening at the Accrington end, and awaited Mr. Robinson's call.

So I was feeling quite cheerful when I walked in through the shop door. Elaine greeted me with an enormous smile, unusual, but pleasant nevertheless.
"Good morning Mr. Jackson," she chirped. "How are you this merry morning ?"
"I'm very well, thank you," I responded, trying to keep the puzzlement out of my voice.

I had never seen Elaine looking so happy, nor had I seen her with make-up on before. She actually looked quite stunning. Her eyes had been somehow made to grow larger and more alluring. I examined her face closely. She seemed to have skilfully used some sort of tawny coloured eye shadow and mascara to achieve this effect. Her cheeks suggested a hint of blusher, and scarlet lip-gloss perfectly complemented her white skin. I wanted even more to paint her ! I could tell she was bursting to tell me something. I probed around a bit.

"So what's new with you ?" I asked. "You look sort of .... different," I added, hoping she wouldn't be offended. "Sort of, well, prettier than normal."
Ouch ! I think I made a bit of a mess of that, but she didn't seem to notice.
"I've been seeing someone for the last week or so," she blurted out with a joy that smacked you in the face.

Old Pals Act

"Excellent, excellent !" I was genuinely pleased for her. "Anyone I know ?"
"Well, sort of," she beamed. "He's been in the shop a few times, buying prints. He actually bought one of yours."

Damning with faint praise, I thought. It was the tone of the word "actually" that struck a chord, though I'm sure Elaine would never mean it in the way I interpreted it. I was just being Peter Jackson, the born cynic.

"Colin had just bought a new house and was looking for some pictures to brighten the place up. I gave him lots of advice on which picture he should have in which room. He asked me if I did an after-sales service."
She blushed at this point, no doubt noticing the wry smile forming on my lips.
"No, not like that, just helping him to get the right position, ... er ....for the pictures," she added as an afterthought.

Poor Elaine was getting flustered, and digging herself in deeper. I raised my eyebrows and looked at her with a shocked expression on my face.
"He wanted them hanging correctly."
I couldn't help but laugh out loud. Another six feet of earth was adroitly removed by Elaine, who, realising what she had just said, decided she had better quit at this point.
"Well, actually, he's a very nice person." she said, jerking her head backwards. "Not smutty like some people."

I apologised to Elaine, she accepted and even had a little giggle herself. I realised this was the first time we had actually had any fun with each other in the shop; she was always so serious. It made a nice change.

"So what does he do ?" I asked, feeling relieved that he was obviously not an artist. I didn't like the thought of anyone painting Elaine in the nude before I did.

"He's an architect, actually, has his own practice in Bury St. Edmunds. Doing well, by all accounts."

"Well, I'm really happy for you Elaine, I really am." I said, in such a way as to suggest that the conversation was now at an end. Not a bit of it.

"I was wondering if you and Sara would like to come to a pub quiz with us on Friday ?" Elaine asked. "Chance for you to meet Colin. He's quite keen to chat with you about a commission."

She had said the magic word. I was hooked. Elaine was wise to me, and just knew I couldn't resist that sort of bait

"I'll have to check with Sara, of course, but I'm sure it will be OK. Can I let you know tomorrow ?"

"No problem, Mr. Jackson, tomorrow will be fine."

Elaine has worked for me for about three years now, and never once has she called me Peter, despite being told to on many occasions. I smiled to myself at the prospect of an evening with Elaine, Colin, Sara and Mr. Jackson. I went into the office to check the post, placed neatly on my desk by the faithful Elaine. I could hear her singing in the shop, totally unheard of. Having a boyfriend was doing her good.

Sara thought it was a nice idea to go out with Elaine and Colin on Friday, when I mentioned it that evening. She, like me, was quite keen to meet Elaine's beau. Neither of us knew what to expect. I felt that at last life was coming together again after the upsets of last month. I suggested a stroll down to the Queen's Head for a drink. The pub was quite busy as we walked in; there were no tables free, so we stood in the space by the door. My eyes roamed the room for Bill Garnett, and sure enough he was propping the bar up in the corner. I nodded across at him. He looked rather uncomfortable, but he nodded back at Sara and myself. It was the first time either of us had seen him since his outpouring several weeks ago.

We talked about my plans for developing the shop. Sara suggested that if Colin were an architect he might be able to draw up plans for the extension. I hadn't considered it, but made a mental note to ask him for some input. My mother would also have thought of that; she and Sara were so alike in many ways.

"So, have you put it out of your mind now, your past and things ?" Sara asked, looking at me with those beautiful green eyes.
"I think so. Whatever mystery surrounded mother died with her, I fear. Still, I would have liked to have found out more, but probably never will," I replied with a resigned tone in my voice. "Unless my father can shed any light on the matter. I really must give him a ring," I added.

We had another drink and set off home again. We hadn't gone very far down the road when an out of breath Bill Garnett caught us up.

"Sorry to chase after you," he gasped, " but I've remembered something else your mother said when she came back from Accrington."
"Oh yes, and what was that ?" I asked, finding it difficult to keep the curiosity out of my voice.
"She kept saying that she understood the quotes, after all these years she now understood."
"What quotes, what did she mean ?" I fired at him.
"Sorry, but I've no idea at all," was his reply. "I just thought it might be important. Well, good night."

With that he turned round and headed back towards the pub. We carried on walking towards my house. Sara sighed. I could tell she would have preferred it to have been left unsaid, even if it didn't seem to make much sense to either of us.

"Please don't start all that puzzling out again," she implored.
"Don't worry. I won't," I answered, though I couldn't help thinking what he could have been talking about.

Perhaps Sue would know. A phone call in the morning seemed likely. I resolved not to mention it to Sara. God, I was becoming as secretive as my mother and the rest of her damned family.

I rang Sue from work the next day. After a preliminary enquiry about each other's health, I related Bill Garnett's comments about understanding the quotes. I asked Sue if she knew anything about some quotes. There was silence at the other end of the phone whilst, no doubt, Sue dredged through her memory banks.

"Quotes for a job on the house perhaps ? Or did she dabble on the stock market ?" Sue suggested.
"Well," I paused, "..... it doesn't sound like mother, somehow."
"No, you're right. Sorry, Pete, I can't honestly think what she might have meant, are you sure it wasn't just Bill Garnett rambling ?"
"No I don't think so, Sue. He seemed pretty certain. Well anyway, thanks. Pop up to Stradbroke and see us sometime soon."

Sue said she would and we rang off. I went back in the shop and told Elaine that we would be delighted to come to the quiz on Friday night. She gave me the name of the pub, The Saracen's Head, and the time it started. I wrote it down in my diary. I watched her as she walked across the shop floor. Were her jeans tighter than normal ? It certainly looked that way. I liked this new sexy image, I decided.

Sara hadn't got back by the time I returned home; the nature of her job sometimes meant that she worked late. I poured myself a drink and started to think about quotes. What on earth had my mother meant ? "Now I understand the quotes". I couldn't imagine. I must have fallen asleep, because the next thing I remember was Sara gently waking me up and calling me lazy.

"So this is what you do when I'm not in," she joked," - fall asleep. Did you tell Elaine we would be going on Friday ?"
"Of course I did. What do you take me for ? On second thoughts, don't answer that !"
I handed over my diary with the date and time written in.

Later that evening I confessed to Sara about my call to Sue. She expressed no surprise.
"I thought you would. I couldn't imagine you letting another "clue" pass you by. This is starting to sound like a detective book."
She smiled across at me, wrinkling her nose at the same time.
"So could Sue help ?"
"Not really."
I related the phone call to Sara.
"Oh by the way, I've invited her to stay sometime," I added.

Sara seemed pleased about that. I felt as though I had done something right. Perhaps I was becoming socially educated. We spent a quiet evening watching television though I had no idea what the programme was about. I couldn't get bloody quotes out of my mind.

Sara could see I was not really concentrating. She knew exactly what I was thinking about. Damn my transparency ! Switching the television off, she slid closer to me on the settee and began to massage my shoulders, I suppose in an effort to make me think more clearly or forget the whole thing. The latter option prevailed. We cuddled together, feeling the warmth of each other's bodies.

"Let's have a cocoa and an early night," I suggested.

I got up to make the drink. Whilst I was waiting in the kitchen for the kettle to boil, Sara called out to me.

"You know, Garnett may have misquoted, sorry about the pun, but he may have meant quotations, a subtle difference."

I was amazed that I hadn't seen this before. Of course that was what he meant. I must be getting more obtuse by the day. Somewhere mother had read some quotations, and she finally got to understand them after her mother's funeral. That seemed the logical answer. But we were no nearer, we still didn't know what quotations mother had seen or indeed where they were. Another tantalising dead end. We went to bed and I promised Sara I would let the whole thing drop.

The rest of the week was pretty uneventful, and Friday night duly came round. The quiz was due to start at 8.30, so we left plenty of time to get into Diss. We arrived at the pub and found a table. Elaine and Colin had not yet arrived. We tried to predict what Colin would look like. The favourite being a small, balding, bespectacled man with a feeble moustache and hollow cheeks. I don't know how we arrived at that conclusion, but we couldn't have been further from the truth. Elaine walked over to the table escorted by a tall strapping six-footer, well-dressed in expensive jeans and a designer label sweatshirt. He positively oozed athleticism as he strolled over to the table. I felt my expanding stomach and promised myself to start jogging the following day.

Old Pals Act

"This is Colin," she said, and we shook hands. "This is Sara and... er ....Peter."
Now that didn't hurt did it ? I thought to myself.
"Pleased to meet you both. I've heard a lot about you," he said in what Sara later described as a dark brown voice. "Can I get you a drink ?"

I gratefully accepted the offer and asked for a pint. Sara, bless her, was driving, as she wrongly called tails at the vital tossing up ceremony before we set off, so she had a tonic water. Elaine, much to my surprise, ordered a gin and tonic. Somehow Elaine and alcohol didn't seem to mix. We settled down round our table and the quiz started. I had never been to a pub quiz before, so I didn't know what to expect. I actually enjoyed it. Little groups of people huddled round tables intently striving for the correct answer. There were different sections and a wide variety of subjects. I was surprised at Sara's wide general knowledge and, indeed, Colin and Elaine's. My own, I confess, was sadly lacking. I ask you, how many people know that Margaret Mitchell wrote "Gone with the Wind" ? Well, everybody in the pub except me, apparently, judging by the speed all the heads in the different teams went down nodding in agreement. At the interval we were lying third. Not, I might add, due to the blinder played by one Peter Jackson !

I got another round of drinks, and by the time I returned from the bar the second half had started.

"Now," said Chris, the resident quiz master, straining to make himself heard, "which hit song by Boney M was based on Psalm 137 ?"

I was amazed to see Elaine writing the answer down. I peered across the table and read upside down, "The Rivers of Babylon". I hadn't even taken in the question. I whispered across to Elaine that I was suitably impressed, thinking what an intelligent employee I had. For some reason that particular question stuck with me as a piece of useless yet fascinating knowledge.

When the quiz finished our team ended up a creditable fourth, only nine points behind the winners. Despite my lack of contribution I felt quite proud of our efforts.
"Well done team," I said, assuming the role of captain.

We had one last drink and got to chatting. Colin would be delighted to call round at the shop to see what would be involved in the building of an extension. I reciprocated by suggesting the subject for an original Jackson painting. All in all, the evening went well. Elaine was totally different, quite the life and soul of the group, laughing and telling risqué jokes. Not at all like the blushing shop assistant earlier in the week. Talk about a personality change when away from work ! I hadn't had as much fun for a long time. Thoughts of mother and her secrets were completely erased from my mind. I could tell that Sara was enjoying herself by the number of times her nose did its wrinkling act.

We said our farewells and made our way home. Both Sara and I were delighted for Elaine. Sara agreed with me about her becoming much more attractive all of a sudden. Actually, I think Sara was more impressed with Colin and his boyish good looks. I, of course, didn't comment. Like most red-blooded males, I never regard another man as handsome.

Sara pulled her car into the drive and we went inside. She disappeared into the kitchen to make a coffee before we went to bed. As she came out, she was tunelessly singing "By the Rivers of Babylon." Sara, alas, hasn't a musical bone in her body. I decided to check the quiz question and went in search of a bible. I knew there was one in mother's box of books we had brought back from her house, so I went ferreting into the loft to retrieve it. I came downstairs carrying the bible, hunting as I walked for Psalm 137. Sure enough, there it was, virtually word for word. I was impressed. Sara took a quick glance at the passage, smiled and nodded, handing it back straight away. As she did so a neatly opened envelope dropped out onto the floor. I picked it up. It was addressed to Miss Anne Lord. I removed the paper from inside and began to read it. Coincidences do happen. It was a letter to my mother written, according to the date, in October 1958. My eyes widened as I read it. It was from her grandfather, the artist, who to the best of my recollections died in that year.

> *Dearest Anne,*
> *You are my only grandchild and I love you very much. I realise now that my life is drawing to a close and soon I will be no longer with you. Please don't be sad when I have gone, for I will no longer have to live in the shadow which has darkened my life for so many years. Your father will be the only one who knows what I mean, and he will decide when you should be told. Hopefully by the time you know the full story, the family shadow will be lighter and will not darken your life like it has mine and indeed your father's. Please, Anne, do not dismiss this as an old man's ramblings. The shadow is real. I pray to God that you will not suffer as I have. Read your bible every day, dearest Anne, just like I told you. Perhaps the shadow is in there somewhere.*
> *Your loving Grandfather and Pal.*

There was another piece of paper folded inside the letter. I opened it and read it carefully. It had six Bible references printed upon it.

ECCLESIASTES 3: 8
2 CORINTHIANS 11: 26

JUDGES 5: 23
MATTHEW 24: 10
1 CHRONICLES 28: 9
PSALM 55: 22, 23

Not being a biblical scholar, I had no idea what these references meant, but I thought it a good idea to find out. I reached for the bible and started to search. I needn't have bothered, because on the back of the paper I noticed my mother had written them out in her teenage hand. I showed them to Sara and we studied them together.

ECCLESIASTES 3: 8
"A time to love and a time to hate; a time of war and a time of peace"
2 CORINTHIANS 11: 26
"I have been in the deep; in journeyings often, in perils of waters, in perils of robbers, in perils by mine own countrymen, in perils by the heathen, in perils in the city, in perils in the wilderness, in perils in the sea, in perils amongst false brethren."
JUDGES 5: 23
"Curse ye Meroz, said the Angel of the Lord, curse ye bitterly the inhabitants thereof; Because they came not to the help of the Lord. To the help of the Lord against the mighty."
MATTHEW 24: 10
"And then shall many be offended and shall betray one another and shall hate one another"
1 CHRONICLES 28: 9
"And thou Solomon my son, know thou the God of thy father, and serve him with a perfect heart and a willing mind: for the Lord searcheth all hearts, and understandeth all the imaginations of the thoughts: if thou

> *seek him he will be found of thee but if thou forsake him, he will cast thee off forever."*
> *PSALM 55: 22, 23*
> *"Cast thy burden upon the Lord and he shall sustain thee: he shall never suffer the righteous to be moved.*
> *But thou O God shall bring them down into the pit of destruction: bloody and deceitful men shall not live out half their days; but will trust in thee"*

Underneath the last quotation my mother had written
   "May 1971, now I understand"

I looked across at Sara with a puzzled expression on my face; she looked as blank as I did.
"I wish I bloody understood," I cursed, hastily placing the bible back on the table before the fires of hell consumed me. We sat and stared at the paper, then at each other, for what seemed an eternity.
"Got it ! Don't you see ?" said Sara, "Look at the date, just after your mother returned from her own mother's funeral. Your father must have told her whatever the family shadow was, making the quotations meaningful. It also means I was right about Garnett, too. Your mother didn't say quotes, she said quotations, grammatically correct."
"What the hell does this nonsense about a family shadow mean ? Why does my family have to speak in bloody riddles ?" I shouted, banging my fist down hard on the coffee table, waking up the sleeping Tiger and causing him to scuttle out of the room seeking a safer haven in which to sleep. "Sounds a complete load of rubbish to me."

I was putting on a show of aggression, born partly out of fear, realising if the so-called family shadow could affect mother's life, then surely it could also be passed on to me. I didn't like it and was reacting in the only way I knew how. I suppose it was a kind of defence mechanism.

"You don't think it could be .... some sort of hereditary illness, do you ?" I asked Sara, praying she would say no.

"Shouldn't think so. If it was, why all the big secret ?" That put my mind at rest.

"So what, then - murderers, rapists, thieves ?"

I could feel myself getting rather irrational.

"And where does my bloody father fit into all this ? Has he got a shadow too ?"

I slammed my hand down again, upsetting my half-drunk coffee onto the carpet. Sara looked pale and shaken as she brought a cloth out of the kitchen to mop up the mess. She had never really seen me as angry as this before. The tantrum in the pub was nothing compared to the red mist that was rising behind my eyes at that very moment. I came out with a long string of obscenities and hurled the letter across the room.

Seeing the effect I had on her, I felt ashamed of myself. I apologised and tried to kiss her, but she pulled back and walked out of the room in silence. I made no effort to follow her. Instead I retrieved the letter and read it and the passages again, but they still made no sense. I gradually began to calm down. I carefully placed them in my wallet I went upstairs to bed.

Sara was sobbing her eyes out when I entered the bedroom. I quickly undressed and slipped into bed next to her. She turned and faced me, her pretty green eyes now red with crying. I felt a complete bastard. I cradled her in my arms and held her close.

"I was so frightened," she sobbed. " Please don't do that again."

"I'm sorry, I really am."

My apology somehow sounded so pathetic as I looked on her tear stained face.

Chapter 8

A NORTHERN PILGRIMAGE

I awoke the next morning feeling dirty and ashamed after my actions of the previous night. I turned over in bed and saw my beloved Sara fast asleep. How could I have lost my temper, frightening her to such an extent ? I felt my stomach tighten when I replayed the whole incident in my mind. Suppose I had actually lashed out at Sara ? That would have been the end.

Tension and apprehension coursed through my body as Sara began to stir. How would she react ? She opened her eyes and looked directly at me. She must have felt my feelings as, thank God, she smiled at me. I was at a loss for words.

" I understand why you did it," she said, "but please don't lose your temper again. It doesn't suit you."
With that she kissed me tenderly. It appeared that everything was going to be all right.

I made a clumsy attempt at an apology and slid out of bed. Relief replaced the apprehension I had felt moments before. What had I done to deserve such an understanding lover ? Linda would have done just the opposite, fought fire with fire, making me worse. I showered and dressed before making my way downstairs. Sara followed shortly afterwards, joining me in the kitchen where I was making a cup of tea and pouring milk on my muesli.

As always I got straight to the point.
"I need to find out more."
Sara nodded, she understood.
"I must discover the family shadow. God knows how but I must lay this ghost once and for all."

Not another word was spoken as we ate breakfast. I kept glancing anxiously across at her, but she avoided my eyes. I finished my tea, placed the cup in the sink, kissed Sara goodbye and left for the shop.

Phil, my father, seemed the next obvious move, but he lived some 200 miles away, and judging from his comments at mother's funeral he was as much in the dark as I was. Nevertheless, he was the final remaining link with mother's past and, ultimately, mine. He had to be contacted. I deliberated what to do all through Saturday, drifting through the work at the shop in something of a dream. Sara would not be pleased if I set off for the north. On the other hand, I would not be able to settle if I didn't at least try to follow it through. The decision had to be made.

Elaine, still projecting her new glamorous image, made every effort to communicate with me, but she was met with the usual grunting noises, a stark contrast to the pleasant evening we had spent only 12 hours before.

"Colin enjoyed meeting you both last night," she began. "He was quite keen to meet up again, perhaps for a meal or something."

Rather abruptly I replied that we would have to "arrange something." I really didn't want to commit myself to anything at that point, though I was uncertain as to why not. Deep down inside I knew I would probably be spending some time away from home in the not too distant future. Elaine, who appeared to be turning into a social animal, seemed rather disappointed with my rather cool reply, and she busied herself around the shop, making no further mention of the idea. Luckily we had plenty of customers popping in and out for the rest of the day so there was no opportunity for the subject to arise again. As we were leaving at five o'clock I had decided what to do.

"I'm going to have a few days away," I began. "You are in sole charge of the shop until I return. Close up if you want some time off, or employ someone part-time. Do what you think fit. I've some business to take care of in the north of England."

Elaine looked puzzled, but she made no comment, except to say that she would do all she could to ensure the shop ran smoothly. Poor Elaine; I had put upon her rather a lot lately.

"I'll make it up to you of course, " I added. "Wage increase and whatever. And yes, we would like to go out for a meal with you, when I get back."

My conscience fully clear, I walked away from the shop towards where my car was parked. The drive back to Stradbroke still remains rather hazy. I honestly don't remember much until I turned into the drive and parked behind Sara's car. I half expected it to have gone, and who could have blamed her ? She met me at the door with a loving cuddle, my sins of the previous night seemingly forgotten.

" You realise I nearly left you three times today, but I love you too much. I couldn't do it," she blurted straight out.

I could feel relief spreading throughout my body. For once I was at a loss for words. I just carried on holding her tightly.

"I hope you worried a lot today. Serves you right, perhaps you'll think in future," she continued. "Well, I think you've got something to tell me, about a trip north ?"

How she knew of my decision I'll never know. She obviously understood the importance of finding out the truth, and made no attempt to talk me out of it, realising, as I had earlier in the day, that I would not be able to settle until I had at least made the effort to find out more. I knew I just had to find out what the family shadow could possibly be, and more to the point how it might affect me and ultimately my life with Sara.

"Just get it out of your system once and for all," Sara said.

I rang my father after our evening meal and arranged to drive up to meet him on Monday. I could, of course, stay at his house and "meet the family", a comment that intrigued me. I apparently had some more relations I knew nothing about. He gave me directions, telling me to ring him when I reached the outskirts of Halifax.
"Leave the M62 at junction 26, follow the A58 towards Halifax, through some traffic lights at a crossroads. There is a lay-by on the right hand side of the road. Park there and I will drive out to meet you."

I rang off and consulted my road atlas. I located the exact spot. I noted with some degree of sadness that I would be travelling very near to the place where mother was killed as I journeyed north up the A1. Still, these things have to be done.

The rest of the evening was quiet to say the least. Sara, I could tell, was not exactly overjoyed at the prospect of me leaving for a few days, but she said nothing. She just sat curled up on the settee reading. Sara is an avid reader. I never cease to be amazed at the speed she can finish a novel.

"You do understand why I'm doing this ?" I said, interrupting her train of thought.
Sara nodded and placed a bookmark at the correct page and put the book down.
"Of course I do. Just be careful. I couldn't stand it if anything happened to you."
I took her hand in mine and squeezed it gently,
"Don't worry, nothing will," I said, and began to massage her neck. She tilted her head on one side and rubbed her cheek on my hand.
"Why don't you come with me ?" I asked. "I'd enjoy the company."
She declined, saying that she was too busy to take any more time off work.
"Besides," she added, " you don't want me there when you meet your father, any more than you did when you visited Sue."

I agreed, but in reality I would have been glad of the moral support she would have given. We watched television for an hour or so before going to bed, sleeping soundly in each other's arms.

The next day was Sunday, so we indulged ourselves with the traditional lie-in. When we eventually did make a move, it was nearly 10.30. I went downstairs to make breakfast and busied myself in the kitchen, thinking I would treat Sara to breakfast in bed. However, she followed me down so we sat round the table and planned what to do with the day. We decided we wanted to set off to the coast. It was still early in the year, so we wrapped up well and headed off in Sara's car towards Southwold, still one of my favourite coastal towns in East Anglia. The fact that Adnam's brewery was situated there had nothing to do with it ! We arrived early in the afternoon and spent an enjoyable time walking on the beach, breathing the fresh, clean air one associates with a seaside town. Damn the woman, she could skim pebbles better than I could. We walked past Mr. Jones' house so that I could show Sara my latest commission. We both felt refreshed and invigorated as we got back into the car and made our way back to Stradbroke.

We arrived home early in the evening and I started to pack the things I needed for my journey. I was uncertain how long I would be away, so I packed enough to last for a week. Sara fussed around, helping me fold things neatly in my suitcase and making sure I didn't forget anything.

"Take a jacket and tie," she said. "You never know."
Women understand about these things, and who was I to argue?

I suggested a drink in the Queen's Head. Sara was none too keen, fearing we might run into Bill Garnett again. She made me promise not to get talking to him if he was there, before finally agreeing to go. A customer of Sara's was playing pool with her husband, so we challenged them. Sara amazed me once again, this time with her mastery of the intricacies of the sport. Was there anything, apart from sing, that she couldn't do ? As usual, I was completely hopeless, drawing forth tutting noises from Sara as I missed easy shots. Feeling relaxed, we put our coats on and left. Bill Garnett gave us a salute as we passed him on the way out of the door. We both smiled back at him but said nothing.

The alarm was set for seven o'clock the next morning, and we both awoke with a simultaneous curse. I showered, dressed and made breakfast in record time; I wanted an early start. Sara had her first appointment at 9.30, so she offered to wash up after I had left. I loaded the car and prepared to leave. The parting was tearful, to say the least. Since mother's funeral we had only been apart the one night I stayed in Oxford, and neither of us liked the prospect. I promised to ring at the first opportunity as I drove away, catching a glimpse of my beloved waving me off as I pulled out of the drive and accelerated towards what I hoped would be another link in the chain. I guessed the journey would take about four hours, which would mean I would arrive in Halifax at about 12.30, to find goodness knows what.

The trip north was uneventful. The traffic was fairly light and I made good time. I felt a lump come to my throat as I passed the place near where mother had been killed. My speed increased noticeably as I made a subconscious effort to leave the area as far behind as quickly as possible. I negotiated the assorted roundabouts on the A1 until I spotted the turn off for the M62. Already I was further north than I had ever been in my life; all my holidays had been spent on the south coast or in France. I drove steadily through the road works on the motorway until I saw the sign for junction 26, one mile away. I carefully left the M62 and found the road leading towards Halifax. It was just as father had said, a crossroads followed by a lay-by. I pulled across, took out my mobile phone and made the call to announce my arrival in West Yorkshire. A woman with a lovely northern accent answered my call. My stepmother ? I told her who I was and asked to speak to Phil, and after a minute or so I heard his now familiar voice. He said he would be there in about fifteen minutes, driving a blue Renault Espace. I said I would wait.

I got out of the car and leaned on the wall looking across the fields. The landscape was different to the East Anglian one. Here there were hills and valleys, offering a wealth of material for an artist. Directly opposite from where I had parked was a garden centre. Should I buy Sara a plant ? I decided against it on the grounds that it might die before I got it home. It felt noticeably colder than it had in Suffolk, so I was glad Sara had insisted I packed my fleece jacket, which I zipped up to the top.

I lit a cigarette and inhaled deeply, I felt I needed something to do with my hands as I nervously waited for my father to arrive, thinking chiefly about Sara and her ability to forgive. I had a nagging feeling that I would not have been so tolerant had the boot been on the other foot. I put this thought right out of my mind. It was about twenty minutes later when Phil drew into the lay-by, got out of the car and shook me warmly by the hand. I still felt ill at ease in his company, but I remarked,
"Good to see you again."
"Follow me back to my house, " he said. " I've brought the big car because it's easier to see in traffic. Can't lose you, so soon after finding you again."

As we pulled out of the lay-by I thought to myself that he must be doing OK. "The large car" suggested he had at least another one tucked away somewhere. He drove slowly towards Halifax. It was quite a pleasant journey, down a tree lined road masking the houses on either side. We dropped down to some traffic lights and then climbed steeply. On arriving at the top of the hill I could see the town of Halifax spread out in front of me. It looked like exactly what I thought a typical industrial town should look like, especially the large mill complex on my right. We drove over a bridge perched high above what I assumed was the centre of the town. I counted four blocks of high rise flats as we negotiated the roundabout, sights rarely seen in my part of the world. I followed Phil carefully.

He was right, the Espace was easy to see in the traffic, enabling me to keep track of him as he wove his way through Halifax.

We eventually ended up at a large grassy part of the town, which Phil later told me was called Savile Park. The houses here were all large and expensive. We turned onto the gravel drive of a smart detached house and stopped. It was large, stone built, with bay windows. The ivy climbing the walls gave the impression of a country manor house. Would there be liveried servants appearing to open our car doors ? Phil jumped out of his car and ran towards the front door.

"Welcome to chez Jackson," he laughed as he made a mock bow indicating with a sweep of his arm that I should enter. I walked in and found myself in a long entrance hall, beautifully decorated in a pale green pastel shade. There were several rooms leading off the hall. A flight of stairs was straight in front of me, turning a right angle half way up in front of a magnificent stained glass window, the light from which made lovely colourful patterns on the stair carpet. There was a large aspidistra on a stand at the bottom, probably the biggest in the world, judging by the number of leaves pointing out in all directions. I gazed round and my mouth must have dropped open with surprise.

"Not bad is it ?" he asked me with obvious pride. " The boy done well."

I agreed with him, the boy had done well; it was obvious there was no shortage of money in this house. A small, fair haired, attractive woman, probably in her late 40's, appeared from one of the rooms, beaming all over her face. She was expensively dressed in a pale blue suit and white blouse. She moved towards me to shake hands.

"This is Victoria, who is, I suppose, your stepmother."

There was no disguising the love in his voice.
"Pleased to meet you," said the same northern voice I had spoken to on the phone earlier in the day.
"It's a pleasure," I replied.
"Phil has told me all about you since he met you at your mother's... er.... since he saw you a few weeks ago."

I felt rather choked that he had seen fit to mention me, a man he hardly knew, but his son nevertheless. I wished I could have said I had heard all about her, but I hadn't, so I just smiled and shook her hand. It felt warm and soft, but with just a hint of moisture, perhaps indicating a nervous reaction about meeting me.

"How about a cup of tea and a spot of lunch ?" Phil asked, indicating the way to the kitchen.

I realised I had not had anything to eat or drink since I left home that morning, and was feeling rather hungry. I was shown into a large modern kitchen, with every conceivable labour-saving device on show. Victoria had made a buffet lunch with the traditional ham sandwiches, sausage rolls, and a variety of things on sticks. I sat down and ate ravenously. Phil looked across at me and smiled.

"You always did have a good appetite, even as a small boy," he joked.

I think I was warming to the man by the second. He certainly had tried to make me feel very welcome. He did not give me the impression of a man who would walk out on his wife and four-year-old son without good reason. I wondered what the truth behind his action would be, though I suspected he was likely to be very much the innocent party in the whole miserable affair.

Victoria went out after lunch, saying she had to do some shopping. Phil smiled across at her with a resigned look on his face.

"Giving my credit card some grief," he added when she had taken her leave.
"I'm forgetting my manners. Let me show you your room," he said.

I collected my bag from the car and followed him upstairs. He showed me into the guest room, which was small but comfortable. The single bed stood along one wall, with a wardrobe facing it. A pine table stood next to the bed, on top of which was an angle poise reading lamp. I unpacked my bits and pieces and went downstairs to where Phil was sitting in the lounge reading the local paper.

"You must see my pride and joy," he said.

Phil stood up and led the way out of the back door and into the garden. It certainly was well kept, with little flower beds forming a border round the lawn. He explained that gardening had become his passion over the last few years, a perfect antidote to the pressures of running his own business. Being early in the year, the garden was not really in full bloom, he explained.
"Come back in the summer and you will really see a spectacular display."

I made appropriate comments, typical of one who regards gardening as little more than a necessary evil. My own garden was well kept, in a bland sort of way. Perhaps Sara would change that, I mused to myself. I dutifully inspected his greenhouse and all that it contained before we headed back inside once more. As we settled into the lounge there was a noise at the front door, and my life was dealt another shock. In walked two teenage children, a boy and a girl, both wearing school uniforms and carrying school bags.

"Hi dad," they both said in unison. "Anything to eat ?"

On seeing me sitting in an armchair they both stopped dead in their tracks. Phil stood up and introduced us.
"These two are your half brother and sister, Emma and Richard. And this gentleman," he spoke to the children, pointing with his open palm, "is Peter, my son."

The three of us stared in stony silence, none of us sure what to say or do. I made the first move, standing up and shaking their hands.
"Pleased to meet you both," I smiled across at them. They smiled back at me, but at the same time looked rather wary. Both children were fair-haired with fresh open faces, just like their mother. As far as I could tell neither of them bore any resemblance to me.

"Emma is 17, and Richard is 15," went on Phil, with obvious pride in his voice. Since the introduction neither of them had spoken. I began to wonder if Phil had told them of my existence. Surely he had, especially as I was due to stay with them for a while.

"Dad has told us a lot about you, but only recently," said Emma answering my thoughts. She smiled at me, showing a set of perfect white teeth.
"Excuse us for being quiet, but I'm sure you must realise it was a bit of a shock to us."
She spoke with the same accent as her mother. Richard didn't speak, he just nodded, grunted and smiled in agreement with his sister. I made some remark about being surprised as well. An awkward silence followed, but Phil, bless him, did his best to get a semblance of conversation flowing.

"Emma is doing her A levels this year. She wants to go in for law, whilst Richard would like to be a mechanic, like me. Better change the name of the business to Jackson and Son." He laughed.

"Both very creditable careers," I commented. "I'm an artist myself. I have my own shop in East Anglia."
Both children nodded in approval. I asked how was school, not a very original question I agree, but it was all I could think of to say. Another silence followed. This was becoming awkward.

The day was saved by the return of Victoria, who exploded into the room weighed down with parcels and packages. Phil smiled and kissed his wife. I observed his face as he was doing so. He clearly loved the woman. Had he ever shown that kind of love towards my mother ? Once upon a time I suspect he had. Victoria took over. She started to show off her purchases, clothes mainly: new trousers for Phil, designer tops for the children and an expensive looking skirt and silk blouse for her. Phil seemed used to this, and sighing, he made the appropriate comments. I suppose he was used to being married to a fashion-conscious lady with expensive tastes, after the years with mother.

"I thought we could go out for a meal tonight, instead of cooking," she said. "You two as well," indicating Emma and Richard.
Both children declined, pleading homework as an excuse. Undaunted and without pausing for breath, Victoria said she would reserve a table at the Blue Ball. Feeling as though I was being swept along by the tide I said that I thought it would be a good idea. I asked if I could ring Sara from the house or would he prefer it if I used my mobile.
"Cheaper to use ours," he pointed out.

He took me into his study and left the room, closing the door after him. Sara answered the phone more or less straight away.
"Hi sweetheart," was her instant reply. If the caller had not been me, goodness knows what they would have thought.
"Hi there," I responded. It was good to hear her voice again. She sounded relieved that I had called her.

"No problems ?" she asked. "Good journey ?"

I answered in the affirmative and went on to tell her about the house and, of course, my stepmother, not forgetting Emma and Richard. We chatted on for several minutes. I think I must have apologised for my behaviour the other night at least five times, until I finally rang off, promising to call her the next day.

I went back into the lounge, which was deserted. I sat down on the black leather settee and looked around the room. It was beautifully decorated. In the corner was a display cabinet with a glittering array of cut glass and what looked like Chinese pottery. On the mantelpiece were photographs of Phil and Victoria and the two children. A large television stood in the corner, with the video recorder underneath. In another corner was an impressive looking CD player, the speakers for which I noticed were mounted on brackets around the room. My artist's eye was drawn to several gold-framed pictures. I stood up and examined them more closely. One of my own particular favourites was on view, "Dance at Bougival" by Renoir. The young lady dancing has always reminded me of mother, a pretty oval face, with auburn hair poking out of a bright red bonnet. Two Monets were on either side of the fireplace, "Les Coquelicots" and "L'etang aux Nenuphars". Van Gogh's "Paysage a St. Remy" adorned the wall behind the settee. I was pleased that I could bring the titles to mind so readily, but there again I was on my own territory, so to speak.

"I wish they were originals, and not just prints."
Phil's voice startled me as he entered the room and sat down in an armchair. I resumed my place on the settee.
"Just casting a professional eye over them. Nice to see that the opposition haven't done anything original for years," I joked.
"Victoria selected them, saying something about adding to the ambience of the place. I hardly ever notice them now."

I promised Phil that the first painting I did of a northern landscape, I would give to him and Victoria.
"Now that *will* add ambience. Especially if it were personally signed."

Small talk over, we stared at each other in silence, not sure what to do next. Simultaneously we stood up and put our arms round each other. I found myself fighting back tears. Phil, I'm certain, was having similar problems. I looked him straight in the eye and simply said,
"Why ?"
"I'll tell you everything I can later," he mumbled, a tear in his eye.

We sat down again, both feeling that we had bonded after all those years.
"Can I call you dad ?" I asked.
He nodded in happy assent.
I now had a father again. Phil went over to the drinks cabinet and poured us both a whisky, adding some ice he fetched from the kitchen.
"Victoria will have to drive now," he grinned mischievously. "She won't like that."

It was probably the most enjoyable drink I had ever had. I was reunited with my father, and things seemed to be on a happy footing. I had a family, relations to visit, extra names on my birthday and Christmas card list. It felt good, but it was a shame it had all been brought about by the death of my mother. I stared intently into my glass, mindlessly twirling the ice cubes round and round. After several minutes of this, I asked the question he must have known was coming.

"Why didn't you contact me ? All those years of knowing nothing about you, thinking you were some kind of thoughtless creature who left us alone. Why, dad ?"
There, I had called him dad for the first time in over twenty-five years.
He looked me full in the face and replied almost apologetically.
"I tried, but Anne wrote back saying she didn't want me to be part of your life again, and that I was a monster."
I looked enquiringly for him to elaborate on that last remark; he must have read my mind ,for he shook his head.
"I don't know what she meant."
"What about access ? " I asked, "You know, Saturday afternoons at the zoo, and all that."
"I tried, to start with, but she made it so difficult that eventually I gave up. Then when I moved back up north, it was impossible."
I looked across at him with a curious stare as if to say, " you gave up easily."
"I know what you're thinking, but, as you know, Anne was used to getting her own way, so I knew it would be useless. Plus, I didn't want to upset your life any more than it already had been. I sent money of course, for your upkeep and stuff."

I couldn't help but think that he must have been a rather weak person to simply give his son up without some sort of fight, but I kept these thought to myself.
At that moment, Victoria came back into the room, and seeing our drinks, she smiled and said,
"I'll drive tonight, shall I ?"
She moved across the room and kissed Phil lovingly on the cheek. They clearly had a good relationship, and I felt happy for my father.
"I've booked a table for 8 o'clock," she said.

We both said that would be fine. I blessed Sara once more, this time for convincing me to pack my only jacket and tie, garments I seldom wore, preferring the casual look of jeans and a jumper.

"We need to leave about 7.30," continued Victoria. "If you want a shower, Pete, do feel free. I've put some towels on your bed."

I gratefully accepted, feeling a little travel stained after the long drive earlier in the day. I made my way upstairs and had a refreshing shower and a shave. After getting dressed I came downstairs resplendent in my light grey jacket, black trousers, clean white shirt and red tie. I felt uncomfortable as I walked into the lounge, especially when I saw Emma sitting there alone watching television. Politely she turned off the programme and turned to face me.
"An artist ?" she began. "What sort of pictures do you paint ?"
I explained to Emma about my particular specialities of landscapes and buildings. She seemed quite impressed, especially when I mentioned the lucrative commissions I had been given over the years. I told her about the shop and she seemed puzzled about the name.
"Chiaroscuro is the distribution of light and dark masses in a picture," I explained, giving the well rehearsed answer I often have to give to many puzzled customers who come to the shop. "My mother thought it up."
"Tell me about dad's first wife," she asked. "What was she like ?"

I really didn't know where to start; after all, I was still finding things out about my mother after all these years.
"She was a very beautiful woman."
I showed her the photograph I always carried in my wallet. She looked carefully at it and handed it back, nodding in agreement. She caught sight of the photograph of Sara, also a constant resident in my wallet.

"Who's that ?" she quizzed.
I passed over the photograph and explained that she was my fiancée.
"She looks nice. What does she do ?"

Again I found myself opening up to Emma, thinking that, with her ability to ask questions and put people at their ease, she should do well in the law profession. I couldn't help but like my half sister; her openness and honesty made a refreshing change from the revelations and secrets of the last month or so. Phil and Victoria entered the room at that point, ready to set off for the pub.

"I like my half brother, " Emma said. "Can we go down to East Anglia and visit him and Sara ?"
The no-nonsense, no frills approach of my father, a trait once levelled at me by Sue Greenwood, had surfaced in another of his children. Her parents looked at each other saying,
"We'll see."

My father began to look a little ill at ease. Perhaps going back to Stradbroke would be too difficult for him, too many ghosts perhaps. I didn't pursue the idea, though I must admit I liked the idea of having relatives come to visit.

We travelled to the Blue Ball in the Espace. Victoria drove carefully down one hillside and up another to a place called Norland. I was taken with the pub as soon as I walked in through the door. There was something about the friendly greeting of the landlord that made you feel welcome. Phil and Victoria were obviously well known. Phil proudly introduced me to the people standing around the bar area as his "Number One Son".

The evening was a great success: the food was excellent, and plenty of it, the beer was good, and too much of it. Victoria was easy to get on with. Apparently she used to be a nurse at the Halifax Infirmary, working in the casualty department.

"Or A and E, as it is known nowadays," she pointed out.
She explained that she met my father when he injured himself at work, when a falling piece of machinery nearly took the end of his toe off.
"I patched him up, though of course the doctor helped as well, " she laughed.

Phil had asked her out, and that was that. They had married in 1978 and Emma was born in 1980. Richard followed two years later. I looked across the table at them. They were happy, feeding off each other like a loving couple should. I want it to be like that with Sara. I offered to pay for the meal, but Phil would have none of it.
"Can't have guests paying," he said, his northern accent becoming more pronounced the more he drank. "Especially my own son."

I could feel tears welling up again as he said that, and I gracefully accepted his hospitality. We left the restaurant and moved back into the bar. Phil and I leaned on the beaten copper top, whilst Victoria sat on a barstool. We ordered one last drink before we returned to the house. Phil and I had a brandy, whilst poor Victoria had a fruit juice. We left shortly after that. I had enjoyed the evening immensely, though I did miss Sara. I felt sure she would like Phil and Victoria.

It was around 11 o' clock when we arrived back at the house. I declined the offer of a nightcap and retired straight to bed. The day had been tiring and I needed to get some sleep. I made my way upstairs to my bedroom and was asleep within a few minutes of my head touching the pillow.

It was about 10.30 when I woke the next morning. Feeling rather embarrassed about sleeping so late, I hurriedly showered, dressed and went downstairs. The smiling face of Victoria met me. She was wearing a pink jogging suit and trainers; her hair tied back with a matching ribbon.

"Good morning, sleepy head," she said. "Phil has had to go to work, but he'll be back by mid-afternoon. Breakfast ?"

I said I would love a cup of tea, as the alcohol the night before had left me somewhat parched. I sat down at the breakfast bar and Victoria made me a drink. A round of toast and marmalade accompanied it. I glanced out of the window and saw the day was fine, with just a faint hint of watery sunshine filtering through the clouds. Victoria sat next to me also drinking a cup of tea.

"He did try to get in touch with you," she began. "He sent you birthday cards and letters, but he never got any reply, so he eventually gave up."

I felt a bitterness towards my mother for keeping these from me, but said nothing. I let Victoria continue.
"He even drove down to see you once, but your mother refused even to open the door to him. I eventually persuaded him to give up his quest; there could be no future in it. Reluctantly he agreed, but he always held out hope that your mother would have a change of heart, and let him see you, but of course she never did."
Again I couldn't help thinking that if he had been more forceful he could have got to see me.
"Did he ever tell you why they split up ?" I asked.
"He genuinely had no idea. All he knows is that she came back from her mother's funeral and the rot set in from there. She wanted nothing more to do with him, almost to the point of obsession. She

went out of her way to drive Phil out of both of your lives and she succeeded, as you well know."

"Mother was very good at getting her own way," I confirmed, my mind going back to the time she spent at college with Sue.

"When our own children were born, Phil became wrapped up in them, so he tried to forget about you, though I think he never really put you out of his mind. He could never do that, he's not that sort of person."

I was starting to believe what she said was true. My father, once more, was emerging as the innocent party in all this. The warmth I started to feel towards him was growing. I pitied him, knowing as I did that mother could be a formidable adversary.

"I got the other side of the story," I blurted out. "Mother told me my father had left us both, that he was a drunkard, a womaniser, a man who didn't care for his family and wasn't worth knowing. She used to tell me that I should have nothing to do with him. I believed her. Well, a child would. It was ingrained too deeply to change my opinions when I became an adult."

I was beginning to realise the extent of the lies mother had told me. There was no way any of it could be true, certainly not on the face of it. Yet there must have been some reason for mother's sudden change of heart towards him. It seemed apparent that Phil did not know, or if he did, which was unlikely, he had not seen fit to tell Victoria the reason. No, it must be something rooted in the past, the family shadow, whatever that was.

"All I know is that I love Phil very much, and I have done all I can to help him build a new life," Victoria said with an air of finality.

I agreed with her. Phil had built up a new life, and as a family they seemed a strong unit. I was glad I could at last be a small part of my father's happiness. We moved into the lounge and sat facing each other across the room.

"How did Emma and Richard take the news about me ?" I asked.
"We told them straight after your mother's funeral. They seemed surprised at first. Emma took it in her stride, but Richard, bless him, found it more difficult to come to terms with. The idea of having a step-brother seemed to throw him at first, but he seems to have accepted you now. Don't expect him to communicate with you, though, he keeps his own council rather well. Phil and I were quite worried about him when he was younger. The doctor thought he might be slightly autistic. It was if he were in a world of his own, always staring, but never communicating. He got much better as grew up. Emma will be much more forthcoming. She repeated at breakfast how much she liked you."
I felt flattered.
"In fact," continued Victoria, "she is very keen to learn more about you and to meet Sara and, of course, see your shop. She likes the idea of having an older brother."

We sat in silence for several minutes before Victoria got up and asked if I would like a walk. I thought that would be a good idea. I had not really seen much of the surrounding area. Mother's death had certainly enabled me to see more of England than ever before. Victoria left a little yellow post-it note on the fridge door.
"Just in case Phil comes back early," she explained.

We walked out through the front gate and down the wide avenue. Almost straight away we turned onto a road that in my mind resembled a mantelpiece on which we were perched. Over a low wall were some rocks and trees, behind which was a truly magnificent view. You could see both ways up a valley, the road in the bottom winding its way west towards Lancashire, I presumed, mentally picturing the map in my road atlas. Victoria told me we

were on Albert Promenade, which offered one of the finest views in the whole area. She pointed out, across the valley, the pub where we had been the night before. The artist in me took over, and I wanted to get out my easel and brushes and try to paint the rather spectacular view. Yes, this would be the painting I would do as a present for them both. Victoria pointed out a large white building nestling in the bottom, more or less directly below us.
"That's the data centre of the Halifax Building Society, shortly to become the "Halifax" when it goes public."

We continued walking along Albert Promenade until we stood almost at the base of a huge ornate tower, tapering up to a point at the top. It looked to have windows all the way up. Even more strange, there seemed to be some sort of gallery just below the summit. I had noticed it driving in yesterday and was curious to know its origin. I looked enquiringly at Victoria.

"That's Wainhouse Tower. Originally it was built as a chimney for a dye works. The local rumour is that it was then turned into a viewing platform so that Mr. Wainhouse could spy on his rivals. You can go up it four or five days a year. I suppose it could now be classed as a folly."

We followed the road round onto Savile Park itself. Judging by the marked out pitches it seemed to serve as the playing fields for various schools and football teams in the area. The children's school was just up the road, she told me. All around, no matter which way you looked, the views were wonderful, an artist's paradise. I really must return one day and do some serious painting. However, I had to resolve my mystery first. I was enjoying myself so much in the north I had almost forgotten the real purpose of my visit.

We walked back to the house and waited for the return of my father. I begged the loan of some paper and a pencil and returned to

Albert promenade to make a quick sketch. Satisfied with my efforts, I returned to the house and proudly showed it to Victoria. It was just at that point, about 2.30, when my father returned. He was wearing a filthy pair of overalls and covered in grease. Victoria ushered him out of the lounge before he had chance to sit down.
"For goodness sake, Phil, get changed before you come in here, just look at the state of you !"

Rather sheepishly, Phil left the room and went upstairs to get washed and changed. Victoria looked across at me and raised her eyes heavenwards. He was obviously a real "hands on" boss.

He came down about half an hour later, wearing jeans and a tee shirt. He jokingly asked Victoria if he could sit down now. The three of us chatted about what we had been doing that day. He seemed impressed with my sketch. I felt like a small child showing off, to my father, what I had done at school that day. An experience totally alien to me.

I really wanted to speak to Phil alone to find out more about his past life with my mother, but it was difficult with Victoria sitting there. I think Phil realised this, so he suggested he took me to look at his garage. I readily agreed. We made our way to the door, only to be met by Emma and Richard returning from school. After the customary greetings, the children headed off, I suspect, towards the fridge, whilst Phil and I got into his other "car", a white and orange pick up truck with "Jackson's Garage" emblazoned on the side. We pulled out of the drive and set off; I wondered what the next set of revelations would be.

Chapter 9

PHIL'S STORY

The afternoon traffic was starting to build up as we drove steadily through the centre of Halifax and out on the road towards Keighley. Phil's garage was an impressive place on the left about a mile out of Halifax. Phil pulled onto the forecourt and we both got out. I was quite relieved, as the pick-up was a noisy affair with a fine set of assorted rattles, which Phil assured me were standard on this model. JACKSON'S GARAGE was written in large red letters across the top of the white building. On one side was a small, glass-fronted showroom containing a selection of used cars, whilst on the other side there appeared to be a fully equipped workshop. A body, wearing the filthiest pair of overalls I had ever seen, appeared from underneath a Ford Mondeo as we walked inside.

"Hi Phil," said the man. "Didn't expect you back today."

"This is Pete, my son, from my marriage to Anne," Phil nodded in my direction, "and this is Ian, the best mechanic in West Yorkshire."

Ian stood up and wiped his greasy hand on the side of his overalls before offering it to me, a token gesture judging by the amount of grease which transferred onto my hand. Ian looked about as old as Phil, but not as tall.

"Ian was my best man when I married your mother," Phil said. "We've been mates a hell of a long time, right back to the Oswaldtwistle days."

The name Ian triggered something in my memory. Here was another character from the past - my mother's escort when my father had gone to Ambleside for the first time. Of course, as far as Phil was concerned, I didn't know the role of Ian in the story, so I just said I was pleased to meet him.

"A lovely woman, your mother," Ian remarked. "Didn't take to me though, not once she'd seen him." Ian jerked his head in the direction of my father. "What was her friend called, you know, the one that fancied you Phil ?"
"Sue," Phil and I answered simultaneously.

Phil looked curiously at me, but made no comment. We left Ian to his work and went into Phil's office. Around the walls were posters and calendars from various companies involved in the motor trade. On the untidy desk was a computer.
"How did you know Sue fancied me ?" Phil asked, getting straight to the point.
Thinking quickly, I answered, "I think she mentioned it at mother's funeral." I was a little surprised at the ease with which the lie tripped off my tongue. Phil nodded in understanding, adding,

"Now why did she mention that after all those years ?"

I shrugged my shoulders, offering no answer. Instead I made a move towards the computer, aimlessly moving the mouse across the mat, causing the screen to change. Terrified I had done some damage, I hastily let go, putting my hands behind my back in a "never touched it" gesture. I must own up to not being computer literate, deaf to the pleadings of Elaine to get one for the shop.

"This is where it all happens," explained Phil, swinging his arm round in an arc. "The nerve centre of my whole operation."
He explained how, by using the computer, he could check on the authenticity of cars coming into the business, if they had been in accidents, if they were stolen, were showing genuine mileage, or had any outstanding credit owing on them, using a system called H.P.I. or Hire Purchase Information. He demonstrated by typing in the registration of my car. Sure enough all the information appeared. Much to my relief, I was the rightful owner of the car and there was no H.P. outstanding on it. I must admit I was quite impressed with the set-up. He seemed to be doing something he loved and was good at.

"Ian more or less runs the breakdown and repairs side of the business. We've got our own tow truck," he said, glancing out of the office window. "It seems to be out at the moment."
"How many staff do you employ ?" I asked.
"Besides me, there's Ian, two mechanics, a salesman and a junior who valets the cars after a service. I help out on the mechanical side of the business, like today, hence the oily appearance back at the house, but I also get involved in the used car sales. An oily finger in both pies, as it were. Richard sometimes helps on Saturdays, providing he has no school work, of course."
"So why Halifax ? It seems a strange choice for a Lancashire lad like you."

"It was Ian's idea originally. When I returned to the north, I got in touch with him again. He told me he knew this place was up for sale, but he hadn't the capital to buy it. We drove over, saw the premises, and the rest is history. Neither of us have ever looked back."

We settled down in the office, and Phil made us both a cup of coffee. I lit a cigarette, pulling the full ashtray towards me. I breathed in deeply, looked across at Phil and simply said,
"Well, go on then, tell me about you and mother."
"Victoria says I get to the point straight away, but I can see I've still got a lot to learn from you."
He lit the cigarette I had belatedly offered him, rocked back on his chair and started to talk.

> *It goes back to the early 60's. I was an apprentice motor mechanic at a garage in Oswaldtwistle. I honestly don't think I wanted to do anything other than work with cars. They were my passion from being a very small boy. One Saturday night, a mate and me finished work early and decided to go through to Burnley to have a night out. You know, I can't even remember his name, not Ian, he was never one for dancing and the like. So we got scrubbed up and set off on the bus for Burnley. We hadn't a lot of money, but enough to have a good night out. Things never seemed expensive in those days.*
> *We arrived at the bus station and headed off towards Burnley Mecca. I remember walking in and being hit by a wall of smoke and sound. I loved it. We went to the bar and got a drink. We turned and faced the dance floor and watched the dancing. Pretty soon we were joined by some other lads we knew from Ossy, so there was quite a group of us. There were quite a few girls around, dancing together. None of us had the confidence straight away to*

ask for a dance. It would take another drink before we got to that stage. Actually it was the other way round. Gerry, yes that was his name, and I were just standing there minding our own business when up walked your mother. She was never short on confidence, even in those days. Straight out, she asked us if we would like to join her and a friend for a drink. We were both shocked at this. Remember, girls did not ask boys for a drink in the early 60s. Certainly not in Lancashire....

"Mother was always one for breaking the mould," I interrupted.
"I'll say," agreed Phil. "She never failed to surprise me with some of the things she said and did in the early days. Though she calmed down after you were born, until - well, you know."
He paused before uttering the last phrase.

*Feeling flattered, we both agreed, and went over to join them. I remember thinking that our luck was in, as both of the girls were attractive and obviously out for a good time. Gerry and I went to the bar to get a drink and discuss tactics. As we waited to be served we looked across at the two girls. Gerry seemed to fancy Anne; they all did, so I said I would talk to the other one. We needn't have bothered, your mother had it all organised. Within minutes Anne had got Gerry on his feet and whisked him away on to the dance floor. I started to dance with Sue. She was a good dancer, and I found I liked her company. She was, and still is, an intelligent woman. We spent the rest of the evening together, getting on really well, you know, comparing backgrounds, swapping addresses and things. I think I even offered to walk Sue the seven miles back to Accrington.
At the end of the dance, Anne returned to us, without Gerry. He was long gone. Though I remember your*

> *mother pointing in the general direction of the entire dance floor, saying he was over there somewhere. I remember kissing Sue and saying good night to Anne. I wandered across the room and found a miserable looking Gerry. Anne, it turns out, had had one dance with him and then walked away, leaving him on his own. Anne was like that, you know. Poor lad - knocked his confidence good and proper. As we caught the last bus home, I thought to myself that I got the best of the deal that night. That other one sounded like a real cow.*
> *I wrote to Sue in Oxford and she replied more or less straight away. We seemed to have built up an affinity with each other. We would probably have been happy together, but things don't always work out as they should....*

There was a tinge of bitterness in my father's voice as he said those last words. Like Sue, he had been made a victim of circumstance. "So what happened ?" I asked, deciding not to mention my talk with Sue.

> *I wanted to see Sue again, so I wrote to her at college asking her to ring me. She was very keen so I heard from her more or less straight away. I had managed to borrow a car for the weekend and Sue and I arranged to meet up in Ambleside. Sue was happy that I was taking a friend to keep Anne company. That was typical of Sue, always thinking of other people. I took Ian up with me. He had always wanted to visit the Lake District.*
> *We all met up on the Saturday and spent an enjoyable day together. It was obvious from the start that your mother was none too keen on Ian, but she joined in as much as she could, to make Sue happy. Quite unusual for your mother, selflessness was not a trait you would associate with her. I walked Sue home to her hostel and I think I*

> *tried it on a bit, but she was having none of it. I respected her for that, but felt rather frustrated all the same. When I arrived back at our digs, I was met by a pretty fed-up Ian. Anne, it seems, had made it rather clear that she had no interest in him, and that she was only doing it for Sue's sake. Put yourself in his place and imagine how he must have felt....*

I glanced out of the office window and saw Ian walking across the yard, with the practised ease of a motor mechanic, carrying a toolbox and whistling to himself.

"He seems to have got over it," I said. I realised the stupidity of that remark as soon as I had uttered the words. "35 years is a long time. Has he married since ?" I asked.
"Oh yes, got three children has our Ian, quite the family man, grandfather as well."

I felt pleased for this man who had been one of mother's cast-offs. Everything she did in the past seemed to be in her own self interest. So unlike the mother who had scrimped and saved for me in my youth. The paradox of her character confused me.

Almost as if he knew what I was thinking, Phil smiled at me and said,
"Yes, I know, she was a strange mix, your mother, as I found out as time wore on. Come on, let's go back to the house. Victoria will wonder what has happened to us."

"A strange mix....." Sue had used the phrase "a funny mix" in describing my mother. Both suited her equally well.
Phil glanced at his watch. Another clock-watcher, I thought. It was nearly 5 o'clock. We stood up to leave, but just as we were doing so, Phil opened his desk drawer and pulled out a photograph which

he handed to me. It was a picture of my mother, taken outside her house in Stradbroke. She was smiling that beguiling smile which was guaranteed to make any male melt. I turned it over, and on the back was a message, written in my mother's familiar handwriting.

> *My love always,*
> *Anne.*

I glanced across at my father; he had a distant look on his face. He had truly loved my mother dearly, and she had loved him just as much in return.
"Don't mention this to Victoria," he said, as I handed the picture back to him. "She'd skin me alive if she found out I had kept it."
He replaced it carefully in the drawer; it was obviously a prize possession.

I promised not to say a word. My sympathy was ever growing for this man who was caught up in some mysterious event in the past, affecting both our lives. We got back in the car after saying goodbye to Ian. Phil drove slowly back into Halifax and headed towards his home. As we made our way through the traffic, Phil was silent. He had said all he was going to say for the time being. I knew that when we arrived back at the house the presence of Victoria and the children would prevent any further discussion on the subject. Perhaps I should suggest a walk or a drink after the meal.

As we entered the house we were met by a delicious smell of cooking. Victoria had been busy in the couple of hours we had been away. Phil sniffed the air, pretending to be a bloodhound.

"Smells like roast beef and all the trimmings," he smiled.
"Your favourite," replied Victoria, giving him a kiss.

I was starting to miss Sara once more. I wanted to be greeted by a kiss. I went upstairs for a shower and to change for the meal. My ablutions complete, I lay on my bed staring at the walls, pondering the events of the day. The love between my mother and father was apparent, so why, then, had it all blown up so suddenly after her mother's funeral? What could her father possibly have said to turn love into hate so rapidly? I racked my brains for a solution; I came up, as usual, with precisely nothing. I took the biblical quotations out of my wallet and studied them again, just like my mother must have done. They were still meaningless, yet there was something nagging at my brain that should have been obvious, but it wasn't. I returned them to the wallet and lay on the bed thinking of Sara. My thoughts were finally interrupted when I heard Phil calling upstairs announcing that dinner was ready.

I made my way to the dining room and took my seat at the table. Richard was sitting next to his father, and I was directed to sit opposite my stepbrother. Of Emma and Victoria there was no sign. As we waited I looked directly at Richard's face, his eyes especially. They seemed curiously void of emotion, looking back at me almost as if he were in a trance.

"Here we are then," said Victoria entering the dining room, distracting my attention from her son.

She was carrying a willow-patterned, oval plate on which was perched an enormous Yorkshire pudding. She put it down in front of me and indicated a gravy boat, full to the brim with onion gravy. Emma followed behind carrying a similar plate, which she put down in front of her father. I poured on some gravy and sat and waited for the rest of the meal to arrive. When everyone had their plate in front of them, they all started to eat. I must have looked puzzled, but I was rescued by Victoria, who said,

"You're in Yorkshire now, Pete, this is the starter. It's supposed to fill you up so that you don't want a big main course."

I nodded in understanding and began to eat. It was rather good, better than I had expected. My experience of Yorkshire pudding was the little, round, rather dry efforts served up in pubs.

"It confused me at first, too, being a Lancastrian, " laughed Phil, "but when in Rome, as they say...."

I ate heartily. The starter ploy worked, and by the time I had eaten the Yorkshire pudding I really did feel quite full.
"That was delicious," I complemented Victoria, at the same time handing my plate to her as she stood up.

The rest of the family all laughed at my gesture. I looked at them puzzled.
"Rule two," giggled Emma. "You keep the same plate for the main course, saves on washing up."

Rather sheepishly I put my plate back on the table in front of me, and for some reason apologised. This brought more smiles from the family.
"Southerners !" said Richard, speaking for the first time, with a tinge of disgust in his voice.
Phil looked across at him reprovingly,
"That will do, Rick."
There was a stern tone in Phil's voice, one that I had not heard before. Richard looked rather contrite and mumbled an apology. I sympathised with the lad; it couldn't have been easy finding out that you had a brother after all these years. Victoria and Emma disappeared into the kitchen, and after a few minutes reappeared with a huge joint of beef and all the trimmings.

"You're honoured, Pete. This is normally a meal reserved for Sunday lunch," Phil remarked.

I tucked in, wondering whether I would be able to finish it all. I managed to clear my plate without displaying any more ignorance of Yorkshire protocol, though I was feeling rather bloated by the time I had finished. Pudding was home-made apple crumble, which, although it was one of my favourites I could not do justice to. We went into the lounge and Emma made us all coffee, whilst Richard loaded up the dishwasher. I thanked Victoria once again for a splendid meal. We settled down to chatting about nothing in particular and the evening wore on rather pleasantly. All the time, I wondered how I could get Phil on his own to question him further. I need not have bothered. Victoria suggested he and I went for a walk.
"You probably need it after such a large meal," she joked.
"Perhaps we could manage a pint," suggested Phil.
I assured him that I could always manage a drink, a fact that seemed to please him. I half expected him to say "that's my boy" but he didn't.

I asked if I could make a quick call to Sara before we went, and disappeared upstairs to my bedroom, where, I had noticed earlier, someone had thoughtfully placed a phone on the bedside table. I glanced at my watch. It was about 9.30, so Sara would still be up. The phone was answered almost immediately and I heard Sara's happy voice on the other end.
"Hi sweetheart," I said. "How are you ?"
"Fine. Missing you, but just fine."
"Anything to report ?" I asked after we had gone through all the lovey-dovey bits and yet another apology.
"Well," came the reply, "Mr. Robinson, the solicitor from Accrington, rang. He wants you to get in touch with him as soon as

it's convenient. I explained you were in the north and you might be able to actually call in to see him. He seemed quite pleased at that."
"He didn't say what he wanted, did he ?"
"Something about a box left in a hotel by your mother, and to sign some document or other."
"OK, I'll see how far Accrington is from here and drive over."
"When are you coming home ?" Sara asked in a pleading tone.
"Soon, I hope. I don't think I could cope with many more starters."

I didn't enlighten Sara despite the puzzled noise she made down the phone. After a kiss, sadly only down the telephone, we rang off. I put on my fleece and made my way downstairs.

"How's the little woman ?" Phil asked.
I grimaced. If there is one thing I cannot stand it is Sara being referred to as "the little woman". Bill Garnett had once called her that, and I could have willingly hit him. However, I quickly reverted to a smile and simply said she was fine.

"How far is it to Accrington from here ?" I enquired.
"A little under thirty miles, give or take, why ?" Phil replied.
I explained the situation to Phil, saying I would probably drive over to see Mr. Robinson.
"A good man," said Phil, " or at least his father was. He dealt with some problem over my grandfather's death many years ago. Apparently he died, my grandfather that is, under strange circumstances. I was too young to remember anything about it, though I remember my father mentioning it once."
"Your father, is he..... ?"
"Still alive, yes, but he's as nutty as the proverbial fruitcake. He lives in an old folks home in Lytham. Near Blackpool," he added, guessing correctly I had never heard of the place. "I go and visit him from time to time, but he doesn't know who I am. He just rambles on about reservoirs and cuts of beef. He used to be a

butcher, you know. Goodness knows where reservoirs fit into the picture."

"He is my grandfather, though," I added, stating the obvious. "What about your mother ?"

"Died years ago, heart attack."

Phil looked at the floor as if in remembrance.

"Still enough of this talk, how about that drink ?"

We called out our farewells to the rest of the family and made our way out of the gate towards Phil's local, a pub called the Murgatroyd Arms only a few minutes walk from the house. We entered the pub, and I was relieved to find that it was not too crowded. I went up to the bar and ordered a couple of pints. We sat down at a small circular table and took a long drink. I still could not get used to beer having a head on it. Suffolk beer tends to be flat. I think I quite like the creamy northern style of serving it.

"I suppose you want me to tell you some more about me and your mother ?" Phil said, getting right to the point.

"Please, " I answered.

"Now where were we ?"

"Ambleside, " I prompted.

"Ah yes, I remember."

> *I suppose you could call that first visit to Ambleside a bit of a failure, but I was keen to pursue my interest in Sue, so I continued to visit. On my own from then on. Poor Ian, he didn't like the experience of rejection one little bit. Sue, being Sue, insisted that Anne went with us if we set off anywhere, so it turned out that the three of us spent a lot of time together. I think Sue was a little afraid of being alone with me after the incident during my first visit. Anne, to my surprise, had no boyfriend at the time, and was quite pleased to be with us. I dropped a few hints,*

> *about going somewhere on our own, but they fell on deaf ears. Sue would never desert Anne if she for one minute imagined she would be on her own and in need of company. We managed an afternoon together only once, when Anne was confined to bed with a bad cold on the chest. She was prone to that, always was.*
>
> *At the end of the year, the girls left for their respective homes. I suppose that was when it started, me and your mother, like. Sue had been staying in Accrington with your mother for a few days. When Sue was due to leave, Anne promised her that she would keep an eye on me and not let me get involved with any other girls. Not that I had any intention of doing, I liked Sue too much.*
>
> *However, your mother had her own agenda. She started to ring me up asking if we could meet up. With Sue's blessing, she would always add. I suppose I felt rather flattered. Your mother was a stunning beauty, as you well know. Well, things sort of happened from there. We became closer, until I became totally obsessed with her. She could manipulate me anyway she wanted.*
>
> *By their third year at college Sue was out of the picture. I didn't feel too guilty, as Anne assured me that Sue had lost interest in me. Apparently two hundred miles was too great a distance to keep a relationship going, was what she had said in one of their girly chats....*

I almost choked on my beer at that point; this was not how Sue had told the story. I said nothing, pretending I'd had a coughing fit.

> *We planned to marry as soon as Anne had qualified, and I was taken to meet Anne's parents formally, not so much to get their blessing, but to tell them Anne's decision. What a disaster that turned out to be....*

Here, Phil stood up and went to the bar for another two pints. I watched him as he leant against the bar, with one foot resting on the rail on the floor. Here was another person who had been placed under my mother's spell. He had emerged, but not totally unscathed. Few people did, it seemed. I thought of Sue and, of course, Bill Garnett, and the scars mother had left on them. Phil arrived back at the table, offered me a cigarette and continued his story.

> *I remember it very clearly. Anne had invited me to meet her parents, officially, one Sunday afternoon. We had the traditional afternoon tea, scones, made by your mother, If I recall correctly, and of course tea, drunk out of the best china cups. I think I made a good impression on them at first. They were pleased by my desire to go into the motor trade. I think Frank, her father, actually made a joke about having his car done at my garage. I said I would be only too happy to oblige. We chatted on quite pleasantly. Yes, Frank and Emily would be delighted to have me as a son-in-law. After a while, Anne and her mother went into the kitchen to make some more tea, or was it coffee ? I forget....*

"Coffee," I said straight away, remembering mother's letter to Sue. "I expect."
I could have bitten my tongue off. How the hell did I know that ? "Mum always enjoyed a cup of coffee," I improvised, trying hard to extricate myself from the hole I had jumped into. Phil gave me another sideways glance, but he said nothing and carried on speaking.

> *When the ladies were out of the room, I happened to mention that my father was Thomas Jackson, a butcher in Oswaldtwistle. He went silent for a few seconds, and then he just went berserk. He grabbed me by the throat and*

tried to throttle me. I thought I was strong, but he was like a man possessed. He backed me against the wall, with a hell of a thump, a murderous look in his eyes. I swear he would have killed me had not Anne and her mother come back into the room at that very moment, wondering what all the noise was about. He told me to stay away from his daughter, forget about the marriage and to leave at once. I didn't take second bidding, I can tell you. I shot off into the street. Normally, I would have stood my corner, but here was a man who seemed determined to kill me. Anne came after me and asked what had happened. I said I didn't know, and carried on walking. Anne said she would sort it out and contact me later.

The next day Anne turned up on my doorstep, complete with two suitcases full of all the clothes she could carry, and moved in with us. It was pretty crowded, but we managed. She had my room and I slept on the sofa downstairs. No sleeping together in those days. My parents were very good, but it soon became apparent that the set-up would not work. Fortunately, after several weeks of this, Anne got a teaching job in Ipswich, so we moved to East Anglia.

We rented a flat in Ipswich. It wasn't ideal, but we managed. I soon got a job as a motor mechanic, and things started to get better for us. Anne told me that her father would not explain his reasons for his sudden hatred for me, so she had walked out on them. She was like that, your mother. She didn't know how to compromise. Not a bad thing most of the time, but I'm sure in this case father and daughter could have talked things through and sorted something out. That was back in 1965. We got married in April of that year. My parents and grandmother came to the wedding, but there was no representative from the Lord family, of course.

> *Eighteen months later we moved to Stradbroke. My father had decided to sell his business and retire. Some of the proceeds of the sale he gave to me, which enabled me to buy the garage in Diss. Your mother was pregnant when we moved, but she carried on teaching in Ipswich as long as she could. She finished at Easter, and you were born in May.*
> *After your birth, we spent some of the happiest times imaginable. We were content. Anne doted on you. I was doing well with the garage. We had made some good friends in the village. Things were good. Over the next four years the business did well, so we became nicely off. Then, in 1971, Anne's mother died. That was when the rot set in....*

Phil glanced at the time. It was getting late, so we decided to drink up and return to the house. The pub had got quite stuffy, so we were glad of the fresh air as we walked back. Everyone had gone to bed when we returned, so Phil made us both a coffee and we sat down in the lounge.

"Let me finish my story before we turn in," said Phil.
I was only too pleased to let him carry on. I was still feeling rather full from the meal, and welcomed the chance to let it settle even more. I knew I would not be able to sleep. Phil moved across to the CD player and put on what sounded, to my uneducated ear, like Mozart. Whatever it was, it was lovely muzak for the time of night.

"Your mother loved Mozart," mused Phil.
I congratulated myself on recognising the music,
"She used to play it all the time on the piano."

> *When she came back from the funeral, she was a different person. God knows why, she never did tell me. All she would say was "now I understand, you bastard, now I understand." What she understood is still a mystery. All I knew was, she suddenly hated me. I had done nothing to upset her, and was at a loss to explain her change of heart over the period of four or five days. I pleaded with her to tell me what had gone wrong, thinking we could try to work it out, but she flatly refused. How quickly love had turned into hate....*

Here Phil stopped talking and stared dreamily into his coffee cup, as if remembering the good times he had spent with my mother. He must have loved her, and I suspect he still did. What did Bill Garnett say ? "In love with her memory."

> *She went out of her way to make life difficult for me. She ridiculed me in front of our friends, she made it blatantly obvious she wanted rid of me. When I pressed her for a reason, she simply cursed her father for not telling her earlier....*

"Telling her what ?" I asked.
"She wouldn't say. I tried and tried to think what it could be, but I never came up with a plausible reason for her strange behaviour."

> *Things went from bad to worse, but the final straw was the Bill Garnett episode. She was, on the face of it, having an affair with him. I could stand it no longer, so I walked out. I sold the business in Diss and moved back to live with my parents in Oswaldtwistle. I went and confronted Anne's father on one occasion, but he refused to even speak to me. So that was that. I knew it was useless to try to get back together, though I did drive down to see her once,*

> *but she wouldn't even open the front door to me. The divorce came through in 1975, and I never saw her again. A sad story, I'm sure you'll agree, but that is it....*

"Did you ever hit her ?"
This was one thing I had to clear up.
"Now why do ask that ?"
"Its just something someone said," I replied evasively.
"Once, I slapped her across the face. Anyone would have done the same, but I regretted it the moment I had done it."
He hung his head in shame.
"Me ..... did you ever hit me ?"
"No never ! Honest to God !"
The tone of his voice was such that I believed him. Tears were appearing in his eyes.
"I'm sorry, dad, truly I am."
I moved over towards him and put my arm round him. He looked me straight in the eyes, fighting back the tears at the same time.
"Son, I'm the one who should be sorry," he said.

I sat down again and lit a cigarette. I felt slightly guilty that I had put my father through this, but I suppose he had really wanted to get things off his chest, to put his side of the story and perhaps clear his name with his son. He had certainly done that. Our emotions soon subsided.
"So, going back to the afternoon you were attacked. It was after you mentioned your father ? Did he know Frank Lord ?"
"No, that's just it. I asked him, of course, but he said he'd never heard of him. Dad rarely strayed far from Oswaldtwistle throughout his life. Except for the annual holidays to Lytham, of course."

I shook my head in bewilderment. I could make little sense of this. Why should Frank go ballistic on hearing the name Thomas Jackson ?

"Mother never mentioned a ... a family shadow, did she ?"
I felt ridiculous asking that last question, but it had to be done. Phil looked at me as if I'd gone mad.
"Family shadow ?" His voice sounded genuinely mystified. "No, I don't ever remember her talking about anything like that. Sorry, can't help you son."
"No matter. It was just something I read in one of her letters."
I didn't enlighten Phil any further; there seemed little point.
"Changing the subject once again, did she ever mention her grandfather's paintings ?"
"You mean Albert, her pal ? Yes, she said he was some sort of artist, but I never got to see any of his pictures. She adored the old fellow and talked of him often. A First World War hero, by all accounts. Not that it will mean much to you Pete, but he was an original Accrington Pal, which would make him one of the bravest men in the north of England at the time. They all were. I would have loved to have met him, but he was dead before I knew her."

When the CD ended, Phil asked if there was anything else he could fill me in with. I couldn't think of anything else to ask.

"That being the case, I suggest we get off to bed," he said.
I readily agreed as I was now feeling tired. A combination of the large meal and northern beer was starting to have its effect on me.
Despite my weariness, I could not get to sleep straight away. I lay in bed turning over Phil's story in my mind. I was no nearer the truth, yet something was nagging at me. Something he had said, but I couldn't for the life in me think what it was. No doubt I would think of it in time.

Chapter 10

ACCRINGTON

I woke early the next morning, dressed and went downstairs. The family were already up and having breakfast. Richard and Emma were ready for school, Victoria was still in her dressing gown, whilst Phil was dressed smartly in a grey silk suit. No wallowing under a car bonnet for him today.

"Going to Luke at some cars in the auction," he explained.
I smiled to myself; Bill Garnett was right about his double O sound. I sat down at the table, poured myself a cup of tea and buttered a slice of toast.
"So what are your plans for today ?" asked Phil.
"I thought I might go over to Accrington, to see Mr. Robinson, to attend to some business." I replied. " I'll probably go straight back

to Stradbroke from there," I added, "so I suppose this is farewell, for the time being."
"You're welcome to stay on, if you want," Victoria responded.
"More than welcome," agreed Phil.

I thanked them for their kind hospitality, but pointed out that I really wanted to visit Accrington, adding that the desire to see Sara again was growing stronger. Phil and Victoria nodded in understanding.

"I'm happy you found someone like Sara," Phil said, looking across at his own second wife. I wondered if he knew about my disaster with Linda. Perhaps Sue had mentioned it to him.

The children got up from the table to go to school. I solemnly shook hands with them both, and promised that they would be welcome to visit me anytime. Emma said she would love to come down. Richard was less enthusiastic and merely grunted, in exactly the same manner as his father, and, of course, me. With that, they left. I wondered when next we would meet up again.

Phil had, in the meantime, fetched a map and proceeded to show me how to get to Accrington from Halifax. The route seemed quite straightforward, but to be on the safe side the road numbers were carefully jotted down. I returned upstairs and packed my suitcase. It didn't take long, and very soon I was standing in the hallway. I gave Mr. Robinson a call and made an appointment to see him at 3 o'clock that afternoon. Victoria insisted we had a final a final cup of coffee before I embarked on my journey, so it was about 10.45 when I was finally ready to go.

Making all the usual pleasantries about hospitality and how it was a pleasure to meet the family, I picked up my case and made ready to leave. Phil and Victoria invited me back whenever I wanted.

"Next time bring Sara," they both said.
"That's a promise, " I replied, walking slowly out of the door towards the car.
I put the case in the boot and turned towards my father. We shook hands, and after giving Victoria a kiss on the cheek, I started the car and pulled out of the drive, calling out of the window,
"Thanks once again. And see you soon."

Phil had given me instructions to find the Burnley road, so I negotiated my way through a complicated junction at a place called King Cross, drawing curses from a taxi driver as I switched lanes rather hastily, before heading towards Lancashire and, of course, Accrington. I contented myself with blowing him a kiss as he shot past me. This could very well be the final destination in my search for the truth.

Driving slowly in the heavy traffic, I made my way along the Calder Valley, smiling with delight at the amazing names like Luddenden Foot and Mytholmroyd as I passed through them. Arriving in a small town called Hebden Bridge, I parked up and found a flower shop. It took only a few minutes to find a florists, quaintly called Fleur de Lys, and organise for a bunch of a dozen red roses to be sent to Victoria, by way of thanks for making me feel so welcome. Sara would have approved of my idea, though she would probably have said I should have given them to her personally.

I continued on towards a place called Todmorden, and turned right at a roundabout towards Burnley. A strange feeling came over me as I gradually got nearer to Accrington, a place of mystery to me, and yet I felt a certain affinity with the place due in no little part to its connections with mother. Within a few miles of leaving Todmorden, the road started to climb and twist through a narrow, steep sided valley. I soon found myself crossing the Lancashire border and the landscape began to change once more. The narrow valley was replaced by a much wider one, but none the less spectacular. I found myself warming to the north of England with its beautiful and contrasting scenery.

Feeling quite light hearted, I pulled into the car park of The Ram Inn, on my left, ventured inside and ordered a chicken sandwich for lunch, the time now being about 12 o'clock. I took my road atlas into the pub and began to study just exactly where I was. It seemed I was only about six miles from Accrington, far too early for my appointment, but I consoled myself with the prospect of wandering around Accrington, to see for myself where mother lived in her youth. I opened my wallet searching for the address of Mr. Robinson's office. I pulled out the piece of paper on which the address was written, Cannon Street. As I did so, the photograph of Sara also dropped out. Her smiling face looked up at me. I wanted to give her a big hug there and then. I replaced the photograph and the address back in my wallet.

After paying for my sandwich, I returned to my car and headed off towards my goal. It appeared that I had to follow the signs for Blackburn, until directed towards Accrington itself. Phil told me the route would take me round the outskirts of Burnley, which was a relief, as I didn't fancy tackling the traffic of a town totally unknown to me, though I would have liked to have seen Burnley Mecca, if indeed it still existed. The place where my parents met each other for the first time all those years ago. Perhaps another time.

I climbed up the road towards Blackburn, and as I reached the top, just after a set of traffic lights, my heart gave a little leap. I saw my first Accrington sign, five miles, that was all. I crested the top of the hill and began to drop down again. I was met with a truly magnificent view. Stretched in front of me were acres of green fields, interspersed with houses and factory buildings. In the background was a long flat-topped hill. This just had to be Pendle Hill, home of the witches. My mother used to tell me frightening bedtime stories about the place when I was young boy, my face well and truly hidden under the pillow.

I pulled into a lay-by just below the crest of the hill and took a long look all around. The artist in me was surfacing again. Here was another place I wanted to return to and paint. Suddenly the low, rolling terrain of East Anglia seemed very unspectacular.

"Luke out of the window, let me have a Luke, Luke here," I practised to myself as I slowly pulled back onto the road. You never know when it might come in useful !

There was a filling station at the bottom of the hill, so I pulled in and filled up. Petrol seemed much cheaper here than at home. Turning left at the next set of lights I just knew I was getting close. I smiled to myself as I crossed the Accrington boundary. Had I come home ? Not really, but this was as near as I could get to my roots. Driving slowly and dropping down yet another hill, I entered the town of Accrington.

I stopped the car and asked a passer-by where Cannon Street was. The directions I received didn't seem too complicated, so the offices of Robinson and Robinson, Solicitors and Commissioners for Oaths, were soon located. I parked in a side street nearby and heaved a huge sigh.

I strolled into the centre of the town, killing time until 3 o'clock. It seemed a pleasant enough place, boasting a Marks and Spencers and a Woolworths. Walking into the charming shopping precinct I located a jeweller's shop, where a silver necklace, matching the bracelet I bought in Ipswich, was duly purchased for Sara.

I found the tourist information office and asked about the local art gallery, which apparently was just off Manchester Road, heading out of town. I recalled that Sue said mother and her parents lived on the same road. I promised myself that if there were time I would call in to see if I could find any paintings by Albert Lord.

I strolled back towards the offices of Robinson and Robinson. A shiny metal plate proudly announced the name beside a smartly painted green door. It was shortly before 3 when I presented myself to the receptionist sitting behind a desk. Gill ? I wondered.

"Ah yes, Mr. Jackson. Take a seat, and I'll tell Mr. Robinson that you have arrived."
Yes, it was Gill; I recognised the northern lilt. She pressed a button on her intercom and announced my arrival. A door opened to my left and a tall, thin man appeared, the lack of hair on his head more than made up for by a thick, slightly greying beard and moustache.

"Mr. Jackson ?" His voice was very deep, not how I had remembered it when I had last spoken to him over the phone.
"Mr. Robinson ?"
I stood up and shook his hand; he had a good firm grip, generating confidence.
"Do come through."

I followed him into his office, and he indicated that I should sit down. A huge bookcase filled one wall, crammed with legal books. He sat down opposite me and brought the tips of his fingers together.

"Things finally seem to have been sorted out," he began. "Your grandfather's estate, not an inconsiderable sum, I might add, has now been added to your mother's estate, to which you are the sole beneficiary. You are now a wealthy young man."

He smiled across at me.

"As per your grandfather's instructions prior to his death, the house in Manchester Road has been cleared and placed on the market. All contents of a non-personal nature have been sold and a firm offer has been put in for the house. Personal belongings, such as papers, jewellery and the like, are lodged in the storeroom of this very office."

"So what do I have to do ?" I asked.

"Actually, its all been done. You just need to sign this." He passed a legal looking document across the desk. "Then we shake hands and that's it, as simple as that. The cheque for the final balance of the estate will be forwarded to your mother's solicitors in Diss, less our fee of course, and they will send you the final balance, less their fees."

"It all seems so straightforward."

"Well, basically, it is. You were the sole beneficiary, there was nobody to contest the will, we acted as executors, done, easy."

Mr. Robinson smiled across at me. "Now if you could just sign there."

He indicated the place.

I duly signed, we shook hands, and that was that.

"You said something about personal items being stored here ?"

I couldn't imagine what they might be.

"Yes, of course. Your mother left them in her hotel room by mistake before she was .... er .... went south, after her father's funeral. Just wait a minute will you ?"

He pushed a button and within seconds, the ever-obliging Gill entered the room once more.

"Can you show Mr. Jackson where the box is, and perhaps help him load it into his car ?"

"Of course, Mr. Robinson. This way, please, Mr. Jackson."

I shook his hand again, and followed Gill out of the office.

"Any problems, don't hesitate to call me, " he said as I left the room.

Gill led me into a small, seemingly little used side room, where I saw a large cardboard box, neatly taped up, with my mother's name written across the top in blue felt tip pen. Between us, we managed to transport the box out of the room, Gill opening the doors, whilst I carried it out of the offices and into my car. It was too big to go in the boot, with my suitcase already being in there, so it took up residence on the back seat. I thanked Gill for her help and she returned inside. I was on my own again. Glancing at my watch, it was nearly 4. The prospect of a three-hour drive back home again loomed large in front of me. It did not appeal; I was tired and hungry. Perhaps I should stay the night in the north and return to Stradbroke the next day.

Call it morbid curiosity if you like, but I decided to try to get a room at the same hotel my mother had stayed in when she came for the funeral. Now what was the place called ? I remembered it was in Haslingden, just up the road. I looked at my map and plotted the route out of Accrington. I could ask somebody where the hotel was on my arrival.

After getting lost once, I eventually found myself climbing out of Accrington heading towards Haslingden, coincidentally up Manchester Road. As I drove I noticed one or two houses with "For Sale" boards up. One of them surely must be the one where the Lord family had lived. Still, there was no way of finding out. I suppose it was just curiosity again, another part of my history. I saw a sign for the Howarth Art Gallery, but I decided against stopping, wanting to get booked in at the hotel. Another time, I said to myself. I was convinced this would not be my last visit to the north. I drove on, climbing steadily, eventually arriving at a large roundabout. Haslingden was the second exit. I followed the road until I reached what appeared to be the centre of the town. I stopped at the side of the road and tried to locate someone who might be able to direct me to a hotel. It would be easier if I could remember the name of the blessed place.

"Excuse me, could you tell me if there's a hotel near here ?"
The question was directed at a young woman with two small boys hanging tightly onto her hands.
"Well, there's Sykeside House, about a mile down there."
She pointed, along with the child currently holding her hand, in the direction my car was facing.

As soon as she said the name, I remembered that was the same place mother had mentioned when she rang up all those weeks ago. I thanked the lady and carried on towards my goal, finding the place easily enough, next to some traffic lights on the left. I drove into the car park and made my way to reception. I was in luck. They could accommodate me for the one night only, the receptionist muttering something about a conference coming in for the rest of the week. I returned to the car, collected my bag and was eventually shown into a comfortable single room overlooking a quiet country lane. I lay on the bed and lit a cigarette. I suppose it would be too much of a coincidence to suppose that this had been my mother's room, though I did not intend to find out. Some things are best left alone.

Getting an outside line on the telephone located on a small table next to my bed, I rang through to Sara. There was no reply, so I left a message on the answer phone, telling her I'd decided to stay another night in the north and would try to ring later. Feeling grubby, I undressed and had a delicious shower, followed by a shave. I put on a clean pair of trousers and a pale blue shirt. I glanced at myself in the mirror and noted my visibly tired appearance. I needed a break. Perhaps Sara and I should set off for somewhere warm for a few days. Yes, that idea had definite appeal.
I made my way down to the dining room, was directed to an empty table, and ordered an evening meal. I glanced round the room. It

was not terribly busy. A group of businessmen were seated in the corner, enthusiastically discussing the latest marketing techniques. A young couple were on the next table to me, staring into each other's eyes. The waitress arrived at my table, and took my order of steak and chips. I decided to lay off the beer, and asked for a small carafe of red wine. The meal was a good but solitary experience, contrasting greatly with the friendly banter I had experienced the night before with Phil and his family.

As soon as I had eaten, I returned to my room and tried once more to contact Sara. Luck was with me this time. Her happy voice answered the phone after only one ring. It was good to hear her again. I told her all that had happened with Mr. Robinson, and explained that I could not really face the drive home that night. She called me morbid, when I told her where I was staying. I suppose she was right, but she agreed that it was probably a good idea to rest for the night. I rang off, promising to drive carefully the following day. At a loose end and feeling in need of fresh air, I decided to go for a walk and explore the local area.

I couldn't have gone more than a hundred yards towards the town centre when it began to rain. Not wanting to get soaked through, I decided to curtail my walk and headed back. Force of habit led me over to my car to check it was all locked up. I noticed the box on the back seat. Why not take the box inside, I thought, and examine the contents ? If mother had seen fit to keep them, they must have some sentimental value. Perhaps they might even provide a clue to my mystery, though I was getting the feeling I would never find out the truth. My father had been my last contact with the past, and he hadn't really unlocked any doors.

I opened the car door and carefully slid the box out. Doing an amazing balancing act, I managed to lock the car door without letting the box rest on the ground. I carried it into the hotel and up to my room. It wasn't terribly heavy, but the bulk made it awkward to carry. After struggling upstairs I inserted the smart card into the door lock and entered my room. With a sigh of relief I deposited the box on the bed and rang down to reception and ordered a small bottle of whisky, which duly arrived in a few minutes. Getting myself comfortable, I proceeded, with the assistance of my Swiss army knife, to cut the thick brown tape, in order to study the contents.

How like mother, I thought, as I peered inside. Everything seemed to have been individually wrapped in newspaper. I opened some of the bundles, which seemed to be chiefly ornaments, which no doubt meant something to mother. There seemed to be an inexhaustible supply of lustre ware jugs of different sizes and patterns. There was a delicate figurine of a ballet dancer in the process of doing an endless pirouette. Other similar artefacts appeared as I unwrapped the various bundles. Beautiful as they were, they held little interest for me.

Events started to take a different turn as I got to the bottom of the box. I removed three jewellery boxes. I opened the first and was greeted with the sight of a multitude of rings - wedding rings, engagement rings, dress rings, signet rings, you name it. These were certain to be valuable. The second box contained a gold pocket watch attached to a heavy linked, golden chain. Inscribed on the back were the simple words

"To Frank, many thanks, Dad 1948"

This, I presumed, was a gift to Frank Lord from his father. I naturally didn't understand the significance of the date. The third box contained three medals. On closer inspection I found one to be the Military Medal, which I remembered was presented to Albert

Lord, my Great-grandfather, sometime during World War 1. The silver medal had the inscription,

"FOR BRAVERY IN THE FIELD"

beautifully engraved on the back, and also the letters GVR, which I presumed referred to King George the Fifth. Fastened to the medal was a red, white and blue ribbon. I wondered what he had done to gain such an honour, and why mother had never mentioned it to me. More damned secrets. I replaced it carefully in its box, feeling quite sad, remembering how much my mother had apparently loved her pal. The other two were probably some sort of campaign medals. I would have to look them up in the library sometime. I bet great-granddad Lord wore those medals with pride.

Right at the very bottom were three large brown envelopes, which I carefully removed. One envelope was considerably newer than the other two. I looked inside this first. It contained the birth certificates of Frank and Emily, and their marriage certificate. I noted with sadness that both their death certificates were also inside. Mother had obviously decided to keep them, planning, no doubt, to put them in her scrapbook. A tear came in my eye. I promised myself that they would be put in mother's book as soon as I got back to Suffolk, the last ever entry.

I needed a drink, so pouring myself a large whisky, I slipped off my shoes and lay on the bed. I spent several minutes like this, just thinking of mother and how much I missed her and how much I would like to ask her. Why was she so bloody secretive?

Shaking myself from this fit of reverie, I reached across and looked at the other two envelopes. They both had faded writing on the front. It took me quite a time to make out what they said, but I eventually managed. One had the inscription

> *"Albert Lord, my story"*

in that beautiful scrolled script I had seen before when I read the letter written by Albert to my mother. The other one simply had

> *" For Anne"*

written in a less impressive hand. I caught my breath. Perhaps contained here, in these two envelopes, was the key to the mystery. With shaking hands I opened the first one and took out a sheaf of papers, neatly tied together through a hole in the top left-hand corner. The handwriting was less ornate and much easier to read. As I lifted up the manuscript a couple of faded photographs dropped out from between the pages. I decided to examine them later, as I was keen to see what Albert Lord's story could possibly be about. I settled down on the bed and began to read.

Chapter 11

ALBERT LORD'S STORY: MEETINGS

I do not really know when I decided to write this story; perhaps if things had turned out differently I probably would not have bothered. However, there comes a time in one's life when you feel that committing your story to paper is a good thing. I have also given a lot of thought as to where to begin the tale, and I think I have got it about right. I realise that very few people will ever read it, just my family and maybe their families. This is just as well because it is not a glorious story, rather one of deceit and betrayal. Nor is it a happy tale, quite the contrary. It is full of sadness and despair. If you read this and then decide to destroy it, well, so be it, that is your choice. One thing I do ask is that you do read it all and make your own judgement.

It all started, I suppose, in the early summer of 1914. I was just 20, and I regarded myself as a man, though I had not yet reached the official age of manhood. I worked alongside my father at Howard and Bulloughs, in Accrington, makers of textile machinery, and unlike many of the other men who also worked there, I was reasonably satisfied with my lot, being happy in my work. I lived with my parents in a terraced house just off Blackburn Road. Rarely for those days, I was an only child, though strictly speaking I did have a brother, who unfortunately died of pneumonia when he was just seven. I was five at the time so my memory of him is only limited. I do remember he was called Peter, but that was about all.

The summer of 1914 was as hot as I could remember, and the days seemed to stretch on forever. The town itself, however, was charged with a certain amount of uncertainty. June 27th saw the closure of a cotton mill in the town, putting some 500 workers out of work. This led to worries about the future of the other mills in and around the town, and, indeed, the future of the cotton industry itself. My own factory was also a source of unrest at the time. The skilled engineers were demanding a pay increase of ten per cent, bringing them up to thirty-six shillings a week, comparable with engineers in textile mills in other parts of Lancashire. I remember the workers giving the mill owners a deadline of July 1st to pay up or else.

The deadline day arrived, and so did a huge thunderstorm, flooding the factory, stopping production and taking the impact out of our planned action. However, we still walked out on strike later that day. 4,000 workers were idle. Not working meant that I could spend more time with my sweetheart, Amy Chadwick, an unemployed cotton mill worker, with whom I had been walking out for several months. She, like me, lived with her parents and two older brothers. I didn't know that Archduke Ferdinand had been assassinated in Sarajevo only three days before. Indeed, had I known I probably wouldn't have cared. It couldn't possibly affect me.

I suppose youth smoothes all problems, and neither of us worried over much about the future. Luckily, I was in a union, so I was drawing £1 a week strike pay. Amy was happy to spend time with me. I remember we used to walk through Oak Hill Park.

So the month of July wore on. The 25th saw the start of the local holidays, and the town seemed to be in a holiday mood. I remember glancing at father's paper and seeing that the situation in Europe was worsening. Austria had broken off relations with Serbia, which meant other countries would take sides for or against a war. England, it seemed, was trying to be a peacemaker. I had no doubt that they would succeed.

Amy and I spent six bob each and took a charabanc trip to Blackpool, where we enjoyed a lovely breath of sea air. It was grand. Feeling like royalty, we walked arm in arm along the promenade, marvelling at the magnificent tower. Neither of us had seen anything like it before. I proposed to Amy on the way back and she accepted. Parental blessing was needed, as Amy was still only eighteen. We both felt sure that everything would be fine. Young people in love rarely think the worst. We had big plans, first to marry and then move away and seek our fortune. We fancied moving to London, where I was told jobs were easy to get. True or not, it seemed like a good idea. It's surprising how plans can be thrown so easily into a right mess.

The Accrington holidays ended on August 1st, and things started to move. Germany had declared war on Russia, and volunteers were being asked for to join a British Expeditionary Force. Amy and I didn't care, her parents had agreed to our marriage and we were suited. I remember walking home from her house and doing a silly jig down the street. I burst through the door, wanting to share my joy with my parents. I was greeted by the stony face of my father, who, in his blunt manner, said, "It looks like bloody war."

He explained that he had been down to the post office, where an order had been stuck up calling for army reservists to join their regiment. I was not convinced that this would touch me personally. After all, Britain had a good army, soldiers prepared to fight for their country, and they would sort out the problem, I was certain of that. After all, that was what they were there for. Almost as if my father had not uttered the last sentence, I blurted out, "Amy and I, we're to be wed."

Father did not take kindly to my outburst, so instead of congratulating me, he gave me a right good telling off, saying it was a bloody serious business. Mother just sat and stared at my father. That was all she ever did, except of course sew, clean and cook. Feeling rather upset that they had not shared in my happiness, I apologised and went to my room, laying on my bed for a long time thinking about Amy and would this trouble affect us. Probably not, was my decision. How wrong can a person be? Three days later, on August 4th, Britain and Germany were at war. My life was about to change forever.

Unless you were actually there, it is difficult to express the thought that went through the minds of the people at that time. I overcame my lack of interest and began to take a note of the worsening situation, a state of affairs which pleased my father but greatly upset Amy. I walked around the town with my father, and everywhere you could feel the tension mixed with excitement. Each day we would turn up outside the Town Hall looking for notices telling us more about what was happening.

I remember joining the crowds on Wednesday as the special reservists departed Accrington on special trains. We all cheered wildly as they marched through the town towards the station. I don't think any of us realised that many of these men would never see Accrington again, or perhaps we shut that thought out of our patriotic minds. In the days that followed, other marches took place, and again father and I were there to watch. The St. John's Ambulance Corps came and went, the Territorials followed suit. The excitement of the situation was increasing with every pounding boot. We were overcome with pride for the brave body of men setting off to fight for King and country.

As father and I walked back to our house, he expressed his concern. He didn't think that the war would be over quickly, and suspected that forces would have to be added to prevent us from being defeated. My father was an intelligent, deep thinking man, possessed with the ability to read a situation with surprising accuracy. I listened to his argument, and somewhere down inside I could see the sense in it, yet I believed that our army would win through in the end and peace would be restored, just as it had in the past. Father simply shook his head as I put my over optimistic thoughts to him. We walked the rest of the way home in silence.

I walked out with Amy later that day and tried to reassure her that our lives and plans would not be greatly affected. Amy was not convinced. Her two elder brothers were both in the Territorials and had marched off to goodness knows where and to what fate. I walked her back to her door and kissed her lightly on the cheek. As I made my way towards home I little realised that any plans we had made would be blown apart in the next few weeks.

It soon became obvious that my father was right. More soldiers would be needed to add to the regular army, and by September 1914, John Harwood, the then mayor of Accrington, had received permission to raise a battalion of 1000 men drawn from Accrington, Chorley, Burnley and Blackburn, including, of course, the surrounding small towns and hamlets. These regiments were Lord Kitchener's fourth new army, and consisted of men recruited from the same area, the idea being that men would go to war with friends, possibly from the same street, generating a comradeship which would last through thick and thin. This was how the "Pals" regiments were born. Father and I carefully read the recruiting poster in the town. Men between 19 and 35 were required. An unspoken thought passed between us and I knew what had to be done. Father was, of course, too old to volunteer, but not so me. I decided that I would represent the family in fighting for King and Country.

On meeting Amy that same night, I told her of my decision. A look of disbelief spread across her face as my faltering words came out.

"What about our plans, our life together?" was all she could say.

I of course had no real answer, except to point out that this was more important than any plans we may have made. Besides, we might not have a future together if this war were not won. That, surely, was a cause worth fighting for. I didn't say that I was still unsure of what the war was all about, but was merely repeating my father's words. *By the time we parted that evening, Amy had realised that the decision was made and that I was determined to volunteer. I was always a stubborn person, and once my mind was made up it stayed made up.*

So it was that on Monday, September 14th, a day forever stuck in my memory, I set off from home wearing my best suit, white shirt and black tie. I hadn't reached the end of the street when a bootlace snapped. I ran as best I could back to the house, and put another lace in. This made me about ten minutes later than I intended and the queue was quite long when I got to Willow Street to take my medical. It was whilst I was waiting in the queue that I first met up with Sam. We were standing next to each other in the line, both of us feeling nervous about the task we were about to undertake. Sam was very tall and thin and, in common with many tall people, he had a slight stoop of the shoulders. He had a pale complexion. Like me, he was dressed in a dark suit complete with a matching waistcoat, white shirt and tie, a flat cap perched on his head with little wisps of sandy-coloured hair poking out. We nodded to each other and eventually began to talk. Sam, it appeared, lived with his parents and his younger sister on Avenue Parade. His family was not from Accrington, but had moved here from London several years ago, though he never told me why. He talked with a curious mixed up southern and northern accent, unlike anything I had heard before.

He too had decided to join up after seeing the recruiting poster. Like me, he was unsure of what the war was all about, but having lost his job as apprentice tackler in the cotton mill in July, the thought of earning the promised 21 shillings a week greatly appealed. His family depended heavily on any wage he could bring into the house. His one great passion, he told me, was walking the hills around Accrington, allowing him to be on his own with his thoughts. I told Sam a little of my background, but not, for some reason, about my plans involving Amy. Our conversation helped the time pass.

Eventually I was called before the doctor. Knowing I was quite fit, I had no doubts that the examination would be anything but successful. My heart and lungs proved to be sound and my eyesight good. The doctor signed the form and I was taken into the next room where a Bible was placed in my hand and I was sworn in. Sam followed soon afterward, and was likewise asked to swear to serve His Majesty the King. We both kissed the book and made our way to the town hall to collect our pay. We were in the army. We were Pals.

We came out of the Town Hall together, and sat down on the low wall outside. I don't think either of us was sure of what we had done, but we were both determined to see it through, no matter what. As the two of us sat there, we promised each other to try and stick together as far as possible. We didn't know it at the time, but this was exactly what Pals regiments were all about.

"Just think, Sam, if my Bootle hadn't snapped, we may never have met."

I told him how I had to return to the house for a new one. He smiled and replied,

"It must be fate."

Our homes were at opposite ends of the town, so we parted on the steps, promising to see each other the next day at the drill hall for our first taste of military training. I called to see Amy on the way home, eager to tell her about my morning. I think she had come to terms with my actions, and she seemed to accept them.

"After all, it will probably be all over soon, if the papers are to be believed," she said as we sat in the parlour, carefully chaperoned by her mother, drinking a cup of tea. I promised to call round to see her the next day after my training, and so we made our farewells. I walked slowly the short distance to my house, where my father, visibly swelling with pride for his son, warmly greeted me. I found it difficult to sleep that night, and when sleep did finally arrive my dreams were of glorious battles and famous victories.

The following morning came all too soon, and I awoke with a start. My mother was calling me to breakfast. She had obviously taken on some of my father's pride and was preparing me for the rigours of the day with a magnificent breakfast of porridge and toast. Quite a luxury in our family. I gulped everything down, keen to move on to my first full day as a soldier. I walked briskly towards the drill hall and awaited further orders. I was still dressed in my best suit. No doubt the proper soldier's uniform would be given to us at a later date. I arrived to find Sam was already there and waiting. We were marched to a place called Ellison's Tenement, a large open space, where we were ordered by a retired sergeant major to form fours and proceed with our drill.

A strange sight we must have looked, wearing our civilian clothes, trying to produce some sort of order. The large crowd of civilians watching must have thought it amusing to observe us in our first disorganised parades. Some of them were not as well dressed as others, displaying obvious poverty. The promised uniforms would stop all that, and we would all look the same, no matter what our backgrounds were. Sam and I managed to march and drill side by side, taking comfort from each other's inability to keep in step. We didn't mind if the onlookers thought it *funny. We were doing our bit for Accrington, King and Country, in that order.*

At the end of the first day we were both tired and ready for a break, proud to have done our first military training. We felt as if we were ready to face the enemy there and then. Sam and I walked together to the centre of the town, where we sat down, once more, on the wall outside the town hall. We had become firm friends, laughing and joking our way through the first day disasters, and were determined to stick together. I remember remarking to Sam how I now felt like an important person, and the call to arms could not come soon enough. Sam smiled back at me, saying he totally agreed. We decided to meet up later that evening and go for a drink to celebrate our friendship.

It was while we were walking home after our drink that I first observed a strange character trait in my friend Sam. As we made our way down Manchester Road from the public house we had chosen to meet up in, there, at the side of the road, was a cat. A carriage or some sort of heavy vehicle had obviously struck it. The poor creature was evidently in pain and wanting putting out of its misery. Sam, seeing the poor creature, walked slowly towards it and kicked at it with his foot. This action caused untold suffering to the cat, needlessly in my eyes. I wanted to grind my heel into its head, killing the poor creature. Sam stopped me from performing this act of mercy, by placing his arm in front of me, preferring instead to toy with the dying animal. Feeling pity welling up inside me, I brushed him aside and killed the poor beast with a kick to the head. Sam stared emptily at me with a look of disdain, his eyes curiously lacking any sort of emotion. I shuddered as I saw them. Just a trick of the light, I decided. Neither of us referred to the incident again as we made our way towards the place where our paths homewards took us in different directions. For some reason, that single act of cruelty stayed with me, and I could never look on Sam in the same light again. Still, they were cruel times, and the death of a cat seemed nothing compared to the horrors we were both to encounter in the months to come.

Day followed day, and we were drilled on Ellison's Tenement until we were quite brilliant at marching in fours. No doubt we would put the fear of God into the enemy. At the start of each new day, new recruits who had enlisted joined us in the regiment. Faces I recognised from the factory, some worthy of a cursory nod from me, the experienced soldier. Sam and I were inseparable, almost like brothers as we drilled interminably around the large open space.

I remember one Saturday, late in September, when all the recruits were called upon to march through the town towards the Town Hall, where John Harwood would watch us and take the salute. We followed the Accrington Old Band and felt very proud. There was a distinct swagger in our step as we marched through the streets lined with cheering crowds, many of whom had watched us in our endless drilling over the last few days. The promised uniforms had not yet arrived, so we still wore our civilian clothes, some of which were now looking the worse for wear. I had walked past the Town Hall many times, but never, until that day, had I felt like a king. I'm sure Sam, keeping in step next to me, felt the same. As we marched, my eyes darted to and fro to see if I could catch sight of my parents or Amy, who had promised to be there. I was unlucky, the crowd was much too large to pick out individuals.

The year of 1914 wore on, and we followed the same old routine of drilling, an exercise no doubt designed to turn us into soldiers. We often marched up Avenue Parade, a dead straight road heading towards the Coppice, a hill overlooking Accrington. Sam pointed out his house as we went past. We stopped in the open space at the top. It was here that we were instructed in the art of digging trenches, not for the last time, I might add. Ready for the real thing when we arrived in France, we were told.
So our strange sort of half soldier, half-civilian existence went on. Things moved forward slightly in November when we were given a treat; our promised uniforms arrived and were distributed to the men before parade one morning. Eagerly we pulled them on. Blue melton with red piping on the collars and cuffs. One comedian in the company said we looked like bloody tram drivers. Still, we were pleased to be wearing some sort of uniform and not our civilian clothes. We felt a little more like the real thing, having gained a sense of identity. It would still be some time before the Accrington Pals would wear khaki. We were gradually becoming soldiers. We were expected to salute officers if we saw them around the town. Some of the lads found this hard, but I had no difficulty in doing it. Amy, swept along by the feeling in the town, was now proud of me, and she loved to walk out with her arm in that of an Accrington Pal, though it became harder to see her, due to soldiering commitments. One evening after parade, I finally introduced her to Sam, who commented that I was a lucky man to have the love of such a fine woman. I noticed he could not take his eyes off her all the time we were together, and I felt proud that she could have that affect on someone else. He appeared to have no love of his own at the time.

It was about that time I became more interested in religion. I had always attended church each Sunday, but now I had taken to reading the Bible more regularly. I suppose it was realising that I might have to kill someone, which made me try to seek help from God. Up to now, facing the foe had been only a distant possibility, but as the year wore on, it seemed increasingly likely. I tried to persuade Sam to go to church, but he always declined the offer. He gave no reason for this. I didn't mention it again after his first two or three refusals.
Christmas 1914 was not a festive time. My parents tried their hardest to make the occasion as normal as possible, but talk was all over the town that the New Year would see the regiment leaving home. I suppose by January the novelty of troops in the town had begun to wear thin. The East Lancashire Regiment, the regular soldiers, had suffered heavy losses. Amy's brothers had both been posted abroad somewhere. Our regiment had not, as yet, been even close to the action, and the people of Accrington began to wonder why we had not been called to fight for our country. After all, we had been training since September!
It was sometime in February 1915 that we were informed that we would be moving out of Accrington. We were to go to Caernarvon for further training. Word was out that we were to leave Accrington on February 23rd. Some kind of farewell parade would have to be organised. Sam and I greeted the news with mixed feelings. I would be leaving Amy, possibly forever, a prospect that didn't appeal to either of us. Sam, on the other hand, was leaving nobody special behind. I appeared to be his only friend in the town, and his family didn't seem to count for much in his eyes.

The night before we were due to leave, Amy and I took a final walk through Oak Hill Park. There was a real possibility that we would not see each other for a long time. Both of us accepted this state of affairs, accepting that this might be the end of all our hopes and dreams. I kissed her on the lips for the first time, as I left her at the door of her parent's house. I wished I'd had the confidence to go a little further, but I didn't. It was with tears in my eyes that I walked home and tried without much success to fall asleep. In the end, this blessed release not forthcoming, I lit my oil lamp and contented myself with reading the Bible, which I always kept by the side of my bed. The text I chose was Ecclesiastes 3: 8, "A time to love and a time to hate; a time of war and a time of peace."
Somehow these words were quite appropriate and seemed to bring me comfort. I eventually fell asleep, dreaming of Amy, so much nicer than battles and bloodshed....

I put the text down and glanced at my watch. It was about 9 o' clock. I had read the story with strange thoughts going round my head. Here, I felt sure, was the key to the mystery, and the biblical quotation virtually guaranteed it. I couldn't help but wonder if I had been named after Albert Lord's long dead brother Peter. This was a distinct possibility when I remembered my mother's deep love for her grandfather. I poured myself another drink, lit a cigarette and sat back on the bed. I flicked through the remaining sheets of paper. There still seemed some way to go before I reached the end, and I doubted my ability to stay awake long enough to finish it all. I was really tired and had a heavy day coming up. Was it too late to ring Sara and update her ? I decided it wasn't, so I put a call through. She sounded surprised to hear from me twice in one evening.

"You're not going to apologise again are you ?" were her first words as she realised who was speaking.

As I told her about the manuscript she sounded relieved, probably because she thought that my quest might soon be at an end and we could pick up our life together again. I put the phone down, and couldn't help drawing a slight parallel between our lives and those of Albert and Amy some 80 years ago. We both had our plans disrupted through no fault of our own. I picked up the manuscript once again and continued reading.

> *I awoke early the next morning. I made my way downstairs and had a wash in the kitchen using a jug of warm water which my mother had got ready for me by heating it over the fire. I returned upstairs and with trembling hands I dressed in my blue uniform. We had to report for our first parade at Ellison's Tenement at 6.30 and then carry our luggage to the railway station ready for leaving. This being done, we were allowed to return home once more, to have breakfast with our families. The three of us ate in silence, each thinking the same thoughts. This could be our last meal together. We might never see each other again. I finished the meal and stood up ready to leave. Tears were in my mother's eyes and she hugged me tightly as we kissed goodbye. Father was much more reserved and he contented himself with shaking my hand and wishing me good luck. They both promised to walk into the town to watch us leave. I hoped Amy would do the same. I tucked the bible in the pocket of my coat, opened the door and walked away. I looked back just the once, to see my father, not normally a man given to outward shows of emotion, with his arms around my mother. I felt a tear prickle the back of my eye, but I continued walking. I didn't look round again.*

I arrived back at Ellison's tenement just before 8.30. Sam was standing in his usual place, he was always early when we arranged to meet up. As I walked towards him, I noticed that, like me, he had filled out a bit during the training and we were both much fitter than we had been those few months ago. The drilling and marching had also given us a discipline neither of us would have achieved in civilian life. I walked over to him and shook his hand. This was it. We were going to war. The bond had formed strongly in the regiment and somehow we drew courage from seeing each other. My hands had stopped trembling and I felt fully prepared for the adventure. I took out my Bible and kissed it, glad of the comfort it afforded me. Sam smiled as he saw my action, but said nothing. We walked over to where two other lads we had become friendly with, Tom and John, were standing, and waited patiently with them for the order to fall in. Conversation did not flow freely as we stood by the wall. In fact there was a subdued quiet over all the men. However, this did not hide the determined look on all our faces.
At last the order went out for our company to line up and begin the march to the station. As we set off down Blackburn Road, the number of people lining the streets to wish us farewell amazed me. There was no marching band to send us on our way, but the cheers of what seemed to be the entire town deafened us. I scanned the crowd for Amy, but once more I was out of luck: there was no sign of her anywhere. I felt sad not to have seen her, but I was comforted by the certain knowledge that she would be there waving with all the rest. I fleetingly glimpsed my father, who had pushed his way to the front of the crowd. I smiled across at him, and he gave a cheery wave back at me. Some of the lads broke ranks and went

over to the crowd to shake hands with loved ones. I had never seen so many Union Jacks in my life. Goodness knows where they had all come from.

The steep slope up into the station was completely blocked by the crowds, and the police on horseback had to clear a way through to allow us to get onto the platform. Sam and I managed to get in the same carriage, but we were separated from Tom and John. We leaned out of the window and waved madly at the masses on the platform, pushing and shoving to get a better view. I felt like a hero, without actually doing anything to warrant it. After a stop further down the line at Church and Oswaldtwistle, our train finally headed towards Wales. My father later told me that once the excitement of the departure was over, a silence overwhelmed the town as people made their tearful way back to their own homes. He also told me that there was a lot of ill-feeling in the town due to the fact that there was no band to play as we marched away. It didn't really worry me, but I know some of the men felt a little upset. Sam remained indifferent to the whole proceedings. He was a strange, unemotional fellow, sitting there, just staring out of the carriage window, but I couldn't help but like him. He was my Pal....

Chapter 12

ALBERT LORD'S STORY: BONDING

Feeling my eyes starting to ache, as the print was faded and difficult to read, I put down the manuscript once again. It seemed like a good place to break off anyway, as Albert had finished what could only be described as a chapter of his story and, indeed, his life. I stood up and looked out of the bedroom window at the country lane outside. A man walked along, taking his dog for a walk. I was pleased to see that the rain had finally stopped. I tried to empathise with old Albert Lord. Whatever must he have felt like leaving his loved one and parents to go to war ? I felt bereft without Sara and we had only been apart for a few days, and I knew I would see her again, while Albert had possibly seen Amy for the last time. I lay back on the bed, put my hands behind my head and thought about the story I had just read. The First World War was rather a mystery to me, as indeed it is to many of my generation, but these words written by my great-grandfather made me determined to find more about it. All I really knew was that I bought a poppy every year, feeling I had done my bit. Albert had obviously done his bit all those years ago. There seemed to be no comparison.

What of this character Sam ? Where did he come in ? The incident with the cat seemed to be a terrible and unnecessary act of cruelty. Smiling to myself, I promised to give Tiger an extra stroke when I got back home. Amy - could she be my great-grandmother ? What had happened to her ? Mother seemed to have an affinity with Albert, but nowhere in her scrapbooks was there a reference to Amy. Judging by the story, she and Albert were very much in love. However, it seems that their plans to move to London had come to nothing.

I lit a cigarette and inhaled deeply. There was something in the story that had jingled some more bells in my mind, but I could not for the life in me think what it was. It was no good, it simply would not come to me. I presumed that mother had read this story at some point in her life. Not for the first time, I wished I could talk to her.

As I made myself comfortable on the bed ready to start reading again, I caught sight of the sepia photographs that had dropped out from between the pages. I reached across and looked at them carefully. One was a picture of a fresh-faced young man in uniform, a peaked cap perched on his head. He was sitting on what appeared to be a coffee table in front of a white sheet. There was a look of determination on his face. This, without doubt, was Albert Lord. I knew this before I read the faded writing on the back. I had seen him before, in mother's scrapbook, the picture of the soldier with the other half missing. I gazed for a long time at this image in front of me, trying to get inside the mind of this man whose story was at the moment occupying all my thoughts. What secrets were hiding behind that face ?

The second photograph showed a couple on their wedding day, standing arm in arm. I gave an involuntary gasp as I saw the bride. The man was Albert again, looking older than the first picture. I turned over the picture and read the fading words. "Albert and Amy at their wedding, Saturday May 10th 1919." I turned the picture over again and stared at the bride. It was frightening. I could have been looking at a photograph of my mother. The same eyes, the oval face, and the way the hair framed her head. I wondered if it was auburn, but the picture gave no clues, of course. It was no wonder Albert was so fond of his granddaughter. What had happened to Amy though ? I eagerly picked up the manuscript again, turned to the new page and continued reading.

The good people of Caernarvon were obviously expecting us. We were greeted at the station by the important folk of the town, accompanied by a huge crowd waving and cheering. I remember there was a thin layer of snow on the ground, but the warmth of our welcome stopped us from feeling the cold. We all got off the train and collected our kit. You can imagine the chaos that ensued as we tried to find our own bags. Luckily Sam and I located ours quickly and we were in the first group of men to be marched out of the station along a wide road where we were told to remain and await further orders. As usual, the two of us contrived to stand next to each other, hoping to be billeted together. It appeared that we were to be sent to a variety of boarding houses around the town. Just as we had planned, Sam and I were put together, along with six other men, in a pleasant house just off the main square. The door was opened by a plump, cheerful looking lady with a twinkle in her eye, who introduced herself as Mrs. Hughes and insisted we all call her "Mum". She directed us into the living room, where a warm fire was burning. We were squashed in, but we didn't care. After so long on a train it was a little piece of heaven on earth.

After a welcoming cup of tea, Sam and I were directed into a room containing two beds and a small chest of drawers, and little else. It was comfortable enough, and we nodded approvingly at each other as we put our bags down on the beds. Sam said he preferred the one nearest the window. I didn't really care which bed I had, so I sat on the one next to the door. Sam lay back on the bed and put his hands behind his head. I sat on the edge of the bed and looked across at him. I don't think we spoke for several minutes, as each of us took in the situation. I was feeling very homesick, missing Amy and my parents. Sam just stared at the ceiling, content to be alone with his thoughts. I knew he would not divulge what he was thinking about. He was not that sort of person.

Unsure of what to do next, we stayed in the room that evening until we were called downstairs for our meal. It consisted of a wholesome stew, and it was the most delicious food I had ever tasted. Probably because I had eaten nothing since breakfast, earlier in the day. To my pleasure, Mrs. Hughes insisted on us saying grace before the meal. Sam merely bowed his head and remained silent. The conversation during the meal was mainly about our various backgrounds. "Mum" was keen to hear about Accrington and our families. Sam never once volunteered any information, indeed he seemed quite content to sit and stare around him, taking in his new surroundings. After the meal we went back up to the bedroom, where I started to write a letter to Amy. I wasn't as good with words in those days, so it took me a long time to say what I wanted to. However, I managed in the end, and put the letter inside an envelope ready for posting. Father had *thoughtfully put some paper and a supply of envelopes in my bag. I also wrote to my parents, taking only half the time as I had taken with the letter to Amy. Sam and I settled down to sleep quickly after that, and neither of us knew anything until the next morning, so tired were we after such a long day.*

We were woken the next morning by calls summoning us to breakfast, which proved to be a bowl of thick, creamy porridge, served piping hot. Afterwards we made our way to Castle Square, where we were joined by the rest of the battalion, including the lads from Burnley, Blackburn and Chorley, whom we were meeting for the first time. I suppose we all treated each other with a certain amount of wariness at first, but after a short time friendships were made. We were drilled, much to the delight of the assembled townspeople, who watched us with what I hoped was admiration. Young children of the town marched along with us, pretending to be soldiers preparing to fight the foe. This proved to be standard practice each morning. I think we all enjoyed the change in our surroundings. Caernarvon Castle, which dominated the whole area, looked down on us, no doubt casting a critical eye over the latest batch of soldiers to be posted to this lovely Welsh town.

It was during the afternoons that Sam really started to enjoy himself. He was given the chance to follow his great passion of walking. We used to do route marches up and down the surrounding hills. Marching next to Sam made me realise just how fit he was. He could leave me standing, especially on the uphill sections. It was obvious that he was marching well within himself, but he would prefer to go much quicker. I recall him saying to me one night, as we were lying in our beds, how he would love to be able to walk the hills on his own. I felt quite sad that he would consider doing this without me. We seemed to do everything together.

On our first Saturday away from home a dance was organised in the town. We were all invited, of course. I was keen to go, but Sam was quite happy to stay in the room. For the first time I actually persuaded Sam to do something he didn't want. He was still mumbling about bloody silly dances as we walked, wearing our freshly brushed uniforms, into the dance hall. A band was playing a cheerful tune, people were laughing, and I began to think that perhaps this war lark wasn't so bad after all. We stood rather shyly at the side and watched the merry-making going on all around us. I had little experience of dances and was unsure of what to do. I was happy just to be out of our room, relaxing, and quite content to listen to the music. Amy and I had never gone dancing back in Accrington. Sam stood next to me staring around the room and looking bored by the whole affair. Then it happened. I noticed Sam suddenly stand up straighter and look in the direction of the door. I glanced across, and there was a truly beautiful young girl wearing a blue frock. Sam was obviously smitten, and his eyes followed her across the room. He was not alone in this, as several of the men also watched her progress.

Sam excused himself, saying he had to go to the toilet, and he set off in the direction of this beauty. To my surprise, when he got level with her he tripped up and fell more or less into her, almost knocking her off her feet. Whether it was accident or design he gently grabbed her arm, thus preventing her falling. He said something to her, and she smiled back at him. From my position I could see everything that went on. Sam didn't go to the toilet, but remained next to her, chatting away. She seemed pleased with his attention, making no effort to move away. The band struck up a waltz, and to my surprise, Sam accompanied the young lady onto the dance floor, leaving the people she was with, a couple probably in their fifties, whom I took to be her parents.

I watched them on the floor. They stood quite still at the side for a moment; Sam seemed to be watching the other dancers intently. He then took the lead and started to dance. I was surprised at his ability. Not once did he put a foot out of place, and all those watching were equally impressed. At the end of the dance, Sam bowed at the young lady and accompanied her off the floor. They disappeared from view amongst a crowd of people. It was several minutes later when Sam reappeared at my side. His face was wreathed in smiles; for the first time he seemed to be genuinely happy. Even his expressionless eyes sparkled with pleasure.

I asked him where he had learned to dance like that, but all he would say was that he didn't know how to dance. He just watched what the other people were doing and copied them. Sam was in a fine mood for the rest of the evening, chatting away and joking with some of our friends. All the same, I noticed his eyes wandering round the room, seeking out, no doubt, his former partner. After the dance had finished we walked back to our billet and went straight to bed. As we lay there Sam told me a little about the girl he had met. She was called Bronwen, and was the daughter of a local publican. He confided in me that he had arranged to meet her the following evening after she had been to church. Yes, he did have her father's blessing. They were to be allowed to walk home from church together. Sam was totally happy. I was pleased for him, thinking that perhaps he would at last have someone he really cared for.

Our life in Caernarvon progressed pleasantly enough, and we soon dropped into a routine. Lieutenant Colonel Rickman took over the Battalion on March 1st, and we were finally under the command of a true soldier. Things began to tighten up and we worked much harder at our training. We no longer relied on our landladies waking us up in a morning, no, from now on "Reveille" was sounded throughout the town at 6.45 am, waking us and no doubt all the other poor residents of Caernarvon at the same time. However, the change which had most repercussions, especially for Sam, was the introduction of the 10 o'clock curfew. Since the dance, Sam had been seeing Bronwen most nights. I must confess I felt slightly jealous of him. After all, I couldn't sneak out to see Amy. He used to leave the house after the evening meal and not return until late, certainly later than the proposed curfew time. I was always amazed how he could come in so late, often climbing in through our bedroom window, which I opened for him, and still be wide awake the next morning for the rigours of training. He was worried when he heard the new orders, thinking he would not be able to see his love as much. He lay on his bed in total silence for at least an hour, thinking about the problem. He announced his decision to me. He was going to ignore the curfew and run the risk of being caught and no doubt having serious trouble brought down on his head. I was concerned for my friend, but of course I still agreed to open the window for him when I heard the familiar owl hoot from below.
Sam must have led a charmed life, because he was never caught all the time we were resident in Caernarvon, though I do believe on one occasion he had to hide in a back yard whilst a group of senior officers walked past.

I never failed him; the window was always dutifully opened. I would also cover for him if necessary, but that never happened. What are pals for?

We were encouraged to take part in sporting activities, boxing being a favourite amongst the men. I tried my best in the boxing tournaments, but somehow I was always beaten early on. Sam again proved his worth. He always did well, and became a man to be feared in the ring. I remember one senior officer remarking what a great asset he would be in hand-to-hand combat in France. One more unpleasant incident did take place. Sam was due to box against a private from a Burnley company, who had heard, somehow, about Sam's night-time excursions to see Bronwen. Just before the bout started, he must have mentioned something to Sam about this. I don't know what he said, but on hearing the bell, Sam tore out of his corner and set about the man. In no time at all he had battered him about the head, reducing the poor man's face to a bloody pulp. I had never seen such a frenzied attack. It took two men to drag him off. Sam simply smiled a chilling smile when he saw the mess he had made. I shuddered and walked out of the hall, painfully reminded about the cat all those months ago. Sam never mentioned the incident when he returned, through the window, later that night. I didn't think it a good idea to bring it up.

I enjoyed the training more and more; we were taught the invaluable skill of charging straw dummies with our bayonets, though we still had only one rifle between six of us. One wag pointed out that he hoped the enemy would stand as still when we got to France. We were taught semaphore, map and compass reading. We were shown how to find our way around in the dark, how to dig trenches properly, and how to attack and defend them. I felt as if I were turning into a soldier. Unfortunately, no

matter how much training we were given, we were never really prepared for the horrors we would face in France. Had we known, there would have been fewer smiling faces to be seen around the town.
On a lighter note, the men were encouraged to give concerts. With so many men there was a wide variety of talent available. I discovered I had a feel for the piano. I had never played the instrument in my life, but one evening I sat down and started to play "Tipperary", purely by ear. I made one or two mistakes at first, but I finally managed to play the whole tune from start to finish, a feat which brought tremendous applause from the men standing around. Even Sam seemed impressed, much to my satisfaction. Following this, I was a regular performer at the concerts. I found to my pleasure that I had similar talents with a mouth organ, and managed to buy one in the town. I kept it with me as a faithful companion for the next two years, before losing it in some French mud.
Amy wrote often. Her letters were full of things that had been happening in Accrington. She visited my parents each week and had become good friends with my mother. Each letter she sent always ended with the same phrase
       My love always,
       Amy
I hoped against hope I would see her again before moving overseas.
I began to spend less time with Sam. His time, when not training or on some kind of duty, was spent with Bronwen. I still had only seen her the once and I expressed a keenness to meet her one evening. Sam said he would try to arrange something. I hastily pointed out that I was not prepared to break the curfew. Sam merely replied,
" Of course not. After all, who would open the window ?"

Sam arranged the meeting for the following Sunday, again meeting after church. So it happened that I was introduced to Bronwen. She was a lovely person, real fun to be with. She had jet-black hair and lovely dark eyes. Her skin was white, but had the healthy tone brought on by living near the sea. Her voice had that sing-song Welsh lilt. It wasn't hard to see why Sam took the risks he did to be with her. She had been told about my ability with the piano and expressed a desire to listen to me play and perhaps accompany her. Sam was less than enthusiastic, but we all went into the back room of her father's public house. It being Sunday, the bar was closed. It turned out the only song that both of us knew was Psalm 23, to the tune of Crimond. I played it through once and Bronwen joined in, giving the most beautiful rendition I had ever heard. Her father came into the room just to listen to her lovely voice. Sam stood in silence by the door. He made no comment. I took my leave of them and made my way back to the boarding house. I lay in bed waiting for Sam's call.

It was in the April of 1915 that our khaki uniforms finally arrived. We were also given our own rifles, and were instructed on how to look after them and keep them in good working order. We now felt as though we could face the enemy with confidence. I suppose only an outsider could notice the difference in the Battalion, but we were now almost a force to be reckoned with, or so we thought. The people of Caernarvon had really taken the Pals to their heart, so we felt a great sadness when we were told we were moving out sometime in May to Rugeley Camp in Staffordshire. Nobody took this news worse than Sam. He was totally shocked. His relationship with Bronwen had grown stronger by the day, and now it seemed it was to be wrenched from him. He even contemplated deserting.

*Goodness knows what would have happened if he had. Luckily I persuaded him not to be so foolish, pointing out that many of the men, myself included, had left loved ones behind. I suppose it was the loyalty to his comrades that made him change his mind and remain a Pal.
So it was, on May 13th, that the battalion left Caernarvon. It was an early start, but despite this many of the residents turned out to wave goodbye as we marched to the station. Sam's eyes scanned the crowd for a glimpse of Bronwen. Whether he saw her or not, I never found out. I'm sure all of us were sad to be leaving Caernarvon and, of course, the friends we had made. Sam never said a word on the journey to Rugeley, he just took up his familiar place by the window and stared out. I took out my mouth organ and began to play "Tipperary". Most of the men in our carriage joined in, but somehow the enthusiasm was missing.
We arrived at our destination late that afternoon. It was pouring with rain and there seemed to be an air of misery over all of us. We marched to the camp, arriving wet through with water dripping off the peaks of our caps. We were shown into a hut and allotted a bed. I say bed, but in reality it was just a wooden board covered with a straw mattress. What a contrast from our previous billet. The toilets were outside, and all around the camp was mud. It was not a happy time, but like most deprivations you can get used to them, and after all, there would be far worse to come before the war was over. Sam was totally miserable. No matter what was said to him, he would merely grunt. I felt sorry for him, but a little disappointed in his attitude. There were many men in the same situation of missing a loved one, myself included. After a while less and less sympathy was extended towards him. This did not*

seem to bother him as he continued with his self-pity and became, if possible, less communicative than ever.
We now had a more accurate taste of army life. Training was stepped up and mock battles were fought. Some of these were at night, and confusion reigned on more than one occasion. It was during one of these night battles that Sam and I for some reason were separated from the rest of our group. We were in total darkness and completely lost. I knew roughly the direction we had to go to find the camp again, so the two of us set off. You cannot imagine the difficulties we faced as we made our way over unknown ground. We fell down ditches, tripped over walls and eventually got so disorientated that we no longer had any idea where we were. I could just about make out Sam's face in the pale light of the moon as it briefly came out from behind a cloud. There was complete panic written all over it. Beads of sweat were trickling down his face. This was not the Sam I knew. He looked across at me and began to shake uncontrollably. It was clear that he didn't like the unfortunate situation we found ourselves in. Realising there was no point in trying to find our way in the dark, I suggested that we remain where we were until daylight. Sam willingly agreed to my suggestion, so we made ourselves as comfortable as possible in a small hollow and waited for first light.
Sam seemed to calm down a little as we sat huddled together for warmth, and he explained to me that he had been frightened of the dark since his father used to lock him up in the coal cellar for hours on end as a punishment when he was a child. It was strange to see him like this. Here was the man who had risked all to see Bronwen during our stay in Caernarvon. Here was the man who had beaten a soldier's face to a pulp in a boxing match, shaking with fear because we were in the dark.

I just could not understand him at all.
Being May, it was light fairly early in the morning. We stood up and looked around. In the distance we could just make out the roofs of the camp huts, so we set off walking towards them. We were allowed through the gates by the sentry and were told to report to the sergeant-major straight away. Luckily, he took a kindly view of our shivering state and didn't report us, though he did say we were almost classed as missing and an extensive manhunt would have followed had we not appeared. As we walked to our hut, Sam asked me not to mention the incident. I of course agreed, though I wondered how he would cope in a similar situation in France. Reading my mind he simply said,
"Don't worry. I'll cure myself. You just see if I don't."
One of the things we had to do at the camp was to aid in the construction of an assault course. This was mainly of barbed wire and low mounds of earth. We were then shown how to overcome these obstacles using planks. After this, we had to charge with our bayonets stuck on the end of our rifles to kill the enemy. After two weeks of this we all felt ready for action, and that our departure for the front was fairly close. I wrote to Amy telling her this, preparing her, I suppose, for the possibility of losing each other forever.
Life at Rugeley continued through the rest of May, through June and into July. During that time we developed our soldiering skills and also our comradeship with each other and the other Battalions stationed there with us. We found the training hard, but we enjoyed it none the less, especially the sports. Inter-company football matches were popular and drew good crowds of the non-players to watch. I was more interested in the concerts we used to put on. My musical skills were

developing nicely, and I would be asked to play the piano for community singing, a task I enjoyed greatly.
It was the middle of July that the rumour of a move began to run round the camp like wildfire. I never found out where it started, but in less than two days we were all convinced that we would shortly be on the move. Would it be France, Egypt or even some other far-flung outpost of the Empire ? As it turned out, it was somewhere much closer to home. In fact it was home ! We were told by our officer that we were to return to the Accrington area as part of a recruiting campaign, designed to raise more men to act as reservists for the Battalion. It was thought that the sight of us brave soldiers marching through the streets would inspire more men to join up.
The move came at the end of July, when we marched to the station and boarded the train bound for East Lancashire. We travelled north with happy hearts, sure that we would be able to spend time with our loved ones. My thought turned to Amy, while Sam sat in the corner seat, staring as always out of the window of the carriage....

I could keep my eyes open no longer. Fascinating as it was, I was starting to fall asleep. I looked at my watch. It was now turned 10.30. My eyes tried hard to focus on the words written down in front of me. It was no use, try as I might I knew I could not continue. No, the Albert Lord story would have to wait until I got back home the next day. I carefully slipped the manuscript back in its envelope, took one last look at Albert and Amy and returned the envelope in the box. I washed myself and prepared for bed. I fell asleep straight away, my tired brain not allowing any further thoughts of the story I had just read.

Chapter 13

ALBERT LORD'S STORY: EVER NEARER

I woke the next morning feeling refreshed, if slightly hung-over. I noticed that the bottle of whisky was two thirds empty. I am drinking far too much, I thought, slipping the unfinished bottle into my suitcase. I just wanted to take the manuscript out again and continue reading. However, my longing to return home and see Sara again outweighed this desire. I showered and dressed, before packing my overnight things. I made sure that I had replaced all the items I had taken out of the box before going downstairs for breakfast. I was shown to a table in the dining room, and I ordered a full English breakfast, justifying such extravagance by the fact that I would not have to stop on the way home for lunch. It was served by a lovely little waitress who smiled as she put the feast in front of me.
"Enjoy your breakfast," she said in the now familiar northern accent.

I poured myself a cup of tea and attacked the gargantuan meal set before me. I managed to almost eat everything, just leaving one fried tomato at the side of the plate. I then attacked the toast. I poured myself a second cup of tea and began to study the road atlas, which I had retrieved from the car, to work out the best way home. I found the exact location of the hotel on the map and plotted my route. I decided to follow the M66, then turn onto the M62 going east until I arrived at the A1. This seemed the easiest route, if not the most direct. That being decided upon, I finished my drink and returned upstairs to collect my things.

I loaded the box and my suitcase into the car and returned inside to pay the bill. Once this was settled I drove away towards the motorway. As I pulled down the slip road I took a last glance at Sykeside House, and thought of my mother and her last night on Earth. She probably drove down this exact stretch of road, heading ultimately to her death. I shuddered.

I followed the M62 back towards West Yorkshire, and as I passed the exit for Halifax I could just about make out, across the valley, the folly tower close to my father's house. I glanced at the clock on the dashboard of the car; it was just after 10. Victoria and Richard would be at school, Phil would be at work and Victoria would probably be setting off on another shopping trip. I had enjoyed meeting them all; it felt good to have relatives, real ones, not just those you read about in faded manuscripts.

As I drove back home I kept thinking about Albert Lord's story. He had obviously seen fit to commit it to paper, but as yet it seemed an interesting yet unremarkable tale. No doubt many of the young men at the time could have told of similar happenings. Yet there had to be something. I cursed myself for not being able to stay awake any longer the previous evening. Still, all would hopefully be revealed later that day when I got back to Stradbroke.

The journey south was straightforward, as I wished it had been for my mother. It didn't seem long before I was picking my way through the roadworks on the A1 near my turn-off towards East Anglia. The terrain was much more familiar now; the hills had disappeared to be replaced by the rolling landscape of Cambridgeshire and Suffolk. I couldn't really decide which I preferred. All I knew was that I would be glad to be home again.

It was just after 1 o'clock when I pulled into the drive of my house in Stradbroke. Sara was out working, so I came back into an empty house. There was a little message left on the table, welcoming me back. Sara's last appointment was mid-afternoon, and she would be back shortly after that. I unpacked and made myself a coffee. I fetched the box out of the car and put it down next to the table in the lounge. I took out the envelope, carefully removed the manuscript, found the place I finished the night before, and continued reading.

> *Our first stop was Chorley, on July 30th, where we were given a civic reception. The Chorley lads were allowed the next day off whilst the rest of us marched to Blackburn to attend the Royal Lancashire Agricultural Show. We gave a drill display for the assembled crowds. After that we were marched into the town of Blackburn itself to be allocated places to stay for the night. We were then dismissed. It was still early afternoon. I, along with several of the Accrington lads, decided to leave Blackburn by tram and make the short journey back home. We knew we could march back the following morning to rejoin the rest of the Battalion. Sam elected to stay in Blackburn. His heart lay in Wales, not with his family in Accrington.*

I will never forget the feeling as I got off the tram in the town centre and walked the short distance to my parent's house. They were not expecting me, thinking that the troops would not arrive in the town until the next day. I knocked on the door, something I had never done before, and in a few seconds it was opened by my mother, who on seeing me flung her arms around me. This show of emotion was out of keeping and surprised me. I kissed her on the cheek and we stood for a long time embracing each other. My father, curious to see who was at the door, shortly appeared, slipping his braces over his shoulders at the same time. His face was a picture when he saw me. He shook me warmly by the hand and led me inside. It was as if I had fought the war single-handed, not just spent endless hours of training. The living room was just as I remembered it. The uncomfortable chairs, the small dining table and the dozens of cheap ornaments were still all in their usual place, yet it was, as ever, completely dust-free and spotless. The world had stayed the same despite my absence, something I would have to come to terms with. Mother was instructed to put the kettle on, and soon I was drinking a welcoming cup of tea.

Father was keen to ask questions about my training, and I made every effort to tell him as well as I could. There was much to catch up on, but I think I filled him in as best as possible. I felt truly happy to see them both again, but my heart lay elsewhere, with Amy. I stood up to go and see her when father, anticipating my next move, put his hand on my shoulder and quietly said,

"Her brothers, they were both killed, you know. Got word last week they did - Gallipoli, we think, but reports are confused."

I obviously didn't know, and sat down again. This simple fact brought the horrors of war a little closer. I had been

touched by death for the first time, albeit indirectly. This made my desire to see Amy even more urgent, to comfort her and to reassure her. I put on my cap and walked silently out of the house.
I knocked on her door, which was opened by Amy herself. She looked paler than I remembered and there was a sad look in her eyes. On seeing me she smiled and asked me inside. A house in mourning is not a place for happy greetings. I entered the living room and was shocked by the sight that greeted me. Her parents were seated on the sofa. They looked up, but neither of them said a word. They seemed to have aged twenty years since I last saw them a few months ago. I made a clumsy attempt to offer my condolences, but Amy caught my eye and shook her head.
"They won't hear you. They don't hear anything any more. They just sit there."
I reached across and held Amy's small hand in mine. I squeezed it gently. She looked up at me, her auburn hair catching the evening sun as it streamed in through the window. I suggested we went for a walk. Amy glanced across at her parents, but they made no movement.
"Just going out for a while," she said.
There was no response.
We left quietly and walked arm in arm towards Oak Hill Park. I wanted to tell Amy how much I had missed her, but the time did not seem appropriate somehow, so we walked in silence for a while. Amy eventually spoke.
"They haven't spoken since they got the news. They just sit there. People have called in at the house, and they look up, expecting to see my brothers, but when they don't appear they look into space again. They're dying a slow death."

Tears came into her eyes, and I kissed her gently on the cheek. I didn't know what to say. No words of mine would have made any difference at that point. We sat down on the grass and gazed across at the hills opposite. There was so much I wanted to tell Amy, but all my little adventures seemed so meaningless compared to her tragedy. I didn't know it at the time, but many similar scenes would be played out over the next few years, not just in Accrington, but in every town and city in the country.

We walked slowly back to her house, where we found her parents just as we had left them. I took my leave and made my way to the door. Amy followed me, and apologised as we stood on the step. I kissed her once more, and promised to call again when the battalion was dismissed after our march through the town the following day. She seemed comforted by this. I walked slowly home, thinking of my loved one and her family and how much they were suffering. God forbid that anything should happen to me. It was with a heavy heart that I walked in through my own front door. I looked hard across at my parents and wondered how they would take it if I were killed. I closed my eyes in an effort to put the thought right out of my head. Mother had made a simple meal of bread and cheese. As we ate I told them of the condition of Amy's parents. Neither of them commented. They, too, were probably thinking of similar news arriving at their house. The war was starting to bite. Father and I treated ourselves to a drink in the public house that night. It was good to be back home again.

It felt wonderful to sleep in my own bed once more, certainly after the straw at Rugeley, though I had to rise very early to make my way back to Blackburn. On arrival, I sought out Sam. He was wandering aimlessly around

outside his billet. I told him the news about Amy's brothers, which he greeted with indifference.
"It happens," was his only comment.
How cold hearted, I thought to myself, and walked away to where we were due to assemble for our march to Accrington. For the first time ever I made no effort to stand next to him in the line, disgusted as I was with his attitude towards poor Amy and her family.
It seemed as if the whole population of Accrington was lining the streets as we entered the town, and they were all waving and cheering. We marched past the Town Hall where John Harwood, the Mayor and the Battalion founder, took the salute. Surely everyone must have noticed how fitter and stronger we looked as we marched effortlessly by. We were to remain in Accrington for three days. We paraded, drilled and gave demonstrations, all designed to recruit a reserve company.
After we were dismissed I went straight away to Amy's house to see if I could offer any assistance. The scene remained the same. If anything, her parents seemed to grow older each time I saw them. It was sad to watch. Amy and I both felt powerless to help.
Following our dismissal on the second day, Sam sought me out and apologised for his thoughtless comments about Amy's family. I accepted his apology and we shook hands. I was relieved to have made up with Sam, who, despite his strange attitudes, was still a good friend. As we sat together in the town centre we discussed the future. Things were not going well with the recruiting. The sense of patriotism seemed to have worn off after reports of how the war was going wrong filtered back. It seemed inevitable that some form of call-up would have to be introduced in the not too distant future, just as my father had predicted many months ago.

After the three days the battalion was once again assembled and we set off for Burnley, where a similar recruitment campaign was to be held. Several other men and I took off overnight and returned home to visit family and friends. I knew that Wednesday would be our last night in the area, so it was with tears in my eyes that I said what might be my final farewell to both my parents and Amy, not knowing when, or indeed if, I would see them again. As I kissed Amy goodbye, she whispered in my ear,
"Don't die, please."
I didn't really know how to respond to that, so I kissed her again and took my leave, walking away in silence.
I rejoined the battalion the following day, and we set off for Ripon in Yorkshire, for what was widely believed to be our last training before leaving for the front. Though this was not strictly accurate, our introduction to active service was drawing ever nearer.
There was a great difference between our billets here and at Rugeley. The camp had been built in a much better fashion. The huts were more comfortable, each fitted with electric lights, I might add. There were recreation rooms and properly organised training routines. There was a rifle range, which all the men used to great effect until we became proficient with the weapon, something which might save our lives at a later date, a fact our sergeant-major never tired of pointing out.
Our huts were in an area known as South Camp and, as the name suggests, stood on the southern edge of Ripon, near the tiny, picturesque village of Studley Roger. Occasionally we walked into Ripon, about 2 miles away, to have a drink. There were several public houses to visit, but for some reason we congregated in one called The

Turk's Head, down a slight slope just off the main square. The Unicorn, round in the square itself, was strictly for officers. Sometimes I wandered off alone exploring the nooks and crannies of this lovely town. I often went and sat inside the Cathedral, enjoying the piece and quiet of this huge building, quite the biggest church I had ever been in. I never actually attended a service there, much as I would have liked. I also enjoyed the horn blowing ceremony performed every night at 9 o' clock in the town square by Thomas Hawley, the hornblower of the day. This was a tradition dating back hundreds of years.
It was during my stay in Ripon that I discovered another of my hidden talents. After we were dismissed one day, Sam persuaded me to go on one of his walks over the hills. He promised to keep to a steady pace and not go racing ahead. So it was we set off on a beautiful August afternoon, having first received permission from our Captain. Sam wanted to walk to Brimham Rocks, a distance of some 8 miles. In our high state of fitness this would present no problem. When we arrived at our destination we sat down on a curious rock formation, looking across the moors. I was quite taken with the view and took out a piece of paper and pencil I always carried with me, and began to sketch. As with my music, I had not received any training, but I found that with careful observation I could produce a passable picture. I passed the finished product over to Sam, who nodded in appreciation, though he didn't say much.
Folding it up carefully, I replaced it in my tunic pocket and we set off back to the camp. We decided to return by a slightly different route going through the grounds of Fountains Abbey, a fine example Norman architecture, or so an old man also wandering around the grounds told me. Its closeness to the camp meant that I had visited the

> ruins several times, content to just sit and stare across the tranquil river Skell at the graceful structure.
> I told Sam I would like to stay here on my own for a while and do some more sketching, since I was feeling flushed with my original success. Sam was quite happy to walk the rest of they way alone. I sat down on the bank and taking out another sheet of paper, began to sketch the east window. The fading light meant that the shadows stretched across the grass. The effect was stunning. I experimented with a style of shading to bring out the lights and darks of the scene. The finished picture pleased me greatly. I decided to send the picture to Amy, thinking that perhaps it would cheer her up. In later years I did many pictures using this style. I'm sure there must be a term for it, but I was ignorant of it at the time....

"Chiaroscuro," I said aloud as I put the manuscript down, hearing the door being opened.

So that was where mother got the name of the shop from."
Indeed, the picture drawn by Albert Lord was at present residing in mother's scrapbook upstairs in the loft. The initials A.L. must have been Albert, and not Anne, Lord. Yet another echo of the past was reverberating into my life.

Sara walked into the room and flung her arms round me. After hugging for a very long time, my whimsical side compared the reunion of Albert and Amy some 80 years ago, when light kisses on the cheek were the order of the day.

"Well ?" said Sara when we eventually disentangled ourselves. "So have you unravelled the Gordian Knot ?"
"Very nearly, I hope."
I indicated the half read manuscript on the settee.

"I'm finding out a lot about my great-grandfather, anyway."
"The Pal ?"
"Yes, the Pal," I replied. I was now more aware of the significance of the term.
"Well, forget that Pal, and be my pal for a while," she rather brazenly whispered. "Let's go to bed."
No red-blooded male could refuse an offer like that, so we went hand in hand upstairs to the bedroom.

It was dark when we came down, and the effects of the breakfast were wearing off, so I suggested a meal at the Queen's Head. Sara took no second bidding so we showered, got changed and walked the short distance to the pub. The place was virtually empty as we walked in, so we went straight into the restaurant area. As usual, I banged my head on the beam as we did so. We ordered our meal and chatted non-stop about what we had both done over the last few days. I had only been away for such a short time, but I was so glad to be back in her company. How must Albert have felt after so long away from his loved one ?
After the meal we went as usual into the bar area, where Bill Garnett had, almost inevitably, manifested himself. We nodded across to each other and I bought him a drink. He walked slowly in our direction. I caught a glimpse of Sara tensing slightly as he drew nearer. She really didn't like him.

"Not seen you around for a while. Been away, have we ?" he asked.

I replied that I had been up to the North to sort out a few things to do with mother's estate, cursing, for some reason, the fact that he had noted my absence from the village. He nodded in understanding. With that he thanked me for the drink and returned to his usual place by the bar. We found an empty table near the door and sat down. We talked about everything and nothing, just glad to be back together again. Yet I could feel my mind wandering back to the manuscript still on the settee at home. I thought it prudent not to mention these thoughts to Sara.

Sara wanted to know about Phil and his family. I told her about the beautiful house, the garage and, of course, Victoria and the children. She seemed keen for them to come and visit us at the earliest opportunity. I promised to arrange it, saying I would ring my father the next day. We had another drink each. I soon slipped back into drinking beer with no head, two pints going down in quick time. Sara was much more reserved, sipping away at a solitary half of lager. We returned home, strolling the short distance hand in hand, not arm in arm as Albert and Amy tended to do.

Sara went straight to bed, but I searched about in the loft until I found the picture I now knew to be of Fountains Abbey, drawn some 82 years ago. I carefully spread it out on the coffee table and stared at it again. It was a good picture, there was no doubt of that. Old Albert had a feel for art. I thanked him for passing his talents down to me. I closed my eyes and imagined a young soldier sitting all alone on a riverbank, far from his loved one, deciding to send her this gift. Had Amy liked it? Surely she must have. I decided to have the picture framed and hang it in pride of place in the living room. I carefully replaced the picture in the book and went upstairs to bed.

The following day we both rose early, Sara had an appointment at 9 o'clock, whilst I decided I would put in an appearance at the shop. We parted with a kiss at the front door. I drove steadily to Diss and parked in my usual place. I entered the shop and was greeted by the still glamorous Elaine. Just as I expected, she had held the fort immaculately in my absence, seeing no need to employ extra staff, though she did admit to closing early one afternoon in order to do some shopping. I jokingly suggested she had better put some extra hours in on Sunday. We both laughed at this and Elaine went to put the kettle on.

Feeling kind-hearted, I gave her the rest of the day off, the least I could do under the circumstances, and Elaine gratefully accepted.
"But be in all the earlier the next day," I almost quoted Charles Dickens.

Left alone in the shop, I went through the post. There was nothing of great importance, and I soon cleared the pile. I wished I had brought the manuscript with me to read in the quiet times. I settled down on the chair behind the counter and began to sketch, from memory, some of the wonderful northern hills I had observed on my trip. I felt like Albert Lord must have felt when he first sketched all those years ago. I began to experiment with the shading technique he described and found it a very satisfying medium.

I found Phil's number and dialled through to Halifax. There was nobody in at the house, so I tried the garage. My father's now familiar voice answered the phone.
"Pete, good to hear from you. Did you find out anything in Accrington ?"

I described my visit to Mr. Robinson's, and told him of the contents of the box. He seemed quite interested in the manuscript and said he would like to read it one day. I asked after Victoria and the children, to be told they were all well and he would pass on my best wishes. I told him about Sara's keenness for them all to visit, and he suggested some time during July when the children were on holiday from school. I replied we would have to get our diaries together and work out a date. I rang off, promising to contact him as soon as possible.

The rest of the day proved to be fairly quiet, and by five I was ready for home. I locked up and headed off to the car, running through the town as it was pouring with rain. I negotiated the Diss traffic and was soon sitting at home, with a nice whisky in front of me. I picked up the manuscript and continued the story.

> *Life at Ripon proved hard, but arguably more enjoyable than at Rugeley. For one thing, it was easy for family to visit, there being only a three hour train journey involved. I was not one of the lucky ones to have a visit from family and, not surprisingly, neither was Sam. Still, it was nice to see the smiling faces of those who did.*
> *Sam and I spent a lot of time walking round the beautiful countryside, and I suppose I got to know him even better. It was on one of these walks that he really opened up to me, telling of his miserable childhood. His father had treated him badly as a child; beatings were a regular happening, as well as frequent spells locked up in the dark. This had contributed to his somewhat detached attitude to other people, and explained the way in which he often appeared selfish, putting himself first. His own kind of self defence, he used to call it. His little sister, Ruth, had been his parent's favourite, and after her birth he had been very much pushed to one side, almost to the point of hatred.*
> *"Samuel and Ruth, what lovely biblical names," I pointed out.*
> *"My father's idea," he replied. "Great church people, our family."*
> *He must have caught sight of my puzzled look.*
> *"We were made to go to church as children and had it forced upon us. I hated it. God never looked after me in that coal shed, so I look after myself, without his help, see."*

I found it difficult to understand why his father, a Christian, should treat him so badly.

"But why... ?"

Sam held up his hand and stopped me from finishing.

"I know, I know. Why was he, a churchgoer, so cruel to me ? Well, go on, bible scholar, read Proverbs, Chapter 13 Verse 24, then you might understand."

I took out my Bible and found the reference. I read it out aloud.

"He that spareth his rod hateth his son: but he that loveth him chasteneth him betimes."

" My father followed it to the letter. He used to shout it at me time and time again, through the door as I cowered in the dark. At other times he used to hit me sixteen times, shouting it out as he did so, one belt for every word ! Call that love ?"

There was real hatred in his voice. My sympathy was with him. We both went silent. Sam eventually spoke, confessing he had told no other living soul that story. I felt flattered that he had chosen to treat me like a brother and open up his heart.

He rooted around in his bag and produced a crumpled piece of paper that he handed over to me. It was a picture he had drawn, more or less an exact copy of my first sketch of Fountains Abbey.

"I always was good at copying," he explained. " Just show me some handwriting or such like and I will copy it. I did this one afternoon when you left it on your bed."

I passed it back to him, and to my surprise he ripped it up and threw it away, shrugging his shoulders at the same time. I could not make him out at all.

As time wore on at Ripon, the battalion began to receive supplies it would need for active service. We had kitchen and ammunition wagons assigned to us, along with what seemed like hundreds of mules for drawing them. An thrill of excitement rippled through the men. It seemed at last that we were ready for moving to the front. Nobody knew where it would be, but the general feeling was that it wouldn't be long.

With our departure about to happen we were all granted a weeks leave. Sam and I travelled down to Accrington together. He told me he would spend a day with his family before travelling once more to Caernarvon. This cheered him up, and the journey home was one of jollity, with me playing my mouth organ and leading the inevitable chorus of "Tipperary". As soon as the train pulled into the station, men grabbed their bags and dived off in every direction, keen to spend every available minute with their loved ones. Sam was true to his word. He disappeared after one day, but not before I persuaded him to join me at the photographers for a picture of the pair of us together, wearing our army uniforms. He dismissed this act as sentimental rubbish, but he had it done all the same.

I divided my time between my parent's house and Amy's. Her mother and father had both become worse, and they were literally fading away before our eyes. Amy was understandably distressed. I did everything I could to comfort her, but I could tell they were both going to die sooner rather than later. Is it possible to die from a broken heart ? It seemed likely in both their cases.

When not sitting with her parents, Amy used to walk out with me, usually to our favourite place in the park, where we would sit and talk of the future when the war would be over. I suppose this was our way of putting what might happen out of our minds. I had a terrible feeling that we might not have a future together, that our plans might be brought to a cruel end by a bullet through my head. I said nothing of my thoughts to Amy; she was depressed *enough. I gave her a photograph of me in full uniform, without Sam, this time. She promised to keep it for always, placing it on the mantelpiece next to my sketch of Fountains Abbey.*

The week went all too quickly, and before we knew it we were heading for the station. There were no cheers this time, they were replaced by our families openly weeping as we said goodbye. I hugged mother and Amy before I walked along the platform and boarded one of the special trains taking us back to Ripon. I leant out of the window as it pulled out to take a last loving look at Amy, her pretty face awash with tears. My father remained stoical as he stood with his arm around my mother.

There was no singing on the return journey. All the men wanted to sit quietly thinking of their families. Of Sam there was no sign, but I felt certain he would be on the train somewhere. This proved to be correct: as I got off the train, he appeared as if by magic at my side, his tall angular body looming over me. We marched back to camp together, telling each other about our days on leave. Sam was once again full of Bronwen. He had promised to try to stay alive and return to her. How many similar promises had been made, only to be broken by a bullet?

Final preparations for the move were made, and so it was that at the end of September 1915, one Friday evening, the battalion headed south for Hurdcott Camp near Salisbury, widely regarded as a stopping off place before going to the front. I remember the journey took about 12 hours, during which time we had little to occupy our minds, though we were given tea in the early hours of the morning.

We got off the train, feeling stiff and thoroughly miserable, only to be told we had a five-mile walk to the

> *camp. It was pouring with rain and the deep mud on the road slowed down our marching speed.*
> *"Like bloody Yorkshire in 'ight a summer," one of the Oswaldtwistle lads called out.*
> *We all laughed, in spite of the discomfort we were feeling. Sam walked beside me, and I actually heard him singing to himself. Try as I might, with rain running down my face, I could summon up no such enthusiasm....*

I shot up in the air as the strident tones of the telephone echoed around the house. I put down the manuscript and picked up the phone. It was Sara.

"Pete, can you come and get me ? The car's packed up. I'm stuck in Laxfield, just outside the Low House."

I replied that I could, and said I would be there as soon as possible. Cursing inwardly, as this meant my reading of the manuscript would have to be curtailed yet again, I put on my coat and ventured forth. It was still pouring down; little rivers ran down the main street as I headed towards Laxfield. I knew the Low House very well, though I had not been there for a long time. It was a pub, actually called The King's Head. It derived its affectionate name due to the fact that it stood in a dip in the road. It was a journey of about seven miles so it took me a good quarter of an hour to get there. The rain sheeted down, just as it did during Albert's march to the camp, no doubt. I spotted Sara's car straight away and pulled up in front of it. It transpired that she had driven through a flooded section of road and the car had stopped and refused to start. So it was a very wet and miserable Sara that climbed gratefully into the passenger seat of my car. We drove swiftly back to Stradbroke before she caught her death of cold. By the time we got back to my house Sara was starting to steam up the car, and I was relieved to shepherd her in through the front door into the warmth. She went directly upstairs to get out of her wet clothes and have a shower. I lit a cigarette and went into the living room.

I could hear Sara singing in the shower as I once more picked up Albert's story and took up where I left off.

> *We found after several days at the camp that our free time grew less and less. Never before had we been so busy. We were given brand new rifles and ordered to get to know them well.*
> *"As well as you know your bloody girlfriend !" barked a Sergeant-Major.*
> *"Have you ever met my girlfriend ? You wouldn't want to get to know 'er," one lad called out, adding "Sir," as an afterthought. Such was the spirit we had built up over the months we had trained together.*
> *Other items of field equipment were handed out, and machine guns, medical supplies and signalling bits and bobs arrived. We were trained now by soldiers who had recently returned from the front. They really put us through our paces. We were shown how to spread barbed wire and to dig trenches, properly this time. We spent full days in the field in atrocious conditions. The somewhat sparse camp seemed like the best hotel in Lancashire, when we arrived back tired and filthy in the evening.*
> *By the time November arrived the weather was cold and frosty. We had to endure nights spent outside in the muddy trenches. Sam stuck close by my side in the dark, often shaking with fear, but nowhere near as bad as before.*
> *"I just think of Bronwen, and then I don't feel half as bad," he whispered out of the side of his mouth.*

I remember writing home asking for some cocoa to be sent down in order to make a warm drink. Eventually it duly arrived, accompanied by a letter from my father, informing me of the death of Amy's father. He added that her mother was expected to follow shortly. I wished I could go home to be with her, but this of course was not possible, especially as the rumours had started again. It appeared we were to move out within days, if the latest batch of stories were to be believed. In fact an advance party had been sent to somewhere in France. Surprisingly, this party was recalled after only a couple of days. We never did find out why.

The middle of November saw Sam being summoned to see the Commanding Officer. With a puzzled expression on his face, Sam left the rest of us and made his way to the office. He was gone for about half an hour, and when he returned I was sure he had been crying. I walked over to him with a questioning look on my face. He told me that his father had died suddenly, and he had been granted compassionate leave to journey back to Accrington for the funeral. He was due to leave in an hour. I asked him if he would call and see my parents and Amy. He gladly agreed and I hastily scribbled brief letters to them both. I felt a pang of sorrow as I said farewell to the tearful Sam as he headed towards the gates of the camp, head bowed. Tears I never thought he would shed for the man who beat him and locked him in the coal shed as a child, unless it was all an act to gain some sympathy. I put that thought out of my mind, dismissing it as totally unchristian.

He returned a few days later, but it was quite a while before he would look me full in the face, let alone talk to me. I assumed he felt a little ashamed of his tears before he left. Sam did not like his emotions to show.

The good news came early in December. We were to be given some leave prior to our departure from England. We all were excited at the prospect of going home again, though Sam seemed rather worried about the thought. There was even a special train at the station ready to take us home. There was great excitement amongst the men as we prepared to see our families once more. Our hopes were dashed when we were told all future leave was cancelled, and that we were to be ready to move out within days. Not to France as expected, but to Egypt. We were informed that we were to leave camp for the journey to Devonport, where we would set sail on the 19th of December 1915.
"Perhaps it will be a bit bloody warmer there," suggested one of the men.

Shivering in my bed, I really hoped so....

Sara finished her shower and came into the room wearing a fluffy pink dressing gown. She selected a CD and set it playing softly in the background. She poured us both a drink, and joined me on the settee and snuggled up. I put down the manuscript. Sara looked into my eyes, her head resting on my shoulder, and said,

"Don't mind me, you carry on reading."

The music of M People filled the house, something about searching for a hero. I wondered if I was about to read about a genuine one. Sipping my drink, I picked up the document once more and carried on reading.

Chapter 14

ALBERT LORD'S STORY: ABROAD

As the ship, the White Star liner S.S. Ionic, pulled slowly out of the harbour I had an awful feeling in the pit of my stomach. A question impossible to answer formed in my mind: would I ever see England again? I took one last look at the retreating harbour wall and then simply stared out to sea. I asked myself further questions. Was I ready for a fight? Had I trained enough? Would I fail if I were asked to shoot somebody dead? Would I be killed before I got the chance to fight for my country? No doubt the other men were asking themselves similar questions. There could be no answers. Only time would tell.
Sam joined me leaning over the rail. I was glad to have him with me. We had known each other for over a year now and, strange as it may seem, we both felt happy in each other's company. Yet since the funeral of his father,

he had been rather distant with me, not really uttering a word. I put this down to his normal attitude and general lack of communication. He seemed quite relieved to be leaving England.

"Shame our leave were cancelled," I said, trying to open the conversation.

"I suppose," he replied. "Perhaps it's better to get off though. Waiting, can't stand waiting."

"I would have liked to have seen Amy again. Tell me, Sam, was she well when you called on her?"

"Aye, she were OK. In tears when I left her."

I wished I could have been there to comfort her. I wished this damned war had never happened. Leaving Sam leaning over the rail, I returned to my hammock and scowled as I watched it swaying gently with the movement of the ship. How I was ever going to sleep in it I could not figure out.

After several days of sailing south we entered the Bay of Biscay. That is, if Charlie Sykes were to be believed. Charlie knew a bit about geography, and so became the unofficial guide to his friends. Here the weather deteriorated and the passage became rough. I was walking on the wet, slippery deck when a large wave rocked the ship, knocking me over. I fell like a stone and banged my head on the ship's rail. I was carried unconscious to my hammock, where the ship's doctor visited me. He said I had concussion and told me to stay put for two days. My condition worsened and I became delirious. Sam later informed me that I was rambling in my sleep, cursing and swearing.

To make it worse, I began to imagine all sorts of horrors. The day before my fall, I had been reading the Bible, 2 CORINTHIANS 11:26, which conjured up in my mind all sorts of perils rising out of the sea and crawling towards me, all wearing the distinctive spiked helmets of the German army. In my puzzled state I thrashed out at them with an imaginary bayonet. It took three men all their time to hold me down. Eventually my illness subsided and I began to be more rational. It was a good job Sam told me how I had been, for otherwise I would never have believed it. Something else in the biblical quote was to return to haunt me in a totally different way in the months ahead. Apart from my accident, there was one other incident worthy of note on the journey. This happened on New Year's Eve. We had just left Malta where we had stayed for two days, not that we saw anything of the place, as only officers were allowed shore leave. A cry went up that a German submarine had been sighted a few hundred yards away. The alarm was sounded and we were put at lifeboat stations. We all held our breath as the torpedo slowly edged past us, about a hundred feet away. Feeling shaken by our close brush with death, it was a subdued group of men who went to sleep that night. It was the first time any of us had seen the enemy's desire to kill us at such close quarters.

Luckily we escaped, though we later found out that another ship had been sunk with the loss of over three hundred souls. You can imagine the relief that spread over the ship as we docked, unscathed, in Alexandria the next day. Once again we were denied shore leave, but many men defied this order and swarmed ashore. Sam and I were not among the group that jumped ship, so we escaped the confinement to quarters, the punishment meted out by Lieutenant Colonel Rickman. After this incident all the men had another sharp reminder that we were not on holiday, when we could do as we pleased. We were in the army, and a code of discipline had to be followed.

Five days later we arrived at our destination, Port Said, where we were, at last, allowed off the ship to move into tents near the rather primitive railway station. For me and many others it was the first night we had spent away from England, not counting Wales of course. If only it had been the last. How good it felt to fall asleep without the constant rocking from side to side of my hammock.
As we awoke the next morning, the thing that struck us all was the heat. I suppose in real terms it was not particularly hot, but remember we had just arrived from a cold, wet England, and a temperature in the mid sixties, as it was, felt pleasantly warm. What was unbearable though, was the wind blowing the fine sand into our faces, stinging like a thousand tiny needles. Still, there was nothing we could do except make the best of it. Something the Pals were becoming good at.
To our horror, we were told that rations were to be cut. Something about a break in supply lines was the reason given. Not good news, and of course the morale of the men began to suffer. This was worsened by the middle of January, when the 6th East Lancashire Regiment arrived in the next camp on their way back from Gallipoli. Many of the Pals had relatives serving in this regiment as regular or territorial soldiers, and so there were several family get-togethers. The news conveyed to us by these men was bad. Over two hundred of their comrades had been killed at Gallipoli, dying in terrible conditions and with little hope of victory according to some of the more outspoken regulars. Even the survivors were a terrible sight to behold. It was one of our sergeants who remarked, as we headed back to our camp one night, "Their eyes are dead, died through seeing too much death."

How right he was. They were here, and no doubt grateful to be alive, but part of them had died in Gallipoli. I wondered how Amy's two brothers had met their end. Quickly, I hoped. Sam went very quiet on hearing their stories, and he spent long hours not speaking to anybody. Goodness knows what thoughts were going through his head.

Our stay in Port Said was not too difficult or arduous. Our tasks consisted mainly of guard duty or travelling to the Suez Canal acting as lookouts on ships. Eventually our mail from home arrived, and I received a letter from both my parents and Amy. All seemed well with them. Many of the women in the town had got jobs acting as replacements for the men, but strangely not Amy. In fact her letter seemed rather subdued, probably because of the imminent death of her mother. My parents were both keeping up with the news of the war, and father, as ever, was not optimistic about the outcome. I looked up from his letter and glanced at our body of men, thinking there was no need to worry. The Accrington Pals are ready for action, we'll save the country, single handed if need be. I wrote back to them, but all our mail had to be read and censored, so I kept my messages as brief as possible. I did manage to tell Amy I loved her. No doubt the censor would let that go, after all no details of our whereabouts could be gleaned from that. Sam didn't get any post from home, but he got a letter from Bronwen, which he took away and read in private. He only ever wrote to her, nobody else.

On our rest days, I used to go across to the harbour and sketch the ships entering and leaving. It was only later that I found out that my actions were closely watched. Someone had suggested I might be a spy, using my sketches to record the movements of the British ships. I soon gave up that little hobby when I found out, destroying all my sketches at the same time. I stuck to playing the mouth organ after that.

We didn't know it at the time, but the start of March was to see us enter a new and bloody chapter in all our lives. We set sail from Port Said on March 2nd on S.S. Llandovery Castle, bound for France. When we found out our destination there was a feeling of relief running through the men, mixed, I suspect, with a feeling of trepidation. Word had got through to us that the war in France was not progressing too well, and that we were being shipped over to take part in a huge battle in order to drive the Germans back across the border into their own land. We Pals felt proud to be involved. We Pals couldn't wait to fight. We Pals couldn't wait to die.

After a week at sea, we finally arrived in Marseilles on March 8th. The following day we set foot on French soil for the first time as we marched to the waiting trains. We all looked sunburnt, fit and well. Our time in Egypt had done us good. We were ready, or so we thought.

The train journey was terrible. There seemed to be several carriages too few to accommodate us all. As a result of this, we were squashed into the compartments, made to sit on uncomfortable wooden seats, making sleep and relaxation very difficult. Food appeared less and less and the weather turned colder as we journeyed north. Our nightmare train journey ended, two days later, at a place called Pont Remy. We were herded off the train feeling cold, hungry and thoroughly miserable. We were marched about six miles to the village of Huppy where we were given billets in an assortment of farm buildings. My barn was in the corner of a farmyard; it was here that I first came across the horror of rats. They were everywhere, scurrying across the floor and the beams. We slept on filthy straw, and very quickly we became infested with lice. I don't think I was ever free of those obnoxious little things until the end of the war. It was no good complaining, though some did, but sympathy was in short supply as everyone was suffering the same problems.

So this was France. We had all joined up knowing we might end up here, but deep down most of us never actually believed it would come to this. The weather was freezing, and several cases of frostbite were reported. The featureless landscape stretched before us under a grey humourless sky. The jollity of training had now gone, to be replaced with an air of depression. My thoughts were constantly of Amy. Would I ever see her again? The prospect seemed to be growing more unlikely as the days wore on. Hunger was a new threat to our well being. I seemed to have a gnawing pain in my stomach most of the time. A group of us managed to make the local farmers understand that we wanted to buy some eggs, in an effort to supplement our meagre rations. I knew no French, but soon picked up the fact that "oeuf" meant egg.

Before long we were on the march again, heading ever nearer to the front line. Finally, after a journey of some eight days, we arrived at a place called Colincamps, about a mile behind the lines. As we arrived, all we could do was gaze in amazement at the place. Wherever you looked there seemed to be soldiers, every one of them busy rushing around from place to place. There were ambulances, staff cars, supply carts, all making our progress through the camp difficult as we had to keep stepping to one side to allow them to pass. The roads, so important for a supply line, were constantly being repaired by men who looked tired and worn out. Everywhere we looked there seemed to be burnt out ruins of buildings, destroyed by heavy shelling. Spent cartridge cases littered the streets. Worse than this, we could hear in the distance the sound of the cannons, barking out their defiance to the enemy. The night was worse, when the glow of burning buildings lit up the skyline. I suppose we finally got used to this and closed our minds to the horrors. I hoped I would never witness these weapons of death at close quarters. A forlorn hope.

We were given billets in a barn at one end of the village. Inside were wooden bunks arranged in tiers. This was to be our home for an unknown period of time. We were, of course, in a state of readiness to move at a moment's notice. Uncomfortable as it was, it would come to seem like heaven compared to the trenches we would inhabit barely a mile away.

As the month of March wore on, we got used to the squalor in which we lived. Perhaps I should have said tolerated. It was normal to see rats running about, seemingly unafraid of human presence. Indeed, some of the soldiers returning from more advanced positions said that they had actually seen the rats feeding on the remains of their poor dead comrades. Hard to believe as it was, I saw no reason to dispute their stories. Sam spent more time deep in his silent moods. It was almost as if he had decided he was not going to come out of this nightmare with his life. Occasionally, I noticed him smiling to himself and nodding. If he saw me looking he would quickly turn away, averting his empty eyes, as if embarrassed by his thoughts.

Much of our time in reserve was spent doing fatigues and general jobs around the camp. Many of the lads were keen to see some real action, and constantly asked their sergeants when they would move forward. The answer was always the same: wait and see. I suspect that information

was known only to officers much further up the chain of command.
During our rest periods I tried some more sketching, having begged some paper and a pencil from a Lieutenant. I sharpened the pencil with my bayonet and positioned myself to one side of the camp and tried to take in all the destruction around me. The half ruined buildings, the skeletal trees, the groups of soldiers sitting round waiting for their next job, wondering when they would be called into action. I even did a quick sketch of Sam as he leaned against a tree. I never showed him the picture; the haunted look in his eyes was too accurate. A Captain happened to see one of my pictures and asked if I could sketch him. He wanted to send the picture back to his wife and family. I felt pleased that my talents had been recognised by an officer, and gladly obliged. He positioned himself leaning against a ruined wall, with his pipe in the corner of his mouth. He was delighted with the finished picture, and rewarded me with half a crown.
After this, more and more men asked me to sketch them, I had quite a good little business going. The money I got I hid carefully at the bottom of my kit bag. One of the lads joked with me, saying that he had heard that Lieutenant Colonel Rickman wanted his picture drawing, but was afraid to ask. So I became one of the unofficial Pals' artists. Some of the scenes I sketched became the basis for my paintings after the war.
By early April, a buzz went around the battalion. We were supposed to be moving closer to the action, and after the weeks of waiting this proved to be a relief. As with all rumours, you were never sure of their accuracy until they happened. But happen it did. Sam and I were in one of the first groups of men to be guided down the communication trenches leading towards the front line. We marched in

total silence, not knowing what we would be called upon to do. Perhaps our party were to go over the top and attack the Germans right there and then. Ridiculous thoughts, I agree, but at the time they seemed very real. Our progress was slow. The ground was thick with mud, which stuck to our boots making a horrible squelching noise as we moved, and slowing us down terribly. The only relief we got was when we walked on the duckboards, until they, too, sank in the horrible slime. All trenches were constructed in a zigzag style so that there was never more than a few yards of straight trench. This, I was told later, was to stop an enemy soldier arriving in the trench and firing straight down the line and wiping out a long line of men all at once. One thing it did do was to slow down our progress. Carrying full kit made life even more difficult as we picked our way forward. I walked behind the stooping frame of Sam in the line. He said not a word, nor did he turn round.

As we neared the front line, the trenches gradually got deeper and better constructed, and the sides were shored up with sturdy wooden supports. We soon realised that going over the top was to be reserved for another day, and were told to perform repair and construction duties on the advanced trenches. This was backbreaking work, but we did it as well as we were able, knowing one day a solidly constructed trench wall might save our lives. As Sam dug away in the trench, he unearthed a previous occupant, long dead and forming part of the wall. Neither of us had seen a dead body at such close quarters before, and were unsure of what to do. Our Corporal came across and helped us dig him out. We called for a stretcher-bearer to take the body to a communal grave behind the lines. To the day I die, I will never forget the

sight of his half-eaten face and twisted, blackened limbs being carried away.
Each section of men remained at the front for 24 hours before being relieved. We positioned ourselves in a dugout towards the back of the trench and well protected by sandbags. Here we were given hot tea and a meal of bread and cheese. As we ate, to our horror, rats, even bigger than the ones we had seen back at camp, appeared. This war must have been wonderful for the rat population of France, with all the dead bodies to feed on. Shortly after the meal we got our first taste of what was to become an accepted part of our life for the next months. As we stood at the front of the trench, positioned on the fire step with our heads just below the sandbag barrier, there was a loud screaming noise, getting louder and closer by the second. As if by instinct, we all threw ourselves onto the ground, putting our hands over our heads as we fell. A shell burst uncomfortably near us and a shower of muddy, wet soil tumbled into the trench. This was followed by another, and another, until I was sure that one shell must score a direct hit in our trench. I offered my soul to God and closed my eyes and thought of Amy. This was how I was going to die.
It seemed like hours, but it must only have been a few minutes later, when the shelling got less and eventually stopped. One by one we lifted our heads up and stared at each other, the smell of burning powder stinging our nostrils and making our eyes water. I wanted to retch. One young lad, only sixteen, started weeping and crying out for his mother. He stood up and made to climb out of the trench next to where Sam was brushing the soil from his uniform.
"Stop him !" yelled someone.

Sam looked up at him and, to my horror, took no notice. A corporal dived across the trench and held onto his feet, pulling him back just in time. The lad fell back into the trench shaking with fear. Sam remained unmoved by the incident, and continued brushing away the soil. Nobody commented on the incident, but I had another example of Sam's coldness and apparent indifference to the plight of others. I wondered if he would have done the same had it been me. I hoped never to find out the answer. I looked straight into his eyes across the trench; they seemed even more expressionless than usual. Not for the first time, I shuddered.

That night, as we settled down for sleep, we placed our helmets over our faces in an effort to stop the rats feasting on us. I remember waking up from my fitful slumbers to see an enormous rat crawling across my leg. I flapped at the monster with my hand, but it just gave me a look of total indifference before moving away. We were relieved the following afternoon, and we made our way back down the communication trench, arriving at Colincamps some three hours later. We had seen our first real action and, more important, we had survived.

We sank into our beds, uncomfortable as they were, and slept soundly, disturbed only by the distant rumble of the guns serving up another helping of death and destruction. The horrors were truly being driven home to us. As parties returned from the front line in subsequent days, we heard of our friends being wounded or killed by the shells or flying shrapnel. I suppose our group were lucky, as none of us received so much as a scratch, certainly not delivered by the enemy, though Sam did fall and twist his ankle quite badly and had to be almost carried back to Colincamps by myself and another Pal.

Our third visit to the front line was quite a frightening experience. We were directed to open up some new trenches deep into no man's land, to serve as listening or observation posts. This meant we were really under fire for a while. I remember coming back to the trench almost deafened by the noise of the shells. On one such excursion forward some Germans, having guessed our intentions, had also advanced and started to throw hand grenades towards the trenches we were digging. One man I later found to be a sergeant called Rigby dashed out carrying some of our own hand grenades and attacked the Germans, totally alone. That single act of courage earned him the Military Medal, and proved to be the Pals' first battle award. I watched his return to the trench, thinking I would never be able to bring myself to perform such an act of bravery. It is amazing the reserves of courage you can muster when you have to.

At the end of our first eight-day front line duty we were stood down and rested for two weeks. I say rested, but this was not strictly the case, as we were found plenty to do behind the lines. For example, we had to carry ammunition to the forward positions. Back and forth we went, often in the dark and in pouring rain. This was described as "donkey work", and it was not hard to understand why. All this was in preparation for what was called by officers and men alike the "Big Push". Nobody knew what this would entail, or indeed when it would take place. I had a sinking feeling that it would not be long. Despite the terrible conditions we had to endure, the spirit of the Pals remained as good as ever. I knew as I looked around the camp that I would be proud to fight and die with any one of them. I felt sure Accrington would not be ashamed of its sons when the time came.

Sam and I spent a lot of time together talking about all we had done since our first meeting in Accrington. He confided in me that he didn't think he would come out of this alive. I tried to be more optimistic, pointing out that we had a far superior army and we were being led by professional soldiers who knew how to conduct a war. Sam was not convinced, and he repeated that he wouldn't see the end of the war. Nothing I said could persuade him otherwise.

May became June, and we had done our second spell at the front line. We were now much less terrified by the noise of the shells bursting overhead, and indeed hardly even noticed it. The knowledge that the next day might be your last takes your mind off small discomforts. The rats were still there, but we treated them now as an inevitable part of trench life. What we didn't like were night patrols, when we climbed out of the trench and laid down more barbed wire. This was a dangerous occupation, especially when a flare went off and you were silhouetted against the skyline. This often brought a volley of fire from the enemy snipers. The only answer was to fling yourself to the ground and pray. It seemed to work, as once again I always managed to tumble back to the relative safety of the trench. Every night I thanked God for having lived through anther day. I wondered as I prayed, did the enemy thank the same God ?

When we were replaced at the front line, for the last time we rehearsed for our part of the action. Our battalion was to form part of an attack on the village of Serre, perched on top of a hill. The more astute of us realised this would place us at a disadvantage, having to advance uphill. Our fears were allayed by the officers who assured us that after the bombardment on the enemy's trenches no

Germans would be left alive. This gave us great heart. It was almost as if victory was assured.

So rehearsals began. We were all told of our objective and how to go about achieving it. The attack was practised until we all knew what we were doing, or so we thought. All we had to do was to leave the trench system when we were told, and walk slowly towards the enemy lines. They, we were assured once again, would all be dead, and any barbed wire laid to prevent our progress would also have been destroyed by the heavy shellfire. We would capture the enemy trench and then move forward once more. This was to be done in waves. It was hoped that the town of Serre would fall later that day. The plan worked a treat on the mock battlefield, marked out with tape, well behind the lines.

We knew things were getting near when the battalion headed towards the front line trench system on 24th of June. I remember the date clearly as it turned out to be Sam's birthday. I remember playing "Happy Birthday" on the mouth organ as we marched along. The senior officers didn't seem to mind too much, but I still only played it the once. He never commented. This day also coincided with the start of a huge artillery onslaught which went on for five days non-stop. I thought that no German could ever survive such a pounding. What we didn't know was that the enemy trench system was much deeper than ours, meaning they were well protected. We prepared ourselves for the off on the 28th of June, only to be told that the bad weather had delayed the attack for a couple of days. Some of us were relieved whilst others suffered the agony of waiting even longer. Sam seemed to be oblivious to it all, staring as usual at nothing in particular. If only I could have got behind that blank look and discovered his thoughts.

The barrage of artillery fire seemed endless. Surely the enemy and their murderous barbed wire must now be destroyed, making our advance more or less a formality. We got to talking as we waited, about how we would all be treated as heroes when we returned to Accrington. The parades, the cheering, the celebrations. Those that weren't with us would want to buy us a drink and listen to the tales of our bravery. Amy kept appearing in my mind's eye. Her smiling face, her beautiful auburn hair, our marriage. Never had I felt so positive. Things might be all right after all.

June 30th saw the battalion paraded for the last time. We were to set off for the front later that day. Each man was issued with his pack, consisting of a gas-helmet, a groundsheet, a water bottle, iron rations and four empty sand bags, to repair any trenches we were lucky enough to take in battle. On top of our rifle, bayonet and bullets this amounted to about sixty pounds, quite enough to carry given the difficulty of the ground we would have to advance over, pitted as it must be by now with hundreds of shell holes. We marched off to take our places at the front line. As usual we made our way along the complicated system of communication trenches, not an easy journey, and progress was slow. The zigzag system proved to be difficult for us, especially where the water, mud and slime covered our knees. We followed a carefully laid out system of direction tapes no doubt positioned to speed our way to the front and almost certain glory. Some of our comrades fell in the difficult conditions, but we always managed to help them back onto their feet to continue their journey. I remember marching past a number of small wooden crosses, stacked row upon row against a pile of stones, no doubt for future use. I could not hazard a guess at the number. Would my name be carved on one of them, I wondered?

After a break for some hot tea and a hard biscuit, we were soon moving again. The officers urged us forward, conscious of the strict time schedule to be kept. Just before three in the morning we arrived at our forward trenches near two small wooded areas called Matthew Copse and Mark Copse. The trenches were in a poor state of repair, but hopefully we would not have to fight in them, only advance. There was no thought of defence in the mind of our generals. Meanwhile the artillery was still pounding away at the German front line. We stood or sat in the trenches and waited for the order to attack, which was due to be given at 7.30 a.m. On our previous visits to the front line, there had always been enough room to be relatively comfortable. Not so now; we were all squashed in together. The smell of sweat and unwashed bodies permeated the whole atmosphere.

According to our captain, we had some four hours to wait before we would be called into action, so we settled down in our particular trench to wait. Some of us sang our favourite songs and smoked. It was a pleasant and normal way to pass the time, and it took our minds off the next few hours. I suppose there was a sense of relief that soon the waiting would be over, permanently for many of our number.

As the daylight slowly appeared over the horizon, I got down on my knees in the filthy slime and prayed, then I leaned against a wall of sandbags and thought of my parents and Amy. Still the bombardment went on. Surely there could be nothing left alive. At 7.20, the word went down the line that we were to fix bayonets. At the same time the tremendous roar of our guns ceased and there was a deathly hush. The silence made as much noise as the artillery fire. The order went up to fix bayonets. My hands were shaking as I pushed the weapon of death into position on the end of my rifle. Sam was doing the same, having contrived to be next to me in the trench. I looked across at him and mouthed "Good luck". He smiled back at me, without any emotion at all. We faced the front of the trench and waited. Shortly after that, whistles blew and the order went up that we were to go. I scrambled up, the wet loose earth making me tumble backwards. I tried again, not really thinking what I was doing. I was conscious that to my left Sam was doing the same thing. Not one man flinched or turned back. Our heads appeared over the parapet of the trench at exactly 7.30, and all hell broke loose....

Chapter 15

ALBERT LORD'S STORY: BETRAYAL

Sara's head was resting gently on my shoulder. She was fast asleep. I put down the manuscript and woke her gently. She was none too pleased to be woken from her slumbers, and said as much. I carefully gathered her in my arms and carried her upstairs. I deposited her on the bed and let her resume her sleep, covering her with the duvet cover. I kissed her lovingly on the cheek and returned downstairs to carry on with the rest of the text. I poured myself a whisky, lit a cigarette and took up the document once more and continued reading, feeling sure I was getting to the end. I flicked through the remaining pages; there was not much to go. I felt fully awake; this time I was determined to finish.

> *I suppose even the best laid plans sometimes go astray. No sooner had we climbed out of the trench, the murderous onslaught of the German machine guns*

started, followed by artillery fire. Sam and I walked forward up the slope towards what seemed to be certain death. My heart gave a little leap of pride as not one man flinched, retreated or showed any signs of fear. We would show them. We were the Accrington Pals. The noise of gunfire was overwhelming. Smoke filled the air until we were unsure of which direction we were walking in. On either side of us, men were falling slowly to the ground, bodies arching backwards as they breathed their last. Not certain of what to do - our training had not prepared us for this - we kept on moving until we, too, would be cut to ribbons. I saw Charlie Sykes, the Pals' geographer, on my left getting his face blown in two by the murderous crossfire of the enemy. Sam and I kept together step for step. Then it happened. Sam was hit, his body falling slowly forwards as he joined the ranks of those lying face down in the mud. I gave a little cry of sorrow, before I too felt a searing pain in my thigh, causing me to tumble into an old shell hole. My helmet flew off as I hit the ground, my head struck something hard, and I remembered no more.

When I regained consciousness, I was still lying in the hole, which afforded me some protection. It was still light, though the sky was thick with smoke, and there was a tremendous noise going on all around me. Men were calling out, shouting to each other or just crying in agony or fear. I was aware of a terrible pain in my leg. I looked down and saw my khaki trousers were covered in blood. I examined the wound and saw to my relief that apparently the bullet had only hit the side of my thigh, and the bleeding had almost stopped. I pulled myself up and tried to crawl to one side of the hole. This movement gave me great pain, causing me to sink back to the ground, putting my hand out to steady myself as I did so. To my horror, I touched something soft and sticky. I looked across and saw I had put my hand in a dead soldier's face. In truth it was only half a face. The rest was goodness knows where. Pulling my hand away quickly, I looked around the shell hole. Other bodies were all around, at least five. All were dead, their eyes staring into oblivion. One poor soul was virtually cut in two, his insides spilling out into the mud. I was promptly sick.

My desire to get out of this hellhole was foremost in my mind, so, trying to ignore the pain, I attempted to pull myself to the lip of the crater. Carefully easing my head above the rim, I looked around. The scene of death and destruction still lives in me today. Bodies were everywhere. Bodies twisted in agony, bodies caught on barbed wire and, even worse, wounded men writhing on the ground and wailing. The wound in my leg was worsening. I glanced down at it, and at my trousers soaked in blood. I knew I would not be able to move far without some sort of assistance. Once more I slid down, the mud, or was it blood, speeding my return to the bottom of the crater. I was doubled up with the searing pain in my leg, caused by the exertion of dragging myself around. To make matters worse, my leg was bleeding worse than before. I had to stop the blood somehow, or die. I managed to pull the shirt off one of the lifeless bodies and made myself a makeshift bandage, pulling it as tight as I dared round my leg. The effort of this caused beads of sweat to roll down my face. I was almost passing out with the pain. This torment seemed to be worth it, though, and the bleeding was finally reduced to a slight weeping through the bandage. I lay there for goodness knows how long. I suppose I prayed as the battle raged around me. I lapsed back into unconsciousness.

A shower of soil hitting the ground nearby brought me round. I suddenly became aware of someone else in the hole behind me. Rather unsteadily I turned round, pointing my rifle in the general direction of the movement, not knowing if this new arrival were friend or foe. I looked straight into the expressionless eyes of Sam. I cannot put into words the feeling of relief that came over me at that moment.
"Sam, dear Sam ! I thought you were killed ! I saw you fall," I called.
My eyes examined him. There was no evidence of him being wounded at all - no blood, no torn uniform, nothing.
"Things aren't always as they seem," he replied.
"But how .....?"
"Let's just say, it seemed like a good idea to hit the ground at that moment," he said, cutting me short.
Realisation flooded through my slowly recovering brain. He hadn't been hit at all, it was a clever trick. He knew I had worked it out, and for a second or two he looked ashamed.
"I won't tell, Sam," I whispered. "Just let's get back to our lines. I need help, I can't walk."
He looked down at my leg, which was still weeping blood. "I can't do it," he replied. "I'm not going back to the lines. I've worked it out. When it gets dark, I'm going to head that way."
He nodded in a northerly direction, running roughly parallel with the lines.
"The fighting is less up there. I think I can hide out and escape. I'll try to make my way to the coast, and then we'll see."
"Sam, you can't ! They'll catch you."
He held up his hand again, pointing out beyond the mud.

"Have you seen the mess out there?" he snarled, nodding towards the battlefield. *"There are men cut in two, men with their heads blown off, corpses hanging from trees. No one will even know I'm missing. In fact they'll think I'm some poor sod that's been blown apart."*
We both ducked instinctively as a shell burst nearby, showering us with earth.
"It's foolproof," he laughed. "The only problem is you. All the bloody shell holes around, and I had to pick the one you were in! Now what do I do?"
He looked across at me, as if turning all the options over in his mind.
"I'm sorry, but I can't let even you spoil my plans. I leave when night falls. It's odd that you helped me overcome my fear of the dark. Thank you, Albert."
He gave me a mock salute.
It was all too clear to me. He intended to leave me here to die. He wasn't going to help me back to the safety of our trenches.
"You can't leave me here like this," I groaned at him. "It's murder."
He smiled his chilling smile at me.
"Murder, you say? So tell me, what's that?"
Again he flung his hand towards the carnage all around.
"The Generals, they're the murderers. We have to survive the best we can. It's people like us who keep this bloody war going. Well, I've had enough of this stuff about being desperate to get at the evil Hun. Tell me, Albert, what would happen to their precious war if we all turned round and went home, eh? No, I'm sorry, you'll have to take your chance, though I don't hold out much hope for you."
I knew he would not change his mind. I would be left here to die, by someone I thought was a friend. I had to do something. I made a move towards my rifle in an attempt

to take him prisoner and force him back to the lines. Seeing my intention, he took a mighty swing at me, connecting with my shoulder, and sent my rifle flying across the hole out of reach, knocking me further into the mud. Shock waves of pain passed through my body, causing me to pass out. When I came round again, nothing had changed. He was still sitting staring at me, his face showing no emotion or regret. I knew I could expect no mercy or assistance from this man.
"Doesn't our friendship count for anything, all we've been through?" I pleaded.
He shook his head, saying not a word, and looked the other way.
We remained in the crater until nightfall. Neither of us spoke again. The sounds of battle diminished, to be replaced with the howls of wounded men lying in No Man's Land. Sam cautiously stood up and began to climb to the top of the crater. Without even saying goodbye, he disappeared into the darkness, leaving me to die. With a tremendous struggle, I managed to pull myself just above the lip of the hole. Better to be shot by a sniper than die in the foul earth at the bottom. It was useless. Pain overtook me once more, and I slipped back into a fitful state of semi-consciousness....

I put the manuscript down on the table and took a large drink of my whisky. I lit another cigarette from the first, and blew the smoke out across the room. I was repulsed by this callous action, but what was worse was that the light was beginning to dawn on me. It was a situation too horrible to contemplate. I continued with the text, hardly daring to read what was to come next.

The next thing I remember was a pair of rough hands turning me over, and a voice -

"Here's another. Still alive, but only just."
I opened my eyes and saw a dirty, half-smiling face staring down at me. Relief spread through my body. How the stretcher-bearers had found me, amongst all the other wounded men, remains a mystery to this day, but they did.
"Don't worry chum, we'll soon have you out of here. Harry, bring the stretcher."
I felt myself being loaded roughly onto a stretcher and carefully being carried out of the hole and back to safety. As I bounced along, the agony from my leg doubling with every movement, I prayed as I'd never done before, giving thanks for my deliverance from death. The next few hours passed in a daze, but eventually I arrived at a dressing station where my wound was attended to.
"Another hour, and that leg may have had to come off. Infection would have set in," said a medical orderly, as he indicated I should be moved to join some other wounded men lying on makeshift beds.
"As it is, it's back to England for you, for some rest and convalescence."
I smiled at him and weakly asked,
"Where's Sam?"
" Sam ? Sam who ? There are probably dozens of Sams in here. Which one do you want ?"
I shook my head.
"It doesn't matter," I replied. "No doubt I'll find him sometime."
Just before I fell asleep I vowed to myself that if Sam were still alive I would move heaven and earth to confront him with his actions. With that, I closed my eyes and pulled the coarse blanket over my head, in an effort to drown out the groans of the wounded men lying all around.

The next few days were something of a blur. I recall being loaded up onto a stretcher and being carried onto a train, every movement sending waves of excruciating pain through my leg. Gradually, I drifted off into a merciful sleep. I eventually woke up again in a proper bed. I propped myself up as best I could and gazed around me. I was in what appeared to be a hospital ward, with many beds down both sides of the room.
"Where the hell am I?" I groaned.
A man in the next bed turned his head towards me.
"In hospital," came the rather obvious reply. "Etaples, I think."
I collapsed back onto my pillow, the hell from my leg proving too much to bear. I closed my eyes and tried to recall what had happened. It came flooding back to me all too easily. The attack, the wound, the shell hole, and Sam. I shuddered to think of his action. I began to wonder what had become of him. Had he escaped? And where was he now? This proved too much for my tortured brain, and I once again fell into a blissful sleep.
I suppose it was the next day when I awoke again, feeling much better. The pain in my leg was subsiding into a dull ache, and I was starting to think more clearly. Amy came over to my bed and changed the dressing. She seemed pleased that there was no sign of infection. I smiled at her kind gentle face and I closed my eyes. Amy was looking after me. I opened my eyes and it was not Amy, just a nurse I had never seen before.
Later that day a doctor came and told me I was to return to hospital in England, until my wound had recovered. So in the early afternoon I was put on a train bound for Calais and my return to England. I wasn't afforded the luxury of a stretcher on board the ship, I was just propped up on an old wooden bench. Sitting next to me was a

soldier, not much older than I was, with a bandage round his head and over one eye. We got to talking. His name was Joe, and he had apparently been wounded at the same time as me, but further along the front. He was from Barnsley and also a volunteer. He had heard that the battle had gone badly and that the " Big Push" had been a disaster. He also said that the stretcher-bearers who had taken him to a dressing station had told him that most of the battalions in our part of the line had been virtually wiped out. This proved to be correct. Like Joe, I was one of the lucky survivors. Both of us felt terribly alone. We had lost our Pals.

The channel crossing passed without incident, and before long we had arrived in Dover. The white cliffs were a beautiful sight as we docked in the harbour. When the boat was tied up and made secure, gangplanks were put in place and we were taken off the ship and sent to hospitals for our convalescence. Being from the north of England, Joe and I ended up near Manchester. I cannot remember exactly where it was, nor can I remember its name. It was good to be away from the horrors of war, though I was told that my wound was not bad enough to keep me from the front for too long.

As soon as I could, I wrote to Amy and my parents informing them of my whereabouts, and to tell them I was still alive. I got a letter from my father telling me about the disaster of the battle. Many of the men who had volunteered with me had been killed in action, their names recorded endlessly each day in the paper. The town of Accrington was in mourning for its brave sons. Amy's letter said much the same thing. I felt depressed. I almost wished I had been killed with so many of my friends. Since I was so close to Accrington, my parents, accompanied by Amy, actually managed to visit me on one

occasion. I cannot tell of the joy I felt seeing them again. Yet their visit was tinged with sadness. As expected, Amy's mother had died, and she was now alone in the world. My parents had spent more time with her. The three of them exchanged secretive glances, but said nothing further. They were looking forward to her becoming their daughter-in-law as soon as the horror was over. I looked across at Amy, and noted her face was much paler than I remembered, with perhaps sadness in those eyes, a feature I had not seen before. She saw me studying her, and hastily looked at the floor.
I asked my father if there was any news of Sam. Apparently he had been posted as missing in action, but his body had not been recovered. Again they looked at each other and changed the subject. It was as if they knew something but were not prepared to share it with me. I didn't pursue it at this the point, I was just too weak. No doubt I would find out everything in good time. When they had gone I was left alone once more, allowing me to brood on what had happened.
Joe became a constant companion, and we helped each other through a difficult time. You can imagine the shock I got when he finally had his bandages removed and I found he had lost an eye. For him the war was over. It was a sad day when he finally was allowed to return to his native Barnsley. We embraced each other like brothers as he left. We promised to keep in touch, but we never did.
I spent many long hours reading my Bible, which by some miracle had been returned to me, rescued from the inside pocket of my uniform. The mud-stained book was a comfort to me, as always. I jotted down four more biblical quotations, which to me seemed more than appropriate under the circumstances. I smiled to myself at the irony of the word, or in my case name, "Lord" that seemed to

crop up. I felt sure one day someone would read the quotations and understand.

I had a long time to think about the incident with Sam. I could not believe he had done this despicable thing. I even got to thinking I had imagined the whole affair. Yet how could that be, when everything else was so real? I was unsure what to do. I knew nobody would be interested if I told the officers at the hospital. They would probably put it down to the ramblings of a wounded man. I felt I had to do something, but I could not think what. In all probability he had been killed within a short time of leaving me. Then again, he might just have managed to escape. I doubted I would ever find out.

As soon as my leg was able to support my full weight again, I was encouraged to walk with the aid of crutches, initially in the ward, and eventually around the grounds of the hospital, using just a walking stick. My increased mobility meant that I could talk to the other wounded men. I counted my blessings, seeing some of them. Many had limbs missing; one poor soul had lost both his legs, after gangrene had set in before he could get treatment. One man, who had had his arm blown off, he told me he was a keen cricketer in civilian life. I felt a fraud, my injury being so slight compared to theirs.

My leg was finally fully healed, and the day came when I was discharged, pronounced fit to return to active service. Needless to say, I did not wish to go back to France, but I had little choice. I was posted initially to the training reserve battalion in Shropshire before being sent back to join my old battalion in France in October of 1916. I managed to write one more letter to Amy before I boarded the boat at Plymouth, taking me back across the channel. As always, I expressed my love for her and promised to write as soon as possible.

I suppose I could count myself lucky to be sent back to my own battalion, since many men were being sent to different areas of the front, away from their friends. Such was the fragmentation, after what everyone was now calling the Battle of the Somme.

When I arrived back at Warnimont Wood, I was shocked to see so many men I did not recognise. There were one or two familiar faces, of course, who greeted me like the long lost Pal I was. However, it did not seem like our old battalion somehow. The comradeship of training together somehow seemed to have gone. Some of us old campaigners did try to keep the spirit of the Pals alive, telling some of the new recruits of our adventures earlier in the year. I asked around if anyone knew what had happened to Sam, but there was little response. One man thought he saw him fall shortly after leaving the trench, another swore he spotted him later in the day. Unfortunately everything was confused, and unless a body was found and identified it was impossible to know fully the fate of any one man, just as Sam predicted would happen whilst we were together in the shell hole. He had thought this out very carefully.

The rats were still there, as indeed were the lice. I think it was about a day before I started to feel the familiar itching sensation all over my body. I managed to get into billets with some of the original Pals, and this made me feel much better, though none of us were as naive as before. The excitement of fighting for our country had gone. The disaster of July 1st had driven this out of us. We all realised the futility of it all and the waste of human life - perfectly natural for anyone who had just seen so many friends wiped out in the space of a few minutes. Friends we had trained with for nearly two years, living as we did in one large family. We regarded ourselves as the survivors, and were determined to see this bloody war out for the sake of our fallen comrades. Some of us managed it, thank God.

Christmas came and went, and the year of 1917 finally arrived. Little had happened to upset the routine of life over the last few months. The war seemed to have stopped, except we knew it hadn't because occasionally the guns could be heard booming death over the countryside. There was no mention of another "Big Push".

It was the middle of February when we found ourselves on the move again. We arrived back near Serre, believe it or not, sometime in March. Apparently the enemy had withdrawn and the area around Serre needed filling and fortifying. It was here that we had the most horrible of duties to perform. A party of us was sent out into what was the old No Man's Land to recover bodies that had lain there since the previous July. The Germans had, thankfully, buried some corpses beneath wooden crosses with their names on, but there were still the remains of many lying just as they had fallen eight months ago. Many of these rotting skeletons were our old Pals, listed as missing. We buried each body with the respect it deserved, and a Lieutenant recorded the names as best he could. Sam was not amongst them, though there were many bodies which could not be identified. He could have been any one of them, or of course none of them. Each day, after this duty, many of us were physically sick, and all were mentally scarred for life.

I suppose we should count ourselves lucky that the sector of the front we were on was one of spectacular inactivity and the battalion was able to reorganise, supplemented as it was by the arrival of more new recruits in late February. Being one of the old hands, as it were, I was promoted to corporal and given the job of keeping my eye on some of the ridiculously young newcomers. Probably they were only one, maybe two years younger than I was, but years behind in terms of experience and bitterness. They were keen to hear of the battles, and what it was like to go over the top, but I was always reluctant to tell them too much. They would have to face it themselves one day. My mouth organ had disappeared - no doubt it is still buried in the mud somewhere - but I managed to borrow another one and continued my duties as section musician. I also resumed my sketching duties; there was a new crop of faces to be drawn.

I think it was towards the middle of March, though many of us were unsure of the date by now, that we were given the orders to march north, away from the accursed Somme. I remember the road we took ran parallel to the front line, but a considerable distance from it. The roads were in a poor state of repair and were often ankle deep in mud. This hindered our progress, as we continually had to dig out the assortment of carts and gun carriages that we took with us. My leg ached every night, and I found it very painful as we set off the next day. One morning it was so bad that I was allowed to ride on a cart for the whole of the journey, much to the envy of some of the others.

It was nice to go through the towns en route and actually see buildings that had not been totally destroyed by the enemy's heavy artillery. French people were selling food from little tables as we marched past. Many of us took advantage of this service, and we feasted heartily on cheese and fresh bread after our long walks. It was a taste of normality, after the unreal world we had lived in for so long, though I suppose I was luckier than some, having spent time in England resting in hospital.

Many of the little villages we passed through were very picturesque, and I would have loved to have stayed in any one of them and done some sketches. Trees, they were my latest source of enjoyment. Around the battlefield of the Somme, they had been blasted to tiny stumps; here they were whole, and at that time of year were just starting to show their new crop of leaves. I think that despite the long march and the poor living quarters most of the men benefited from this period. I certainly did. It was at night, as I lay in my bed, that my thoughts turned to Sam. I could still not come to terms with his action and, I am ashamed to admit it, I was starting to think of some sort of revenge. Not the best sentiments from a committed Christian, but I couldn't imagine the situation would ever arise. No, he would be long dead by now.

We eventually arrived at our latest destination, the town of Merville, about a week after our departure from the Somme. It was heaven to think that the next day would not see us leaving for yet another weary walk. We were billeted in the town itself, which gave us time to look around the shops and interesting buildings, many of which I sketched and gave to my comrades as souvenirs. How many of them ended up, like their owners, in a pool of blood, I couldn't hazard a guess.

There was even a restaurant in the town, and we had our evening meals there. One of the lads, called Stephen, announced to our table that he thought he had died and gone to heaven. Not the most tactful remark ever made, knowing that any day we could be called back to action, and really go to heaven, but we all understood what he meant and heartily agreed.

Our peaceful existence continued up to Easter. It was hard to imagine there was a war on as myself and some others stood in the square at Merville watching a religious procession, accompanied by the local band. It reminded me of the old days in Accrington, when the bands played in Oak Hill Park. This, in turn, reminded me of Amy, I wondered how she was coping with life. I felt sure my parents would be looking after her. Since my return to France I had received no mail, and I was starting to feel strangely detached from my loved ones. I attended the church service later in the day, along with many others, who would be going to church for the last time.

The following week, on Easter Sunday to be exact, we were told to move out again. Much to our horror, we were heading south. Surely not back to the Somme ? We found out as we marched that we were to go to a place called Vimy Ridge. This proved to be partially correct, in that we only stayed in that area for a short period, seeing no action. No, we were to continue marching, with only the occasional rest, until we finally stopped about two miles from Arras. Here, to our distress, we were once again issued with the equipment needed for a return to the front. After such a relaxing early spring some of us older hands were sickened by the thought, whilst the youngsters, although showing some nerves, were keen to see action. I didn't know it at the time, but my war was very nearly over.

We moved to the front line on May 3rd, taking over a section called Oppy. Our trenches were very close to the enemy, only yards away it seemed. We were briefed to throw bombs into the enemy trenches, and they, of course, threw their own back. We were truly living in hell, each of us knowing that at any moment we could be blown to bits. This knife-edge existence continued for many days, with only brief rests away from the line. A fortnight later it happened. The day was fairly quiet, but at night all hell

broke loose. Bomb after bomb rained down on our trenches. It was decided that a party should leave the trench and attack a strong German position. I was selected to go with the party. We climbed stealthily out and advanced across No Man's Land. I thought that my time had surely come. There was no way I would survive this. Unfortunately the wire had not been cut, and we struggled to force a way through. By this time the enemy had crept up on both sides and was attacking our party on the flanks. One of the captains on my right found himself entangled in the wire and could not free himself. The enemy was getting ever closer. The order went out to return to the trench, but the captain was stuck, he could not move. To this day I do not know what came over me, but I grabbed the man next to me, shouting to him to try to and untangle the helpless man. Seeing what had happened, he started to tug away at the wire. I knelt down and faced four or five advancing Germans. I began to shoot in their direction, praying my rifle would not jam. It didn't, and the enemy was halted in their tracks, diving for cover right and left.
This bought enough time, and the captain was released, with only a badly gashed leg. I carried on facing the enemy, who had regrouped and were advancing again. I fired once more, hitting one in the stomach. His body arched backwards. Glancing over my shoulder, I saw my two comrades had almost reached safety, and I made to move after them. Keeping low, I scurried towards the trench, and then, turning once more, I was faced by a German no more than two yards away. I fired. Nothing. This was it. He advanced closer. I could see a murderous look in his face, or was it fear? I suppose everyone has a built-in desire to survive, and I was no exception. Without thinking, I thrust forward with my bayonet. It struck home,

not a mortal wound, but enough to put him out of action. Here I turned and fled. About a yard from the trench, I stumbled and fell. I heard a bullet whistle past my head and thud into a sandbag, so that trip probably saved my life. I was not so lucky the next time. Just before I tumbled over the top, I felt the pain of a bullet tearing into my left shoulder. I collapsed into the trench straight into the arms of a sergeant who had witnessed the whole incident. I vaguely remember someone saying, "Well done, lad !" before once again passing out.

I was in yet another dressing station when I came round. My tunic had been removed and discarded. My shoulder was being expertly bandaged. I was sick with pain. I looked questioningly at the doctor.

"It's a bad one, son. Bullet lodged in the shoulder. It will need surgery. That's it for you, lad."

I felt a mixture of relief and nausea as I was transported to a field hospital well behind the lines. The operation, such as it was, took place a day later, and I was told it had been a success, and that there should be no lasting damage as far as they could tell. I lay in my hospital bed, not able to decide if I was unlucky to have been wounded twice, or lucky not to have been killed. Later that day Captain Booth, the man whose life I had probably saved, visited me. He shook me, very carefully, by the hand, offering his thanks at least a dozen times.

"The whole incident was witnessed by several of the men, and your name has been put forward for the Military Medal, for bravery in the field," he announced.

I was lost for words, just managing to stammer out "Anyone would have done it."

I knew one person who wouldn't, but of course I didn't say it out loud.

I was eventually transferred yet again to a hospital on the south coast of England, where a doctor examined my wounded shoulder and proclaimed me unfit for service. Apparently the bullet had damaged the muscles in the shoulder, and to this day I cannot raise my left arm above my head.
Officially discharged, I was allowed to return to Accrington, where I was welcomed back by my parents. I took up residence back in my old room. I had survived the Great War, unlike so many of those brave souls who had marched away with me in 1914.
Accrington had changed. It was a town in mourning, and there was no longer any air of happiness about the place. Few families had come out unscathed. I suppose we were one of the lucky ones. A whole generation of Accrington's sons had been wiped out. I had returned a war hero, with a medal to prove it. My father was enormously proud of his son, but I was more modest about it and only reluctantly told of my time in the trenches to father's friends. I suppose it pained me to be reminded of such a terrible time. Never once did I tell the story of Sam, not to my parents, not even to Amy.
When the war finally ended in 1918 there was great celebration in the town, and I remember going to a street party, where I met some of my comrades. So many were missing. I asked if anyone had heard of Sam, but nobody had. He had not been seen since that fateful day in July 1916. In all probability, he was lying buried in the mud of France. Sam had gone out of my life forever.
Amy and I were married in May 1919, and I was starting to feel much happier with life. The mental and physical scars of the Great War were healing gradually, and I was starting to live a more normal life. The only source of worry was Amy. The first three months of married life

were surprisingly strained. She was reluctant to let me make love to her, always backing off at the crucial moment. I could not understand this, but I did not try to force the issue. I felt sure that everything would take its natural course. I tried hard to persuade Amy to tell me what was troubling her, but always she pleaded for me to give her more time. Even my parents seemed to understand the problem, but they refused to tell me anything, insisting it was a matter to be resolved between man and wife.

It was one night in early August that the final, awful revelation was disclosed to me. It was one of those warm sunny evenings that seem to always stay in the memory. Amy and I were walking through the park, something we did nearly every night during the summer. We sat down on a grassy slope and looked across towards the hills overlooking the town. I knew by now that it was useless to ask Amy about her problems, so I aimlessly sucked a piece of grass, enjoying the peace of the evening. Amy slipped her small hand in mine and kissed me hard on the lips. I was somewhat taken aback by this action and began to respond. As always, Amy pulled away, wiping tears from her eyes.

"I'm so sorry, so, so sorry," she sobbed.

I held her tightly in my arms, her whole body shaking with emotion. I just knew she wanted to tell me something, but she still showed a reluctance. We stayed like that for several minutes until it all came flooding out like a torrent.

"It's Sam," she began.

I spun round, expecting to see his tall frame lumbering towards me.

"No, no, not here. Back in 1915."

I looked in puzzlement at her face,

"What in 1915 ?" I asked.
"He .... brought a letter to me, when he came for his father's funeral."
I remembered the incident quite clearly.
"You never replied."
I looked accusingly at her. Surely this was not the reason for her unhappiness ?
"Well, he called at the house, a big smile on his face, holding your letter. I took it from him and read it, whilst he stood looking out of the window. I remembered my manners just in time, and offered to make him a cup of tea. He accepted and sat down. Father was dead by then, of course, and mother was upstairs in bed. We sat chatting for some time. He told me all about life in the army and how he thought you would soon all be sent off to war."
Amy was crying even more at this point, and I was beginning to fear the worst.
"As he stood up to go, he shook hands, but instead of letting go he .... he held me firmly, by the wrist, and pulled me towards him. He .... kissed me. I struggled and pulled away backwards, but he was too strong. With his free hand he pulled at my blouse, ripping it off at the front. I struggled even more fiercely, and managed to pull my hand away from his, so that I fell backwards onto the floor. He was on me before I could cry out. Oh, Albert, he .... he lifted up the front of my skirt, tearing at my underclothes. I tried to stop him, I did, Albert, but it was useless, he was too strong. He pinned me to the floor and, well.... I'm sure you can imagine what happened next."
Amy threw herself into my arms crying "sorry" over and over again. I held her close to me in silence and total disbelief. She looked up into my face, her eyes red and swollen, awaiting my reaction. Countless thoughts went

through my mind. Everything was clear now. I honestly didn't know what to do or say. We walked back to the house in silence. Somehow the warm evening had turned cold, and I was actually shivering as we arrived back at the front door. I suppose it was shock. Finding out your wife has been raped is bad enough, but to find out she was raped by someone you thought you could trust is even worse, especially when you, yourself had asked him to visit her. If Sam had walked up the street at that point I would have killed him with my bare hands.

We entered the house and went straight upstairs to bed. There was so much more I wanted to know. Amy was feeling relieved that she had told me her dark secret, but questions still had to be answered.

"Why didn't you tell me straight away, a letter or something? You knew where I was at the camp. I could have...."

"Exactly," Amy interrupted. "You would have killed him, and then you would have been hanged for murder. What good would that have done?"

I stared into space, realising the sense of her remark.

"The next day, I went round to see your parents and told them everything. They were so kind, bless them. Without them I probably would have jumped in the canal. They advised me not to tell you, saying you had enough to worry about at the time, so .... we kept quiet."

I nodded in understanding, and put my arm round her and stroked her silken hair. I looked into her eyes and knew immediately there was more to come. I prompted her to continue. She looked up at me with tears welling in her eyes again.

"I think you've guessed," she whispered.

I averted my eyes, fearing the next sentence.

"I discovered in January that I was carrying a child. You can imagine the shame I felt. Your parents were very kind, and they helped me all they could. My own mother never knew, of course, thank goodness. She died without suspecting a thing."
"What happened .... to the child ?"
"I lost it after ten weeks, which I suppose was a blessing in many ways."
I fell silent for several minutes, trying to take in the awful revelations. I could feel the hate inside me welling up. This man, who had left me for dead in France, had blighted my life once again. I clenched my fists in a gesture of despair, not really knowing what to do or say.
"I'm sorry, I'm so sorry," Amy said once more.
"You've nothing to be sorry for," I replied, holding her closer to me. "It's not your fault."
I could not really look at her, or at anything, for the murderous thoughts that were swirling round my head. We lay in each other's arms for a long time, neither of us speaking, until sleep spared us the misery we both felt. In the days that followed, that great healer, time, took over, and the whole sordid affair was talked through over and over again. There was little either of us could do. Amy seemed greatly relieved that she had finally told me what had happened in 1915, and if anything our relationship became even closer. We finally consummated our marriage a month later, and my son was conceived. My parents realised that I knew everything and they awaited my reaction. I did nothing. After all, what could I do ? Sam was probably dead and beyond any earthly revenge. No, his punishment would be handed out by a power far greater than mine.

So it was that the incident was never mentioned again, yet the hatred was still boiling inside me, a hatred that would go on until the end of my life, a hatred of the name Sam Jackson. A shadow blighting my life. A burden to be carried or an episode to be forgotten?

Albert Lord.

I put down the finished manuscript and stared into space. My suspicions had been growing for some time now. Sam was my other great-grandfather. Everything fell neatly into place. The loathing shown by Frank Lord towards my father, my mother's change of heart towards him, it was all too clear. The incident in the trenches 80 years ago had come down through the generations. Far worse than that was the other sorry happening, the rape, that most terrible of crimes. It was no wonder mother suddenly loathed my father, when she discovered he was descended from a rapist. Come to think of it, so was I. An ironic twist of fate had brought the two Pals' grandchildren together and between them they had produced me.

This was going to take some time to sink in. No wonder my mother kept it from me, when she found out. Presumably, her father had shown her this very manuscript when she went to her mother's funeral. Her love of her grandfather had been great, and she could not stand the thought of anyone doing harm to him, even all those years before she was born. It was hard to imagine how so much hate can cross generations: hate handed down from father to son, to daughter. The family shadow. I sat contemplating the situation for a while longer. Eventually I went upstairs to bed, thoroughly drained by the situation.

Chapter 16

EAST ANGLIA: REALISATION

I woke up next morning with a start, my mouth dry from the whisky and cigarettes. I had, without doubt, over-indulged myself the night before. Sara was still asleep next to me. I peered at the bedside clock; it told me it was 7.30. I knew I couldn't stay in bed any longer, much as I would have liked. It was Saturday, so the shop would be open and I would be expected to put in an appearance. Elaine had done enough for me recently, so I couldn't for shame to leave her alone again. Sara turned over as she felt me moving and smiled up at me.
"What time is it ?" she asked.

I told her and she snuggled back down deeper into bed. I took it that she had no appointments that morning. I did not feel like talking much; there were too many thoughts going round my head. I made a curious assortment of grunts which, roughly translated, meant that I would see her later that evening. I needn't have bothered; she had already drifted back to sleep. I made my way downstairs and put the kettle on to make myself a cup of tea. This done, I slipped a slice of bread into the toaster and moved through into the living room, hoping that the manuscript would have disappeared. It hadn't. There it was, just as I had left it on the coffee table the night before. I picked it up and read the last few lines again. The name Sam Jackson shouted at me from the page.

I heard the kettle boiling, so I went to get my drink. Holding a slice of toast in one hand and a mug of tea in the other, I went back into the sitting room and pondered. There was little else I could do. There could be no mistake, could there ? After all, Jackson was a pretty common name. No, this one was definitely my other great-grandfather. It all fitted so perfectly. The reaction of Frank Lord, mother's strange behaviour, everything. Even the quotes from the Bible made a sort of sense, albeit somewhat convoluted. The torn photograph now fitted, too: the other half was obviously Sam. I wonder who ripped it in two. Probably my mother in a fit of temper, when she found out what he had done to her beloved pal.

There were still questions to be answered, though, not the least of which what had happened to Sam. I was living proof that he had survived the war, but where had he got to ? I had a feeling the second envelope addressed to my mother would contain the answers to these and the other questions that were forming in my mind. I knew I would have to read it at some point, but funnily enough I wasn't sure I really wanted to. The revelations of Albert's story had shocked me enough. The description of Sam's eyes kept flashing into my brain. Why did they keep ringing bells ?

Taking the easy way out, a family trait ? I left the envelope on the coffee table and set off for the shop. I would be very early, but what the hell, I had a lot to think about. I was sitting in the office when Elaine arrived bang on 9 o'clock. She seemed very surprised to see me.

"Morning Mr. Jackson. Quite the early bird this morning."
She hung her coat on the peg and looked me full in the face.
"Excuse me for saying this, but you look like you've seen the proverbial ghost."
"I think I have, Elaine. Well, read about it, anyway."

She didn't ask and I didn't enlighten her any further. We busied ourselves around the shop. That is to say, Elaine did. I remained at my desk and went through my list of jobs to do. Absence from the shop meant that my commissions were behind, but try as I might, I couldn't make any headway with any of them. I just stared at my easel, pondering. No, they would have to wait. An artist needs a clear head to produce his best.

I went early for my lunch, but instead of buying my usual sandwich and returning to the shop to eat it, I went to the public library. I asked the librarian where I could find out about the First World War, and she directed me to a row of books in one corner of the room. After studying the titles, I took a book off the shelf, deciding it was the one I wanted. It was called "The Battle of the Somme". I thumbed through the index and found a reference to Serre. Eagerly, I turned to the page, and there it was. An account similar to Albert's, though without the personal touch, of course. There were photographs of the place as it is today, and one of the ruined village compared with modern Serre. There was even a picture of a wooded area, the trees now growing healthily again after the devastation of the artillery fire. I remembered Albert had mentioned a copse. Perhaps he and Sam had stood on that very spot. I felt a tingle run down my spine. I knew at some point I must pay a visit to Serre and see this place for real. I looked through the index again to see if there was any reference to the Pals. There was just a paragraph saying that Pals regiments were formed so that men who lived near each other could go to war with their friends and not strangers. Go to war ? That was a laugh. Go to die, more like. The article went on to say that many of the Pals regiments had been wiped out on the Somme, not due to any fault of their own, but because the strategy for the battle had gone horribly wrong. Too right, by the sound of it.

I dug deeper into the book. Apparently 600,000 allied soldiers had been killed or wounded in the five months the battle lasted. Another alarming statistic was that on 1st July 1916, 130,000 allied soldiers went over the top, just as Albert and Sam had done, and 57,000 of them were either dead or wounded by the end of the day. Of course, I knew there had been great loss of life during the war, but never before had I felt it touch me so closely. I closed my eyes and imagined Albert and Sam standing next to each other waiting for the signal to climb out of their trench. I thought of Albert lying wounded in hospital and Sam, somewhere in France, making good his escape.

I closed the book with a shudder, and replaced it on the shelf. Leaving the library, I headed back towards the shop. Halfway back, for whatever reason, the penny dropped. Eyes ! Eyes ! I had it ! Richard's eyes were exactly as Albert had described Sam's. The cold emotionless stare had reproduced itself in his great-grandson three generations later, as indeed had the long periods of silence, described by Victoria. My temper, did I get it from Sam and not mother, as I had always believed ? A mixture of the two sounded like a potent combination ! I continued walking back to the shop. Elaine took her dinner break as soon as I returned, leaving me alone to mull some more over Albert's story.

The phone rang, me back to the present day. It was Sara.
"Hello darling, " she said as soon as I answered. "Look, I hope you don't mind, but I've started reading that .... manuscript .... er...."
I heard a rustle of papers.

"Albert Lord's Story. It's quite a piece of living history as far as I can tell. I'll have finished it by the time you get home. Just thought I'd tell you."
"Prepare yourself for a surprise," was all I could manage in reply.
"You won't forget my car is still in Laxfield will you ? Love you lots. Bye."
With that Sara put the phone down.

So by the time I got home she would know the full story. At least I would have someone to discuss it with. I could think of nobody better than Sara. Knowing that a trouble shared is a trouble halved, I felt better, and actually settled down to do some work that afternoon. I managed to finish off Mr. Jones' house in Southwold; another trip out to the coast would seem to be beckoning.

I drove home after I closed the shop feeling as if I had been tarred and feathered by an eighty-year-old crime. Sara must have heard my car in the drive, because she was standing in the doorway as I emerged from the car. I saw there was a look of understanding and sympathy on her face. She kissed me on the cheek and stood to one side to allow me to enter.
"You know ?" I asked.
"Yes. I finished it about ten minutes ago. I didn't put it down, except to ring you up."
"So what do you think ?"
"It's hard to know what to think, but it certainly explains things."
"So what next ?"
"It all happened so long ago, there needn't be a next, though you must tell Phil, of course. I mean, all the players in the story are dead."
She smiled at me.
"Though it must feel rather strange knowing that you are the fruit of both their loins. I bet Albert would be mortified if he knew."
"Just like my mother was, and her father before her."

I shook my head in exasperation.

"I wish mother had told me. I could have understood it better coming from her. Why, oh why was she so secretive about everything ?"

"Well, you are a rather special case in this instance," Sara pointed out. "How would she have begun to tell you all the details ? Where would she start ? By the way Peter, just thought I'd better mention that your great-grandfather and your great-grandfather..... and so on."

She smiled at me, shaking her head. She was trying to cheer me up, but I could not see the funny side.

"What about the rape ?" I continued. "Why did he do it ? He had Bronwen. What was the point ?"

"Who knows what went through his mind when he saw Amy ? Remember the story says earlier that he couldn't keep his eyes off her."

"He must have known Albert would find out, surely ?"

I shook my head as I said this, unable to come to terms with the appalling action.

"Perhaps he was gambling that Albert would never find out. After all, they were due to go to war any day. The chances of survival were not high, were they ? Sam probably thought that they would both be killed."

"I suppose leaving Albert in the crater would more or less guarantee Sam's safety. It was good luck, or bad luck, depending on your point of view, that he was discovered when he was. Another hour and Albert may well have died."

It felt good to be able to discuss matters with Sara. She was always so down to earth and straightforward. There were no hidden secrets lurking behind those lovely eyes.

"Could you continue to love me if you found out I had raped your grandmother and left your grandfather to die ?" I asked, fearing the answer she might give.

"It's not quite the same, is it ? After all, it was Sam that did the deeds, not Phil. Your mother stopped loving your father as a result of events that happened way back in the past. She was quite a lady, your mother, though rather unforgiving."

Mother had decided she could not forgive the Jackson family in the form of her husband, yet blood was thicker than water, as they say, at least far as I was concerned. She had not rejected me, as Frank Lord had apparently suggested. I was descended from Sam Jackson, just like my father, but I was also descended from Albert Lord. My mother must have been faced with this dilemma when she read the story. My head was spinning. I needed a drink.

As if reading my mind, Sara had poured me a whisky, for which I was grateful, so we sat down and looked at each other.
"You do realise that there is another envelope in the box, don't you, addressed to my mother ?"
Sara shook her head.
"No, I didn't look inside it. I just read this because you left it out."

I rose and crossed the room and pulled out the other envelope and the medal case.
"These were Albert's," I said, handing the velvet box across to her. She opened it and took out the medals admiringly.
"Good old Albert. I bet he was a fine fellow to know, just like his great-grandson."
"What about Sam ? I'm *his* great-grandson too ! He doesn't sound like a fine fellow."

I could see Sara wrestling with this conundrum. Like me, she could come up with no reply.
"Did you see the photographs ?" I asked.
"No, where are they ?"

I delved to the bottom of the envelope and pulled them out. Like me, Sara gasped a little when she saw the wedding photograph of Albert and Amy.

"She's just like..."

"Yes, I know, my mother," I interrupted.

"He doesn't look like you much," she said, her eyes rapidly comparing me with the picture.

"Don't you mean I don't look like him ? He was born seventy years before me."

"Suppose you look like Sam ? You're certainly tall like he was."

That thought had crossed my mind earlier, but I didn't want to contemplate it. I wondered if Phil had any photographs of his grandfather. I made a mental note to ask him when I next contacted him.

"Let's just leave it for now," I suggested. "My brain can't cope with this any more."

I finished my drink, whilst Sara went into the kitchen to prepare the evening meal. Soon the aroma of liver and onions found its way into my nostrils. I went into the kitchen and laid the table

After the meal we drove over to pick up Sara's car. Giving it a good spray with water repellent, I managed to start the blessed beast and we drove home in convoy. Settling down to a coffee, I began to prepare myself mentally to read the next manuscript.

"Well, here goes," I said as I removed it from the envelope. This one was not as thick, but it no doubt contained more revelations, I was sure of that. Sara said she would go and have a shower and start to read it when she came down.

"I'll make it a long shower. You read so slowly," she laughed and headed for the bathroom.

Old Pals Act

I took the first sheet and started to read another chapter in my family history. Surely, I thought, the contents couldn't be just as awful as before ? I was shortly to be proved horribly wrong. The family shadow still had not been fully revealed.

Chapter 17

FOR ANNE: EARLY DAYS

I was greatly relieved, as I pulled out the document, to see it had been neatly typed. This would make reading much easier. I don't think my eyes could have coped with wading through another manuscript with the handwriting of Albert Lord. With an understandable feeling of trepidation, I began to read.

> *December 1995*
> *Well, Anne, if you're reading this, it means I'm dead. I left strict instructions with Robinson not to give you this envelope until after my death. Perhaps when you have read it you will understand fully the reasons for my behaviour towards you over the preceding years and realise the true darkness of the family shadow. Everything would have been fine if you had not met that damned Jackson boy. You could have married anyone. Why did you have to pick him? After your mother's funeral, you did realise the hatred we all felt for his family, and you*

actually agreed with me. I was relieved to find out that you felt the same way. I was afraid you might dismiss it all as being too far in the past to be of any further importance. I'm sure your grandfather would have been pleased with your decision to leave Jackson. Why, oh why did you not leave that child of yours with his father? Then they could have left our world forever, and my last years could have been spent in happiness with you, with no more of that family blighting our lives. I really loved you, Anne, and I would have done anything for you, but I couldn't bring myself to even look at the offspring of such a hateful character as Sam Jackson. The position you found yourself in must have been very difficult. You made your choice, and I respect you for it. You loved your son, and nothing could change that. Unfortunately it was a choice I could never come to terms with, and it had to be said after your mother's funeral. I suppose it is the curse of the Lords, the inability to bend for the sake of peace. Blame your grandfather Lord for that. He started it all. As he became older he became more and more intransigent, and I suppose it rubbed off on me and, inevitably, you.

So why am I writing this now? Well, I'm 75, and I have just learned I have a weak heart. The doctor doesn't know how long I have left to live. I might die tomorrow or go on for several more years. So I thought it would be a good idea to fill you in on some facts you were not aware of regarding this sorry tale.

You know, of course, about the shell hole, and how my father was left to die by that man. And you know about the rape of my mother. Those two incidents were the primary cause of all this ill feeling, and they can never be forgiven. However, I will now reveal to you the rest of the story, much of which is known only to myself and, of course, your grandfather. You will be aware of some of the details, but I've left them in regardless.

I never knew my mother, Amy. She died giving birth to me. She was only twenty-four. I was brought up by my father and his parents, in the house off Blackburn Road, the same house in which your grandfather had lived all his life. It must have been a struggle for the three of them, to bring me up, but somehow they managed. My father would always manage. You don't live through what he did without having some resilience. Luckily, he got his job back at Howard and Bulloughs, which brought in enough money to keep us from starving. I think he may have got a pension from the army, but I was never sure. I didn't care how difficult it was for them, as long as I had a full stomach.

My first real memory was when I was about eight, and my father took me to the war memorial in Oak Hill Park. He explained it was for the "Pals". I didn't follow; my pals were Jimmy and Charlie, two lads on the street, with whom I played out and went to school. He just said I would understand one day. How right he was.

I suppose the next event I remember was in the early 30s when I was aged about twelve or thirteen. My grandmother died. She was followed eighteen months later by my grandfather. Even at the funerals, father shed no tears. He had been surrounded by death too much to let his emotions show. I remember squeezing his hand tightly as we walked back home after the funeral of his father. We were alone now, just the two of us.

I left school at fifteen, and was lucky to find a job helping out on the market. An old comrade of dad's in the war ran a clothes stall, and was prepared to take me on as a general helper. I enjoyed the work and the money was

useful, though dad sold some of his paintings, which also brought in some much-needed cash.
I remember those paintings well. They all seemed so sad. Even the landscapes he painted somehow held no joy. The ones that really fascinated me were his war pictures. They were so vivid, you could almost feel the horror bursting off the paper, especially the eyes of the soldiers. They were what I used to call "dead eyes". Dad said he had a good model. I didn't understand what he meant by that, not for many years. I tried to paint like him, but never managed to get the same feel.
When I was eighteen, I began to take an interest in the Great War, especially as the talk at the time was the continuing rise of the Nazi party in Germany. Father used to shake his head whenever he read the reports in the paper and say "My God, not again !" I used to beg him to tell me about his time in the war, but he always refused, until one day I found his medals. It's funny, he had never mentioned getting a medal for bravery. It was as if it was part of his life he wished to forget. But I pestered and pestered his life out - does that remind you of anyone, dear Anne ? - and finally he agreed.
We sat in front of the fire that night, and he told me everything, exactly as was written down in the document I showed you at your mother's funeral. He told me about Sam. I was the first living soul he had ever spoken to about the shell hole episode. I could feel my blood boil as he related the tale. You could tell there was real hatred in his voice as he relived the brush with death brought upon by his so-called friend. I couldn't bring myself to use the word "pal", as the connotations were wrong in this instance. He even showed me the Bible quotations he had written down whilst in hospital. I understood them, though they seemed a little contrived, but they were important to

him. *My jaw dropped open with horror when he related the rape incident to me. This man had truly cast a shadow over our lives. The family shadow, father used to call it. I knew then I could never forgive him, or any of his descendants if indeed he had lived to produce any. My father was a good church-goer, so to see this anger was quite a new experience for me. I asked the question he could not answer.*
"What happened to Jackson ?"
Father sighed deeply and explained that after the war he made every effort to find out if he had lived or not, but he always met up with the same dead end. He visited Jackson's house in Avenue Parade, but the new tenants said mother and daughter had moved away in 1917, to goodness knows where. I asked him if he had thought to go to Caernarvon. The chances were that if he had managed to get back to England he would try to see Bronwen again. He had toyed with the idea, but transport was not as easy back then, and what with his wedding and my birth there seemed so little time. He never mentioned my mother's death. He disappeared upstairs and returned with a photograph of himself and Jackson in full army uniform. Remember it, Anne ? It was the one you tore up at your mother's funeral when I showed you the manuscript. What a temper !
I looked at the picture, and that staring face was forever etched on my memory. I would recognise it anywhere. I wanted more than anything to see that face in real life and confront the man behind it with his despicable actions. I was due a holiday so I said I would take a trip to Caernarvon to see if I could find out anything. The autumn of 1938 saw me heading for Wales in search of someone who might have died over twenty years ago. My father had described the lovely town of Caernarvon very

accurately, and as I got off the train and looked around me, it was as if I had been there in a previous life.
I headed for the square in the middle of the town and wandered around looking for a place to stay for the night. Eventually I found a boarding house, quite close by to where father and Jackson must have been billeted all those years ago, though from memory it was on the opposite side of the square. I settled in and headed towards where father had said Bronwen's parents ran the pub. It was too much to expect them still to be there, but I hoped I would meet someone who remembered them.
The man, probably in his mid thirties, polishing glasses behind the bar, looked at me suspiciously when I began to ask questions. After all, I was English and worthy of a certain amount of distrust. I explained to him that my father had been stationed here during the last war and I was trying to visit some of the places he had been and, of course, meet some of the people he had met. He thawed a little when I mentioned this fact. Yes, he remembered the troops from East Lancashire.
" I'd be a boy of about 16 when they were here," he said, beginning to open up. "We used to watch them drilling in the square, and quite a sight they were. Us lads thought the Germans would soon be on the run when they arrived. We used to march behind them, pretending we were part of the battalion. My sister got quite friendly with one of them, as I recall."
His lovely Welsh voice tailed away as if thinking of his past life, and he stared into space. Shaking his head, he regained his senses and looked at me.
"I remember the old landlord, " he continued, after my prompting, "and his wife. They used to chase me away from the yard at the back when I used to try to steal the

beer bottles to throw stones at, you know like, pretending to be soldiers."

"They had a daughter," I casually mentioned. "Bronwen, I think her name was."

He grinned at me.

"Oh yes, pretty girl. Jet black hair, I remember. We all loved her, but she took up with a soldier, tall chap, never seemed to smile, scary eyes. Frightened us lads he did. He came a-visiting quite often. We used to follow him back to his house and watch him climb through a window. I remember once we pretended to be wild animals, howling and the like. He would have killed us if he'd caught us."

That certainly sounded like Jackson, especially knowing that he used to go and visit Bronwen virtually every night. I smiled at the thought of him being followed through the streets by a gang of small boys, making noises.

"You don't know what happened to the family, then?"

"Not really. You see, I joined up a year later, lied about my age, I did. I never saw any fighting. They'd sorted it out before I finished training."

There seemed to be a hint of regret in his voice.

"When I came back in 1919, they'd all gone, mother, father and daughter."

"So when did you start to work in this place?" I asked.

"Two years ago. Lucky to get this job, I was. Lot of unemployment around here," he added with a hint of relief in his voice. "Got a young family, you see. Now old Huw over there," he said, nodding to an elderly man sitting alone in the corner, "he might remember what became of them."

I thanked him and went to sit down next to an elderly man nursing a half-pint of flat-looking beer. He looked up at me as I approached, his coal black eyes staring intently at me. We fell into conversation, helped by the drink I

presented him with. It was quite difficult, as Huw spoke only a little English, though probably more than he let on, and I, of course, spoke no Welsh. However, with a little help from a man sitting nearby I discovered that Bronwen had married a soldier at the end of the war and moved away, to England, or so he thought.
"Tall chap, he was, bit of a stoop."
He stopped talking at that point, as if recalling events of long ago.
"Never smiled much," he continued. "Met him once or twice. War hero, so he said. Lot of them about at that time."
This certainly sounded like Jackson, except the war hero bit. That he certainly wasn't.
Her parents had gone to live in a village called Llanrug, about five miles away. They were now both dead, he believed. I thanked him, and returned to the bar and asked the barman to give him another drink. Just as I was leaving, old Huw called out to me in his curious English. "They went to church. We laughed when we found out." From what father had told me, that didn't seem at all like the Jackson he knew. Probably why they laughed. If the soldier had been Jackson, as seemed likely from the description, then Bronwen must have converted him back to Christianity. Something my father had been unable to do.
I walked round the town, taking in all the sights and places my father must have seen during his stay in Wales. He had spoken very fondly of this place, and I could see why. I would have dearly loved to explore the hills and dales, and possibly look round the castle. Still, I was not there for sightseeing. Jackson's trail had gone cold. The only thing that did seem certain was the fact that he had survived the Great War.

Old Pals Act

I returned to Accrington the next day. There seemed little point in staying away any longer. I walked from the station up to the house, a route my father must have taken when on leave. Funny, I had walked that way many times, but it was only now that I considered my father striding home, his kit bag over his shoulder. I told him of my findings. He simply said, with hate in his voice, "So he lived."

I nodded in agreement. There seemed to be no doubt about that. The description given by the man in the pub seemed to confirm that Sam had somehow escaped the horrors of France, made it back to England and, finally, Wales, to be reunited with Bronwen. Father sat for a long time with his head in his hands, rocking gently backwards and forwards. I wanted to do more, but there seemed no way of moving forward in the matter. Anyway, I had other things on my mind.

I had recently met Emily, your mother, and we were trying to spend some time together. She appeared one day looking through the dresses on the stall, we got talking and that was that. I asked her out, she agreed, so there you have it, that's how I met your mother, Anne. She came from a well off family. I think her father was in munitions during the Great War. They lived out on the Burnley Road, near the cemetery. I used to walk up and meet her most nights. That hill kept me pretty fit, I can tell you.

By the middle of 1939, there was a certain inevitability about there being another war. Hitler had already marched his troops into Czechoslovakia, and apparently he was turning his attention towards Poland. Father read the papers each day and became increasingly uneasy about the worsening situation. Remember, he had seen it all before, in 1914. I thought he was concerned about being called to war himself.

"You needn't worry, dad," I said. "You're a wounded veteran. You won't have to fight again."

"Don't be stupid, lad ! It's not me, it's you who might have to go this time !"

I suppose, like many men of my age, I had not considered that a possibility until that very moment. Of course, he was right, I might have to fight for my country just as he had done. I shook at the prospect of spending time in the trenches, covered in rats and lice. I was only nineteen, a year younger than he had been when he joined up, and very naive. I shut the thoughts of war out of my mind and tried to pretend it would all go away.

I'm ashamed to admit it, but I neglected him during the golden summer of 1939. My relationship with Emily had got stronger and we wanted to spend time together, just like he had wanted to spend time with my mother over twenty years before. This meant he was on his own a lot, thinking, I suspect, about Jackson. Other than reading the Bible and any books he could lay his hands on, his main source of enjoyment seemed to be his painting, but his pictures were even more sombre than before, and people stopped buying them. I suppose they had their own war to worry about, without being reminded of his.

I came home one night and he took me into the sitting room and showed me a thick manuscript. You know which one I'm talking about, Anne. He told me he had written down everything he could remember about the events of the Great War, well, his part in it, from volunteering to being discharged, and his subsequent marriage to my mother. He had become a great reader over the years, and had developed a way with words, unusual for people of his generation and class. I read through it, saddened by the

tragedy of his life, yet at the same time impressed by the way he had managed to tell accurately of his early life. I suppose the act of me writing this to you is keeping up the family tradition of wanting to tell our stories. Perhaps you will do it one day.
"You must keep it safe, Frank," he said, "and let your children read it when you think fit. They can then decide what to do with it after that."
He sealed it in an envelope, where it remained until you read it after your mother's funeral. I've long regretted the fact that I didn't show it you sooner, but you were off before I got the chance.
War with Germany was finally declared in September of that year, and within days of the announcement poor father suffered from a nervous breakdown. He was ill for many weeks; he just used to lie in his bed, mumbling to himself. The doctor said he thought it was triggered off by the latest confrontation. Not the most inspired of diagnoses in the world, was it, Anne? He had seen too much suffering in his life and he was only in his mid-forties, remember. I used to hear him at night ranting and raving, shouting for Sam and crying for help.
Time is a great healer, and against all odds, he woke up one morning in early January 1940, laughing and saying, "They've gone to Church."
After that he became more lucid.
I looked after him as best I could, and he was soon restored to full health. It was when I felt he was fit enough to take it that I thought it was time to tell him that Emily and I were to be married in June of that year. It's funny, Anne, but we seem to go in for getting married young in our family. Though I suppose I wanted to marry her before I was called away to war.

> *I think father was pleased with this latest turn of events. He had always liked her company whenever she came round to the house. After the wedding, Emily left the comfort of her own large house and came to live with father and me. Our first married home - a bit different from our last, I'm sure you agree....*

I put the document down and smiled at Sara as she entered the room, looking all warm and cosy in her dressing gown. Her hair was still wet from the shower and she had combed it back over her ears.

"Well ?" she asked. "Any new revelations ? Have you found out that you are also related to the Kaiser, and your great uncle was Adolf Hitler ?"

I smiled across at her laughing face. Joking apart, though, being described by the phrase "offspring of such a hateful character" hurt more than a little. The more I found out about Frank Lord, the more relieved I was that I never got to meet him.

"No, not quite, but I appear to be related to Casanova, on my father's side."

I pulled her down onto the settee and kissed her lovingly. We sat in each other's arms for several minutes before I went over to the drinks cabinet and poured out a whisky for me and a gin and tonic for her.

"Cheers," she said.

"Cheers," I answered. "Happy reading."

We snuggled together on the settee. I passed over the pages I had read, whilst I continued with the rest.

> *After our marriage in June 1940, the war took a turn for the worse. It became apparent that Hitler was going to invade England. Starting in Accrington seemingly. We had only been married for about four days when there was*

an air raid. A German bomber, presumably heading for Manchester, had got slightly off course and proceeded to deposit its bombs on Whalley Road. We heard the sirens and rushed to shelter in the cellar. My father was in a terrible state as he heard the bombs falling. He kept crying out "Into the dug out ! Into the dug out ! Helmets on, there might be gas !" I tell you, Anne, he was a wreck when we finally were given the all clear to go back up into the house.
Less than a month after that, German attacks on the British ships in the channel were reported, whilst bombs were falling around the southern ports in an effort to destroy our Fighter Command. This was termed the Battle of Britain by Winston Churchill. There was further bombing of London and certain other major cities. This continued until the end of the year. To my knowledge, no more bombs fell in Accrington. There was to be no mass volunteering as had been the case in 1914, though I knew my turn to go and fight would not be far away. My father knew this too, and he just sat and waited. He had been through all this before. He knew what to expect.
1941 saw the extension of conscription; all men aged between 18 and 51 were likely to be called up. I watched the post every day, waiting for my papers to arrive. Sure enough they did. The brown envelope dropped through the door in the spring of that year. Father knew as soon as it arrived what it meant. So, Anne, I too was called to arms. You must feel proud to be descended from such a patriotic family. When I went away, Emily was a great source of comfort to my father, who was beside himself with worry. My exploits in the war are not really of any importance to this story, so I will leave them out. I cannot claim to be a hero like Albert. In fact I never saw any real action. I came home on leave in February 1942, and you were born

in the November of the same year. A proper little war baby, you were. Your lungs alone would have repelled any invasion force. Luckily I was away for most of your screaming stage, so I missed all the sleepless nights. Your granddad took a special liking to you from the moment you were born. He pointed out from your first breath how like Amy you were. I obviously couldn't see the similarity, but I took his word for it. I suppose the fact hat you eventually grew a beautiful head of auburn hair helped matters.
At the end of the war I was demobbed and I returned to Accrington and my little family. Although he was not yet fifty, father had aged rapidly during the years I was away. Doubtless he relived all his old memories, thinking that his son would be going through hell like he did. This was not actually the case, but no amount of explanations would convince him that I was not in a trench somewhere n France. He was old before his time.
Life returned to something like normal after the war. I went back to my job on the market, though I now was in sole charge, buying out my old boss. Rationing was still on, and I won't pretend that life was easy. I suppose we were luckier than most, in as much as we were becoming quite well off. The dress stall was doing great business. I had developed some good connections in the army and I could supply most things that people wanted, officially or unofficially. Say no more ! I eventually sold the stall and bought the shop in the town, with the help of money given to your mother by her parents.
One night in the summer of 1947, father and I walked into Accrington for a quiet drink. This had become quite a habit of ours recently. I enjoyed spending time with my father. Emily didn't mind, she was totally absorbed in our four year old daughter, who was proving to be a very

demanding little girl. Nothing new there ! As we settled down with our drink, he looked me in the eyes and said, "I think I know where he is."

I knew instantly who he was talking about. Sam Jackson. "I've been thinking about it for the last eight years," he said. "I must be right."

"Well go on then, tell me more."

"I'm surprised you didn't see it," he replied. "Think about the man in Caernarvon."

"Old Huw ?"

I was surprised that my memory had retained the name for so long.

"Yes, Old Huw. What did he call out to you as you left the pub ?"

I admit I had to think for several minutes until I recalled.

"They went to church, or something like that," I said.

"Jackson would never go to church." *Father stared across at me at me.* "You know that."

"That's what Old Huw said - they went to church."

"OK, OK. Now how do you spell church ?"

"c - h - u - r - c - h," *I spelt out.*

"Now spell it with a capital C at the start. What have you got now ?"

"Church, with a capital C," *was my obtuse answer.*

"Think, boy !"

I thought, and then I twigged.

"Church ! Bloody Church ! Not the place of worship, but the town."

"Exactly. He went to Church."

Church was a small village about a mile from the centre of Accrington, two at the most.

"There was no way Sam would ever go to church, but Church, that's a different matter. He returned to the north of England, presumably with Bronwen. I realised when I*

was ill, just before the war, and I have been thinking about it ever since. I must see him again. I need to confront him. I must."
His voice was almost pleading.
"Don't worry, we'll find him if he's there, that I promise," I said, hoping for all the world I could keep my promise. We finished our drinks and walked slowly back home. Your mother was still up waiting for us. She made us a cup of tea and then went to bed. I sat down with my father and he told me he had it all worked out. He was going to be avenged. I must confess, Anne, that I was worried about my father. I didn't know how he would take it, should Jackson not be living in Church.
"Suppose, just suppose, he's not there ? He would be taking a big risk, coming back so close to home. He might be recognised."
"Would anyone care any more ?" Father asked. "Would anyone remember him ? Don't forget, he wasn't from around here originally, and he was always a bit of a loner with no real friends. Except me, of course."
I smiled across at father.
"If you were his friend, then God help his enemies !" I said ....

I put down the document and rubbed my aching eyes. Sara was close behind me.
"So did they find him, do you think ?" she asked.
"The answer is in here," I said, tapping the document with the back of my hand. "All neatly written down. I think I'd rather let it go for the night. My mind can't cope with any more just at present."

We made our way up to bed, leaving the unfinished document lying on the table. I took a final glance before turning out the lights. What secrets did it hold ?

Chapter 18

FOR ANNE: DISCOVERIES

We slept late the next morning, enjoying a well-earned Sunday lie-in. I was eventually awoken by Sara as she slipped out of bed and headed downstairs to prepare breakfast. I followed her down, having first taken a shower. I kissed her lightly on the cheek. We sat down and ate breakfast in virtual silence, both of us thinking about Frank Lord and his letter to Anne. I was keen to get back to it and find out once and for all the ending to the whole sorry tale. Sara, on the other hand, ever practical, wanted to go for a walk and get some fresh air.

"Come on," she said. "We spent all last night stuck inside. We need a break, so let's go up to the shop and get a paper."

On sufferance I agreed, and we strolled to the paper shop near the church. Instead of heading straight back we wandered down the road to the graveyard. I wanted to visit mother's grave, complete now with its simple headstone. We both stood looking at it for

several minutes. Even in death, my mother was still with us somehow; her spirit was contained in the two documents at present residing on my coffee table at home. Her little character traits showed through in the writings of her father and grandfather. I suppose, in certain ways, so did some of mine. I knelt down at the side of the grave, soaking my trousers in the process, and quietly whispered,
"Oh mother, what next ?"

She knew everything, but only for a few hours before her death. Not for the first time, I wondered what she would have told me had she lived. Sara and I walked hand in hand back to the house, feeling refreshed after our short walk. The red light was flashing on the answer phone when we got back. I pressed the button and Sue Greenwood's voice filled the room.

"Hi Pete, hi Sara, how are you both ? Out again. I honestly thought I might catch you in on a Sunday. I was just wondering how your delvings into the past were going. Do ring and let me know of any developments. Bye."
"That poor woman," I laughed. "She never manages to catch us in. She'll begin to think there is some sort of conspiracy against her."
"We should keep her informed, you know," remarked Sara. "She's going to get quite a shock when she hears all this."
"I know. There's too much for the phone, though. Let's invite her down next weekend. She said she would like to pay us a visit sometime."

I looked at Sara as if asking permission, and she nodded in approval. I picked up the phone and rang her back. Yes, she would love to come, and she would drive down on Saturday morning and return home on Sunday. That being fixed, I made a coffee, sat down on the settee and continued reading, whilst Sara started to prepare lunch.

*We decided that it would be best if I tried to locate Jackson, thinking he would not know me, while he would in all probability recognise Albert. So the following Saturday, some time in September 1947, saw me walking the couple of miles along Blackburn Road towards Church. You recall Church, don't you, Anne ? A town, no, more a village - or was it merely an extension of Accrington, or a part of Oswaldtwistle ? The inhabitants of Church would argue that it was its own town with its own identity, and I think they are probably right. However, whatever else it is, it is a small place. In 1947 it was a collection of terraced houses with the usual array of shops, a mill and, of course, a pub. When I arrived in what was the centre, I suppose I was uncertain what to do next. I could wander around hoping to bump in to him, but that might not produce any results. So I decided to ask at a small grocer's shop if they had heard of a man called Sam Jackson. I entered the shop to be met by a sparse collection of food for sale. Remember, Anne, rationing was still going in 1947. I made a pretence of looking round the poorly stocked shelves, when a thought struck me. Suppose, just suppose, word got back to Jackson that someone was asking about him: that might make him a little suspicious. After all, as far as we knew he was a deserter from the Great War, so might the authorities still be after him ? I didn't know, but I didn't take want to take the risk. Luckily, the shopkeeper was serving someone else, so I left the shop without speaking to anyone.
In the street again, I wandered up the road, under the railway bridge, towards Oswaldtwistle. I saw Moscow Mill on my left, a collection of low buildings where cotton was processed. Being Saturday, the mill was closed and there was nobody about. I walked up to the gates and looked into the yard. Could Jackson work here ? After all,*

he had worked in the industry before the war. I remember my father telling me that he was an apprentice "tackler", one whose job it was to look after the "tackle", or the machinery. Perhaps he had returned to his former occupation when he came back to Lancashire all those years ago. Maybe Bronwen also worked here. This being the case, did he have any family, and did they work there, as often happened in the industry ?

All these question were left unanswered as I turned around and strolled further up into Oswaldtwistle centre. It was, and indeed still is, a pleasant little town, boasting solidly built terraced houses, presumably for the mill workers. The main street has a variety of shops, similar to the one I went in earlier. I began to think how lucky I was in my business. Rationing had been a problem I had overcome, due to my contacts. I was proud that I could supply almost anything, for a price of course, and as a result I was now becoming a wealthy man.

It was a pleasant autumn day, so I walked back over the tops, enjoying the wind in my hair as I dropped down into Accrington along Willows Lane. The walk had given me time to consider what to do next. I had decided to return to Church the following Monday morning to watch the workers entering Moscow Mill. I felt sure I would be able to recognise Jackson if I saw him. I was beginning to warm to the task of being a detective.

As I entered the house, my father looked expectantly at me. I shook my head very slightly to indicate I had not seen him. You and your mother were in the room, Anne, so we couldn't discuss my next step. It was only when you were being put to bed that we were able to talk. Father agreed with me that he might have got a job in the mill, and it was worth a try. He would not let go of this until

Jackson had been found, or we knew for certain that we were on the wrong track.

"Of course, if I do see him, we have to decide what to do next," I pointed out.

"Oh I know," said father, smiling to himself.

I somehow didn't like the sound of that, but I was prepared to listen to his idea and to help him carry out any plan he came up with. Understand, Anne, I loved my father and I was sickened to hear of how he had been left to die, by the callous, selfish actions of one man. I never knew my mother, but I knew something must be done to avenge her ordeal at the hands of this monster.

Father had by now given up his job at Howard and Bulloughs. His chest had become worse over the last few years, due, so he said, to sleeping in wet trenches in 1916. Though I suspect it was the number of Woodbines he got through each day that was the real cause. However, he did occasionally help me in the shop, and this he promised to do on the Monday morning, as I set off early for Church and Moscow Mill. Your mother must have wondered what was going on, seeing me leave at about 6.30 to be outside the mill gates before they opened at seven. I drove my little Morris 8, a car I had bought for a good price, about £75, earlier that year and was my pride and joy.

I parked the car out of sight, and casually positioned myself across the road, where I could see everyone going in. I watched everyone as they walked towards the mill. I tried to keep myself as inconspicuous as possible, my coat collar pulled up, half covering my face.

"There's no jobs, mate, if that's what you're after," called out one of the workers as he passed me by. I nodded back to him and moved away. I stopped a few yards down the road and continued my watch.

It was just before quarter to seven when I saw him. There could be no mistaking that tall figure with the slight stoop, and I felt sure the haunted, cold eyes would be there if I got close enough. He was dressed in filthy overalls, covered in grease, with an equally dirty flat cap on his head. There could be no doubt. I had found Sam Jackson. Walking next to him was a homely looking woman, wearing a long navy skirt and a shawl around her shoulders. She had very dark hair, touched now with the occasional streak of grey. This just had to be Bronwen. They chatted to each other as they entered the mill yard and disappeared from sight.
I could feel excitement welling up inside me as I drove back to Accrington and the shop. Father could see the look on my face as I walked in through the door, and he knew that I had located Jackson. I promised to fill him in with all the details that night. He said his farewells and returned home. I could have sworn there was a spring in his step as I stood in the shop doorway and watched him walking away.
After the evening meal, I spent some time playing with you on the rug in front of the fire. You used to enjoy me rolling you over and bouncing your teddy bear on your tummy. I remember how you giggled with delight as I snuffled it over your face, making silly growling noises. Even Albert joined in that night, playing his mouth organ as I pretended to make the teddy sing along. Simple pleasures, Anne, but it was always nice to see you smile and hear you laugh. Later, whilst your mother was putting you to bed, father and I began to talk. We kept our voices low so as not to involve your mother. To her dying day, Anne, she knew nothing of what we were planning. In fact she didn't know about Sam Jackson's existence until I

briefly told her about his terrible deeds, that awful day you brought his grandson to the house in 1964. She certainly knew nothing of the events contained in this story.

"You're sure it was him?" Father shot the question at me. "Certain. He looked just like the photograph, much older of course, but there was no mistaking him. Even the stoop was just as you described. There was a woman with him, probably Bronwen."

"Well, this is my plan," he whispered.

When he had finished telling me, I was amazed at the simplicity of it, yet it was perfectly foolproof. We were going to get revenge on Sam Jackson, poetic revenge. That night as I lay in bed I shuddered, thinking of the cold calculating way my father had worked out all the details. It was planned to the point of obsession. How he must have dreamt of this moment. Now was the time to put his ideas into action.

I started to move the very next day. Albert worked in the shop again whilst I drove into Church and parked the car a small distance away from the mill down a quiet side street. I realised that there were not many cars on the road in 1947 and it might cause a few raised eyebrows, but that was a risk I had to take. This time, I was there at the end of the day's work to watch him on his way home. I wanted to find out where he lived. Sure enough, he came out with the same woman and they made their way, under the railway bridge, towards Church centre. Thrusting my hands deep in my pockets, I adopted a shuffling gait, blending in with the other workers leaving the mill. I followed them, under the railway bridge towards the main crossroads in Church. Eventually they turned off into a small side street and walked up to a smart looking terraced house nearly at the top. Here they went inside. I made a mental note of the location, went back to the car and drove home.

The next part of the plan was not quite as straightforward. I had to make his acquaintance, as if quite by chance. Once more, father had worked it all out to perfection. Jackson was always a great walker, and father figured he would still enjoy rambling round the hills. We could not be sure of this, of course, but if this plan failed there would be other ways, I was certain. I was to take on the guise of another keen rambler and ask directions to the village of Guide, which I had heard was a pretty place, with plenty of good walks and scenery. I had to tell him I was from Burnley and didn't know that part of the world too well. The plan was to involve Jackson in conversation about good walks in the area. I knew he would be reluctant to talk, but I felt confident I could do it. I was then to engineer a situation whereby we would go for a walk together, gaining his friendship and trust. Albert had truly worked this out to the last detail. Just how long he had been brooding over this plan I had no idea. Years, probably, hoping against hope that Jackson might be found.

One Saturday, I watched him come out of his house and down his street and walk towards the main road. I, complete with stout walking boots, stick and a good thick coat, stopped him and asked for directions. I heard his voice for the first time as he told me how to get to Guide village. I shuddered as I thought of his last words to my father in the shell hole. I looked into his face, sickened at the hurt he had caused my mother. I continued the conversation, explaining that I enjoyed walking, but I wanted to try something new, having grown tired of the walks around my native Burnley. He told me there were many walks in this area, and as luck would have it, he *himself was a keen walker. There was no luck involved, I thought to myself. We chatted about some of the local walks.*

"You sound like a perfect guide to Guide," I said, and we both laughed at my little pun.

I took my leave of him and set off down the street. I had only gone about ten yards when I turned and called out to the disappearing figure.

"How about going on a walk together?"

He turned round and made his way towards me. Now I saw the eyes quite clearly, and they were studying me deeply. I looked away and pretended to cough.

"Well, what do you say?"

He thought a walk together was a good idea. We arranged to meet the following Saturday, near the Commercial Hotel in the centre of Church. I set off once more in the direction he told me. When I was out of sight, I looped round over the tops back to Accrington. I had no desire to see the sights of Guide village that day. Father was delighted when I told him of my arrangements.

"The trap is sprung," he said, hardly able to keep the thrill out of his voice. "Now we must make things develop."

The following Saturday, I drove into Church, parked the car and waited for him to arrive. I had driven down the road from Burnley, just in case he was there waiting for me. It would have looked rather odd if I had appeared from the Accrington direction. I leaned on the bonnet of the car and waited. Sure enough, I soon saw him strolling down the road from his house. He looked admiringly at the car.

"Nice machine," he said. "I've a little grandson who would be thrilled with that. Thinks about nothing but cars, he does."

My heart missed a beat. So he had children, and at least one grandson. I suppose I must have realised there was a good chance of this, but to have it confirmed seemed rather odd.
"We'll have to see if we can't arrange a ride for him some time."
As soon as I had uttered those words I regretted them. I didn't want to meet any of his family.
"You do realise I don't know your name?" he said. "I'm Sam Jackson."
"Pleased to meet you, Sam. I'm Frank Holt, " I replied. There was no way I could tell him my real name, well not just yet. We shook hands. I don't think he noticed the little shudder I gave at this moment.
We set off on our walk. He had worked out a route heading towards Blackburn, through the village of Knuzden Brook. Father was right, he was a good, strong walker. I was roughly half his age, and it took me all my time to keep up with him. Seeing this, he slowed down and we managed to keep pace with each other. The day was fine and quite warm, so we stopped after about an hour and sat on a wall for a rest. He took a bottle of water out of his rucksack and offered me a drink. I accepted gratefully.
"Thought you would have some of your own, being a walker, like," he said.
Damn! I thought. A mistake. I had to think quickly,
"I must have left it at home. I was in a bit of a rush when I set off."
"But you were early," he pointed out, giving me a sideways glance.
I muttered something incomprehensible under my breath, but made a mental note to be very careful. Here was a

clever character and no mistake. I changed the subject by asking him the only thing I could think of.
"Are you from round here, then?"
Again he looked sideways at me.
"Where else would you think?"
"Oh, I don't know..."
I was digging myself deeper in.
"I'm originally from the south of England," *he said eventually.* "Moved to Accrington when I was a small child, moved to Wales, and then came back here with my wife, OK?"
The answer was rather abrupt, but I had expected this. Father had warned me he was not the most forthcoming of people.
"Accrington... er, I'm not really that familiar with it. Been once or twice, but that's all," *I lied.*
I hoped I could remember what I had said. To be a good liar, you need a good memory.
"So what were you doing in Wales?"
"You ask a lot of questions of a relative stranger," *he replied in a prickly fashion,* "but if you must know, I was stationed there during the first war."
I nearly said that I knew someone who was there as well, but I checked myself in time.
"Whereabouts?"
"Caernarvon, then on to Egypt, then to France. I was in the Battle of the Somme. Look, if it's all the same to you, I'd rather not discuss the war. It's a time I'd rather forget."
I apologised, and didn't mention it again. I wasn't surprised he didn't want to mention it, knowing what I did. We continued on our way. We walked in silence for a while. This was not going to be easy. I had to be careful not to upset him, in case he didn't want to go out on

another walk. I asked him no more questions for the rest of the day. I was exhausted when we arrived back in Church. We parted company at my car. I suggested another walk in a fortnight and he agreed, saying it was nice to meet someone who liked walking. None of his family were in the slightest bit interested. We arranged to meet at the same time.

I drove back home again, taking care to go up the Burnley Road, before heading into Accrington. Emily greeted me at the door with a puzzled look on her face.

"So where have you been all day?" she asked.

"Business," was my reply.

Emily knew never to ask what kind of business. She was well trained! I could see father was bursting to question me about the day, but we had to wait until later that evening before we could discuss matters.

He seemed pleased with the progress I had made, and was delighted about our proposed walk in two weeks.

"Things are progressing. Well done, Frank."

"What about Emily? She's bound to be puzzled by my days out."

"Don't worry, just tell her you are out looking for a new house. She's always saying this place is too small for all of us."

"A full day?"

I was not convinced, but at that moment she walked back into the room after putting you to bed, Anne....

I put the document down as Sara walked into the room, carrying some cheese on toast. She put it down in front of me.

"Well, how goes it?" she asked.

Without speaking, I passed the pages I had finished with over to her, indicating that she should read them. She did not seem overjoyed at this prospect, putting them down straight away.

"Let's do something this afternoon. I'm fed up with reading bloody family histories."

This was a bad sign. Sara rarely swore, and if she did it was serious. I apologised and replaced the document in its envelope and started on my lunch. It was about two when we had finished. I wanted to read on, but I thought better of it.
"What would you like to do ?" I almost added " then" at the end, but decided against it.
"Oh, I don't know. Something. Anything."
After the outburst on the night of the quiz, I had been doing a lot better in keeping my temper, but it nearly flipped at that point. I gave an exasperated sigh and said,
"Well, suggest something."
Sara must have caught the edge in my voice, because she looked across at me and apologised, with a resigned tone in her voice.
"I'm sorry, Pete. I know this thing is important to you. Just carry on reading. I'll not mention it again."
She kissed me on the cheek and took the document out of the envelope. Picking out the pages she had not yet read, she handed the remainder to me, thinking, no doubt, that the sooner I got to the end the better it would be for both of us. I apologised in return for snapping at her. There was a prickly silence as we carried on with our reading.

> *During the next two weeks, Albert got more and more excited. I think he could see the day when he would meet Jackson again drawing ever closer. Every time we were alone he kept asking me if I knew how to proceed. Your mother could not understand the air of expectancy in the house. Even you noticed it, Anne. You kept asking why was granddad singing all the time. It was Friday, after work, that I told your mother I would be out all the*

following day. She took it calmly, but father jumped in saying,
"Tell her, Frank. You know, about the house."
I cottoned on at once,
"Well, you know about wanting a bigger house ? I'm going to have a look round tomorrow, to see what's about."
She seemed thrilled at this prospect, though I felt she would have liked to have gone with me.
"Best go on my own, to start with, you know."
I don't think she did know, but she made no reply....

"Lies, lies, more lies and bloody secrets ! That sums my family up. On both sodding sides," I shouted, making poor Sara jump up in shock. I apologised for startling her. I think she must have thought I was going slightly mad. I was starting to think that way myself.

Like the previous Saturday, I detoured round on the Burnley Road and arrived at the usual place. This time he was there waiting for me, holding the hand of a small child, of about six as best as I could tell, wearing a pair of grey shorts and a filthy blue jumper. A little urchin if ever there was one. You realise who it was though, don't you Anne ?
"This is my son Tom's lad, Philip, the one I told you about, the one who loves cars."
The child took no notice of me, and made to climb into the front seat. He played with the steering wheel, making loud engine noises.
"Come on Philip, that's enough. Let's get you back to your dad."
I was beginning to feel sick. The last thing I wanted was to meet anyone belonging to the Jackson family. The little boy was fine; he hadn't even looked at me, but his father

might be another matter. Taking his now weeping grandson by the hand, Jackson headed off down another street close by.
"Won't be a minute," he called over his shoulder.
It was just as well that he couldn't see the cold sweat that had come over me. By the time he got back I had just about recovered.
"Nice little boy," was all I could think of to say.
He smiled that chilling smile of his back at me, but said nothing.
The walk proved uneventful. I tried to find out more about his family, but all he would tell me was that his son worked for the local butcher in Oswaldtwistle, his wife worked in the mill with him and his eldest son had moved to London after the last war. I suppose that was the best that I could have hoped for, knowing what an uncommunicative character he was.
We both realised that Christmas was coming, and that the opportunities for our hikes would be limited for the next few weeks, so we parted, our friendship forged, arranging to meet the second Saturday in January for another tramp round the hills. January 10th was the actual date, I believe. I remember it because you started piano lessons that same day, much to Albert's delight.
Christmas 1947 was, in spite of the rationing, quite a good one for our family. We managed to get a turkey and all the trimmings. I even arranged for a wide selection of presents for you, Anne, something many of the other children did not get. I suppose you could call our little family lucky, given the circumstances. So 1948 dawned, and with it new hope for the country and revenge for the Lord family.
I met Jackson on the Saturday, knowing full well that my father's plan was not far short of coming to fruition. It

was a cold but crisp day as we set off towards Great Harwood. He asked me about Christmas, to which I replied it had been quiet, with the family. I said I had spent it with my wife, daughter and father. He asked no further questions. I actually enjoyed that walk, knowing that I would not have to endure the company of this man for much longer. As we strolled back to the place where I had parked my car, I made my suggestion.

"I was talking to a friend at work about our walks, and he suggested that we should try walking up the Grane Road, towards Haslingden, and around the reservoir. Do you know where I mean?" I asked him.

"Yes, but it's quite a long way. Several miles. At this time of year, it would mean an early start to get back before dark."

"My friend said it was worth it. Let's try, just for a change. Are you game?"

He finally agreed, asking me if I thought I was up to a return walk of about ten miles. I assured him I was, and was looking forward to it. We arranged to meet the following Saturday, at an earlier time, to go on our long march.

Albert was overjoyed when I told him that the walk was planned for the following Saturday.

"Now is the time for the final piece of the plan to be put into place," he said.

I smiled across at him, knowing exactly what he meant. During the following week, father and I went over the plan time and time again. Everything had to be right. We would never get another chance if it failed.

So on the Friday afternoon, the day before I was due to meet Jackson, I drove the car to Haslingden and left it parked in a country lane about a mile from the Grane reservoirs. I followed the path leading off the road; the same route we would be taking the next day. It was just as father had said. I hid a crucial piece of equipment under a bush and made a mental note of the exact spot. My walking with Jackson had left me quite fit, and I was only twenty-seven, so it took no time at all to walk the few miles back to Accrington. I did actually meet some friends I used to know from my market days, who asked me what I was doing walking when I had a car to travel around in. I grinned at them, muttering something about needing the exercise, and tapping my belly.

As I arrived back at the house Emily greeted me. She had a puzzled look on her face, especially as the car was nowhere to be seen. Luckily, she asked no questions, as usual, though she must have wondered just what was going on. I did not enlighten her. Like a dutiful wife, she disappeared into the kitchen and put the kettle on. Had you been old enough, Anne, no doubt you would have questioned me until I gave you an answer. Albert appeared out of his room and glanced across and raised his head in a questioning manner. I nodded almost imperceptibly back to him, indicating that everything was in place. The plan was going well.

We went to bed that night, all of us thinking different thoughts. Your mother must have wondered what was happening to her husband. Albert was probably contemplating seeing Sam again. Whilst I kept turning the whole plan over in my mind. You, Anne, were probably dreaming about your latest doll that I had managed to get for you earlier in the week....

Chapter 19

FOR ANNE: FRUITION

The following morning was bitterly cold as I set off even earlier to keep my appointment with Jackson. I actually arrived a good quarter of an hour before the time we had arranged. Seeing that tall frame walking towards me made me realise how glad I would be to put an end to this matter once and for all, hopefully within a few hours. I told him as he stopped beside me that I had lent my car to a friend for the day and he had dropped me off, thus explaining my being on foot. He merely grunted, and we set off, heading towards his destiny. We tramped over the fields, our feet crunching on the still frozen earth, until we arrived at Haslingden Old Road. We were both quite breathless as we got to the top, so we rested, leaning on a wall. The clear crispness of the day meant we had magnificent views across towards Blackburn.
From here we headed towards Haslingden, following the road and dropping steadily until we saw the reservoirs on

our right. We left the road and made our way down a narrow path leading to these impressive man-made lakes. I must admit it was a pleasant walk, the cold frosty air making our breath condense in small clouds.

We dropped down from the main road and walked along the path, which formed part of the dam wall. On our left as we walked across we had a view of the small town of Haslingden, nestling in the bottom. It was too nice a scene for what was to follow. I suggested we stopped at the other side of the reservoir to have our packed lunch, before completing the circuit and heading back. It was about 1 o'clock when I suggested we stopped and ate lunch. The surface of the water, especially round the edge, had a thin film of ice forming on it. As we ate we admired the view, though I could not really concentrate, knowing what was to come. Jackson pointed out that some clouds were building up in the north and remarked that he thought there was snow in the air and that we should not linger too long. I agreed with him, but for a different reason, and finished my sandwich as quickly as I could, though I could not tell you what I ate even to this day. My mind was too full of what was to follow.

As we stood up, I said I had to answer a call of nature, and headed up towards some trees, just off the path. I actually relieved myself by a stream that cut a zigzag down the hillside. He waited patiently for me to finish. As I approached the path again, I pretended to fall and twist my ankle. I cried out in pain, and he walked slowly towards me, a look of frustration on his face. He asked me what was the matter. I pointed to my ankle, saying that I thought I had twisted it. He left the path to try to give me some assistance. How different his actions were in 1916.

As he got within range, I stood up, and with the heavy spade I had left there for this very purpose the day before, dealt him an almighty blow across his shins, rendering him incapable of movement. He sank to the floor, grabbing his legs in pain, cursing and swearing as he rolled in agony.
"What the. . . .?"
I hit him again in the same place, shattering one or both of his shinbones, judging by the crack. The agony and puzzlement on his face was obvious. He rolled on the floor, trying to stand and crawl all at the same time. It was useless. There was no way he could move more than a few yards.
"Why?" he gasped. "Why?"
Before he could utter another word, my father appeared from behind a clump of trees, where he had concealed himself, and whispered in a deathly voice,
"Hello, Sam."
The look on his face was one of recognition, followed by fear and then understanding.
"You? You survived?"
"Oh yes, and so did you, more's the pity. But now comes the reckoning. We need to finish some business."
Sam looked across at me, more carefully than ever before, until slowly an ironic smile spread across his face.
"You're his son, aren't you? I thought you were familiar the first time I saw you. You planned all this between you, you bastards."
"You left me to die, Sam. I was lucky, no thanks to you. Why did you do it Sam?"
I could see my father was getting emotional. I hoped the confrontation would not prove too much for him. I took his arm - how frail it felt - and eased him down onto the ground next to Jackson. Seeing the two of them together

felt strange. These two old friends who, lets face it, Anne, had suffered together, were now meeting for the first time in over thirty years. Jackson was almost grey with pain, and even in the gathering gloom I could see that he was about to pass out. However, drawing on tremendous reserves of strength, he managed to blurt out,
"I just had to get out of that hell hole. I wouldn't have survived otherwise. It was the only way. I once told you how I always looked after myself. It was my natural instincts again."
"Many brave men felt the same as you, but they stayed to fight and die ! What made you so special ?"
My father almost screamed out those last words.
"We all went through hell ! God, I had to go back for more ! Many brave men died, and not one of them thought of running away. Except you. You let them all down. Coward !"
Jackson looked across and shook his head.
"Wrong ! You're wrong, Albert. I'm no coward, nor did I let you down. I climbed out of that trench like everybody else. I would have died, like so many of the others..."
I could see my father was not convinced. He just shook his head.
"Can he walk ?" my father asked me.
"I doubt it. At least one shin bone must be shattered. I hit him hard enough."
"So, Sam, now you know how it feels to be immobile. To be totally helpless. Sorry I couldn't arrange for some shells to be bursting overhead, or maybe a sniper firing at you if you dared to move."
There was no reply. Sam Jackson realised that he was beaten.
"What was it you said, Sam ? I'm sorry, you'll have to take your chance, though I don't hold out much hope for you ?

Yes, that was it. I made it., though, Sam. Will you ? By the way, Sam, how did you escape from that nightmare ? I've wondered that, ever since I found out you were alive. Come on, tell us."

"Go to hell !"

"That place is reserved for you, Sam," my father replied, "and sooner than you think."

I had never seen my father like this before. He hardly ever lost his temper, but now the anger was shining from his eyes.

"I want to know how you got away, Sam," he insisted.

To my horror, my father picked up the spade lying on the ground and threatened to hit him again across his legs. Jackson flung his arms up and flinched backwards. My father brought the spade to within an inch of one of the shattered legs before he stopped.

"OK, OK, I'll tell you, though there's nothing much really to tell."

Father put down the spade and sat back and listened.

"After I climbed out of the hole, I almost went back for you, but I realised that would probably mean a certain death. I crawled along the ground, keeping as flat as possible. Most of the fighting seemed to be over, so I knew I had a good chance of reaching a quiet part of the line, or at least somewhere I wasn't known. I was nearly caught once, by a group of the wounded making their way back to our pathetic trenches, but I lay face down in the mud, feigning death. It worked, and they passed me by.

"Everywhere you looked there were bodies lying on the ground, so no one was going to worry about one more. I suppose the screams were the worst thing. Men howling in pain, crying for help, calling for a stretcher, but none came. That was to my advantage. I knew I had to get well away before it became light again, so I pressed on. I

actually crawled over a dying man in the dark, adding to his agonies and, I think, hastening his death. After what seemed to be an age I reached a small clump of bushes not blown into oblivion by artillery fire. It was probably about a mile behind the lines. It was July, so the day was breaking early and the first shafts of light were appearing. Here my luck held yet again. There was nobody about. I crawled into the middle of the bushes, trying to make myself as invisible as possible.

"*I stayed there all of that day. I could make out sounds of a battle going on, not too far away, but no one came anywhere near me. As the night fell again, I knew I had to move on. Feeling very stiff and very hungry, I made my way silently, as far as I could tell in a westward direction. You know how much I hated the dark, Albert, but it was the only way. Moving during the day would make capture certain. I was so far behind the lines now to be classed as a deserter, which would have meant a firing squad. No, I had to make this succeed.*

"*Travelling by night, I managed to get further away from the front and nearer to the coast, though I never really knew exactly where I was. I slept where I could, in barns, behind walls, in the middle of woods. The army training had taught me that much. I stole food as I went along. It's amazing how the odd egg followed by a bit of mouldy fruit can sustain you. After about three or four days of this terrible existence, I settled down for a rest during the day. I could smell sea air and hear seagulls so I knew I could not be far from the coast. What I would do then was anyone's guess. I would cross that bridge when I came to it.*

"*I suppose weariness, brought on by hunger, was setting in, and try as I might I could not stir myself to move on when it became dark. I must have fallen asleep again, for when I opened my eyes I could see dawn breaking in the distance. I slowly poked my head out from under the bush. I couldn't see much, but somewhere close at hand I could hear voices. It was an indistinct sound, a low mumbling, but they were voices all right. I retreated back into the safety of the branches, cursing myself for not having moved sooner. The prospect of spending another night under the bush was not a pleasant thought. I dare not move. I had not come this far to be caught and shot as a deserter.*

"The voices got louder, clearly heading in my direction. As they drew closer, I could tell they were English. Peeping out from the bush, I could now see three men dressed in uniform gradually getting nearer. They passed within two yards without seeing me. Or so I thought. Suddenly I felt someone grab me from behind through the back of the bush. I struggled out and put my hands up in the air to indicate surrender. The men smiled at each other, and two positioned themselves at either side of me whilst one walked in front. I had no choice but to follow them."

Jackson stopped at this point, his face creased with pain, and in spite of the coldness of the afternoon, beads of sweat were rolling down his forehead. My father gave him a drink, which he took thankfully. He was soon able to continue.

"As we crested a small rise, there spreading out in front of me was a huge army camp. I went sick at the sight. This was my destination, where I would be court-martialled and then shot. Believe me, Albert, I wished I'd stayed with you and carried on fighting. These thoughts lasted only a minute because, much to my surprise, the three soldiers started walking away from the camp, entering a hilly, wooded area about half a mile away as near as I could tell. By now it was fully daylight, and the men hurried to make the tree line before we were spotted. They rushed me along, still not saying a word.

"When we made the cover of the trees, they slackened their pace down to a slow walk. They obviously knew exactly where they were heading. As for me, I was now totally lost, so there was no danger of me making a run for it. They knew this and they became less vigilant in their guard duty. I almost thought they were going to speak to me, but they didn't. This silent journey went on for another ten minutes or so until we entered a clearing, around which sat about twenty more men, dressed also in the uniforms of British soldiers and talking to each other in small groups. The chatting stopped as they noticed me. The thing that surprised me was the wide range of ranks on view. There were privates, corporals, sergeants, and I swear I even saw a captain amongst them.

"I was taken in front of a soldier who was sitting on a tree stump, smoking a cigarette. He indicated I should sit down. He offered me a cigarette, which I thankfully took. He glanced across at the men who had brought me to the camp, and told them to bring me some food.

"Now, soldier, tell me your story, and then we'll decide what to do with you," he said.

His accent was undoubtedly southern. I recognised it from my early life in London.

"So I told them more or less what I've just told you, leaving out, of course, the part where I left you in the crater. All the time he sat there, nodding occasionally, especially when I mentioned going over the top. Before I had finished, some food had arrived. It was a simple meal of bread and cold meat, washed down with a mug full of hot tea. Hardly a banquet, but to me it felt like the best meal ever set before a king. I continued telling my story as wolfed the food down. When I had finished I looked expectantly at him, like I was waiting for the verdict in a courtroom.

"After what seemed an eternity, he smiled and welcomed me to their little camp. There were questions I wanted to ask, but, you know me, I was never curious, so I just thanked him. I had stumbled, quite by chance and a little help from my escorts, upon a band of fellow deserters who had made their homes in the woods and hills outside the camp at Etaples. Some of them had been there since 1915. The army knew of their existence, and from time to time sent out search parties, but only rarely were any captured.

"Apparently, there were many such groups in and around the area. They offered me the chance to stay with them. I accepted, but I pointed out that I would really like to return to England, to be reunited with Bronwen. They said that they could probably arrange for me to cross the Channel if I was sure, but pointed out the risks involved. I was prepared to take these risks if it meant seeing Bronwen again.

"So I spent a couple of months in this little haven, secure in the knowledge I was amongst my own kind. Actually, I became quite useful to them. As you know, I could always copy things carefully. Signatures, handwriting, even the way people spoke and walked. I was given the job of forging various passes and documents, enabling them to walk freely around the town of Etaples. Even to enter the vast camp unhindered, leaving again with quantities of food.

"I suppose my crowning glory was forging my own discharge papers, stating I had been wounded in battle and was no longer fit for combat. I didn't really know what such a document looked like, but probably neither did anyone who was likely to stop me. So I managed to get on board a ship heading back to England, carrying soldiers going on leave and, of course, the many wounded. I was never challenged.

"The papers and some English money I had earned forging various documents helped me travel through England, right into Wales and on to Caernarvon. They also gave me an air of respectability in the town. Everybody likes a war hero !"

"Didn't you ever once think of your friends, who were still fighting, or me, in the crater ?" asked my father.

"Not once," came the unashamed reply. "I just wanted to get away and see Bronwen again."

I glanced across at Jackson in disgust. I just might have felt sorry for him had he not said that.

"Look," pleaded Jackson. "When I joined up I never thought it would be like that ! I never believed we would actually have to fight and kill people, or even get killed. Besides, I hadn't met Bronwen. She would have changed my mind."

"None of us anticipated the horrors that we were going to face, but we didn't run away," father spat at him.

Jackson looked at the ground, possibly in shame, or more probably in defeat. Father was not finished yet; he jumped to his feet and pointed accusingly at Jackson lying on the ground.

"Curse ye, Meroz, said the Angel of the Lord, curse ye bitterly ! . . . I am the Lord, and you are Meroz. Curse ye, curse ye !"

I laid a restraining hand on my father's arm, trying to calm him down, but he would not be stopped.

"They came not to help the Lord - that's me, see, Sam, Lord - to help the Lord against the mighty."

I don't know if it was the emotion of the moment, but my father broke down and wept. I put a gentle arm around his

shoulders. Jackson continued staring at the ground. I think he knew his fate was sealed. Perhaps he realised that death, so successfully cheated in 1916, was about to catch him up some thirty years later.
"Do you want me to go on?" Jackson asked.
His face betrayed real signs of pain as he moved his position. I knew he could not move very far.
"Not really," I replied. "I think we've heard enough."
There was silence for a few moments. The first few flakes of snow drifted slowly down. My father moved over towards this beaten man, kneeling down once more, putting his face no more than six inches from Jackson's, and hissed out the words,
"You raped my wife! She died because of you."
I was shocked to hear that last statement. What did he mean? I looked questioningly at my father, but all he could see was Sam Jackson.
"Oh yes, you killed her, just as sure as if you'd put a gun to her head and shot her."
Thinking he had gone mad, I placed a restraining hand on his shoulder once again. He shook it off and carried on speaking.
"She lost your baby. She had a bad time of it, made a mess of her insides, and she died because of it. No one said that was the reason, but I knew. My son lived, but she died."
He waved his hand at me.
I don't know much about babies and childbirth, Anne, but I think Albert was wrong on this. It seemed unlikely that a miscarriage three years or so before would have brought about my mother's death. I didn't say anything to my father. It would have been no good, anyway. He evidently did believe it, and that was why he was accusing Jackson of murder.

"Why did you do it?" father implored. "You had Bronwen! Why did you want Amy as well?"
Jackson shrugged his shoulders, causing a further spasm of pain to pulse through his body. He had no defence. My father got to his feet once more, turned away from his one-time friend and walked several yards up the path, beckoning me to follow. I reached into Jackson's inside pocket and removed his wallet and his pocket watch. I met with no resistance.
"Look, Sam," father said. "It's starting to snow, and it will soon be dark. Dark, Sam. No lights around here. Bit like a trench, this stream, isn't it? Come on, son we must get going."
I took one final look at Sam Jackson, and followed my father back to the path, hurling the spade, his wallet and his watch far out into the black waters of the reservoir. We left that monster, lying in the zigzag ditch made by the stream. We walked slowly back to where I had left the car the night before, my father limping quite badly as his war wound started to hurt him. I had to support him over the last few yards to the car. Neither of us said a word. We both knew we had left him to die in agony. No more than he deserved.
"You must be exhausted," I said to my father as we drove back to Accrington. "You walked all the way from home this morning."
"I am, but it was worth it. I have done what I vowed to do all those years ago."
"Do you think he'll survive?" I asked.
"He might, but it's unlikely, I would think. It must be nearly a mile to the road, and with that leg. . ."
Strange as it may seem, I felt no remorse for him as we headed back down the hill towards Accrington, only relief that we had succeeded in what we had set out to do. Now

it was in the lap of the Gods. I suppose it was possible that he could be rescued, but what could he tell ? It would all come out then, him being a deserter and a rapist. No, we were safe even if he lived, and we both knew it.

The snow was quite thick on the ground as we skidded to a halt outside the house, to be greeted by an anxious Emily.

"Where on earth have you been ?" she called.

"Put the kettle on, love, we're both freezing," was all my father would say.

Emily didn't ask again. She knew better.

So there you have it, Anne, the full story. Well, almost. We watched the papers for a day or two until we saw it. A short paragraph was all the incident merited:

> CALLOUS ROBBERY AND MURDER.
> The body of an Oswaldtwistle man, Samuel Jackson, was found at Grane Reservoir yesterday. A heavy instrument had broken Mr Jackson's legs, before he was robbed and left to die in the freezing cold.
> Police wish to talk to anyone who saw Mr. Jackson and a companion, believed to be a Mr. Frank Holt of Burnley, on Saturday of last week.

I hoped the real Mr. Holt, if indeed there was one, didn't suffer too much at the hands of the police and could prove his innocence.

The next few days proved anxious for us both. Albert asked time and time again if any of Jackson's family had seen me. I assured him they hadn't, although Jackson had apparently mentioned the name I had made up. Eventually he believed me. There was no knock at the door; no policeman ever came to see me. Murder by person or persons unknown, was the verdict. The police didn't have *much to go on, and let the case drop. Jackson's family did try to get the investigations going again, but failed despite the pleadings of their solicitor, Mr. Robinson Senior. If only his son knew what this letter contained, he wouldn't be so happy to store it for me until my death.*

Well, you know the rest. We moved to Manchester Road two years later, though without Albert, who said he preferred to stay in his own house. As you grew up, you and he became closer and closer. He kept calling you his new Amy. You spent a lot of time together, going for walks or going to church. He even used to take you up to the war memorial in the park, as he had with me when I was young. It was your grandfather who helped you with your piano lessons, though you could never draw as well as he could, a big disappointment to him.

I remember when he died in 1958 you were inconsolable for a long time afterwards. You had lost your special pal. But time is a great healer, as they say, and you finally got over it, and by the early 60s you'd decided you wanted to become a teacher, so you went away to the Lake District. Everything was fine until that fateful day when you brought that cursed Jackson boy into the house. The boy who had played with my car all those years before, though of course I did not recognise him at the time. It was only when he said he was the son of Tom Jackson, the butcher in Oswaldtwistle, that I caught on. I suppose your sins come back to haunt you. Perhaps you realise now why I tried to stop you from marrying him, without success.

So that is it, Anne, the full story. What you do now is your business. I'm dead, somewhere with Albert, Amy, Sam and your mother. Now it's up to you. But perhaps now the reasons for my actions are a little clearer to you.

Goodbye, dearest Anne, and God Bless.

There were no more pages. I put down the document, wiping a tear from my eye, though who it was for I couldn't say. I walked over to the drinks cabinet and poured myself a stiff whisky. Sara looked across at me with a puzzled expression. I could not bring myself to say a word. I sat down in the chair with my head in my hands and waited for her to finish.

Finally she, too, put down the last pages and hugged me tightly. She realised what I must be feeling. It isn't every day you find out your grandfather and great-grandfather murdered your great-grandfather, who had raped your great-grandmother. It was a long time before either of us spoke. Sara could sense the mixed emotions welling up in me. Whose side should I take ? Was it, indeed, a matter of taking sides ? I could sympathise with Albert and, to a lesser extent, Frank, but I had an overwhelming feeling of sorrow for Sam, his wife and offspring. It felt strange to read about my father as a child, actually meeting Frank Lord. I wondered if he remembered the incident.

"How do you feel, sweetheart ?" Sara's voice broke the silence, dragging me from my thoughts.
"How do you think ?" I whispered in reply. "Like a man who has had his family ripped apart by...." I paused, ".... by his family, I suppose."
"If it's any consolation, I agree with Frank. Amy probably didn't die as a result of the miscarriage, so you can't lay her murder at Sam's door."
I suppose Sara was trying to lessen the impact of the story when she said this. It didn't work.

I wanted to be alone. I said I would have to go out for some fresh air. Sara, understanding the situation, tactfully remained in the house. Without thinking, my steps led me once more to mother's grave, where I knelt down in virtually the same spot as I had earlier that day.

ANNE LORD, LOVING MOTHER OF PETER shouted at me from the headstone. I sat quietly for a while, wishing, not for the first time, I could discuss things with my mother. She would have known how to proceed from here, or would she ? I was in a unique position; neither she nor my father could understand how I felt.

I do not know how long I remained at the graveside, kneeling as I did in complete silence. Eventually I pulled myself to my feet. I was feeling better, though not any less confused, as I made my way back to the house, where Sara was busying herself making the evening meal. She held me close as I entered the kitchen.
"Get drunk," she said. "That'll help."
She passed me another large whisky. I took it gratefully and downed it in one go. I did get drunk that night. I do not remember even going to bed, but I suppose I must have done, as I woke up in a crumpled heap the following morning. The prospect of going to work did not appeal one little bit, but I forced myself.

Heaven only knows what Elaine must have thought of me that day. I hardly spoke, either to her or the customers. I was a bit short with Mr. Jones on the phone when he rang up to ask when his painting would be delivered. It was awful. I made my excuses and left early, leaving a very puzzled Elaine to close up the shop.

Sara was out when I arrived back at the house. I glanced at the clock. It was barely 3.30, so my father would still be at work. I needed to talk to him, to tell him of the horrors of both our pasts, our family shadow. Sue, also, had to be told, though that could wait until her visit the following weekend. I slipped slowly into a doze in the armchair. I was eventually awakened by Sara arriving home from work. It was nearly 6 o'clock. We embraced each other. She

didn't mention the revelations of the day before, instead she slipped upstairs for a shower. I remained in the living room and pondered my next move, though deep down I knew what I had to do. I had to call Phil, who would be home now. I poured myself a stiff drink. My liver was probably past saving after the excesses of the past months. I picked up the phone and dialled his number. It took several rings before the chirpy voice of Emma answered.
"Hi Peter !" she cried, her voice smiling at me down the phone. "How are things ?"
I was not really in the mood to make small talk, but I felt obliged to reply that " things" were fine. Hardly a truthful or accurate answer, but it had to suffice under the circumstances. I asked to speak to Phil, hoping that I didn't sound too brusque. I heard the receiver being put down at the other end. Several seconds later I heard the now familiar voice of my father.
"Pete, how the hell are you ?" he asked.
"Dad, I know it all now," I blurted out. "Prepare yourself for a shock."
There was complete silence at the other end of the phone as I began to relate the story.

Chapter 20

VISITS: THE SHADOW LIFTS

It was not an easy conversation I had with my father. He was totally confused by the whole thing. He didn't believe me at first, and my potted version was greeted by a stony silence at the other end of the phone, but as I revealed more and more of the two documents he began to accept the situation as its reality began to dawn on him.

"That would certainly explain the hatred shown to me by Anne's father," he said, his voice sounding a little flat. "And by Anne," he added. "But why the hell didn't they tell me, and why should anyone bear a grudge for so long ? It was fifty years ago, for God's sake !"
"I suppose it was Albert more or less cursing the Jackson name. Son and granddaughter took it literally. I suppose my arrival must have blown Frank's mind, and Mother's too when she found out about Sam."
"So what now ?" Phil asked.

"Well, I'm the offspring of both families, a living reconciliation if you like. So I suppose that's an end to it. If only Frank Lord could have seen it that way, and destroyed Albert's story when I was born, instead of showing it to mother, then all this would never have come out."

Subconsciously I was searching for a happy-ever-after scenario.

"They did murder my grandfather," Phil pointed out.

"But only because. . . " I paused, realising the futility of trying to apportion blame.

"Look, we both know the full story," I said. "How would it be if Sara and I come up north, then you and I can go to Accrington and lay some ghosts to rest ?"

There was a momentary pause before he answered.

"I think I'd like that. I want to be with my son more than ever now." There was genuine desire evident in his voice. I consulted Sara, and we arranged to visit the north in a fortnight's time, since Sue was due to visit us the following weekend.

Like a small child wanting to look at pictures in a storybook, I climbed into the loft once more and brought down mother's scrapbook containing the photographs. I removed the three sepia prints from the envelope and placed them carefully in the book with the others. Almost all the characters were now together. There were Albert and Amy on their wedding day, smiling out at me, masking the unhappiness in both their lives. I studied the two faces, neither knowing the other's tragedy at that time, and Amy little knowing that her life would shortly be at an end. I wished I could have seen a picture of Sam. He should have been there, though somehow I couldn't see mother ever tolerating his photograph in her book. Did my father have a picture of him, I wondered ? I saw Grandmother Jackson, Bronwen. Did she know the full story of her husband's treachery and disloyalty to her ? I looked intently at her face, still pretty even in her seventies. Her smile had frozen in time, on the day of my parents' wedding. I imagined the anguish she must have felt when the police told her that Sam had been found robbed and murdered. She would never imagine Albert Lord, the young soldier who accompanied her singing the 23rd Psalm, was responsible. Tom Jackson and his wife, and Phil's parents gazed out from the page. I now realised why the confused old man rambled on about reservoirs.

Sue arrived the following Friday evening, her little 2CV pop-popping its way into the drive. After kisses and hugs on the doorstep, we went into the lounge and settled down with a cup of coffee. I decided it would be easier to tell the stories rather than let Sue plough through the two documents. I related everything, from Albert volunteering, to the incident behind the reservoirs.

She listened in silence, shaking her head in disbelief, as I unfolded the events. Typically her first thought was for my mother.
"Poor Anne ! What a terrible thing to have to carry with you to the grave, knowing your father committed murder in the name of revenge."
"At least she only knew about it for a few hours before she died. Poor mother. She must have been turning it over in her mind when ..... well, you know."
Sue looked down at the floor, staring emptily at the fading coffee stain on the carpet.
"You and Sara need to take a break," she suggested. "Well away from England. Somewhere hot and relaxing."

The idea certainly had appeal, but, as I explained to Sue, I had to visit Accrington at least one more time, as I had said to Phil, to put a few ghosts to rest. Sue understood, but counselled me to put the past behind me after that.
"There can be little point going any further. You and your father know the truth now, and there's nobody else left alive."

"Forgive and forget, eh ? Something my family seem to find hard to do, at least one half of them," I pointed out.
"Perhaps if they had, then things wouldn't have gone as far as they did," Sue said, shaking her head. "Albert Lord isn't the only one who can quote the Bible. Look this one up, Pete: 2 CORINTHIANS 2:7."

I fetched mother's bible, now in residence on the bookshelf, thumbed through it and found the reference Sue mentioned.
"So that contrariwise ye ought rather to forgive him and comfort him, lest perhaps such a one should be swallowed up with overmuch sorrow," I read aloud, before closing the Bible with an air of finality.
"Maybe Albert should have read parts of the Bible preaching forgiveness and taken them to heart, rather than quoting about bloody and deceitful men and the like. That would have been better for all concerned."
"I think you're probably right, Pete, but what's done can't be undone. Let's try to enjoy the weekend."
Sue and I hugged each other, before joining Sara in the kitchen, happily singing along with the radio and preparing the evening meal.

The weekend with Sue was very enjoyable. I tried my hardest to put all thoughts of hatred and revenge out of my mind as we spent the Saturday afternoon pottering around Norwich, looking at the shops and the castle. Sue was good company, keeping us entertained with stories of when she was a schoolteacher, a deliberate attempt, I suspect, to take my mind off things. It worked. We sang happily as we drove back to Stradbroke, for a meal at the Queen's Head. Sara and I were sorry to see her leave the following afternoon.

We made the trip north on the following Friday to see Phil and Victoria and the children. As Sara was introduced to everyone I noticed that she was staring intently into Richard's eyes, comparing them with the descriptions of Sam's, though of course she made no comment. As I anticipated, Sara and Victoria got on well together, spending much of the evening, once again in the Blue Ball, laughing and giggling. It was nice for Sara to have some female company for a change, and not to be spending her time with an obsessive like myself. Phil and I were more subdued, knowing the following day meant a trip to Accrington, and I think we were both rather wary of how we would feel. I showed the documents to Phil later that evening, but he said he preferred not to read them. I suppose he must have felt a certain amount of shame in Albert's story, and an equal amount of anger in Frank's. He did suggest what we might do with them. I agreed, leaving them on the table, ready to take with us the following day.

Sara and Victoria had planned a trip to Leeds to do some shopping and set off in the Espace, with a delighted Emma and a grumbling Richard in tow. Phil and I departed soon afterwards in my BMW. We didn't say much as we headed towards Lancashire, due in no small part to the fact that Phil expressed a desire to drive, which he did, with spirit to say the least, causing me to hold tightly to the edge of the seat with my heart in my mouth, as he raced along the Calder valley and through the hills towards Burnley.
"It's nice to drive a car with a bit of power," he enthused, overtaking a bus and narrowly missing a car going in the opposite direction. "The Espace will feel pretty flat after this."

I breathed a sigh of relief as we parked in the car park not far from the offices of Robinson and Robinson. I suggested that I might drive back, "Share the driving and all that !" He smiled, but there was a tinge of disappointment in his voice as he agreed. We climbed the steps leading out of the car park and headed towards the centre of the town. On my previous visit I had been unaware of the significance of some of the locations in the town, but now everything took on a new meaning. Phil pointed out it was many years since he had lived in the area and Accrington had changed. However, many places had remained the same.

Phil showed me Ellison's Tenement, now a large, empty space, used as a fairground, just off the main shopping area of the town. I closed my eyes and imagined the rows of Pals marching in squares. Could I hear the sound of pounding boots ? Or was it just traffic noise ? We visited the Town Hall, now housing the Tourist Information Centre. Inside were glass display cases containing assorted Pals memorabilia and books on the subject. As we perched on the low wall outside, I imagined Sam and Albert doing exactly the same, discussing their first day as soldiers and arranging to meet up for a drink later that night. Everywhere there seemed to be little echoes.

We strolled along Blackburn Road, searching for Albert's house. Phil was uncertain of its exact location, so we may or may not have seen it. The sound of a modern diesel train, rumbling through the station nearby, made me think of the hundreds of men boarding the train over eighty years ago, each one of them scanning the cheering crowd, hoping for a glimpse of a loved one, before setting off on what, for many, was their last great journey. There were no great crowds that afternoon, just shoppers rushing everywhere; not one of them carried a Union Jack !

Puffing and panting, we walked up Avenue Parade, past Sam's house, though once again Phil wasn't sure exactly where his grandfather had lived. Passing some modern houses and going through a park, we finally made it to the Coppice at the top and turned round. There, spread out below us, was the town of Accrington, rows of tidy terraced houses, occasional mill chimneys and the remaining factories. The view was not vastly different, I suspect, from the one seen by the Pals all those years ago.

A brisk fifteen-minute walk, all down hill on the way back, took us back to the car. Following Phil's directions, I headed up Manchester Road. Phil indicated I should stop outside a semi-detached house.

"You are now looking at the former Lord residence, your mother's home," he announced.

It was more or less the way I had imagined it, a large garden at the front housing a FOR SALE sign, with SOLD stuck across it at an angle. I got out of the car and stood at the gate. A face looking out of the window indicated the new owners were in residence. I wanted to knock on the door and ask to look round, but I thought better of it and contented myself with one final glance as I rejoined Phil in the car.
"Seen enough ?" he asked.
I nodded back at him.
"So now it's time ?"
I nodded again.

I swung the car round in the road and parked a few hundred yards down the hill, outside the gates of Oak Hill Park. I opened the boot and retrieved the two documents and a biscuit tin, provided that morning by Victoria.

"Let's finish it," I said as we went through the iron gates and made our way up through the deserted park, past Albert and Amy's bandstand, to the War Memorial perched proudly at the top. Here was the place my mother had visited many times with Albert, and in later years with Sue. Here was to be the final resting-place for our family shadow. I studied the lists of names, not only from the Great War, but World War Two, Northern Ireland and the Falklands War as well. Brave sons of Accrington and the surrounding villages, who had died so readily for their country.

"The park keeper would kill us he knew what we were going to do." remarked Phil.

I smiled and calmly placed the documents in the tin, took out my lighter and set fire to them. I twisted and turned the papers until all that remained was a pile of charred paper resting in the bottom of the tin. I grabbed a handful of the paper and crushed it even smaller before throwing it up in the air, watching as the slight breeze caught the tiny flakes and whirled them away. Phil and I repeated this action several times until all the sadness and bitterness had finally gone. A symbolic act, but one that we both believed had finally removed the family shadow once and for all.

I drove carefully back to Halifax, a weight lifted from my shoulders. The rest of the family were waiting for us as we pulled into the drive.
"Well, did you discover your roots ?" asked Victoria as we settled down to a cup of tea. "Though why you wanted a tin I'll never know."
She didn't know the full story, and I somehow doubted Phil would ever tell her. There was no real need.

I explained to Sara what we had done as we lay in bed together later that night. She seemed pleased to think that all my puzzling and searching would soon be at an end. We left for home the following afternoon, arriving back in Stradbroke in the early evening. Yet another meal in the Queen's Head rounded off a happy weekend, and even the ubiquitous presence of Bill Garnett didn't seem so bad. I think Sara actually managed a smile in his direction.

There was still one place I wanted to go before I felt all loose ends had been tied up: Serre, that little village somewhere near the river Somme in Northern France. Sara, realising that this was so important to me, took yet more time off work and agreed to accompany me on my pilgrimage. We booked a place on the Eurotunnel service along with a night in Coquelles and two nights in Albert, a sizeable town, near to the Somme battlefield. Quite a poignant place to stay, given the name.

Heading south on the M11, round the M25 and eventually to Folkestone, we set off on our journey to France. After a lightning visit to the duty free shop, we were shepherded down the ramp and into the cleverly designed carriages at Folkestone. I wondered what Albert and Sam would have made of this quick, clean and clever way of crossing the Channel to France. Somehow I don't think either of them would have been over impressed. We arrived at Coquelles shortly after 5 o'clock and checked into the Hotel Copthorne, a modern building, constructed I suspect to cater for the people, like us, driving off the train.

The following morning we left the hotel and headed towards Albert. Mother and I had spent holidays in France when I was younger. I was what you could call a Francophile. I loved everything about the place. Yet this visit was so totally different. This was not a holiday, though I suspect Sara thought slightly differently. As we drove towards Albert, along the road from Bapaume, we were amazed by the number of signposts that came into view indicating the site of a battle, accompanied by the inevitable war cemetery, final resting place for the participants. We actually called at one, named Warlencourt British Cemetery. We entered through a brick-built, square archway. Both of us were shocked by the rows of white headstones stretching into the field, each one standing for a lost soul many years ago. In the space between each one was a rose, just coming into bloom. Never before had I realised the scale of the mass slaughter that was the Great War. We walked silently back to the car and headed off down the road. It felt strange, driving along, our progress unhindered, so different from those valiant young men who died so bravely to advance only a few yards.

On arriving in Albert we checked into the Hotel La Paix, and had a shower. I wanted to find Serre there and then, but Sara stopped me, suggesting we had a meal and rested in the hotel that night. She was right, as usual. We both fell asleep as soon as we got back into the room after consuming the not very ambitious meal of, "poulet roti, frites et petits pois, avec un demi-pression pour moi et une verre de vin blanc pour mademoiselle." I always made a big effort to speak French, though mother always said I had the worst accent she had ever heard.

The following morning, we studied the map and planned the best route to Serre, arriving about mid-morning. The small village itself had largely been rebuilt since 1916, as you would expect. It is now a typical French village, consisting of a main street with the usual array of houses on each side of the road. Looking in the guide book, bought specifically for the purpose, I discovered that there was a monument to the Accrington Pals in the Sheffield Memorial Park, near Mark Copse, the one mentioned in Albert's story. We had to leave the road and go down a lane, little more than a track, until we found it.

I felt a shiver go down my back as I caught my first glimpse of a "W" shaped construction made out of red brick. It looked so peaceful there between the trees, which I suppose had grown since the slaughter of 1916, replacing the dead stumps Albert, and indeed Sam, had known. I am not an impressionable sort of person, but I could swear I smelled death in this now peaceful little hollow. I closed my eyes and conjured up the vivid picture of rows of soldiers waiting for the order to advance, not knowing if those seconds would be their last or not. Trembling hands fixing their bayonets. Albert looking across at Sam, still his friend, and silently mouthing "Good Luck". An aircraft passing overhead broke my reverie, not one piloted by a World War One ace, rather a jet heading for an unknown destination.

I opened a small gate and stood before the monument. There was a simple plaque fastened to one of the sides. I read it silently to myself, holding tightly onto Sara's hand.

> DEDICATED TO THE MEMORY
> OF ALL MEMBERS OF THE
> "ACCRINGTON PALS"
> SO MANY OF WHOM FELL HERE
> DURING THE ATTACK ON
> SERRE 1ST JULY 1916
> IN THE OPENING PHASE
> OF THE
> BATTLE OF THE SOMME
>
> THEIR NAME LIVETH
> FOR EVERMORE

I stood in silence for a while gazing at the memorial, thinking not only about Albert, but also Sam. This was the location of so much misery for both of them. They had come here, one ready to die and one planning to leave that hell once and for all. By a twist of fate they had both survived, in their own way. I thought of the inhabitants of Accrington. How many of them, I wondered, had made this pilgrimage to see the final resting-place of some of its bravest sons ? Sara passed me a little wreath I had had made especially in Diss before we left. It consisted of three poppies wound round a wire frame. In the middle I had written the simple yet poignant message:

"To the Accrington Pals, from Peter, the great-grandson of two of your number."

As I stepped back and bowed my head, I noticed a shallow ditch in the ground, running for several yards. This, I presumed was the remains of one of the trenches. Possibly Albert and Sam had crouched here together, waiting to go over the top. I mentally decided, yes, this was their trench, and I was standing where both my great-grandfathers had stood 81 years ago, though neither of them were destined to die here. Scuffing the ground with my foot, I unearthed a small piece of shrapnel, a not unusual occurrence when visiting the Somme area, according to the notes in the guidebook. No doubt Albert's mouth organ would have been discovered by someone, to be placed on a mantelpiece or in a display cabinet. I gazed around the surrounding area. I suppose I was searching for the remains of a shell hole. I didn't see one, successive farmers had seen to that, as they attempted to reclaim the land for its proper use. We walked slowly back to the car, neither of us saying a word. Before cresting the hill, I took one final look at the memorial, set at the bottom of the slope, there for all time.

We drove in silence back to Albert. I felt happy to have visited Serre and seen for myself the location of the start of so much unhappiness for my family. I felt that somehow my visit had put an end to all the bitterness, another full stop if you like. I prayed that Albert and Sam would see it that way and be reconciled to each other in whatever place they now found themselves in. I was surprised at my musings. It did not feel like me thinking these thoughts, but in the presence of so much sadness and death you tend to have a different set of values. Sara understood how I was feeling and quietly said,
"So.... now it's over ?"
"It's over," I repeated, as we headed homewards.

The last scene of the Old Pals Act had been played out, eight decades after it had started.